Buried Dreams

Marrisse Whittaker

Also by Marrisse Whittaker

To Bob Whittaker, the original January wasp and to the youngsters in the Whittaker Vespidae: Lily, Daniel, Peter, Jas, Sid and Tallulah. Love them all.

Chapter 1

Wrong time, Wrong place

I rina had thought that she might have been about to die many times, prepared for it even. Prayed for forgiveness. But when this, her true heart-stopping moment had finally arrived, it had caught her completely by surprise. It was the second day of the new year and also her wedding day: 2 January 1995. There had been promises of eternal love, or at least a vow of devotion 'until death do us part'...

If Irina still had enough breath inside of her soot-filled lungs, then she might have laughed at the recollection of making those promises and also at the words of the chart-topping song that she could faintly hear playing on a radio from the next-door house, its title 'Stay Another Day'. But instead, one single tear trickled out from eyes brimful of regrets. It traced a salty, sorrowful pathway down to her chin, before dripping onto the lace of her once pure white, but now deathly black, wedding dress.

She had heard that people often glimpsed their whole lives passing before their eyes at the moment of death. When her grandfather had told her about this it had seemed a preposterous snippet of folklore, for how could anyone prove the claim?

1

'If they had lived to tell the truth of the tale, then they couldn't have been about to die in the first place,' Irina had argued. Her grandfather had said that she argued too much. Why couldn't she be like the other girls and just accept what she was told?

But Irina had never felt that she fitted in, never listened to what the men at the top told everyone to do because they always ended up fighting in the end, just like this time and it was always the people at the bottom, the people who always did what they were directed to do, who suffered the most.

Above her, she heard a noise. Her emotions lifted for a heartbeat as her senses reconnected hesitantly, like the fluttering of butterfly wings just before flight. Looking up into the semi-darkness, her arms stretched above her head as though in welcome, she observed a lone wasp spiralling down towards her. Her spirit smiled somewhere deep inside, aware that her body was already numbed beyond any pain, should this lost queen offer a stinging death kiss. Irina hoped that unlike her, the insect would find freedom, escape from this hellish prison.

But the wasp gave up its struggle for survival and suddenly dropped, lifeless, brushing past Irina's outstretched fingers and then falling downwards. There would be no chance of arising Phoenix-like from the dark ashes below. It was winter, black as coal, unwelcoming, airless and bitterly cold. The tiny creature should have still been snuggling up somewhere safe and warm, ready to build a new nest, start a new colony. Instead, it was clear that this particular queen had lost in the lottery of life.

Born at the wrong time in the wrong place. *Fate can be so cruel.* Irina's brain registered the thought as if from somewhere far away, as her body gave a final shivering death jig. No way of telling her grandfather that her whole life really didn't pass before her eyes. Perhaps the reason was that much of Irina's life lately had been too horrific to dwell upon at this irreplaceable moment. Instead, her brain accepted what to many is heartbreakingly unacceptable. *I'm merely another of an uncaring god's creatures. Born at the wrong time in the wrong place. I am a January wasp.*

Chapter 2

A Wedding Favour

Present day

'How much? I'd have to sell both my kidneys and probably an arm and a leg to drum up the dosh for that!'

Ellis Darque was reacting to the sight of the price list on the wedding venue brochure he had just been handed. The wedding promoter looked nonplussed, yanking the glossy booklet back with her manicured talons, painted in pearly Bridal Pink.

Billie Wilde suppressed a smile. She had to agree with the sentiments behind the outburst but unlike Ellis, she was focused on staying true to her undercover character, that of one of many bridezillas at this wedding fair, in a smart hotel in the centre of town.

Ellis had, until that moment, been doing a sterling job of playing the part of her loving fiancé. They were on the trail of an erring husband, on behalf of a client who was paying top dollar for their Wilde and Darque private investigations firm to dig up the dirt she needed for a divorce.

The quite intimidating woman, a district judge no less, had visited the office many times now, addressing Ellis and Billie as though they were defendants in court. District Judge

Pennington had drummed home the fact that they were to deliver evidence, beyond all reasonable doubt, to put before the guilty party but had firmly stipulated that *she* and only *she* would have the triumphant moment of confronting her husband on his infidelity, before passing sentence that divorce proceedings were already underway and she would be claiming everything, including the house, cars, various designer dogs and a substantial French holiday home. The oldest kid was already grown up with some high-flying career of his own and the two afterthoughts, a product of a passion rekindling attempt at some stage, were teenagers at boarding school, so custody wasn't an issue. No one wanted them, but Judge Pennington had made clear that her errant husband would be the one shelling out for their substantial fees.

No love lost there then, on either side, Billie and Ellis had agreed on the way to the event. They had already pinpointed, and Billie had befriended, the husband's latest conquest, hairdresser Pandy Wood, who had confided that her new amour had proposed already. Billie had recorded the conversation, having made an appointment for a cut and condition at the hairdressing shop that Pandy owned.

It was amazing how many personal details someone would give away whilst struggling to tame a mane of unruly curls, Billie realised, tucking that knowledge away for future use. She had requested that the stylist lop a good chunk off her hair, partly because it would allow more time for Pandy to spill vital beans on her relationship and also to make life easier when Billie was required to quickly shove her wayward mop under the various wigs she had to wear these days in order to perform her new investigative duties.

'Taking this amount off your hair out of the blue,' Pandy chirped as she snipped away, 'it's normally what everyone does when they've just been given the chop by a boyfriend, not when they are thinking of tying the knot.' Pandy smiled through the mirror at Billie, who was slightly taken aback for a split second at the revealing insight. Billie divorced herself from that memory immediately. 'Don't know about you, but I can't wait until Saturday,' Pandy continued, fortunately not having paused for Billie to answer, as she struggled with the job in hand, excitedly sharing details of the wedding fair, which she would be attending with Judge Pennington's husband, to finalise details, or so she thought, of their planned nuptials.

'I mean, my Rexy said, "What are we waiting for, babes?"' Pandy had explained. Billie wanted to answer, 'a divorce, perhaps?' but had held her tongue. The poor girl clearly didn't know that he was currently still married. But this was the wrong time, wrong place, to put her straight. She and Ellis had been given their orders loud and clear. If Judge Pennington had brought her gavel with her she would have no doubt slammed it down on the desktop, for emphasis. The job of Wilde and Darque was to gather the evidence, not confront the principals. Took some doing, after a lifetime of kicking down doors, banging wrongdoers to rights, Billie had to silently admit, but she couldn't blame anyone but herself for her new world order.

She had willingly chucked in her job as DSI on the local force, heading up the Murder Enquiry Team no less, to launch a joint effort with Ellis, a former crack Serious Crime Investigation agent. They had form working together, though Ellis was more experienced at operating undercover, whereas Billie was still getting used to her change in status, having to lay low and dance around a situation, telling porkies all the while, rather than getting straight to the heart of the matter.

A shine had broken out on Pandy's perfectly made-up features, mascara smudging beneath her eyes as she had finished the mammoth task of blow-drying and straightening Billie's crazy hair, in between endless wedding chatter.

'Phew! All done,' she had exclaimed, reaching for a back mirror so that Billie could view the resulting shoulder-length helmet from all angles. A defiant corkscrew curl had sprung out, despite the liberal use of unctions and gels in an attempt to instil some sort of order on her head. Pandy had swept in with the hot irons once again. They sizzled on contact. Billie smelled singed hair, grateful at least that it was already red in colour.

'Lovely,' she said, forcing a smile whilst wondering if she had time to nip home and stand under the shower on full blast, before heading back to the office. 'I'll try to keep it just like this until I see you at the wedding fair on Saturday,' Billie had fibbed, but she wanted to be sure of the time of the event. 'Three o'clock, did you say?'

'That's right. Be there or be square. I'll just put a bit more spray on. It'll help it stay in shape.' Pandy sprayed another cloud of shellac from a giant cylinder, which caught Billie's breath and made her eyelashes feel sticky. She thought of a fly choking to death, spiralling to the ground in its death throes. 'I can't wait to meet your fiancé,' Pandy continued. 'I'm sure he'll get on with my Sexy Rexy. My mates say people will think he's a sugar daddy, but I've always liked the older guys. Rexy says that he's matured like a fine wine.'

'They'll probably have loads to talk about.' Billie nodded in agreement. Ellis would make sure of it.

'Aw, you know, I couldn't wish for a better man. He just can't wait to get our new life underway. There'll be over a hundred exhibitors at the fair.' Pandy did a little excited gig. 'Free bubbly, hundreds of dresses, films about different venues, you name it. You can even get perfume piped through the church now, you know, like Meghan Markle wanted at Windsor. I can see where she was coming from. Who wants to say their vows in a pongy old church? Rexy says he wants all the works. Nothing too much trouble. I bet your fella feels just the same. If you set your date for your big day, I'll clear my diary. Come and do your hair just like this. Mates' rates.'

Billie saw Ellis in her mind's eye and almost laughed out loud at the thought. It wasn't that he couldn't brush up well, but they were strictly business partners. What's more, neither of them had *any* interest in romance right now, especially not with one another. Billie had announced, albeit whilst slightly tipsy, over a drink with their joint mates in the local pub, that she would rather have her eyes put out by red-hot pokers than ever think of a wedding again. Ellis had agreed and even offered to eat his own spleen, should he be tempted to visit that scenario. He'd been dragged up the aisle once and that was enough. Now Billie was about to break the news to him that they would be playing love's young dream at Saturday's wedding fair.

The announcement had gone down like a cup of cold sick as Ellis had been planning a trip to the local football match where a big game was due to kick off at the same time. Instead, in a cloud of sweet-smelling room perfume and piped muzak, both partners in the Wilde and Darque PI agency now did their best to put their acting capabilities to the test. The banner above them read, *A one day wedding extravaganza. A lifetime of love and inspiration.*

'Hmmm, great wedding breakfast samples. Only a hundred quid per head too. Fried spleen looks good,' Billie quipped as she viewed menus at a stall.

'Yep and you know where you can stick those red-hot pokers of yours,' Ellis counter-joked, shaking his head in horror as a young handsome man loomed up with a tray of Asti Spumante and waved it under Ellis's nose in what he had possibly hoped would be a tantalising fashion.

'Eyes and teeth now,' Billie answered. 'You were the one who insisted that we can't be picky about jobs, especially in the first year of the business. We just have to grin and bear it.'

'Yeah, well I'd kill for a pie and a pint right now. Bit of luck we might be done in time for me to nip up the road for the second half of the match.' Billie looked around. She spotted Pandy and her lover, Rex, their target, across the room, talking to a wedding planner.

'With the latest intel that's just come in, the job's a good 'un anyway,' Billie agreed. They had just received some news which would turn out to be devastating for both Judge Pennington and Pandy. Even more so for the lothario, nicknamed Sexy Rexy by his currently doting fiancée. A little shadow of sadness passed through Billie's heart on behalf of the hairdresser. She'd suffered her own romance horrors in the not-so-distant past and guessed that the young woman's cheery spirit would be crushed.

'Yep, but best make sure we still record all this extra stuff for Madame le Judge. She was quite precise about the evidence she's demanding before she'll cough up payment. Shame we can't charge her for the surprise blockbuster info, but once we get him on video talking about tying the knot with your barnet terroriser, then our work is done.' Ellis tugged Billie's hair cheekily. It was shorter now, but back to a mass of wild red corkscrew curls. She slapped his hand away.

'You must be impressed with my latest recording gear though.' She glanced down to the lapel of her smart jacket where a wedding corsage hid a tiny camera. 'Think it squirts water too? I could get Sexy Rexy right between the eyes,' she joked. But Ellis was distracted.

'What's a wedding favour then?' he asked. 'Do you offer to do the washing-up a couple of nights a week or something?' Billie rolled her eyes, handing him a tiny gauze drawstring pouch filled with pastel pink- and blue-tinted sugared almonds. It had a large price tag hanging from the bow. 'You're joking!' Ellis looked from the bag to Billie. She couldn't help breaking into a grin. He was clearly genuinely puzzled, rather than playing up his undercover character.

'Or, we could choose these. One for every guest...' Billie picked up a tiny jar filled with a hand-poured candle. A sprig of dried flowers was fastened with a raffia bow around the rim.

'I dry the flowers myself.' A woman with a simpering smile and hawk-like eyes swooped along the table. Ellis pulled a less than impressed face.

'I hate dead flowers,' he explained, 'and what about the flame when you light the things? Death traps. I mean, imagine if everyone lit them at the reception, with all this net and confetti and plastic shit everywhere – the balloons filled with hydrogen for starters–'

'No, they're helium,' Billie corrected him, whilst putting the candle back on the table, smiling apologetically to the miffed seller, but Ellis was on a roll now.

'Place would go up like a bomb. Bride and groom would be a fireball and Granny wouldn't be able to move quick enough to get out...'

'Sorry, he's been watching too many horror movies.' Billie grabbed Ellis's arm and led him away from the stall, whispering, 'Not funny. *You* reminded *me* to stay in character when we came in, remember?'

'Honestly though, it did happen on a job I was on once. Someone had been selling dodgy balloons and we were undercover at this event. Kid had a sparkler in his hand and...'

'I thought I was the one who suffers from PTSD?' Billie answered.

'I'm suffering all right. That sounds like a goal,' he replied as a roar could be heard from the football stadium along the road. From the suddenly raised heads and sorrowful faces of other males present, he wasn't alone. 'Let's get our little bit of filming done and get away, now we know the game's up for our laddo already.'

The news that both Billie and Ellis had alluded to had been received moments before they had entered the wedding fair venue. Their client, Judge Pennington, had without doubt been ahead of the game on the subject of her partner's long-time infidelities. However, the big shock Billie and Ellis were about to report on Monday morning, when the judge had booked in an update, was that he wasn't actually her husband at all. Not legally. He already had a wife and two small children living in Surrey when he had entered into the bigamous marriage with her and her sizeable bank balance.

He was clearly a man of many personalities, reshaped to fit in with each of his latest romance scams. It appeared that he was planning another repeat performance with Pandy Wood, who obviously had absolutely no idea about her fiancé's true past or future intentions. But during the hair-wash stage of Billie's styling saga, Pandy had divulged a large inheritance as a result of a family bereavement and had been talking about investing it. Billie felt honour-bound to protect her new friend, despite the hairdresser having at first appeared to have simply been 'the other woman' in this investigation.

'We're thinking of having one of those photo booths on our big day!' Pandy joined them, holding her fizz in one hand and her new fiancé's arm in the other. He looked at Billie, tracing his gaze up her long legs, pausing at her cleavage before addressing Ellis. Billie mentally bristled.

'Sounds like they've just scored.' He flicked his head in the direction of the football stadium.

'Have you seen that kinky stall over there?' Pandy put her hand over her mouth in mock shock as she whispered in Billie's ear. Billie looked across to the stall full of tacky honeymoon-night toys, including edible knickers and wind-up private parts. Somebody was clearly in for a rib-tickling first night, she guessed, by the look of the interested females crowding around the stall.

'You were asking if there were any handcuffs on there, weren't you, Rexy?' Pandy trilled suggestively, pulling Rex close as Billie put her hand in her pocket and started the hidden camera recording. 'Likes a little bit of naughty light bondage, don't you, Sexy Rexy?' Pandy continued, totally loved up. 'Well, you said there's no harm in it, didn't you, love? Not when you are in a forever relationship.' Ellis coughed. Billie hoped he wasn't going to be sick.

'You know how it is, mate, women like to be kept cuffed to the kitchen sink, right?' The judge's husband winked at Ellis. Billie guessed that he had modified his accent to fit in with his fake personality. She also guessed that he was a mouse of a man at home, wondering what it would be like to be a fly on the wall in that house when Judge Pennington cornered him with the evidence. She was having trouble not grabbing him by the scruff of the neck and pinning him up against a wall herself right now and not in any remotely romantic way.

'Know of any good stag venues?' Ellis fell into the part of fellow randy fiancé. Billie knew he would have his own hidden camera rolling. Rex winked at him, man to man.

'Funnily enough I do, mate. Why don't you two lovely young ladies run along to that wedding-favour stall over there. What the hell *are* those things anyway?' He was playing to Ellis now. 'While we have a man-to-man chinwag...' Pandy giggled like a schoolgirl.

'I told you those two would get on, didn't I?' She nudged Billie, who thought she'd downed a glass or ten too many of the Asti Spumante. 'Now, no naughty boy talk.' She wagged her finger. 'We'll be back in a moment.' Pandy staggered off in the direction of the white frilled and swagged tables decked with wedding paraphernalia.

'See you over at that corner bar table in five,' Billie called to Ellis, who nodded. They needed to get more footage of the engaged couple together as evidence. Rex elbowed him, whilst projecting his voice for Billie's benefit.

'You want to watch her, mate; she's trying to get you under the thumb already. Treat 'em mean, keep 'em keen, I'm telling you, son.'

'You're bang on there, lad,' Ellis answered, through a chuckle, pretending to wave Billie away as he turned Rex in the direction of the bar, well aware that Billie would be finding it difficult to disguise her reaction to Rex's *sage* advice.

'We're having such fun here, we're thinking of setting up a wedding event business ourselves,' Pandy confided in Billie as she reluctantly followed her towards an array of strawberry- and chocolate-flavoured bridal thongs.

'Is that a good idea?' Billie was suddenly on high alert.

'Yeah, well Rex says you've got to speculate to accumulate, and I've got all that money my Aunt Sadie left me, just sitting in the bank doing nothing. I was planning to set up a couple of nail salons but we're going to Rex's bank first thing in the morning to do a transfer. He says that he's an expert on these sorts of things and I've got enough on my plate with Pandora's Lox,' Pandy explained, referring to her hairdresser shop.

'Wouldn't it be wise to wait?' Billie's mind was racing. Sexy Rexy's game would be up when they reported back to Judge Pennington on Monday, but even so, it would still cause all sorts of legal headaches for the unsuspecting bride-to-be, getting the money back into her account. Not least, due to claims that would be made by his two separate families to his assets. It didn't seem fair.

'Don't see any problem.' Pandy giggled as she wound up a

plastic dick that set off at a pace across the tabletop. 'After all, we'll be husband and wife soon. What's mine is his and vice versa. "Till death do us part" and all that.'

Billie was finding it almost unbearable to hold her tongue whatever promises she and Ellis had made to Judge Pennington. Her attention was suddenly distracted by activity outside, beyond the huge glass window separating the Saturday shoppers from the wedding bubble. Billie had developed an almost sixth sense to this sort of thing due to her years as a detective.

She suddenly realised what she had picked up on. An elderly man, obviously visually impaired, wearing dark glasses and being led by a guide dog, was being followed by a hefty youth walking rapidly towards him. He suddenly pushed the man forcefully and kicked the dog hard, before ripping a leather bag from the man's shoulder and racing away across the road in the direction of the hotel. Billie took off like a greyhound, pushing past the wedding fair attendees before hurtling through the front doors, emerging outside to intercept the thief. He was heading for a narrow alleyway that Billie was now blocking.

'Out of my way, bitch!' he snarled at Billie, who swore under her breath when he pulled a razor-sharp craft knife out of his pocket and waved it towards her. She had no intention of letting him pass, but she was hyper aware that a knife often turned out to be a lethal weapon even in the hands of the most inexperienced thug. The knowledge made Billie move quickly, taking advantage of the fact that the thief wouldn't expect a woman in a dress and jacket with a flower corsage pinned neatly on the lapel to do what she was about to.

She whipped forward, grabbing the wrist of the hand holding the craft knife, forcefully pinning the young man's arm back, locking his elbow. At the same time she pushed herself hard against his body and whacked the back of his knee firmly with her foot. He catapulted over and hit the ground, thankfully loosening his grip on the knife as he did so. It dropped to the pavement. Billie kicked it into the gutter, aware of people around her now and the door to the hotel opening. Bodies tumbled out. The thief still held on tightly to the bag.

'Drop it!' Billie shouted loudly, pulling the hand that had held the knife tightly behind his back as he lay face down on his stomach. 'Drop the damn bag!' she bellowed again, pulling his arm tighter behind his back as he squirmed. It was with some relief that she spotted Ellis's scuffed suede boots coming into view. He stood on the hand holding the bag, whilst reaching over to pick up the craft knife.

'The lady says drop it.' His voice was quite calm, but with an air of potential threat. The thief finally gave up as Ellis yanked the bag from his fingers.

'Check the guy and the dog are okay.' Billie caught her breath as she stopped fumbling in her pocket with her free hand, yanked both arms behind the youth's back and clipped on the handcuffs she had pulled out, pleased to find a spare old pair of police gadgetry within the smart jacket that she'd had no need to wear for months now. It had been something of a joke in the past that she would secrete police paraphernalia about her person even when wearing a slinky dress on a night out, hence her one-time nickname, 'Ever Ready'.

'Wow. Did you get those from the stall over there?' She heard Pandy's voice, glancing back to see her looking at her in amazement. 'Good quality, aren't they? Last us a lifetime that pair, wouldn't they, Rex?'

Billie was already pulling out her mobile, pressing in the emergency number, before looking up to see a police minibus pulling alongside the kerb. A uniformed officer climbed out. He looked at Billie, took in the scene.

'I thought you had scarpered from the force, ma'am,' he said. 'Believe I chipped in for your leaving present.'

'You're a copper?' Pandy sounded astonished. 'I thought you said you worked with animals?'

'Same thing, love.' The police officer firmly grabbed the still struggling body. Another officer who had now jumped out of the minibus, joined him in hauling the disgruntled bag snatcher upright.

'I'm making a citizen's arrest, as per section 24A of the Police and Criminal Evidence Act 1974. Charges are assault and robbery on a vulnerable person, animal cruelty and threat with a bladed weapon... That last one alone will definitely get you locked up and off the streets for a bit, sonny boy.' Billie faced the young man, as Ellis rejoined her.

'The guy and his dog are okay,' he told her. 'Bit shaken up, but someone's taking him home.'

'You'll have to come down and give a statement, ma'am,' the police officer added as he and his colleague propelled the disgruntled thief into the vehicle.

'You can forget the *ma'am*. I'm just plain Billie Wilde now,' she replied, running her fingers through her hair.

'But you told me your name's Jayni Knowles!' Pandy looked with a stunned expression, from Billie to Rex who had joined her. He grabbed Ellis's arm.

'Sure you are doing the right thing getting hitched to her, mate? Rather you than me. Great pair of pins, but I hope you're not getting blinded by the bodywork. Make sure you get her to say the "obey" bit loud and clear. For what it's worth, my advice would be you're better off looking for something smoother to handle.'

'Hang on.' Billie stopped the police officers as they were about to get in their vehicle. 'Got you another one here–' She had her hand in her other pocket, had realised that she had another set of handcuffs in there and just couldn't resist the urge

16

overwhelming her as she marched swiftly across to Rex, yanked his arm and clipped the handcuffs on.

'What the hell is she doing?' Rex shouted at Ellis as though Billie was a child that was out of control.

'Making another citizen's arrest,' Billie addressed the gobsmacked officers.

'My Rexy? But what on earth for?' Pandy wailed like a child.

'Bigamy,' Billie announced loud and clear as the people crowded around, some filming on their mobiles. 'Sorry, mate, it's not going to be third time lucky for you.' She yanked Rex's arm forcefully as he tried to pull away, pinning him hard up against the hotel wall, staring into his eyes. 'Let's hope that when you come up in court, it's before your second wife, Judge Pennington...' She yanked the stunned man towards the police vehicle, pleased that Ellis had his head in his hands, shaking it in horror at that moment, so he couldn't catch her eye.

'In the meantime, it'll be li'l old me walking you up the aisle to an appointment with the custody sergeant. As long as you love, honour and *especially* obey, we'll get along just fine.'

Chapter 3

A Sting In The Tail

'Don't judge anyone until you've walked a mile in their shoes.' Billie pretended to be irritated by the ribbing from those assembled at Ellis's newly inherited terraced home, where they had gathered for a house-painting party. They were hugely jollied up by glasses of beer, wine and takeaway pizza and consequently, a devil-may-care attitude to her attempts to whitewash the whole embarrassing situation.

'If I had walked a mile in your shoes then I would have nicked your shoes and I wouldn't like to have been wearing those stilettos of yours when you were hot on the chase, a set of handcuffs in every pocket.' Teddy Cook, Ellis's cousin, was waving the front page of the local newspaper under Billie's nose, finding the whole situation hilarious.

Billie cringed inwardly. It was true that she had blown their undercover operation quite spectacularly. She could hardly deny it, caught here in the full cover shot, legs akimbo across the back of the wriggling crook, leaving little to the imagination as her demure on-the-knee dress had moved thigh high in the skirmish.

'Wilde by name, wild by nature, mate.' Ellis shook his head at the memory.

'And all caught in the flash of our roving reporter's camera.' Boo Mensah laughed, clapping her hands gleefully towards a large woman in her forties, paintbrush in hand, slapping magnolia paint onto the wall of the room.

'Well, what do you expect?' Perry Gooch tried to argue. 'I'm just a poor jobbing freelance journo with two teenage daughters to keep in false brows and tat with a designer logo stamped on it. Billie handed it to me on a plate. Editorial manna from heaven. Otherwise all I had to report was a minor skirmish between a scrawny kid and the owner of Barbara's Big Baps sarnie stall, outside of the footie match. She'd taken offence at his offer to give her a free saveloy dip.' Perry rolled her eyes. 'Kids today, eh?'

'Well at least someone's getting paid as a result.' Ellis filled his roller with paint from a tray. 'Mrs Judge is arguing that we're in breach of contract, despite saving her the divorce fees to get rid of the husband that never was. I'm guessing that she gets off on power. Bit miffed at the embarrassment of a local copper knocking on her door to share the news that her man's in custody and he's actually married to someone else. Trouble is, we did agree in writing to keep the information for her eyes only...'

'I said I'm sorry.' Billie pulled a long-suffering face.

'I'll sort out Pennington, no worries.' Perry Gooch slapped some more paint on the wall, which was now rocking a patchwork display of varying decorating skills due to the age, size and inebriation level of the different painters. 'I'll doorstep her. Put it to her that I'm going to write a story about the judge with no judgement skills. Can't even spot a fraudster when he's been literally staring her in the face for years.

'I'll also mention that it will bring a lot of aggrieved

characters crawling out of the woodwork, determined to tell me how she also judged their convictions all wrong. Actually, that's not such a bad idea for a story...' Perry dunked her brush in the paint pot thoughtfully, before slapping more, haphazardly, across the wall. 'Anyway, putting that mercenary thought aside as we're mates, I'll offer to forget my brilliant feature idea, as long as she pays Wilde and Darque in full for their services.' Perry grabbed a slice of pizza and stuffed it in her mouth.

'Sounds like blackmail to me and aimed at a judge, not wise.' Ash, Billie's best friend, was focusing on painting the chimney breast area of the room, his two older daughters, Happi and Indie, at his feet, happily splashing paint aimed at the skirting boards in all directions. Ellis laughed.

'Oh I forgot; the long arm of the law is in the room. We still have one functioning copper left amongst us. Keep schtum on any dicey dealings we may be thinking of, folks.'

Until just under a year earlier, DS Ash Sanghera had been Billie's trusted wingman within the MIT unit. Boo had been her crack office manager, whipping the team into shape, ensuring that evidence was submitted on time, vital information reported back to Billie and generally guaranteeing that everything ran smoothly. Ellis had been called in to offer specialist support on a particularly harrowing case. They had been a team of best mates as well as colleagues. But there had been a seismic shift, for every one of them, when Billie had decided that she desperately needed to break free. The result was that Ash was now the only police officer amongst the group still in the force.

'Don't remind me,' Ash answered. 'Hey, did you hear about the two peanuts that went for a walk in that dangerous part of town I warned you about?' Ash asked seven-year-old Indie.

'No, Dad,' his sweet-faced daughter replied, a look of worry furrowing her brow.

'One was assaulted.' Ash chuckled.

'God give me strength!' Teddy Cook shook his head in dismay at Ash's terrible joke. He had a reputation for them. Billie laughed.

'Yeah, if I ever have any regrets about leaving the force, I just dredge to mind the dozens of crimes against comedy you hit me with on every shift,' she jibed. Not that Billie had left Ash. He lived in the basement flat below her own house, in an idyllic spot overlooking a white sandy beach. Billie couldn't be happier with the arrangement. It kept her friend close along with Indie, Happi and Tani, her god-daughters, on the weekends that Ash had child access, following his recent divorce.

A car horn peeped outside as a dark Audi pulled up. Teddy dumped his paint roller in the tray, grinning.

'That's my get-out-of-jail-free card, saved from more Christmas cracker jokes,' he quipped in the direction of Ash. 'Got a date with the lads.'

'You never said that you were only putting in half a shift. Can't get the staff these days,' Ellis shouted after Teddy, good-naturedly. Billie clocked that Ellis seemed to have bonded really well with his new-found second cousin. It had been a bit of a year for him. First, the revelation that he had a teenage daughter, Maya, from a brief relationship eighteen years earlier. The stunning young woman had come looking for him after her mother's death and then decided to follow in her father's footsteps, set on a career in crime prevention.

Then, completely separately, the news that he had an uncle whom he had never met, who had died and left him a huge surprise – his terraced home in his will, along with an assortment of far-flung relatives. Billie had suffered her own monumental family upheavals in the past year and had for a time been left feeling utterly bereft. She was so glad that Ellis's discovery of past family secrets had resulted in a much happier ending.

'How's Maya's new room coming on?' Billie asked Ellis. His daughter had earmarked a huge room on the ground floor, with a bay window, as hers and had great plans for the decoration. It would be the first time that father and daughter had actually lived together, so Billie knew that Ellis was desperate to get it just right.

'She's due to text me any minute about her pick-up time from the airport. I was hoping to have her den well underway before she got back, but I've had to wait for a chimney sweep before getting started. He's coming this afternoon. The fireplace is boarded up and she's after some fancy surround that she's seen in a magazine. Got her dad wrapped around her little finger that one.' Ellis grinned at the mention of Maya's name.

Maya had been away for a month during her break from university, helping out at an orphanage in Romania with some fellow students. She had been taking a degree in Professional Policing and had been a very useful member of Billie's team whilst on work experience, during Billie's last investigation as a detective.

'Maybe she's fancying an alternative career as an interior designer?' Billie mused. Boo had confided that Maya had recently shared a few dark moments of indecision about her university course and future career choice. Not exactly surprising after the grizzly work experience she had undergone whilst on Billie's last job.

That particular case had been life-changing for them all and Billie wondered, outstanding team player though Maya had turned out to be, whether her original vocation decision might have been coloured by a desperation to impress her newly found dad. Ellis had a reputation as having been one of the top officers in the Serious Crime Investigation Agency.

Billie had come to realise that her own high-flying career before breaking free, had been caused by the same intention, in connection with her own father, a former chief of police. She didn't want Maya to fall into a similar trap. She hoped that a month away in a totally different environment would have offered the young girl space to think about what she *truly* wanted to do in life regardless of the choices that had been made by those around her.

'Remember I said I would pick her up from the airport,' Billie called across to Ellis, the offer having been made when she was still in the throes of guilt about outing the bigamist so publicly.

'I'll drive you,' Boo joined in. 'I'm on orange juice and let's face it, I'm better at stripping paint off skirting boards than painting them neatly,' she added. It was a fact that no one present could argue with. Boo was legendary for moving at such speed in her powered wheelchair, that she regularly took centimetres off any skirting boards or door frame that might stand in her way.

'Any excuse.' Ellis rolled his eyes. 'It's like rats leaving a sinking ship this. You lot were meant to be helping me turn this into an ideal home...' They all paused for a moment, taking in the view of the hideously applied paint.

'We could have a whip-round to get some proper people in,' Ash offered. 'Didn't you say you've got some distant cousin here who runs a building business?'

'According to Teddy, he owns loads of different businesses, but I've never met the guy. Hardly know any of my rellies, let's face it. I didn't even know I had a dead uncle. Mum's big brother from her dad's first marriage. She never even met him.'

'The joys of blended families,' Billie said with a sigh. Trying hard not to dwell on her own less than perfect mix. 'Okay. We'll just come back tomorrow and put on another coat of paint. It should brush up okay...' She trailed off, looking around. It was clear by the looks on the faces of the others that they were less than convinced. Ellis's mobile rang.

'Oh, here's Maya now.' Ellis clicked on the video link.

'Shouldn't she be on the plane?' Billie asked, before Ellis turned the mobile screen to face the group. They all shouted greetings. Indie and Happi waved their paintbrushes at the strikingly pretty girl who had been their nanny for a while when she had first appeared on the scene.

'Dad–' Maya started to say, before the screen went blank.

'Signal's dropped. Maybe the plane is delayed.' Ellis started punching Maya's number into his phone as Ash took the paintbrushes from Indie and Happi.

'Right, let's go to the kitchen and clean up. Cuppa everybody?' Ash asked. Everyone cheered. There was a sudden rap at the door knocker. 'Chimney Sweeps,' Ash announced, glancing through the window. 'We'll let them in, girls.' The chimney sweeps emerged in the background, equipment clattering as they dragged it into the room across the hall. Ellis listened into his mobile, shook his head and tried again. Billie had started scrolling through her own phone. She frowned.

'Looks like the flight's due in on time. Maybe she's accidentally left her mobile on and it's connected to a roaming system en route.'

'I hope not. That'll come out of the bank of Dad. I know someone who did exactly that. He got charged five hundred quid when his phone connected to the system of some far-flung country they were flying over at the time.' Ellis had a pained expression as he stared at the screen of his mobile phone.

'Best give it a rest from trying to ring her then,' Boo advised.

'Got a moment, mate?' One of the chimney sweeps popped his head into the room. 'Looks like you've got one big blockage in here. Maybe an old wasps' nest. They can stay in place for years, especially if the fireplace hasn't been touched.'

'Yeah, whatever, I don't think that room's been used for yonks.' Ellis shoved his mobile into his pocket and followed the sweep across the hallway. His partner was on his knees in the room, squinting up the dark chimney opening. He shook his head.

'I've just tried to send the digital camera up but it's too crammed to get a proper picture. Might have to charge you extra for the additional time in clearing it out. Is that okay with you?'

'Yeah, it's for my daughter. Her new room.'

'Enough said, mate. Got to make sure that your little princess stays safe, right?' Billie joined Ellis who couldn't resist taking his mobile out of his pocket and trying Maya's number again. Billie smiled. Ellis already had a toddler daughter from his former marriage, but he had been an utterly doting dad to Maya, the child he hadn't even known existed until last year. Making up for lost time... The phone went on to loudspeaker. A single long ringtone rang out.

'Probably dead.' The first sweep was talking to the second now as they assembled their brushes.

'What?' Ellis asked, misunderstanding.

'The wasps' nest.' Billie patted Ellis's arm.

'Yeah. Don't worry, we've got it under control. You aren't in for any nasty surprises,' the first sweep called over his shoulder, as they started the motor of the power sweeping brush. Perry joined them at the doorway, taking a cuppa from the trays of tea and biscuits offered by Ash and his girls, as the brush started to make a loud noise. The sweep stuck his arm up the chimney.

'I've got hold of something. Here we go–' He tugged hard. There was a sudden and huge fall of soot, along with a clattering noise of the blockage collapsing into the grate. A cloud of dust filled the room for a moment, making everyone cough, before it cleared to reveal a skeleton wrapped in a soot-embedded lace wedding dress, various bones detached and scattered. A black, partly mummified skull rolled out, still sporting odd strands of long dark hair. It came to a halt at Billie's feet, eyeless orbs, staring upwards as though crying out for a safe haven.

'Jesus,' gasped Billie, looking up at the others.

'No, it must be Santa Claus?' Happi innocently corrected Billie, before Ash quickly swept the girls out of the room.

The January wasp's desperate flight had finally ended. Billie exchanged glances with Ellis. Was this the reason why he had been left the house by a relative that he had never even known existed? Had his uncle been hiding a terrible secret, one that he had planned to reveal from beyond the grave? Skeleton bride's didn't just turn up in chimneys without a disturbing story to tell. Billie shivered. She suddenly had an ominous feeling that this particular horror story would have a deadly sting hidden within its tail.

Chapter 4

The Lady Doth Protest

'One hell of a house-warming party. You've got to admit that,' Boo said as she headed for the airport with Billie in the passenger seat. Billie was already wondering if that had been a good decision, bearing in mind that Boo drove her car much like her powered wheelchair, now tucked behind them in Boo's specially adapted vehicle. Luckily, she hadn't gone as far as shaving off the sides of pavements as she zoomed by, but it was a close thing.

Billie breathed in as they came within millimetres of taking a driver's wing mirror out whilst overtaking. The driver shouted something abusive that luckily Billie couldn't hear due to the speed at which they were moving and couldn't have pulled him for anyway, not now that she was no longer a serving police officer.

'I wonder how long the skeleton bride's been there?' Boo pulled a face. Billie shrugged.

'Not my problem anymore,' she answered, starting to hum a tune in an absent-minded fashion as she looked out of the car window, hoping a mother pushing a child in a pram wouldn't make it to the zebra crossing before they did. She wasn't certain that Boo would stop.

'Got no strings to tie you down.' Boo glanced at Billie, before slamming on the brakes as the mother pushing the pram stepped out onto the zebra crossing.

'Hmmm?' Billie swallowed hard, trying to appear nonchalant, as she gripped the passenger door handle with white knuckles. Boo had been injured in the line of duty long ago and was defiantly independent. Billie guessed that her gung-ho driving style well predated her disability. She didn't want Boo thinking she was making judgements based on that.

'That's the song that Pinocchio sings, the one you're humming, and I can see your nose growing right now,' Boo joked.

'Well, do me a favour and keep your eyes on the road,' Billie answered as the woman finished pushing her pram across the road and Boo took off at speed once again.

'The lady doth protest too much,' Boo teased. 'Sure you've got no regrets about giving up the force? The skeleton bride would be our case if we hadn't all upped sticks and scarpered.' Boo slammed the gear down and took over a lorry. Billie's life passed before her eyes.

'Too many memories. You can't change history, but you can stop making the same mistakes over and over again,' Billie answered. 'You decided the same thing with Ellis,' she added. Boo and Ellis had enjoyed a professional partnership as undercover detectives years before, that had almost become a romance before fate had struck. They had tried to pick up where they had left off when he had arrived to advise Billie's team a year earlier, but it hadn't worked out in the end.

'We're still great mates though and he was an all right lodger, bar the snoring that I could hear through my bedroom wall.' Boo chuckled. 'Probably be coming back to doss down short term, whilst your successor digs up his new gaff looking for more hidden bodies.'

'That'll take a lifetime if Slug Harris is definitely Senior Investigative Officer. Why they didn't give the job to Ash, I'll never know.'

'Because he's your mate.' Billie already knew that Boo didn't believe in beating about the bush. 'Same reason he elbowed us all aside when he took over from you and we ended up jumping ship. We're all too good for him and he knows it.'

Billie sighed. She tried to put thoughts of the skeleton bride aside, shocking though the unannounced party guest's entrance had been. She'd had a couple of wedding close shaves of her own, so the tragic vision had sent shivers up and down her spine. She didn't want to dredge up any unwanted memories.

'Looks like she's been there a good while. Shame Ellis didn't know more about his uncle...'

'What, like he was a lady killer?' Boo just missed a cyclist as she swept through a set of traffic lights as they were turning red.

'Seems odd that he would have left his home to a senior crime officer, if he did away with the wife and stuffed her up the chimney,' Billie reasoned. Boo shrugged as she took a sharp turn right into the airport.

'Guilt can be a funny thing. You know yourself, sometimes people put on different faces for the separate people they meet.' She glanced at the clock on the dashboard. 'Phew, just made it in time.' She cut in front of a car which was about to pull into a disabled parking space. The driver slammed on the brakes before getting out of his car and irately approaching them, hammering on Billie's window.

'Hoy, what do you think you're playing at? That's my space!' he ranted. Billie so wished that she still carried a police ID. It would usually shut a big mouth up without a word of argument.

Boo poked the passenger window button on her dashboard. It slid down.

'Disabled space, and from where I'm looking you haven't got a badge, mate.' Boo leaned over Billie. 'Take a look in the back.' She flicked her head towards her wheelchair. 'Space is all mine, sonny boy, and I'm a vulnerable person, so don't try and upset me.' The irate man backed off as Billie chuckled under her breath.

'Vulnerable person, you?' She raised a questioning eyebrow at Boo. 'Whose nose is growing now, Pinocchio?'

———

'Plane arrived on time anyway.' Billie scanned the board as people milled around, dragging cases through the thoroughfare. She spotted one of Maya's friends being welcomed by her mother, heading off, out from the airport.

'Here they come,' Boo said. 'Who's going to be the one to tell her that we've just found a skeleton in her new bedroom?'

'Let's take it gently. We don't want her jumping on the first plane back,' Billie quipped, as more students she vaguely recognised as uni friends emerged, looking dishevelled from the journey. As minutes passed and the arrivals crowd thinned out to a sporadic trickle of weary bodies, a girl with long hair dyed every colour of the rainbow appeared alone through the arrivals door. It was Maya's best friend, Lily. Billie approached her.

'Is Maya coming through?' Lately they had been practically joined at the hip. She wondered why Lily hadn't waited with Maya to collect her case. Lily shrugged.

'Maya wasn't on the flight.' She frowned, shaking her head as though Billie and Boo were a bit dense.

'What do you mean?' Boo looked from Billie to the girl. 'We've come to pick her up.'

'Right. I thought she would have sent a message. Told you she's staying,' Lily explained.

'Staying?' Billie ran her fingers through her hair. Maybe that's what the curtailed call from Maya to Ellis had been about earlier, but she was due back at uni in a couple of days, which in practice, meant work experience in the unit Billie had just stopped running. Billie had quietly hoped that Maya might have fed her some juicy titbits about the skeleton bride investigation despite her claiming to have washed her hands of police problems, once the youngster had returned to work.

'For a bit, then maybe travelling with Mitch.' Lily glanced across to her father, who was approaching with a big grin on his face. Billie knew that Ellis wasn't going to be smiling when he got the news. He was looking forward to having some quality time with the daughter who he had met for the first time, so recently.

'Who's Mitch?' Boo asked.

'Just a guy she met. What is this, a police interrogation?' Lily was only half joking.

'It would be nice for her dad to have some information,' Billie persisted, as Lily handed her case to her father. He nodded cheerfully to Billie and Boo.

'I've got to go.' Lily started to move off. Boo moved her powered wheelchair, blocking the teenager's way.

'You're her best friend. She must have told you more about her plans.'

'And you must know something about this Mitch. Where's he from, is he a student?' Billie added. Lily rolled her eyes in response.

'I get what Maya was on about now, all this close surveillance of her all of the time.' Billie and Boo glanced at each other, turning with equal indignation back to Lily.

'Meaning?' Billie asked.

'Well, *obviously* after her mum died she had nobody and yeah, she did go searching for her dad, but she had to fend for herself at first, even been homeless for a bit and now she's getting all this fussing all of the time from the crazy surrogate family. It was only her and her mum in the past. It's all been a bit much.'

Billy knew that Ellis would be hurt if he had heard Lily's words. Maya had been conceived when he was working undercover with an environmental protest group, the pregnancy totally unbeknown to him, confirmed after he was taken off the job. He was desperately ashamed and equally desperate to make up for lost time.

'She's just been finding it a bit suffocating.' Lily looked down, kicking the toe of her trainer against the floor. She bit her lip before adding, 'And the whole police thing. I mean, she was totally freaked out on that last case, working with you.'

Billie was in no doubt that Lily was accusing her. They had all been freaked out by the last case that Billie had overseen as a police detective, but no one could have been more so than Billie herself.

'Now she's got a taste of freedom again, maybe she wants to do something different, perhaps working for a charity like you, Boo,' Lily said. Billie knew that the irony of the words wouldn't have escaped Boo, whose budding romantic relationship with Ellis, way back when they had been acting undercover together, had stopped before it had really started because of his brief liaison with a target. Crazy then, that the child born from that momentary lapse in professional conduct, was thinking of modelling herself on Boo and her new job with a charity that focused on homeless teenagers.

'We all felt that we were doing something useful, you know, volunteering with the orphanage over in Romania. Helping people get a better life, not digging up the dirt once they're like, dead.' That was clearly the final nail in the coffin as far as Lily's appraisal of Billie's former brilliant career went, Billie reflected. Maybe she was right.

'We just want to check that she's okay.' Billie had decided to ignore the jibe. 'Was Mitch another volunteer at the orphanage?' She had to tell Ellis something to reassure him. He wasn't exactly laughing when they had left. He'd been waiting for Billie's successor to arrive, with a partly mummified bride lying at his feet.

'Yeah. But Mitch's a regular. He knows the ropes. He and Maya really hit it off.'

'Sorry, but I'm in the short-stay car park,' Lily's dad politely interjected, a look of apology on his face, 'and her mum's got her favourite tea waiting. We really must run.' He took Lily's arm and led her away. The girl only glanced over her shoulder once as they left through the door, but for some reason the look on her face made Billie shiver.

'What do you make of that?' Boo looked from the door to Billie.

'I think she's keeping something from us.' Billie had her bullshit radar on full alert.

'What, so she doesn't hurt your feelings?' Boo quipped.

'Maybe she's right, I'm insufferable, suffocating and an eternally over-suspicious former copper.' Billie pulled her mobile out, wondering how Ellis was going to react when she conveyed the news.

'Or maybe she's telling a pile of porkies.' Boo turned her wheelchair back from facing the door, having watched Lily climb into her dad's car. Her mobile suddenly rang. 'Ten guesses who this is...' She pulled a face at Billie as she glanced at the screen before answering. 'Hi, Ellis–' Boo started before her greeting was cut short and her face fell. 'You are joking?' Billie heard her friend say with utter disbelief. 'Okay, keep us posted.' Boo ended the call and shoved her mobile back in her pocket.

'What? He didn't even ask about Maya.' Billie was amazed.

'He didn't have much time. Making use of his one call. Slug's trailed over to the house. He's just been arrested.'

Chapter 5

Taking No Prisoners

'Y̶ou're having a laugh, mate. Been doing your SIO exams at kindergarten?' Ellis rocked back on his seat, arms folded, as he eyed up Slug Harris.

'I've got strong grounds for arrest.' Slug Harris's voice sounded like it hadn't even broken properly yet. Ellis remembered Billie having taken some flack in her time, for being a young detective super. Those people who were jealous of her outstanding success blaming it on her dad and then her godfather having both been chiefs of police, but at least she'd earned the respect of her fellow officers, big time. She'd been an absolutely cracking detective who'd led her team in solving a series of shocking serial killer murder cases, not without huge personal cost. Slug Harris wasn't fit to walk in her size sevens. Not by a long chalk – even though whispers were that one of his parents was a big nob in the judiciary.

'Still waiting for those grounds, sonny boy, and the clock is ticking. Let's hear them loud and clear. I've got my daughter heading home from her holidays and I'm not going to be singing "La Cucaracha", if she's sitting on my doorstep, whilst you play at *RoboCop* with me here.' The custody sergeant appeared to have been equally inexperienced and incompetent. It was like a group of kids on work experience. Ellis put his feet up on the desk, staring hard at the young detective.

'Grounds for arrest are necessary criteria, set out in paragraph 2.9, section 24 of PACE, Code G.' The young man puffed up with self-importance.

'Really?' Ellis knew them all off by heart. He raised an eyebrow. Slug flicked a gelled fringe away from his eye, his voice becoming a little more sotto, aware as he was of Ellis's piercing stare.

'The necessary criteria being that it is believed that the person may, a) steal or destroy evidence, b) may collude with co-suspects.' Slug blinked, slightly nervously.

'It's on record that I've regularly risked my life to gather and preserve evidence. Even had a couple of awards for it so good luck with that one and I'm asking, yet again, to see your grounds for suspicion that I've done anything of a criminal nature at all.' Ellis folded his arms. 'You are not seriously saying I stuffed the wife up a chimney on our wedding day years back. A quick check will prove that I've only just moved into the house.'

'Owned by a relative. Therefore you had means of access.'

'I never even knew my poor old unc existed until a few months ago and that body has been up the chimney for a good while longer than *that* by the looks of things. My ex-wife though, is very much alive and kicking.'

Ellis blew out a sigh. That was the truth, and she was still giving him earache two years after they'd parted, especially over access to his toddler daughter, Connie, never mind her less than thrilled reaction to the news that he already had a teenage child, Maya, that she'd never known about during their marriage. Still, Connie adored her big half-sister. He'd been so looking forward to Maya's return, flinging the door of their new forever home open and showing her the progress made with the decoration.

Now this kid was wasting his time on charges he couldn't make stick in a million years.

'In addition, section C clause one, "to prevent the person in question causing physical injury to another person..." In this case me,' Slug Harris added.

Ellis rolled his eyes. Maybe he had threatened a few words when the puny kid had suddenly clipped the handcuffs on out of the blue, when he was pointing up the chimney to demonstrate the skeleton bride's line of travel, but Father Christmas himself would have been tempted to give the geeky kid with the astonishingly high-ranking credentials, a knuckle sandwich as a gift. In truth, he was feeling the urge again right at this very moment.

Chapter 6

Lunatics Have Taken Over the Asylum

'Your breakfast is served, my lord.' Ash entered the cell with a bacon butty and a mug of coffee in his hands. 'Heavy on the brown sauce,' he added, as Ellis rubbed his bleary eyes and dragged himself into a sitting position on the hard mattress. In truth he'd only fallen asleep in the past hour, furious and indignant that the little squirt who had somehow managed to take Billie's place in charge of the Murder Investigation Team had kept him in a cell all night, despite Billie apparently having rang up and bent his ear big time. It had resulted in her being threatened with a written police harassment warning. Slug had a cocky little grin on his face when he had popped his head in his cell before he had clocked off, to pass on that vital bit of info.

'Lunatics have taken over the asylum here, mate... thanks.' Ellis took the bacon roll and bit into it. 'Careful you aren't seen canoodling with the chief suspect. Slug isn't taking any prisoners and you were in my gaff as well, when the corpse popped in to say hello.'

'Yeah, well, Gazza Middleton has just clocked on as custody sergeant this morning, and he's already making his feelings known about the situation. He's waiting for Slug to come in before reading him the riot act. My guess is you'll be out of here in the next half hour.' Ash handed Ellis his mug of coffee. He took a hefty swig, thinking of the corpse in his front room.

'Your little 'uns all right? Not every day you see a dead body appear down a chimney.' Ellis considered that he at least should be pleased for small mercies. If his Connie had been on a visit at the time, his ex-wife would have gone hell for leather to make sure he only had supervised access in future.

'Yeah. Took them home via the ice-cream parlour and told them it was some old Halloween prank left up the chimney. They didn't know any different. Thank God there wasn't much flesh left and what there was didn't look real.'

'Poor woman.' Ellis rubbed his face in thought. 'Probably young. Had the whole traditional white kit and caboodle on.' He pictured his beautiful Maya, possibly around a similar age to the tragic bride. Probably like his girl, she'd also been looking towards a bright new future. 'With Slug in charge, it'll be a long wait to find out the full story. This should have been *your* gig, Ash, mate. Job for the grown-ups.' Ash shrugged.

'To be honest I don't want the top job. Nearly finished Billie off and my top priority is my little girls. I might not live with them full time anymore, but me and Jas, we've got over the initial upheaval and we're agreed that from now on, they come first. Same reason you gave up your big flash job.'

'Yeah, that worked out well.' Ellis took another bite of his bacon sandwich. 'I'm still working long hours and still undercover half of the time and the ex *still* doesn't like me having time with Connie. Tell you what, Maya's been my lifesaver.' Ellis pictured his beautiful daughter with her amber eyes and tawny afro hair, sunny and bright and a brilliant team player during her work experience on Billie's team. 'Funny, never knew that she existed for eighteen years and now I couldn't imagine life without her.' Ellis grinned. Ash cleared his throat.

'Em, last night, Billie rang from the airport–'

'Took her to doss down at her place, did she? CSI lot would have been crawling over my gaff all night.'

'Em, no. Maya didn't get off the plane,' Ash explained. Ellis stopped mid-bite on hearing the news.

'Why not?' Ellis swallowed hard.

'Gone travelling with a mate apparently,' Ash answered.

'What mate? She's due back on work experience tomorrow. Soon as I get out of here and get my phone back I'll have a talk to her.' He swung his legs off the bed and started striding around his cell.

'Billie and Boo have been trying to make contact with her all night.' Ash dodged a surge of coffee slopping out of the mug as Ellis banged his hand on the cell door.

'Get a move on out there. I need to be out!' he shouted, before turning back to Ash. 'So what did she say? I thought she would have had a word with me first.' Ellis felt his heart sink a little. Maybe he wasn't turning out to be the dad of her dreams after all.

'Em, well, it's probably nothing. Maybe she was on a ferry or something like that, but she's not picking up.'

'Have they left a message telling her to call asap?' Ellis banged the door again. 'Hey, the joke's over. Slug's going to cop it for this!' He'd been happy to cut the little squirt some slack as Maya had been due to start work experience on his team when she returned from holiday. But Slug would definitely be straight on her back in any case if she toddled in from her holiday late.

'That's the thing,' Ash said carefully. 'Her line's dead.'

Chapter 7

Fast As A Shark

Billie kicked open the door to an office marked *Wilde & Darque Private Investigators*. It had been a long cold night, one in a lengthy line of long cold nights that she had recently spent on observation duties. She had been mostly following the movements of wandering spouses in preparations for divorce cases, interspersed with investigations into fraudulent injury claims. Both types of jobs paid well, so though Billie often found them to be utterly tedious, she had knuckled down and got on with it.

She and Ellis had been taking turns, along with a couple of subcontractors that they hired on a freelance basis, with the different surveillance jobs. It ensured that the target didn't suss that their every move was being watched. As luck would have it last night, the subcontractors had been tied up with other pressing duties and Ellis was locked up in the clink, so Billie was the only one on duty. Nowadays, she didn't have any other commitments and intended to keep it that way, so the extra time spent working was no skin off her nose.

However, she couldn't shake the skeleton bride away from her thoughts, wondering how the tragic corpse had come to be in a chimney in full bridal dress. Billie wondered what secrets Ellis's dead uncle could have told, if only he had made contact with Ellis before his death. Unless he had been the killer of the bride of course. Billie couldn't help the fact that she still thought with the mindset of a detective specialising in murder investigations, rather than a snoop.

She sat down at her desk, releasing a newspaper from under her arm before biting into a bacon and egg sandwich, the sticky orange yolk oozing out onto the paper serviette it was wrapped in. She closed her eyes for a moment, thinking *heaven*. Eating trash food was her default mode on the job and always had been. After all, there had been neither time nor opportunity for five-star cuisine in her old career and as she was finding out, that was still the case these days, despite the change of job.

Billie decided that Ash would probably turn out to be her lifesaver, now that he was living in the flat below her, after she had converted her house. Her dear friend and one-time colleague was a talented cook, who regularly filled her freezer with his amazing culinary creations, so that she had less chance of furring up her arteries, at least when at home.

Also, the night before, she had an unexpected exercise session, when the woman who had been claiming sickness pay for the best part of a year, insisting that she'd suffered a serious back injury at work, had set off in full cowboy kit towards a village ten miles away. Intrigued, Billie had followed and consequently found herself having to sign up for a line dancing class. Two hours later she had mastered the Cowboy Hustle, how to do an Apple Jack, a Side Shuffle and a Chug.

She couldn't remember her legs ever aching as much in her life, but the target had taken it all in her stride, even moving forward to show off her steps in a particularly taxing dance called Fast As A Shark, to Olympic standards, Billie judged. Personally, she had been hard-pressed not to ricochet into the dancer next to her and risk causing a pile-up. Not a good move for an undercover investigator. The whole exhausting dance workout, with the target taking the spotlight, had been captured on Billie's body camera, masquerading as a scarf toggle, so the client would be happy to pay the not insubstantial bill for Wilde & Darque's services rendered.

A family sized bag of crisps and a hot dog had been required to sustain Billie through the long night spent afterwards in her car during which she filmed an errant husband, allegedly away on a business trip, arriving at his lover's house for the third day in a row, staying all night and French kissing him on the doorstep, whilst squeezing his bum before heading off for work. *Bingo*, Billie had almost said out loud, before heading off to get her present breakfast to celebrate.

At the odd moment, after she had joined Ellis in their new business venture, she had dwelled upon the havoc she was helping to wreak with her work, celebrating moments of surveillance success which would invariably devastate many innocents. Of course, her investigative actions had shattered families in the past, none more so than her own perhaps, but she had been on the track of killers then, people who arguably deserved everything that was coming to them. She had been prepared to do absolutely *everything* in her power to catch those responsible and bring them to justice.

Billie had left the force because she had unveiled past cover-ups at a high level, some involving people close to her and she wanted to step aside in order that the full truth could come out without any accusations of judgements being swayed by her presence. But what had the local MIT ended up with? Slug Harris, that's what.

Still, her driving force had always been the search for truth and her private investigations were still revealing that. Now it was for other people to decide whether to bang the guilty to rights. She was learning to stand back and come to terms with her new role, but not without long nights of soul searching with her surrogate family, Ash, Boo, Perry and Ellis to help her to come to that conclusion.

The newspaper's front page read *Skeleton Found During Home Renovation* with Perry Gooch named as the author in the byline. She'd moved quickly. Billie smiled. The short paragraph didn't give much away but as a freelance reporter Perry would have earned a few quid for it. Just doing what she had to do, regardless of the fact that the body had been found in her mate's house, whilst she was helping paint it. Billie had once been at loggerheads with Perry, but now admired her no-nonsense attitude, dogged determination to follow a story and dedication to earning a crust to support her two teenage daughters as a single mother.

Billie suddenly heard a knock at the door and looked up. A drip of egg landed on her sweatshirt. She quickly wiped it away as a man entered. He was tall, thin, and wore spectacles, a nervous and apologetic edge to his demeanour.

'Hello, I'm looking for a private investigator.' He frowned as though it was the first time he'd ever uttered such words. In truth, Billie reflected, it probably was. She grabbed the serviette that had been wrapped around her sandwich, wiped her hands and held one out.

'Hi, I'm Billie Wilde. How can I help you?' she asked. The man blinked.

'I'm looking for the detective that I saw in the newspapers,' he answered, glancing quickly up at Billie and then back at the floor again as he shook her hand. She didn't blame him for not recognising her from the photo of her straddling the thief outside of the wedding fair. She'd been scrubbed up then, unlike now when she was wearing no make-up, faded jeans, a top with egg stains on it and, she suddenly remembered, a dark bob wig that had kept her head warm all night during her in-car surveillance. It had also been disguising her memorable shock of red corkscrew curls, which she revealed as she dragged the wig off and dumped it on her desk. The man blinked in shock.

'Oh, yes, sorry. I recognise you now,' he said. 'I've come about my son, Ozzie. Full name Ozzie Kingsnorth...' He trailed off into silence. 'It's all so difficult, unbelievable...'

'Right.' Billie reached for her notepad. 'Mr Kingsnorth, is Ozzie in trouble?' For some reason a picture of Maya flashed through her mind, the look on her friend Lily's face, as she had turned when leaving the airport, the long flat tone of an unobtainable number when she had tried to ring her several times after leaving the airport.

'Please, call me Richard. He never said he was in any trouble... such a dear boy...' Billie suddenly noticed tears starting to trickle down the man's cheeks. He reached into a pocket and pulled out a cloth handkerchief, blowing his nose hard. 'Sorry, I'm so sorry. Ozzie's dead, you see.' The man started crying again. Billie got up, shoving her notebook in her back pocket.

'Let's have a cup of tea and you can tell me all about it.' Billie headed to the kettle in a kitchen area in the corner of the room, reaching for tea bags and biscuits, her back turned from the man for a few moments to allow him time to compose himself. Her career as a police detective had taught her that key facts would be lost if a nervous interviewee felt pushed into talking too quickly. The door was suddenly flung open so hard that the man visibly jumped.

'Bleeding hell, you'd think I had all day to sit around!' Ellis bellowed, seriously out of sorts as he marched in, not having even noticed Richard Kingsnorth, now bent over, reaching for his handkerchief that had fallen onto the floor.

'Stuck doing nothing in the cop shop. I told them, my kid's

gone missing, and you lot are arsing around wasting my time. You new plods don't know your arses from your elbows!'

Ellis finally focused on Billie, his mind suddenly back, Billie imagined, from venomous thoughts of what he would like to do to Slug Harris. She flicked her eyes in the direction of Richard Kingsnorth. Ellis clamped his mouth shut, but the man was now holding out his hand in Ellis's direction.

'That's exactly it. That's *exactly* how I feel!' His voice had now turned from sorrow to indignation.

'This is Mr Kingsnorth. He's just lost his son, Ozzie,' Billie explained to Ellis. He nodded, stony faced as he took the man's bony hand.

'Sorry for your loss.' Ellis moved immediately into professional mode. 'Two sugars for me.' He nodded at Billie, who grabbed another mug and slung another tea bag into it.

'And me too, please,' Richard Kingsnorth piped up. 'I'm still recovering from the shock,' he added. Billie piled the chocolate chip cookies onto a plate and handed it to Ellis as they led the bereaved father over to a low seating area at the other side of the room, which consisted of two long modern sofas covered in bright red fabric, facing a coffee table.

'The police, they've been totally useless in my opinion.' Richard Kingsnorth was talking fast now, obviously desperate to get his story out. 'Not that we've ever had any dealings with them before. Not in a thousand years, but the individual we've been interacting with, he's no more than a *child*...'

Billie and Ellis exchanged glances. It sounded like Slug Harris or one of his junior-school cohorts had been looking into the death. Richard Kingsnorth took a sip of his tea and slammed his mug down in anger and stress. A little tidal wave slopped out onto the coffee table. Billie remembered now hearing via her car radio, when she had been doing surveillance on a wayward husband the week before, about a body of a young man washed up in a local river. It sometimes seemed that the dead came to find her, wherever she went.

'He insists that Ozzie simply drowned, postulating strongly that he expected it was suicide and said that was the theory he was putting forward to the coroner. Total poppycock! Ozzie's mum's in bits. We were a happy family and devoted to Ozzie. There's no way that he would have just gone running off without a word and then killed himself. Ozzie wanted for nothing. We mollycoddled him if anything. We're in the middle of decorating his room – he'd seen a picture in some swish magazine and was trying to recreate it. There's no way he would suddenly have done off...'

Billie looked up at Ellis who was out of his seat, rubbing his face, as he started to walk back and forth. He may have looked as though he was simply dealing with an aching back as far as Richard Kingsnorth was concerned, but Billie could tell that his words had an uncomfortable ring to them as far as Ellis was concerned, now that his own daughter appeared to have suddenly gone AWOL, also totally out of character.

'How old was Ozzie?' Billie took her notebook from her jeans pocket and clicked on her pen.

'Nineteen. I mean, he was in the prime of his life – a strong boy, cheery too. Everyone loved Ozzie. He wasn't top of the class at school, but he enjoyed his job, did voluntary work for a charity and seemed to get on well with all of his workmates. Everyone is just devastated...'

'Well, if you wish to take us on to investigate further, then we can request that a second autopsy be conducted and make arrangements...' Billie saw Richard Kingsnorth's eyes scrunch up at the very thought of the body of his precious boy being cut open and examined for a second time, but he nodded his head in agreement.

Billie was aware that a swish new private forensics lab had

opened up just a few miles away. She'd had no need to use it yet in her new job, but it allowed access to areas for a private investigator that had only been open to police before. Whatever Billie and Ellis did wouldn't bring Ozzie Kingsnorth back from the dead, but a thoroughly investigated cause of death might allow his parents to move slowly forward with living.

'What evidence have they given you for suicide?' Billie asked. It seemed to be a spurious claim without having done a thorough investigation involving friends, workmates and family. She wondered who the forensic pathologist was that Slug had got his information from. Josta, her dear friend for many years and the leading forensic pathologist in the area, had left during the recent shake-up that had involved everyone, it seemed, in Billie's sphere. Billie missed her, just like she still missed lots of other people.

'They have no evidence at all! The police didn't even speak to us about Ozzie's state of mind. Not to me or his mother. I understand that they interviewed the people he worked with, they apparently said that he had complained that we were suffocating him at home, and he wanted to get out.' Richard Kingsnorth reached for his already tear-sodden handkerchief and pressed it up against his eyes. It didn't stop one large sad salty droplet from skittering down his face.

Billie saw Ellis squirming with discomfort himself, as he paced the floor, rubbing his hand over his face. It was a sign Billie recognised as his own individual reaction to stress. Billie had been told that she started running her fingers through her hair in situations that upset her equilibrium. She didn't need to guess what was causing Ellis's discomfort. He had already pulled his mobile out of his pocket and glanced at it, no doubt for the hundredth time, checking for signs that Maya was okay.

'We can get a second examination underway quickly then,'

Billie said, making a note on her pad. 'And we will also visit Ozzie's workplace, which is?'

'Silver Darlings up at Sugar Sands Harbour.' Billie was writing but heard Ellis's footsteps stop. She didn't need to ask why. 'They've got a wonderful reputation, export smoked fish all over the world and Ozzie enjoyed working there. Got on well with everyone, even the boss. He'd been first in the queue to volunteer for extra shifts. They've been so busy – expanding and they snapped him up.

'That's why this talk of suicide is all so ridiculous. He was happy at work, had good friends and a devoted family – everything to live for. He was a strong swimmer too, competed in school trials for the county and had swum in that river numerous times. We would have family picnics there when he was a little lad...' Richard Kingsnorth trailed off, his eyes closing again, no doubt, Billie guessed, because sunny memories of happier times were skipping through his mind. 'The whole situation just doesn't ring true.'

'Right, Mr Kingsnorth, this information is very useful. If you would like us to proceed then we have a contract–' Billie didn't mind landing clients with their terms and conditions when Wilde & Darque had been engaged by a big insurance company, to investigate a fraud case, but this was the first time that she had been required to talk money over a probe into a suspicious death. She didn't like the feeling, knowing in truth that she would be happy to do this enquiry for nothing. It sounded like another big Slug cock-up to her, but then unlike Ellis she wasn't short of money, nor did she have two daughters and an ex-wife to support, as well as a crumbling old terrace to renovate.

'Yes, yes, I'm happy to proceed. I don't need to know the terms. At least if our beloved boy is looking down on us from somewhere, he will know that we left no stone unturned to prove that he didn't commit suicide.' He blew his nose on his handkerchief, heaving out a sigh of utter desolation.

'You can be certain we'll do everything to verify the truth or otherwise, sir.' Billie gave a small smile. She was desperately sad for the man, but a tiny spark of excitement was also igniting inside. Investigation of dodgy deaths was her home territory, and she was determined to do absolutely everything in her power to ensure that Ozzie Kingsnorth's death was investigated properly. His devastated dad finally reached for a biscuit, whether because he was calming down or desperately needed sugar to remain upright, Billie wasn't sure.

'His boss's name is Teddy Cook.' He tapped his finger on the table next to Billie. 'I can give you his number,' he added, reaching for his diary from his jacket pocket. Billie scribbled it down as he read it out, glancing up to Ellis as she did so. They both knew that they didn't need it spelling out. Teddy Cook being Ellis's newly found cousin.

Chapter 8

Silver Darlings

W hen Billie and Ellis entered Silver Darlings, it was the smell that hit them first, smoky, salty and fishy with a smouldering undertone of oak. A large window covering one wall showed plump herrings, hanging row after row on tenterhooks above little fires, glowing on whitewood and oak shavings in the cavernous smokehouse. It was certainly a sight to stop any visitor in their tracks. Another large window on the other side of the room showed women wearing white oilskin aprons and matching wellington boots, splitting the shiny-skinned fish in two before washing and brining, continuing from one room to the other on their sea-to-smokehouse kipper journey. Ellis's cousin ran a tight ship that prided itself on its excellence as a traditional business.

Teddy Cook suddenly loomed into view, dressed in yellow oilskin dungarees over a blue boiler suit. He gave a wide grin on seeing Billie and Ellis, swung the door open and in a cloud of grey smoke, stepped out from a herring's version of Dante's *Inferno*.

'Look what the tide swept in,' Teddy greeted them cheerfully. 'Come to have a look at my silver darlings?' He waved his hand towards the racks of smoking fish behind him. 'These are in demand all over the world. We even get orders from royalty, I'll have you know. I'll stick the kettle on.'

Billie remembered that Teddy had also inherited this business and the house attached to it, overlooking Sugar Sands Harbour, from Ellis's uncle, who had started the business way back. He had recounted at the house painting get-together, that his much-loved uncle had taught him all the tricks of his trade. That Teddy had followed him around since childhood, like a faithful puppy dog. He had grown up in the house next door to his uncle and had also lived with him for some time, in the place that Ellis now owned. She reflected that it was a shame that Ellis had never had the chance to know the man, who had kindly thought of the distant, never-met nephew, leaving him his home in his will. He certainly didn't sound like the murdering type.

Teddy seemed happy with his uncle's decision. Probably, Billie reasoned, because of his own generous inheritance. She admired the way that Teddy also appeared utterly at ease in his own skin, staying in the same area where he had been born, carrying on traditions that were generations old. Billie wondered if Ellis envied him that stability in his life.

'Come to pick your brains. First, about the dead body stuck up my chimney.'

'I thought you bent my ear over that until there was nothing left to say yesterday when they let you loose from the nick. Not that you were in any mood to be listening. You are now the official black sheep of the family. Good job you didn't light the fire in the grate in that front room. Now that's what I would have called a killer house-warming party.' Teddy chuckled.

'You've been hanging around Ash too long.' Billie rolled her eyes in response to the tasteless joke but didn't hold it against Teddy. Nobody resorted to gallows humour more than murder detectives to cope with some of the shocking crime scenes that they were confronted with. Billie had been guilty of equally grim remarks herself, in the past. Ellis spotted Teddy's biscuit tin, prised the lid open and started raiding it.

'I mean, did our good old benevolent unc have murderous tendencies that everyone's been keeping me in the dark about? I thought it was too good to be true, somebody just leaving me their gaff like that. Maybe he was on some guilt trip. Should I be digging up the patio next?'

Billie thought that wasn't actually a bad idea but kept the thought to herself for the moment. Chances were that Slug Harris was exploring that possibility right now if he had it in for Ellis. Teddy spooned instant coffee into mugs and poured on boiling water, handing them around.

'Milk's in the fridge here. Help yourselves.' Teddy blew out his lips as he considered Ellis's answer. 'No way it was anything to do with Uncle Tommy. Great bloke. He didn't have a mean bone in his body. What's more, he never married or even dated anyone as far as I can recall and the only woman I ever saw in his house when I was around there when I was a kid, was the cleaner. She used to do shifts here as well and she's still alive and kicking. Got half a dozen grandkids at the last count.' Teddy took a swig of his coffee, thoughtfully.

'Then, when he had his stroke and I took this place over, with him not being able to walk or even speak or anything, he had carers to get him up and put him to bed, but he wasn't in a state to marry one of them, then think better of it and stuff her up the chimney. My guess is your dark skeleton dates back to ancient times, or well before Uncle Tommy bought the place anyway. He never used that room. It's the one that they used to keep for best in the old days, you know, for when visitors came. But I can't remember anyone ever visiting. The family hardly ever called by. I was the only one he took a shine to really...'

Billie took a sip of her coffee, it tasted smoked. The biscuit she bit into in order to cover the taste was worse. The way Teddy was knocking his cuppa back, she guessed his taste buds had become accustomed to it.

'Well, maybe you can help us with another mystery body.' She looked at Teddy, trying to cover a grimace as the taste hung in her mouth.

'Who do you think I am then, Sherlock Holmes?' Teddy dunked his biscuit into his tea, for double the smoke sensation, Billie guessed.

'This one should be easier. The body washed up on the riverbank a couple of days ago. It appears that he worked here. Ozzie Kingsnorth, is that right?' Billie asked. Teddy put down his mug, a pained expression on his face.

'Yeah, that was a real bummer. Poor old Ozzie. Been with us since he left school. Good worker too. First in line to do the overtime shifts. Couldn't believe it, mate, just couldn't believe it. The lad's a big miss.'

'The fuzz have told his folks it was a likely suicide. That sound the business from your point of view?' Ellis put his mug down. It was still full. Billie guessed he hadn't inherited the family smokeproof genes. 'Knocked his mum and dad sideways as you can imagine, the thought of that.'

'Yeah, well you know what it's like, mate. Us crumblies don't know it all. Word from the police was they heard Dad and Mam wanted him sitting at home watching *Antiques Roadshow* all night. The cling-on type. Lad wanted to get out in the world – see a few sights, not be tied down with the old folk. Guess it all got too much for him.' Teddy glanced over to a young man walking across the room with a tray of kippers in his arms. Teddy waved him over.

'I've got to get back, but Smokey Boy Patel here, he was good mates with Ozzie. He'll give you the inside story. Might have been him that the police interviewed. Is it true that Ozzie was at the end of his tether with the old folk, Smokey Boy?' Teddy slapped the young man on the back, taking the tray off him, before marching back into the smoking chamber.

'Smokey Boy, is that your name?' Billie yanked her notebook and pen out of her pocket.

'Yeah,' he answered meekly, looking down at his feet. He had a striking face, even dressed in the uniform of blue boiler suit, yellow apron and wellies. His eyes were green, fringed with thick dark lashes. His jet-black hair cut in the latest style, with shades of caramel, honey and gold, a perfect balance of dark and light, giving a tortoiseshell effect.

'Worked here long?' Ellis asked.

'Yeah, since I left school. Followed my dad into the job. Smokey Patel.' He nodded to a man packing kippers in an area off the smoke chamber. He was an older version of the teenager, although sporting a more sober hairstyle. 'Me and Ozzie started together,' he added, looking up. His eyes had started to fill with tears. He quickly wiped his sleeve across his face to remove them.

'So you knew him better than most?' Billie watched him sniff, take a deep breath and then look at his feet again. He nodded. 'We were like brothers.'

'So he would have talked to you if he was thinking of killing himself?' Billie could see Ellis wasn't in the mood to beat about the bush. Smokey Boy's head shot up for a moment, his expression indignant.

'No way would he have–' He stopped, looked down again. 'He must have just drowned. Maybe had a few drinks when he jumped in.'

'So who told the police he was suicidal?' Billie took up the questioning again. Smokey Boy shrugged, glanced up and across to the smoking chamber.

'Dunno,' he answered. His voice almost a whisper.

'When did you last see him?' Billie asked.

'A few weeks back. I was away for a bit, abroad and when I came back, he'd gone.'

'Away on holiday, were you?' Ellis questioned. 'Ozzie not fancy going?'

'He couldn't get time off.' The young man shrugged.

'This poor lad sounds like a prisoner at home and at work.' Billie remembered Richard Kingsnorth describing Ozzie as a happy-go-lucky lad. 'Did you not have any laughs together?'

'Girlfriends, nights out, that sort of thing?' Ellis picked up the questioning.

'Yeah. Ozzie was a real laugh, the best. We were always messing around. He wasn't the way people are making out...' Smokey Boy trailed off. Billie sensed real sorrow in his voice and indignation at the way his friend's death was being portrayed. 'It was just a terrible accident.'

'What's this?' Ellis waved to a poster on the wall across the room and started marching towards it.

'The firm was sponsoring a fundraising thing for an environmental charity and me and Ozzie volunteered to do a photoshoot with some students from the uni.'

Ellis stopped in front of the poster, so that at first Billie couldn't see what he was looking at. As she joined him, she spotted Smokey Boy in the photo, linking arms with two other young men and two girls.

'That's Ozzie there.' Smokey Boy pointed to a smiling young man who looked almost as photogenic as he did. 'The other guy, Jake, and the girls were uni students. The one with the dyed hair, that was Lily and the other one, can't remember her name, but she was really hot...'

'That's Maya.' Billie nodded towards the beautiful girl smiling out of the photo, arms linked with Ozzie and Lily.

'You know her?' Smokey Boy asked.

'Yep.' Ellis tore his gaze away from the poster for a moment to reach for his mobile again to check it. Billie could see that the action was in danger of becoming a nervous tic.

'I had to leave straight after we finished as I had a flight to catch. I think I remember her saying she was going travelling with some uni friends the next day too. I left her and Ozzie in a dark corner, getting to know each other. Looked like it was going to be a long goodbye. Maybe she took him for a midnight swim.'

'What do you mean by that?' Ellis suddenly squared up to Smokey Boy. Billie caught his arm as the startled boy stepped back.

'Just that they looked really into one another–'

'That's my daughter you are talking about, sonny boy!' Ellis pointed his finger.

'Smokey Boy,' the teenager corrected, biting his lip. The door from the kipper smoking room suddenly opened. Teddy popped his head out, shouting over towards them.

'Hey, can I have my staff member back if you've finished grilling him? Pardon the pun.' He grinned, thumbing the kippers hanging in rows. Smokey Boy looked relieved. Ellis shook Billie's hand away from his arm. She pulled a business card from her pocket and handed it to the lad.

'We're investigating Ozzie's death for his mum and dad. Trying to put their minds at rest as to what actually happened to him. If you can think of anything that might help us shed some light on how he came to be washed up on the riverbank, please get in touch.' Smokey Boy took the card, glancing sideways at Ellis before sliding out of grasping distance and marching towards Teddy, head down. Billie could tell that there wasn't a cat in hell's chance he would willingly head their way again.

'Take it easy.' Billie took in a big breath of smokeless fresh air as she looked towards Ellis, his face dark as thunder as they left the building. This was a side of him that she wasn't used to seeing.

'I can handle myself, thanks. I don't need you to hold my hand. Equal partners, remember,' he snapped back. Billie was startled by his response but reminded herself that he had just found a dead body in his chimney. Most of his investigations to date hadn't been so personal. She, on the other hand, had got well used to the feeling.

'Sorry. I know that you're worried about Maya, but the lad might have been able to give us vital information about Ozzie leading up to his death–'

'Yeah. He has. He was hanging around with my girl and that fact alone gives me the creeps–'

'Aren't you overreacting?' Billie cut across his words. 'She flew to Romania the next day and it sounds like it was the first time they had met.' A picture of Lily's face as she departed the airport arrivals lounge suddenly appeared in Billie's memory. She swept it away. Maybe it was true that working in law enforcement made operatives eternally suspicious that everyone was hiding the truth.

'And now she's missing–' Ellis started, checking his mobile again. Billie wondered if she should perhaps have shared Lily's views at the airport, that his newly discovered daughter was desperate for some space? It had seemed too cruel an insight to inflict on him after a night in a police cell at the mercy of Slug Harris, but perhaps, Billie reflected, it was better to be cruel than to be kind. Ellis might end up heartbroken about her feelings for him but less worried as to Maya's whereabouts.

'Not missing exactly. Just out of contact...' Billie had been trying to calm the feeling herself, that there was something more to Maya being unreachable than a dicky mobile, but right now there was no evidence to the contrary.

'Well, maybe that's the difference between us, mate.' Ellis

clicked his car keys to unlock the vehicle. It stood in a bay next to Sugar Sands Harbour, a dark foreboding space created from whinstone with an opening to the stormy sea at one end. Right now, waves were crashing against the wall under a darkening sky. A spray of salty seawater caught on the breeze, stinging Billie's cheeks.

'What do you mean?' Billie frowned as she strode alongside Ellis and swung open the car door.

'Your main interest is dead people, whilst I'm trying to save the living.' Ellis climbed into the car and started the engine as Billie stood gobsmacked. The comment had hit home like a slap in the face, especially coming from Ellis the jovial joker. It made Billie wonder once again if she had made the right decision in leaving her top job in the police and joining forces to run Wilde & Darque. One thing was for sure. The honeymoon period was definitely over.

Chapter 9

Sleeping Beauty

The first thing Maya was aware of was a pounding headache and the feeling that her tongue was so dry that it seemed stuck to the roof of her mouth. She swallowed hard, trying to turn her body in the darkness before other painful sensations enveloped her with every movement. She heard a moaning sound, that at first seemed very far away, before her brain registered that the keening noise was emerging from her.

'Sleeping beauty awakes.' It was a female voice, heavily accented. Maya now heard others, whispers in the darkness, words trapped in what felt like a dim fug. Was she back in the orphanage? Some of the sounds matched the rhythms of Romanian speech that she had become accustomed to after a month volunteering there, but the smell was different – cheap perfume mixed with a musky smell of sweat and cigarette smoke, an undertone of urine. She started to cough.

'Sssh, stay quiet.' Another female voice now, closer. Did she recognise it? It reminded her of sweet Otilia, fourteen years old and preparing to go out into the world now that she was considered old enough to fend for herself. But hadn't Otilia said goodbye already when Maya had been packing for the airport? She recalled the girl having been in the room with her when she had rung her dad, but then again, her memory was hazy.

Lily had told Maya earlier that their plane had been delayed and they would be leaving later. She had taken the children out to the park to play one last time. Lily had said she was going sightseeing, then... what? She remembered calling her dad to tell him about the delay. It had connected, then everything after that moment was a total blank. Had something fallen on the back of her head? She lifted her hand to try and feel if she had a bump, but her limbs felt leaden.

'What's going on?' Maya struggled to get the words out, trying to open her eyes. It felt difficult, as though she had the worst hangover in the history of hangovers.

'You've got to stay quiet. Here, take some water...' The face loomed over Maya as she felt a small hand slipping behind her head, helping to tip it forwards. She flinched at the contact. Something definitely wasn't right. She struggled to sip from a plastic bottle, coughing, almost choking as the water took a detour, slipping down into her lungs. She pushed up onto her elbows, desperate to breathe, her eyes finally flickering open, focusing on the face of her helper. It was indeed Otilia. She had a worried look on her pretty features that made her appear even younger.

'What's happened?' Maya gasped for breath in between sips of the lukewarm drink. She felt hot and sticky. Maya remembered having been desperate to take Otilia back to England with her, rather than think of the girl fending for herself on the streets. She had wanted to look after her. It seemed the relationship had spun around, just like her head was spinning.

What was it she had just discovered? Something

important... something that affected Otilia... yes, that was it. The girl had confided that she wasn't an orphan, that her family had sold her to the 'orphanage' to pay back moneylenders, that many of the children weren't really orphans. That well-meaning foreigners had been duped into supporting an institution that existed to exploit in all manner of ways, making money by using the children.

Now, she slowly remembered, having been in a state of shock at the story, she had run to find Mitch, recounted the horrific tale and told him she was going to ring her dad. He would know what to do. He would report it, send people to check it out. He had contacts...

'We've been taken away,' Otilia whispered. 'You've got to stay quiet, or there will be trouble for all of us. They'll beat you again.'

Maya blinked and managed to look around now. The room was small and bare. As she turned her head she realised that bright light was shining from a tiny window, behind and high above her. She closed her eyes tightly for a moment. When she opened them again, she found herself staring into several other faces, all of them female. Whereas she was lying on a hard wooden pallet covered with a filthy mattress, the other girls were huddled on scraps of sacking and the odd rumpled blanket. They appeared to be in a dank cellar. A bucket in the corner of the room explained the smell that had caught her breath on awakening.

Outside, she could hear male voices and laughter. The sound of people enjoying freedom. Maya's brain suddenly started to kick into gear as she felt an ache deep in her body, chafing between her legs. It was only now that she realised that she had no clothing on and that dried blood covered the insides of her thighs. She wrapped her arms around her body, starting to shiver, with shock rather than coldness.

'Where's Mitch?' Maya asked Otilia, who shook her head.

'He's not called Mitch,' Otilia answered. 'He gives girls different names every time he comes to the orphanage. I don't know his real name, just that he is British. He's a lover boy.'

'I had a lover boy once. I was stupid. He told me we would go to Rome together. He could get me work, we would eat pasta and drink wine. La Dolce Vita. The sweet life.' An older girl was speaking now. Maya's age, perhaps. It was the first voice that she had heard on awakening. 'I was so in love, so stupid. I never guessed that as soon as he took me to Rome he would sell me to a pimp and then he would trade me on. See, I have three tattoos from each one who's owned me.' Maya was horrified as the girl held out her arm. One of the tattoos looked just like a barcode on a supermarket product. Merchandise to be bought from the wholesaler and then sold on for profit.

'Now, I have the new one, just like you.' The girl moved her hair aside to show the tattoo on the nape of her neck. It was still encrusted in blood, but the shape of a wasp could be made out on her soft skin.

'We all have it.' Otilia lifted her own hair to show Maya. 'It hurt. At least you were unconscious and couldn't feel anything.' Maya clutched the back of her neck and felt encrusted blood. In her case it was only one of the locations of pain and damage to her body, but somehow the small branding affected her more than any of the other horrific indignities.

'Take this. It is yours. They left it for you.' The older girl handed her a short, flimsy and cheap-looking red nylon wrap, with scratchy black lace trim around the edges.

'No.' Maya shook her head even as she grabbed the garment, desperate to cover her nakedness. The other girls were similarly covered in an assortment of short, cheap and nasty garments, all doing little to hide their bodies. One girl in the corner had a bottle of nail varnish in her hand. She was painting her toenails a garish blue.

'What are you doing?' Maya could make no sense of the scene. The girl was around Otilia's age, long haired and plump, a couple of early teenage spots erupting on the chin of her freckled face.

'If I look good, they get paid more when we have sex with men. Trust me. This is the second time the traffickers have taken me. I was only twelve the first time. They toured my home village. If they want us, they take us. Nothing anyone can do. I got away once before and got back to my family, but when my father had to take work abroad, they came back.

'Try to fight and you will get beaten, as you can see. There is no way out. We are on the move. Last time I ended up in Germany. Who knows this time? It is always the same anyway, no matter where we end up. This is our life. We can do nothing but make the best of it. If I'm lucky and he's pleased with my work, my lover boy will keep me this time.'

'This isn't happening.' Maya managed to pull herself upright as she dragged the hideous garment around her body. The faux lace scraped against her already sore legs; sharp, plasticky monochord thread-ends stabbing areas of her body that already felt heavily bruised. She felt sick. 'We've got to find a way out.' She thought of her mobile phone. 'I'll call my dad.' She hardly had the words out before the plump girl laughed.

'They took our phones. They took our passports, they take everything. We don't exist anymore. Nobody is coming to help us. This isn't a fairy tale. They've already taken what they wanted from us when they gave us the drugs for transport. They always test the product before they start selling and still you didn't learn, you still tried to fight back. They just make you suffer more.'

'I'm not staying here. I've got a home and family to go to—'

'Yes, we heard you argue that you were training to be in the police.' It was the older heavily-accented girl speaking now. 'Stay quiet from now on. That only made it worse for you. It's a good job you were so drugged that you don't remember, but we all saw it. Everyone sampled your wares. They laughed and joked whilst they were doing it. Forget your past life. Nobody will find you.'

'My dad will.' Maya was certain it was true. Her dad was almost superhuman in her eyes, and Billie too. They would find a way; she was sure of it. As soon as Lily told them she was missing. 'He's probably got a search party flying out to Romania now.'

'They moved us, in the back of a lorry.' Otilia looked tearful. 'Your lover boy had a gun. So did the older man. We all had to stay silent. That's why they gave us drugs. To help. But you wouldn't, so they gave you more. We thought you might be dead. You've been asleep for maybe two days.'

'So where's this?' Maya suddenly felt sick.

'Who knows? They took our watches. They took everything from us,' another girl whispered.

'We're in Poland now.' The plump girl finished painting her toenails, stretching her legs out to admire the result. 'I came here once before. It's one of the places they buy and sell us for sex. Just like the cattle market in my home village. There are many sellers and buyers from everywhere. Maybe I will go to England this time. They say it's a good place to be taken. Girls can be hidden in plain view there. Nobody notices their neighbours and if they do, nobody likes to complain. It's a free country.' Maya couldn't believe what she was hearing. Couldn't believe that most of the girls appeared to be accepting of their situation. She was determined to get out.

'You won't be going there, of course,' the older girl said to Maya, her voice dropping to a whisper as footsteps could be heard heading in their direction. 'We'll all be split up. You'll be going somewhere your papa has no hope of finding you. The sooner you wise up to that, and forget you ever had a family, the better it will be for you in the end. Now is the time to sing from our lover boy's song sheets.'

Chapter 10

Passing Strangers

'Has he started humming tunes yet?' Boo chuckled as Billie caught up with her in a community café attached to Boo's new place of work, managing a charitable foundation helping young homeless people. Billie waved across to the waitress to request a second mug of coffee, such was her desperate need for caffeine.

'None that I've felt like singing along with. We aren't exactly on speaking terms let alone likely to launch into a duet.'

Billie was still smarting with indignation, having confided in Boo about her fall out with Ellis.

'He'll start doing that. Listen out for it. Great indication about what he's really feeling. He even does it in his sleep sometimes. I swear that I once heard him humming *"Wake me up before you go-go"* one morning when I left him snoring in bed.' She chuckled. 'I'm beginning to feel like a marriage counsellor here.' Billie rolled her eyes.

'Let's not even go there. I've just been to visit a client to tell her that her hardworking husband, allegedly away on business, has been dirty dancing with his boyfriend, only a couple of miles away from her doorstep.'

Billie had tersely asked to be dropped off by Ellis, unable to bear the icy silence in the car on the way back to the office. The day before, after Richard Kingsnorth had left, Judge Pennington had swept in to give an earbashing in person and Teddy had been away on business until this morning. That meant that she'd had time to update various reports and invoices ready to be delivered to clients, so she had good reason to be elsewhere. She looked at her watch and yawned before gladly accepting the coffee refill. She'd been on overnight investigations two nights in a row now.

'Ellis was meant to be handling the office this morning. He was so stressed out yesterday, I insisted he take an early night and doss down at my place. If I hadn't been so kind, I could have left him to deal with poor Ozzie Kingsnorth's investigation alone.'

'That was never going to happen,' Boo replied.

'Don't you start saying I've got an obsession with the dead now.' Billie ran her fingers through her hair. Boo patted her arm.

'I'm sure Ellis didn't mean it like that. And he'll be pleased with the speedy resolution of those two cases the other night. No doubt there's a big lump of dosh due.'

'Dunno. I didn't tell him where I was going. Got out of the car before he'd even stopped it.' Billie's temper flared again at the memory of Ellis's harsh words. 'Come to think of it, he was humming *"We seem like passing strangers now"*.' Boo smiled.

'Look, I love you both. You're my best mates but you are both strong characters, used to getting your own way. It was always going to be a bit of a bumpy ride at the beginning, starting a new business venture. You'll be a great team before you know it.'

'I might be asking you to do a few freelance shifts for us if the work keeps coming in at this rate.' Billie stifled another yawn. 'I was hoping to knock off now, but someone just left a message on my call service saying they have seen us in the paper and are desperate to have a word about a new job, this afternoon.'

'See. There's no bad publicity. But you've been up all night. Let Ellis do it. Here, have some more sugar.' Boo pushed her half-eaten wodge of chocolate cake in Billie's direction.

'Thanks. He no can do. He'll be on a job this afternoon. Another investigation into fraudulent disability claims. Guy says he's got such bad arthritis he can't even use a toothbrush, but word is he makes a living as Kev the Clown, master juggler. Speciality's sink plungers apparently and they're extra hard on the old mitts. Ellis needs to get evidence of him performing. Word is he even balances a kid on each hand for the grand finale. Get a pic of that and the job's a good 'un.' Billie forked a large chunk of chocolate cake into her mouth as Boo laughed out loud.

'So is Ellis taking Connie and playing the party dad?' Boo asked, referring to Ellis's toddler daughter.

'Ha, no way. Can you imagine his ex allowing *that*? He's already had to go to court to get unsupervised access, with her claiming his old job puts him and Connie at risk of revenge attacks. He's undercover as the other children's entertainer.'

'You are *joking*. Ellis?' Boo wiped her eyes as tears of laughter started to leak from the corners. 'He'll do anything to prove he's a real family man right now. No wonder he's so upset about Maya going walkabout. The ex will make a big thing of that, if she doesn't come home soon. Lost one kid, can't be trusted with the other one.'

'I wish I was joking.' Billie finished off the cake as the waitress brought the mug of coffee that Billie had requested. 'Hope he's not billing himself as Mr Chuckles, that's all, because he seriously hasn't had me in fits of laughter so far today.'

'I'm sorry to interrupt.' The waitress was staring at Billie.

'But aren't you the famous private detective, the one who was on the front page of the news stand across the road?' Her voice was heavily accented, Billie noted.

'Well I wouldn't say that.' Billie exchanged glances with Boo. She was hoping that the photo would have faded quickly from the public's mind, that it had already become the proverbial fish and chip wrapper.

'Billie meet Abrihet. Abi, if we're being less formal. She's made amazing progress since arriving at the foundation. Couldn't speak a word of English when she arrived and now she's taking a course in nursing. A real success story.' Billie held out her hand to shake. The girl took it in both of hers, bending forward.

'I need to find my brother.' She tightened her grip on Billie's hand. 'His name is Jemal, Jemal Zerezghi. I lost him.' Her huge eyes, darkly tanned skin and mass of curls made Billie think of Maya for a split second. She shivered despite the warmth in the girl's touch.

'Abi came to the UK by land and sea. A long journey that started in Eritrea—'

Abi cut over Boo's words. 'We had no future, my parents were taken away, forced to join the army. Our country was fighting a border war with Ethiopia. My mother was shot, we never saw our father again. They say that the war there is over, but when we were nearly ready to leave our school the army came looking for us too. We had to do military training, girls as well as boys. In Eritrea, we have no choice and there is no end to our conscription. Most people can never leave, not ever. They said I was free to choose – join the army or marry a man I didn't know. In truth I was free only to breathe. So Jemal and I ran away.'

'These are the people tossed aside as simply tricksters on the make, rather than true refugees, such as those coming directly from armed conflict,' Boo explained. 'People like Abi are the arrivals that we see on the telly news, scorned by many as economic migrants, as though they come here just to get a cheaper weekly shop or something.'

Billie sighed, running her fingers through her hair. She pulled out a chair and nodded to Abi to sit. The girl looked nervously towards Boo for permission. Boo patted the girl's back. 'Sometimes it's good to talk about it,' Boo quietly encouraged.

'We had a long journey from Eritrea, over the desert to Libya. We paid smugglers. It was very dangerous. Eventually we got to Khartoum. We were beaten by police and worse...' Abi trailed off, her face darkening as she dredged up what was clearly a terrible memory. 'Then one of our group was killed by a smuggler. We were hiding in the boot of a car on the way to Libya and he was ill, dehydrated. We were all so thirsty. He started coughing, so they stopped the car in a place out of the way and shot him. We had to leave him there with his face in the dirt. He was like family, like a brother, we had travelled so far together...' Abi trailed off again, deep in thought.

'I'm sorry to hear that,' Billie quietly encouraged.

'At Libya we were kept in a big warehouse, but still I could not sit to sleep. We were all standing. There were over a thousand people in there all tightly packed, hiding, all trying to get to a safe country. Then we were moved around by different smugglers, everyone beating us, or making use of our bodies, until eventually we arrived here.'

'How did you get to England?' Billie asked. Abi shook her head, agitated.

'I can't tell you anything. The smugglers threatened to kill our families and friends if we say even one word. What will they

71

do to Jemal, if I tell and they find out?' Abi looked panicked at the thought.

'Do you think Jemal is still with them?' Billie asked. Abi shrugged, now twisting her hands in fear. Billie sighed. 'I know this is hard for you, but I'm not a magician. Without any pointers I can't even begin to help you solve the puzzle of where your brother is. Have you registered him on the Missing Persons Unit?' Billie looked now to Boo. They had used the facility many times themselves, usually when trying to cross-match an unidentified body via the organisation's database. The downside was that there wasn't anyone still alive on there.

'Yep. Luckily no matches. Abi only has a hazy photo of him taken two or three years back before they left Eritrea, but he hasn't turned up via any of the missing persons organisations that I've registered him on,' Boo said.

'If you can't tell us something about the people who brought you here, then I'm sorry, I can't really help.' Billie didn't want to dash the girl's hopes. It was clear that she was desperate, but in truth it was like looking for a needle in a haystack, even if her brother actually wanted to be found.

'He went to work on a farm when we arrived. Somewhere in Scotland, I think. He had no choice. The smugglers said he had to work to pay for being brought here. We wanted to stay together, but I was told that I must work here in England. It was very bad. I didn't want to do the things I had to do...' Abi hugged her arms around her body. 'With men. It was just like before, every time we stopped on our journey. I couldn't bear it anymore, so I got a chance and ran away. Boo found me. She saved me.' Boo took Abi's hand.

'We found her whilst we were doing outreach with the soup kitchen and luckily we had a spare bed here.' Abi got up and started clearing the table.

'I must get back to work. I don't want to outstay your kindness. If you can think of any other way I can try to find my brother, I would be most grateful.' Abi took her full tray and headed back for the kitchen.

'Poor girl,' Billie said through a grimace. 'Truth is he could be anywhere by now.'

'Yep. Most of the people in the UK haven't got a clue what is going on right in front of their eyes. Victims of slavery hiding in plain view, conditioned not to say a word, terrified that it may fall on an unfriendly ear.' As she spoke, Billie noticed Boo looking over her shoulder.

'Who've you got your eye on?' She turned her head, following Boo's eyeline.

'James Checkley, over there. He's the one who gave the mega-donation to start the charity. Mind you, yours wasn't far behind his.'

Boo was referring to a large sum that Billie had recently inherited but had chosen instead to give to a good cause. She had wanted something positive to come from the unexpected death of a close family friend. Billie turned around, immediately embarrassed to find herself looking straight into the eyes of a strikingly handsome man. He smiled in amusement, picking up the bottle of sparkling water that he had just purchased before walking over to their table.

'Hi, Boo. Thrilled to see that everything is going so well. I've spoken to some of the clients this morning and I'm so glad that we've been able to make a difference.' He glanced at Billie even as he was speaking to Boo.

'Billie, meet James Checkley, one of your super-donor partners in crime on this amazing project.' James Checkley's smile made his strikingly blue eyes crinkle at the corners.

'Ah, the famous Billie Wilde. I've heard so much about you.'

'All lies,' Billie teased, 'if you've heard via this one.' She nodded to Boo.

'Well, I shall find out for myself tomorrow evening,' he answered. Billie realised that she must have had a blank look on her face because Boo rolled her eyes in good-humoured exasperation.

'The charity's awards event tomorrow night, remember? Honouring the kids who've done well on the programme. Some have secured jobs, many in James's businesses, he's helped with accommodation too.'

'The family business, it's hardly down to me alone,' James Checkley corrected. 'I must run, but I am so looking forward to having the pleasure of your company tomorrow, Billie. I believe that you've launched your own new enterprise. I'm particularly looking forward to hearing more about that.'

James turned and walked away, with a smile and a wave, cutting a swathe through the entrance lobby with his fair hair and expensive dark suit. Two women entering the door almost tripped over themselves, distracted by the view. They giggled like love-struck teenagers as Billie watched him through the window as he left the building, popping on sunglasses as he headed for a waiting Bentley complete with driver.

'Hmmm, quite the golden boy.' Billie realised that it was the first time she'd even taken a second look at a man for nearly a year now. Boo laughed.

'That's the first twinkle I've seen in your eye for a long time.'

'Well, I'm a long way off from being in a manhunting mood, but it will be good for the two of us girls to get out and have a good time.' It was also the first time in ages that Billie had truly felt like making an effort. Maybe she was turning a corner and finally coming to terms with her past.

'Tell Ellis the night shift is on him tomorrow if another

surveillance is on the cards. He owes you that, as well as an apology.' Billie could see that Boo was making clear that she couldn't wriggle out of their engagement, as she had done so many times with other events in the past few months. Billie raised her eyebrows.

'Somehow, I don't think that news is going to bring a smile to his face.'

'Jesus bleeding Christ!' Billie checked her watch. She'd been back in the office for twenty minutes now, waiting for the 3pm client whilst she responded to yet another angry email from Judge Pennington, this time complaining that she was being doorstepped by journalists. It sounded to Billie like Perry had been antagonising her as promised.

Hearing another blast of expletives, it also sounded like Ellis hadn't cheered up much in the time that they had spent apart. Not that she'd set eyes on him yet, but he was making a lot of noise in the small shower room off the entrance foyer to the office. Something clattered onto the floor, followed by more cursing. Billie dearly hoped that the commotion would be over before the visitor arrived. Suddenly the shower-room door was slammed open with a noise so thunderous that she actually jumped.

'Are you there?' Ellis called. Clearly, Billie decided, he must have heard her come in earlier, as there was no way he could think he was addressing anyone else. 'Hello?' Ellis shouted again. Billie sighed as she headed out into the foyer.

'What? I'm actually busy.' She sounded hard put upon. Right now she *felt* hard put upon, as well as disgruntled that in her new job, she wasn't in a position to access the investigative files on Ozzie Kingsnorth or the heartbreakingly sad skeleton bride. Had she still been head of the MIT she would have more important things to do than subdue the temper tantrums of a woman scorned and her own uppity business partner.

'Can you give me a hand with this? I can't reach the zip.' Ellis edged sideways out of the shower room. He was dressed as a giant banana. Billie had to put her hand over her mouth to stop a guffaw of laughter. It was clear by the dark look on Ellis's face, the bit showing through the cut-out hole in the costume anyway, that he was still seriously disgruntled.

'You're not planning to drive in that?' Billie folded her arms as she looked Ellis up and down, somehow managing to keep a stern expression on her face. 'I don't think you'd get the seat belt around it and what if any marauding fruit flies are about? You're looking a bit overripe here...' Billie touched the bottom of the banana costume with the toe of her boot. It was bright yellow, fading into black just before the point where Ellis's feet stuck out of two holes. He was wearing overlarge bright-green shoes, made of some foam-like material.

'I'm being picked up, aren't I? Agency's dropping off all the acts at various parties. The target apparently always helps with offloading equipment at each venue and ours will be last, hence the eagerness to get in the outfit. I've finally managed to secure the camera in the stalk bit here.' Ellis stretched his arm up and slapped the top point of his costume. 'They'll be peeping the horn any minute now, so if you'd just...' Ellis flicked his head back towards the zip which was gaping wide open to reveal that he was dressed in nothing but a pair of boxer shorts.

'It's an outside event, isn't it?' Billie asked as she zipped up the suit and stepped back to survey the scene. As soon as she was done, Ellis headed over to the window to see if the vehicle had arrived. 'Best put a bit of sun lotion on your ugly mush then.

You don't want your skin to start peeling.' Billie couldn't help a hiccup of laughter erupting. Ellis sighed.

'All right, all right, give it a rest, will you?' He couldn't help but finally smile sheepishly. 'Look, I'm sorry about this morning. It was so out of order, what I said.' A pained look crossed his face. 'I'm just a bit wound up about stuff at the moment. My ex kicking off all the time about access to Connie, Maya going AWOL, not to mention the skeleton stuck up the chimney... icing on the cake that was...'

'Or the custard on the banana.'

Ellis finally gave a chuckle. 'No hard feelings, eh?' he asked. Billie was willing to forgive, but she wanted to get something straight first.

'Maybe you're having second thoughts about us going into business together?' Billie had to be sure. Ellis had started the PI business alone, before asking Billie to join forces as Wilde & Darque. After all, he was right, technically she *had* always had an interest in dead people. It had been her job. She felt that it was important to tell the victims' final stories, get justice for them. Surely by doing so, she protected the living too?

'Are *you* having regrets?' Ellis answered with his own question. 'I know I'm not always the easiest guy to get along with – ask Boo, no, ask my ex. She'll have a field day picking out my faults.' He sighed deeply.

'Well, it's true that you can go a bit bananas, even without the outfit, but then I've been accused in the past of being a total fruit cake. We're not a duo to be trifled with.' Billie winked. She couldn't stay angry whilst she was looking into the sad eyes of a giant yellow piece of fruit. Ellis groaned in mock despair.

'I'm having second thoughts now with that pathetic joke. You could give Ash a run for his money.'

'Tough. I'm not planning on running anywhere.' Billie was serious now.

'That's good to know. I think we make a great team, Billie. Honestly, let me say sorry, again.' Ellis shook his head as though he was recalling his bad behaviour that morning. It made him look even more amusing.

'Enough. Shut up now and forget it.' Billie had learned life was too short to hold a grudge too long.

'Think I'm going to scare the kids in this?' Ellis gave a twirl, just as the doorbell pinged.

'Saved by the bell,' she answered, heading for the door. They'd started to keep it shut recently due to the number of crazy people who had made their way to the office having seen Billie in the newspaper. As she swung the door open, Billie, for a split second, thought that no one was there.

'Hello, dear.' Billie looked down, to where a tiny old bespectacled lady stood, with what looked like her Sunday best coat and hat on. 'The name's Edith Cutler. I have a three o'clock appointment.' Billie opened the door wider and beckoned the woman to come in. She hobbled on polished shoes that looked like they had been maintained in peak condition since the 1950s.

'There's my lift.' Ellis moved away from the window and nodded cheerfully towards the old woman.

'Nice to meet you, Mrs Cutler.' Ellis held out his hand. The old woman took it, looking a little bewildered, as Billie's mobile phone pinged. She glanced at it, meaning to have turned it off before the meeting. She now did a double take. It was a message from Maya.

Tell Dad not to worry. I'm fine, just spreading my wings for a few extra days. Love, Maya x

'Message for you.' Billie handed her mobile to Ellis, whilst leading Edith Cutler to a chair. 'Cup of tea, Mrs Cutler?' she offered. The old woman nodded gratefully.

'Thank you, I don't get out much now. Haven't been out for tea in I don't know how many years. I haven't got children or grandchildren you see—'

'Yes! I'm one happy banana!' Ellis's face lit up with relief. 'I hid a packet of chocolate gingers in the back of the cupboard there. Break them open. It's party time.' He did a little wiggle of a dance, winking at Mrs Cutler as he handed Billie's mobile back and left the room. The woman gave a small smile as Billie brought the biscuits and tea over.

'He seems like a nice chap. My Cornelius is partial to a bit of banana now and then. I'll get some on the way home. Might cheer him up a bit.'

'What seems to be the problem, Mrs Cutler?' Billie had settled down now at her desk and had opened her notebook at a fresh page.

'Well, we've been together years. Inseparable really. We watched the same TV shows on the sofa together. Turned in together at the same time every night. Always stuck to the same side of the bed, me on the right, him on the left. Had a little cuddle and then I read a bit of my latest book and he was always off like a shot, but now it's all changed.'

Billie waited as Edith Cutler took a sip of her tea and nibbled the corner of her biscuit. It looked as though what she was about to say wasn't going to be easy for her.

'He's started going out at night when he thinks I'm fast asleep. I take pills for that, you see, from the doctor, but I've stopped, now I've realised what he gets up to. I think he's got someone else.'

Billie blinked. The mention of sleep had reminded her that she hadn't managed to get any for the past two days and she was now desperate to get some shut-eye. She was impressed that

Edith Cutler's husband, who presumably must be not far off kicking ninety, still had it in him.

'Have you got any idea who that might be?' Billie asked, taking a nibble of a chocolate ginger. She had an urge to wolf down the whole plateful in order to keep awake but had no intention of hurrying the old woman who was clearly in the depths of despair.

'I've got a pretty good hunch. He's always seemed so devoted. I had hoped we would live out our last years like two old peas in a pod, but now it seems he can't wait to get out of the door at night. I even cooked him a bit of salmon for supper on Wednesday. That's his favourite. Thought it might make a difference, a special mid-week treat, but it didn't stop him... might I have another cuppa, please? This has all been a terrible shock.'

'Of course.' Billie leaped to her feet and headed over to the kettle once again. She made another cup and set it down just as Edith Cutler was finishing off the last biscuit on the plate. Billie stifled a yawn as she sat down and picked up her pen again.

'So, let's get a few details down. Your husband's name is Cornelius–'

'We're not married...'

'Oh sorry.' Billie made a mental note in her befuddled brain not to make sweeping assumptions on people based on age and appearance. She of all people should have learned that by now.

'Cornelius yes, but I call him Coco.' Billie wrote down the information.

'So we can certainly investigate where he is going to when he leaves at night. That will be no problem but are you sure about this, Mrs Cutler? If you are happy otherwise, do you really think you would feel better knowing the truth?'

'Yes, I've thought about it during all the recent long, lonely nights and I do. When you confirm where he is I'm going to put a brick through the other woman's window.' Billie looked up, startled.

'Now, Mrs Cutler, I really don't think that would be a good idea. Let's just remain calm.' She suddenly had visions of the woman handcuffed, hobbling down to a prison cell for a crime of passion at her ripe old age.

'Haven't you ever lost your true love, Miss Wilde – been tormented by their behaviour?'

Billie kept her head down. Edith Cutler had no idea what she was asking. She *really* didn't want to go there.

'I do understand your pain, but it sounds like you would like the relationship back the way it was before, not smashed to smithereens.'

'Yes. I appreciate what you're saying.' Edith Cutler sighed. 'But infidelity is hard to forget. It might be the death of me.' She sighed again, getting a tissue out of her bag and blowing her nose.

'Well, let's not go jumping to conclusions yet. There might be an innocent reason. We can set up surveillance as early as this evening.' Billie was sure that they could wrap the investigation up in a night. If she couldn't catch an octogenarian having a night out on the tiles then she really would have to conclude that she was in the wrong job. 'Can you give me a description of Cornelius please?'

'Dark and handsome,' Edith Cutler replied, rummaging in her handbag. 'I have a picture of us together here, in happier times.' She passed a photo across the desk. She certainly looked happier than today in it, wearing slippers and sitting on her sofa smiling at the camera. On her knee sat a large black cat. Leaning over, the old woman tapped the photo with a bony finger.

'That's Coco there. If you ask me it's the floozy at the top of the road. I followed her in the local supermarket, and she had some of that high falutin' cat food mousse in her trolley. That's what's causing him to stray.'

Billie kept her head down as she stared at the photo, mentally bashing her forehead off the desktop as she did so. The same swear words that she had heard Ellis shout from the bathroom earlier blasted silently through her head.

Chapter 11

Shock & Horror

The gun was pointing at Maya, held by a scruffy man with a thick, dark moustache. She suddenly shivered, feeling shocked and horrified, the sensation of bristly hair against her skin. She tried to fight off a fleeting recollection of being held down, this man pressing hard against her. He moved his free hand to his crotch now and rubbed it. Stained teeth were revealed as he slowly grinned and Maya recalled the smell and taste of cigars on stale breath. Her heart started beating hard against her chest.

'Ah, my lover girl has awakened.' He rubbed his crotch again. 'You were good, very good. I might keep you for myself.' The girl who had been painting her toenails glanced towards Maya and pouted.

'But, Ubi, you said that you're *my* lover boy.' Her voice had a childish wail to it. 'I've painted my toenails for you.' She stretched one of her plump legs out in a childish attempt at provocation. The man glanced at her like someone he could hardly remember.

'Get up and move,' he called to them all. 'The buyers will be arriving soon and they like their produce clean to try before they buy.' He pushed the door wide open. 'There's a shower along the corridor. Let's walk.' He indicated the direction of travel with his gun. Maya suddenly felt Otilia's hand in hers as the other girls pulled themselves upright and started trudging out of the doorway. Ubi slid his hand randomly into their frail wraps, squeezing breasts and bottoms as they did so, a lewd grin on his face, like a glutton handling forbidden fruit. Maya didn't move. Otilia tried to tug her hand.

'We have to go, he has a gun, Maya,' she whispered. Ubi turned to them as the last of the other girls left the room.

'Still putting up a fight, my beauty?' He ran his tongue across his lips briefly. The movement made Maya want to retch in total disgust, but she wouldn't show him that.

'You have no right to do this to us. People will be looking for me at home in England. They'll make you pay–' Maya stopped mid-sentence as the man moved across to her with amazing speed, despite the heavy paunch sticking out from his body leaving a sickening roll of fat between grubby T-shirt and equally filthy jeans. He held the gun against her head.

'Then maybe I'll just have some fun and then shoot you right here,' he threatened. 'Or maybe I'll kill *this* one.' He moved the gun quickly to Otilia's temple. She whimpered in response, gripping Maya's hand even more tightly. Ubi rubbed his crotch again, looking from Otilia to Maya. 'Or maybe I will call one of my best buyers, he's right here, tell him I've got a young girl ripe for the picking.' He moved the gun, rubbed it up and down Otilia's budding cleavage. 'He likes young merchandise for his snuff movies. Or possibly he'll make *you* the star of one of those, with your exotic beauty.'

Maya knew for sure that she'd rather be dead right now than suffer that. She'd learned all about such films in her training, knew that there was a large and totally warped market for films that degraded and then snuffed out lives, but she had a survival instinct. Perhaps it was genetic, picked up from a father who had survived many highly dangerous situations when undercover, or perhaps it had been honed whilst observing Billie Wilde, who had taken her under her wing when she had been head of the MIT. Or maybe she had simply been born to be a fighter. One thing was certain, she wasn't going to let this piece of scum win so easily.

'Come, Otilia.' Maya pulled herself up straight, chin tilted upwards in defiance as she led Otilia towards the door, gritting her teeth in fury as much as fear when she felt the cold barrel of the gun run briefly between her legs under the hem of the skimpy covering. She heard Ubi laugh as he made the movement and wanted so badly to turn around and smash his ugly face in, but now wasn't the time or the place.

Maya could hear other men in a room somewhere to the left as she turned right and joined the queue of girls waiting their turn to enter the grim shower at the end of the bare, dark corridor. She gripped Otilia tightly by the hand whilst silently vowing to escape as soon as an opportunity arose. She wanted to do her dad proud and Billie too. There was no way that she was going to let herself or them down, not even if it killed her. In any case, she was certain that they would have a search party out looking for her already.

Chapter 12

Telling Porkies

Ellis imagined a whole city full of blocked sinks would have to wait that afternoon as Kev the Clown sent plungers spinning through the air in a quite spectacular show of dexterity. The kids and parents were applauding wildly. He was good, Ellis had to give him that, at both juggling and telling porkies. Ellis felt a little sad that the performer hadn't just stuck to the showman side of his talents, rather than claiming for a disability that clearly didn't exist. It was true that all disabilities aren't necessarily on show, but this guy was unquestionably as fit as a flea.

Yep, there he was now, going in for his grand finale pose, picking up both the birthday child and the boy's big sister, a rather porky six-year-old, balancing them on either hand, arms outstretched. It wasn't just Ellis's hidden camera that had recorded his spectacular ability, but half of the parents present, too, on their mobiles. As many had approached Ellis for Mr Banana contact details for their own kids' parties, he could get wads of extra evidence to add to his report for the clients. The day hadn't turned out quite so bad after all, especially as Maya had finally made contact and put his mind at rest.

Boo had rung him and had a quiet word whilst he had been struggling to get into his costume and recounted what Maya's mate had told them at the airport. Now he felt even worse about what he had said to Billie as they had left Silver Darlings. He hated himself sometimes. Didn't know where this dark side of himself came from. But then his ex-wife had also insisted that he'd changed, after a particularly long stint spent undercover, pretending to be a street tramp to catch some big-time drug dealers.

The memory of coming home at last, in undercover gear, complete with straggly hair and long beard and Connie waking up as he bent to give the sleeping child a kiss, still smarted. She had screamed blue murder, thinking he was the bogey-man and still hadn't been keen to come near him after he'd had a wash, shave and brush-up, despite being told that this was Daddy and he loved her with all of his heart.

The wife said that he must be able to see that it wasn't just her, Connie didn't know who he was either and who could blame her, he'd always been more in love with his job than his family, yada-yada... The marriage had never exactly been a match made in heaven. Truth was that the divorce was proving to be hell too, even though he had given up his high-flying career to put little Connie and Maya first in his life. He tried to convince himself that it would all settle down in the end, that it was just the out of step dance routine experienced during the death throes of most failed marriages.

Come to think of it, Ellis couldn't really remember many sparks of passion during the relationship. It had been a whirlwind romance in a break between undercover placements. For a long time now, he had wondered whether at the time of their meeting, he hadn't quite shaken off his covert persona as a Flash Harry type, whilst investigating a drugs and gambling gang. Certainly the clandestine personality he'd just shed before their first date had been much more former model, Storm Benbow's type. The real Ellis was far too down to earth for her high-flying tastes. No marks for guessing how she would view his act as Mr Banana today, or his fetching costume.

Sometimes he wondered if being an undercover operative meant that he would carry different pieces of his make-believe personas around with him forever. Ellis had read somewhere that it takes forty-two days to make or break a habit. He'd done undercover stretches in his time a lot longer than that, taken on the character of some seriously dark people in his heyday. He'd done things at times that he was desperately ashamed of and had never spilled the beans to anyone. Looking at the children's entertainer, Ellis realised that he had been good at juggling personalities and telling porkies too. However, unlike Kev the Clown, he would be taking his own secrets to the grave.

But from now on Ellis was determined to start anew with Wilde & Darque PI, despite the fact that without a doubt, it was a drop in status for both him and Billie. He could see that it riled Billie, in particular, that she couldn't get the access that she had enjoyed before when heading up a murder squad. Ellis cringed once again as he remembered his words to her that morning. She had rightly been keen to get details about Ozzie Kingsnorth out of the kid and he might have scuppered that. He could also tell that she was as upset as he was, although he was careful not to show these things, by the entrance of the poor skeleton bride in what he hoped to be his, Maya and Connie's forever home.

The truth was that he was in awe of Billie's capabilities and the way she handled challenges, especially the amazing strength of character she had shown when her professional life had crashed so badly into her personal. She'd picked herself up, brushed herself down and started all over again, insisting that no matter what had happened, truth was everything. It was her driving force. He loved her for it. No, he wouldn't use that word, he admired her, that was it. They were great mates and would stay that way as long as he kept his big mouth shut, on all of his wayward feelings, bad and good. They were set to be a great working team and good friends. End of story.

As Ellis watched the children racing around the room, chasing balloons, he felt the shadow of that morning lift. His little Connie got on like a house on fire with big sis Maya and Ash's daughters. It was her birthday soon. He planned to really go to town on the decorations in his new house, have a big birthday party, maybe hire this Banana costume and wipe away once and for all the memories of her shock that night when he had come home and almost terrified the life out of her.

'Hey, Mister Banana!' A small boy ran towards him full of excitement, with something in his hand. 'It's for you.' The child held out his tiny, clenched fist. Ellis bent over as best he could in such a constricting suit. He loved the innocence of kids, the fact they trusted him and that he'd made them laugh and dance that afternoon. Storm was wrong. He could be a good dad. He was determined to make his girls happy.

'Thanks, what is it?' Ellis grinned as he took something tiny and hard from the boy's hand. 'Is it a yummy chocolate button?' he asked. He'd seen the sweets doing the rounds all afternoon. No wonder the kids were as high as kites on the sugar.

'No, it's my verruca,' the boy shyly revealed. Ellis didn't even have time to react as the door to the hall slammed open and not one, not two, but four police officers in uniform marched in behind Slug Harris. Ellis was aware of squeals of surprise and then gasps of horror as parents pulled their kids from his vicinity.

'What on earth–' he started to say before Slug Harris cut him off mid-sentence, standing in front of him to loudly announce that he was under arrest before reading him his rights.

One of the police officers meanwhile deftly clipped handcuffs on Ellis.

'You have got to be joking!' Ellis bellowed in the silence that followed.

'He's not a kiddie-fiddler, is he?' The mother of the verruca-free boy tugged at the sleeve of one of the officers, whilst pulling the child tight to her side.

'Give me a break!' Ellis announced indignantly, trying to wrench his arm free, before he was bundled out of the room. 'You are going to regret this!' he shouted at Slug, trying to kick out at him as he did so. The sight of a banana trying to forcibly resist arrest possibly a vision many of the children would keep with them until their dying day.

Chapter 13

Worth More Dead than Alive?

'No, no, he'll kill me, please!' Maya whipped her head around as she stood at the back of the shower queue. One of the girls, who had showered and then returned, as directed, to the dank cellar, was now being yanked out screaming. She held on tightly to the door frame, as Ubi, their gruesome moustached captor, tried to drag her away. Otilia pinned herself tightly against Maya's side. She could feel the young girl's heart beating against her, through their flimsy coverings.

Suddenly a huge man appeared in view, having marched quickly from the direction of the voices somewhere around the corner of the corridor. He pushed past Ubi, lifted his knee and broke the hysterical girl's hold, along with her fingers, with one sickening kick of his heavy, metal, toe-capped boots against the door frame. The girl cried out in agony and dropped to the floor. The large man grabbed a handful of her long, wet hair and dragged her, still screaming for mercy, feet scrabbling for purchase against the rough plaster walls, back out of view in the direction he had come from. Maya heard muttered apologies from her captor.

'This is no problem,' she heard the large man's upbeat, heavily-accented voice say. 'I need feisty girls for this film. They need to run. I have my best hunting dogs ready to chase them. Give me the devils as well as your angels. It gives me extra pleasure to see them fall and succumb my friend.'

'That's *him*,' the girl with the blue-painted toenails whispered, pinning herself against the wall as she waited next in line for the shower. 'That's the girl killer. He films it. If he takes you, you're dead.' There was real fear in her voice for one who had earlier seemed so relaxed about their situation. Maya could hear Otilia whimpering now, wrapping her arms like a limpet around her waist.

'It's okay,' Maya said, trying to calm Otilia in a whispered voice. 'You're talking rubbish!' she said, admonishing the other girl. 'Can't you see you're frightening her?' Maya pulled Otilia even more tightly against her, partly to offer protection and partly out of fear for her own welfare, as another girl left the shower room, dripping wet. The girl pushed past them in the narrow corridor, returning to the cellar, no doubt in search of some rags to dry herself on, shivering madly with the cold of the water or utter terror, Maya wasn't certain.

'I don't care if you believe me or not. You don't have a lover boy, like I do, to protect you and you are older than most of us. That means you are worth less. You're probably worth more dead than alive and they sell the films on the dark web. See her?'

There was another yelp of horror as the girl Maya had spoken to earlier, the girl around her own age, who had told her to forget her family, was dragged out sobbing.

'She knows her fate. She was with me last time when he made a film. Some of us had to be in a crowd having sex, but a lot of girls were snuffed out. She knows it's *her* turn this time.'

The girl ran into the shower, pulling the door firmly behind her, clearly not as sure of her own future as she liked to make out. Maya couldn't quite believe what she was hearing, but she wasn't about to wait around to find out if it was true. She nudged Otilia, putting a finger to her lips as she flicked her eyes towards the corridor which was now empty. Steering Otilia alongside her, Maya slipped back a few steps and then pulled the younger girl sideways, into a deep dark alcove. The noise from the room where the men were waiting was now more raucous, fuelled by strong drink, Maya guessed. Cries of pain and fear were mingling with laughter, grunts and groans. She imagined a nightmare scenario.

'What are you doing? They'll beat us if we don't do as they say. We've got to get a shower and–' Maya cut across Otilia's petrified whispers.

'We've got to get out.' Maya held Otilia by the shoulders and looked into her eyes. 'Follow me and say nothing else,' she whispered firmly. The young girl's eyes were huge and round, like a rabbit trapped in the headlights.

Maya had noticed that in the dark shadows at the back of the deep alcove, was a small wooden door, bolted from the inside. Possibly an old delivery hatch for coal or wine – she had no idea or interest in finding out its true origins, only that it offered their sole means of escape. She pulled Otilia by the arm, aware of the shower running along the corridor and the noise of the room reaching crescendo point. Hopefully if the bolt scraped, no one would hear, but they would have to be quick. Crouching down, she gave the bolt a tug. It didn't move, so encrusted was it in dirt and dust. She waggled it hard, tried again. It moved a little. She gave another yank and it finally opened. Maya let out a sigh of relief.

Suddenly the shower stopped. She knew that they now had to act speedily, before their captors realised that they were neither in the cellar or shower. Maya carefully pulled the square wooden door, holding her breath. It creaked open. She stood on tiptoe and peeped out. The opening seemed to be at pavement level leading onto a back alleyway.

'Here quickly.' Maya cupped her hands together. 'Step on my hands and climb out. Go!' Otilia did as she was bid, scrabbling out with a push from behind by Maya.

'Hey, where are you going?' The girl with the blue-painted toenails was at the entrance to the alcove. Maya didn't wait to explain as she dragged herself up and out onto the cobbled street on her stomach, taking gulps of fresh air. She could taste freedom.

'Where do we go?' Otilia squealed, upright now and hopping from foot to foot, pulling her thin gown around her. Suddenly a door opened only a few feet down the alleyway and Ubi appeared, the girl with the blue-painted toenails at his side.

'Run!' Maya shouted as she rolled over onto her knees and pulled herself upright. But Ubi had already covered the few feet between them. He grabbed her arm tightly. Maya remembered some of her police training, quickly shooting her free arm out at his face, the first two fingers of her right hand making contact with his eyes. Ubi let out a loud yell of pain. Maya pushed down as hard as she could, trying not to throw up with the sensation of fingers heading into eye sockets, but it did the trick. She'd had no time to trim fingernails whilst working at the orphanage. Ubi fell to his knees, screaming in agony as the girl with the blue toenails ran to his aid. Maya took off at speed, turning a corner where Otilia was pinned, shaking against the wall. She grabbed her hand.

'Let's go,' she called, yanking the terrified girl behind her as they tried to put as much distance as possible between them and their captors.

'Where to?' Otilia gasped.

'An embassy, if there is one, or a police station. They'll get hold of my dad and Billie; they'll get us the hell out of this place.'

Chapter 14

A Little Nest Egg

B illie left a message on Ellis's answer service. He wasn't picking up, probably deep in the middle of his Mr Banana act, she guessed, and couldn't help smiling at the thought as she finished yet another yawn. She'd just left him the news that he was on cat-watch duties tonight, because she knew she wouldn't last another night without any sleep and hadn't had the heart to turn poor Edith Cutler away, despite the absurdity of the situation.

'I've got a little nest egg saved up,' she had replied when Billie had outlined their costs, hoping that the finances would put her off. 'And my pension is due on Friday. I'll scrape by,' she had added. Billie had told Edith that it would be cheaper to get the downstairs bathroom window fixed, as the old woman had explained that it offered Coco's means of escape, but she wasn't having any of it, swearing that it was the gust of fresh air through her house that had kept her alive all these years.

Billy mentally kicked herself. She was a sucker for a hard luck story. It had been so much easier in many ways running the MIT – a murder had been committed, the culprit clearly had to be caught, no argument about it – but she had realised that these smaller tales of deceit and loss of love could have as big an effect on someone's life as the front-page news that her murder investigations had generated in the past.

'Oh, no, no, no. He won't like you putting that thing on, love.' Edith had wrung her hands in concern as Billie had fastened the cat tracker around Coco's neck. 'It might make him run off forever.' The old lady had put up a fair argument, which Billie had only just had the final word on.

'It's fine, Mrs Cutler.' She had tried to soothe her voice, cracked by lack of sleep. 'You'll be amazed how much detail this will reveal about the exact route that Coco takes each night. It'll be a real eye-opener and you can have it for keeps. It's a present from me.' The tracker had been fifty quid. Billie could just see Ellis's eyes rolling now, should she tell him that she wasn't going to charge Edith for the device. 'It means that we don't actually have to follow Coco when he leaves your house tonight.' Billie had a sudden mad vision of Ellis having to climb fences, shin up trees and down rabbit holes trying to keep up with the nocturnal activities of the moggy.

'So there'll be no charge at all.' Billie was beginning to accept that she might have been a crack police detective but was showing signs of being a pretty crap businesswoman. Still, a random act of kindness and all that...

'I won't be able to believe it though, all that digital nonsense. No, I really would like you to be on his trail in the flesh. Look, I shouldn't really tell anyone this, but I've got a few emergency pennies stashed under my mattress. I think it's still all legal tender. If I scrape everything together, it should cover your wages for one night. I like to pay my way even if it takes everything I've got.' Edith made to get up from her chair, giving a slight moan of pain as she did so. Billie stood up as Coco, annoyed with his new necklace, tried to swipe her hand with his paw.

'No, look, it's fine, Mrs Cutler.' Billie sighed and ran her fingers through her hair, as Coco attempted to sharpen his claws on the leg of her jeans.

'Okay. Wilde & Darque will do the surveillance on Coco tonight with a member of the team.' She was beaten. 'No charge. All I ask is that you don't feed him any of those pods of salmon mousse I've dropped off until tomorrow. Otherwise he might decide not to eat out after all this evening.'

Now, back sitting in the car recounting the conversation, Billie couldn't believe that she had been so weak. The box of luxury cat food had set her back another thirty quid. She looked down and found herself absent-mindedly rubbing a scar on her arm. She had received it via a machete wielded by a serial killer that she had once apprehended, who had raped and was in the midst of murdering a woman when Billie had intervened. On reflection, the old lady had looked very like Edith Cutler. Funny, she thought, how these things came back to haunt one.

Billie had already decided to pay the invoice herself and slip it through. Ellis didn't need to know all the details. He would kick off enough at the absurdity of chasing a cat doing what cats did in the middle of the night. But she would use his own regular argument back at him, that at the start of their business, they shouldn't turn down any work at all that came their way.

Billie's route home would take her down the street where Ellis's house stood. She couldn't help but turn her thoughts to the tragic vision of the bride who had been trapped in his chimney and in particular, the skull that had landed at her feet, as though it had been the victim's chosen final resting place. In the past, Billie would have taken that as a sign, a cry for help from the dead. It was a sad fact that now it had landed at the feet of the wrong person. The skeleton bride had ended up with Slug Harris now firmly in Billie's shoes. Come to think of it, if the CSI and Slug himself were still crawling around his new house, Ellis would be happier chasing cats tonight.

As Billie turned into Ellis's street, she could see police cars and vans parked, along with an unexpected amount of activity in the vicinity of his home. She frowned, maybe Slug and the new CSI team were doing a much better job than she had imagined. The place was swarming with crew. She slowed down her car, spotting Ash heading towards the edge of the crime-scene taped-off area, which finished kerbside. He gave a wave as he slipped his arms out of his white overall and walked towards her car.

'Still at the scene of the crime,' Billie noted, nodding to the people milling around. 'Are they tearing the whole house apart? Maybe Slug Harris isn't quite as green as he's cabbage-looking after all,' she quipped. Ash didn't respond in his usual jovial fashion.

'Will be now,' Ash answered, looking around before bending his head into the car, lest his conversation was overheard. 'Slug's wetting himself with overexcitement. Just found another body in the back garden.'

'In the jungle?' Billie remembered teasing Ellis that there could be a pile of dead bodies in there when she had noted the length of the grass and clutter. Clearly his uncle hadn't been capable of tidying it due to his infirmity – or could there be a more sinister reason?

'Yeah, rather puts the kibosh on his plan to have that space turned into a playground for his little Connie in time for her birthday party. Called some company in to do it, clear the area, build swings, banana slide, the works. Guy apparently nearly had a heart attack when he turned up today and found it. He's been carted off to hospital for check-ups.'

'Anyone we know?' Billie asked. Ash shrugged. 'Just some local company.'

'No, divvy. I mean the body.' It wasn't unusual to find that a dumped corpse belonged to someone they had already met in the criminal world.

'Not a lot of flesh left on the bones. Looks like a job for a crack pathologist. Shame Josta isn't still around.' Billie felt her stomach tense momentarily. She adored the astonishingly talented forensic pathologist who had helped her solve a multitude of complex killings, but the last investigation had been too much for everyone involved, including Josta. She had taken time off. Sold her old home and headed for pastures new, without leaving a forwarding address.

As far as Billie was aware, no one had come in to take her place, not that in her opinion, it was remotely possible for anyone to do so. If there had been the odd suspicious death in recent months, then a pathologist from the local hospital would have taken on the post-mortem. These were usually staff more familiar with death occurring from natural causes, rather than a decomposing corpse dumped who knows when, under a pile of compost and old junk. Not a job for the faint of heart.

'Anyone told Ellis yet?' Billie reached for her mobile, ready to do the deed.

'Slug whipped off with a spring in his step and lifted him already. Apparently it caused quite a shock at some kid's birthday party. One of the lads has just come back. Said there were lots of parents with phone cameras in their faces, so brace yourself for another front-page story in the local rag. Not many times a giant piece of fruit gets handcuffed and slung into the meat waggon. Word is that Slug was lapping up being in the spotlight, playing the Billy Big Balls.'

At that moment Slug Harris emerged from a police vehicle. Billie whipped out of her car and pushed past the uniformed officer who had been daydreaming instead of ensuring that no members of the public trespassed on the taped-off area.

'What's going on? Why have you lifted my business partner yet again?' Billie yelled at Slug Harris. He glanced over her shoulder, to where Ash was standing by her open car door, looking perplexed, before turning back to Billie.

'News travels fast, Ms Wilde. Unless someone...' – he paused, looking in the direction of Ash once again – 'has been telling tales out of school. Grounds for dismissal, that.' He folded his arms and called to the uniformed officer, 'Please move this member of the public back behind the tape. In fact, it might be wise to put as much distance between this crime scene and yourself as soon as possible.' Slug Harris was staring at Billie once again.

'You think?' Billie poked him in the chest. 'Let me remind you that I've got more experience with suspicious deaths in my little finger than you've had in your whole career to date.'

'Well, you're history now, former DSI Wilde. Quite the has-been, but if you don't want to find yourself arrested right now, I would warn you to get back behind the tape and behind the wheel of your car like a good girl.'

'What a joke. Time you went back to PC Playschool and learned how to do your job, Slug. Quick check would have told you that Ellis Darque only got the keys to this place a month ago. He wasn't even resident in this part of the world until he was brought in to assist me in a major County Lines crime. Seems to me that the body up the chimney had been around a good few years longer than that.'

'You seem to know a bit about it.' Slug Harris raised his eyebrow.

'An embryo would have guessed that much.' Billie rolled her eyes.

'But you've just tried to drum home to me the fact that you are an expert with dead bodies, and I'm reminded that you were a witness to the discovery of that corpse, not to mention that you are cosy with the main suspect–'

'You're a joke. He's my business partner.'

'And I'm now getting suspicious that you are hanging around the scene of the crime. Not unheard of by a guilty party–'

'Bollocks,' Billie replied. 'Teach you that in crime kindergarten?'

'In fact, I have grounds to bring you in immediately for questioning, on suspicion of involvement in a criminal offence.' He beckoned towards the uniformed PC.

'Absolute rubbish. You'll never get that to stick in a million years.'

'And further grounds that you are trying to prevent the investigation of an offence. Cuff her and take her in.'

Billie was filled with outrage as the uniformed policeman who looked as though he was aged about twelve, clipped a handcuff on her wrist and attached it to his own.

'If Gazza Middleton's custody sarge this afternoon, he'll have your sorry arse for this, joker boy.'

Slug Harris smirked. 'Shame for you he's taken the day off then. Wife's birthday. I can read the caution here to you if you've forgotten it already.' Billie's answer was of an unprintable nature as Ash approached, scratching his head.

'Everything okay, sir?' he asked. Billie could see the formal address was sticking in his throat.

'Not for you, mate,' Slug Harris answered. 'Looks like you've been sharing confidential police information. Could have you back on traffic detail for that.'

'Give me a break.' Billie pushed Slug Harris in the chest, before being yanked back, by the young PC.

'Have her charged for assault on a police officer in the

execution of his duty as well as breach of the peace. You can drive them back.' He flicked his head at Ash.

Neighbours who had been hanging around in their gardens, pretending to weed and mow in order to have a front-row seat at the House of Horrors show, had started to leave their gardens now and gather. No doubt some had mobile phones in hand. The last thing that Billie wanted was yet another photo in the paper, this time of being arrested rather than carrying out an arrest. Way things were heading, both she and Ellis would be sharing the same front page, which could mean curtains for Wilde & Darque. She furiously turned for the police car, dragging the young PC alongside her, fumbling in her pocket as she did so.

'What are you doing?' he asked. Billie was certain that his voice hadn't even broken yet, as he tried to play the bully boy.

'Making a damn phone call. Tell the toddler here that's my legal right, DS Sanghera,' Billie snapped in frustration at the situation.

'The boss's right,' Ash confirmed, calling her by the name that he had used over the years that they had worked together. Billie punched numbers into her phone, pinning it to her ear as she yanked the startled PC into the car behind her.

'Is that Perry?' she asked as the call was answered. 'Doing anything tonight?'

'Washing my hair, catching up with the soaps, eating my own weight in nachos, and touting for trade to pay the bills. You know, the usual.'

'Fancy doing me a favour? I need someone to stand in for an all-night job.' Perry was an ace investigative journalist and being freelance, was often happy to take the odd shift for the agency.

'Em, well last time I stayed out all night my girls advertised the fact on Facebook, and I came home to a trashed house, sozzled kids passed out in the flower beds and the neighbours vowing to cross me off their Christmas card lists forever. On the other hand, I need the extra dosh, so what can I do for you?'

Billie looked out of the police car window. There was no way out, at least for tonight. She knew that Slug was going to make damn sure of that. 'Are you good with furry things?' she asked, putting her hand over the receiver whilst she turned to the young PC. 'It's just that I've got a pussy that needs some attention, mate.'

The young officer turned bright puce, as Ash glanced at her through the driver's mirror and shook his head with a smile. 'My friend Perry here is going to come to the rescue.' He turned even brighter pink. Billie reckoned his reaction was almost worth the hassle of being arrested.

Chapter 15

Trapped

A cat cried and skittered away from a dustbin that it had been balanced upon, picking its way through rubbish as Maya and Otilia rounded a corner at speed and banged into it, knocking the metal bin over. It landed with a crash scattering the detritus everywhere.

Otilia skidded on a lump of overripe and mould-ridden fruit, landing hard on the ground. Maya stopped in her tracks and ran back, checking desperately that the sound hadn't alerted Ubi or his cronies. On hearing the soft squelching sound made by Otilia's bare feet trying to get traction on the slippery mass, her mind flashed back to Ubi's eyes as she had pushed her fingers into his sockets, and she felt bile rise in the back of her throat. She wouldn't have blinded him, but he wasn't going to be in any forgiving mood should they bump into one another again.

Otilia was hobbling now, her knees having hit the ground hard, stinking fruit slithering down her bare legs as Maya hauled her upright and pulled the terrified girl behind her. Ahead she realised there was a brick wall. They had run into some sort of cul-de-sac. Stopping for a second, Maya looked left and right, spotting a narrow weed-covered gap in the old wall.

'Come on,' she cried. Otilia was gasping for breath and Maya could see a trickle of blood running from her scraped knee, tears splashing down her cheeks. 'We'll be safe through here,' she said, trying to reassure her. At least Ubi, with his fat belly, wouldn't be able to follow them, Maya noted.

The weeds were interlaced with nettles that stung at Maya's legs and feet, but she knew, even as Otilia squealed little sobs of pain as their skin caught on sharp stones and brick, that this was the least of the injuries they could expect in the scenario into which they had landed.

They seemed to be at the back of a building, perhaps a shop, Maya thought, hoping that salvation was only seconds away. There didn't appear to be a door, but Maya managed to coax Otilia towards the side of the building, despite her sobs coming thick and fast now and her body slowing in pain and shock.

Suddenly, as they rounded the side wall and pushed forward through high tangled weeds, it seemed to Maya as though they had entered another world, into a town, busy with roads and people. Maya's heart quickened as she spotted a man and a woman, tourists looking at a map. The woman took out her mobile phone as though checking something. Maya pulled Otilia fast towards them.

'Please, we need help.' Maya's voice was breathless. The couple looked at them, startled. 'Help, please, your telephone.' Maya pointed to the mobile phone, patted her chest and then mimed making a phone call. The couple obviously didn't understand English. She was hopping from foot to foot in desperation. The woman continued to appear confused, but gingerly handed her mobile across to Maya, who grabbed it from her, nodding in panicked gratefulness as she punched in Ellis's number. The phone connected.

'Dad, it's Maya.' Maya tried to keep her voice clear, forcing herself to calm down in order to explain the situation, show him she wasn't some pathetic kid.

'Look, police!' Otilia spotted a van, with a sign saying *Policja* on the bonnet, coming towards them. She started running towards the road, her thin covering lifting in the breeze leaving little to the imagination. People had stopped to stare. To Maya's utter dismay, Ellis's messaging service had started to kick in. She cut the call and raced after Otilia, still holding the mobile, only slightly aware of the man and woman shouting behind her.

The police van pulled up as the woman and man caught up with Maya, wrestling the mobile from her hand. Two uniformed police officers climbed out of the vehicle, looking Maya and Otilia up and down, as the couple gabbled something about Maya and the phone. Maya cut in, trying to explain.

'Help, we need help!' she cried.

'*Prostytutka.*' The first police officer tilted his chin in a dismissive motion to the girls as she addressed the couple.

'No, no. That's not right. We've been trapped!' Maya grabbed the woman's arm, instinctively trying to seek solace from another female. The woman pulled away, pushing Maya.

'Filth!' she cried, shaking her mobile at Maya.

'No, you don't understand. Sorry, I just...'

The second police officer already had Maya by the arm and was opening the back door of the van. The first had a tight grip on Otilia. Maya wanted to apologise to the couple and talk to her dad. She desperately wished he had picked up. She could have kept him on the line. He would have explained to everyone. He spoke heaps of different languages, probably Polish too.

Otilia wiped her face as the van started to move off, her chest heaving with sobs. Maya leaned forward and tugged at the arm of the police officer in the passenger side. Both officers were talking to one another, seemingly unmoved by the girls' dire situation.

'We've been stolen. Kidnapped!' Maya cried. 'Look!' She moved her hair away from her neck and turned to show the blood-encrusted tattoo of the wasp on her neck, before moving Otilia's head to show the same. The police officer stared for a moment, before nodding and saying something to the driver. Maya breathed out a sigh of relief, sitting back in her seat for a moment and patting Otilia on the leg. 'It's okay, we're going to be safe now.'

It was only a matter of minutes before the van turned off the main road again and down a maze of streets, stopping at the end of a row of houses. Maya suddenly recognised where they were, slapping her hand over her mouth to avoid a squeal of horror spilling out.

'No, no please–' She tried to grasp the arm of the police officer as he climbed out of the vehicle.

'This is the same place we've run away from.' A note of hysteria filled Otilia's tearful voice. Maya tried the door. It was locked. She hurled herself over Otilia's body, trying the door at her side of the vehicle. It was similarly secured. The other police officer climbed out of the driver's side, moving to the front door of the building before knocking.

'Maybe they want us to identify them, so that we can get the others out.' Even as the words left Maya's mouth they sounded hollow. The door was opening, a red-eyed and angry Ubi standing at the entrance, his demeanour changing immediately on seeing the uniformed officer who said something that Maya didn't understand. A joke, a shrug from Ubi, before he turned to Maya in the van and made a throat-cutting motion. The second officer opened the door, taking his gun from his holster to show that they meant business.

'Walk,' he said in accented English. 'We are ready to eat.'

Chapter 16

Just Like Old Times

B illie and Ash tucked into giant bacon and egg butties in a no-nonsense café that smelled of grease, sausages and cheap baked beans. A cloud of fug hung in the air.

'Great sarnies these. Feels just like old times,' Ash managed to say through a mouthful of food. He reached for the tomato ketchup, lifted a slice of his stottie and squirted a large helping over the remainder of his breakfast.

'Least I could do. Sorry I dropped you in it. I'm losing my touch, mate.' Billie had spent the whole night in a police cell berating herself for getting Ash into hot water with Slug Harris.

'No problem. I told him you must have seen Ellis's arrest on the internet. He can't prove otherwise; word was everyone had their mobiles out and were recording. He loves the idea of being famous. Lapped it up.' Billie rolled her eyes and sighed.

'I keep wondering if I did the right thing in leaving the force, Ash.' Billie had thought long and hard about historical cover-ups that had happened in the force, some involving people close to her, and decided that she had to step down so that the full truth could be investigated and told, without any doubt that her position might prevent that happening. She felt it was deeply important that the truth was made public. So many people having suffered as a consequence of the past, not least her.

'I thought no one would believe there had been a full investigation when I was still in a high-flying job at such a young age. Daughter of a former police chief, goddaughter of the one after him. But all that's happened is that most of the good guys bar you have followed me out and Slug Harris has slithered in, son of another high-ranking official.'

'At least you were ace at your job. Gazza Middleton's been kicking off good and proper. Made a formal complaint about the number of random and trivial arrests Slug is trying to make stick. Anyone who tells him he's a dick basically and there's plenty of our plain-talking friends on the street who know a bad cop when they see one. Makes us all look like a joke. Gazza is talking about taking early retirement.'

'No way, Gazza is the best.' Billie was relieved that the experienced custody sergeant had been back at work first thing and had insisted on Billie's release, straight after her interview in which Slug had got his rocks off trying to play the bad cop, just like he must have seen done in some telly series five minutes ago when he was at school. Water off a duck's back to Billie.

She'd had the odd sigh of despair in her time when Gazza Middleton had insisted that a prisoner was set free when she had wanted to question them for longer, but she had to admit that he was a stickler for fair play. The custody officer was king in these situations and Gazza would only okay the depriving of people of their freedom and liberty when absolutely necessary. Slug Harris chucking his toys out of the pram on a whim just wasn't going to cut it with him, no matter if he had relatives in high places.

'It feels a bit odd being on the other side of the track,' Billie admitted, taking a bite from her butty.

'Yeah, well you've always been a control freak.' Ash nudged her arm playfully.

'Let's hope Ellis gets out by tonight. Anyone could see that poor girl had been dead for ages.' Billie felt the overwhelming feeling once again that she wanted to get to the truth of the poor skeleton bride's demise, get justice for her, but now she was just as helpless to intervene as any other member of Joe Public.

'Yeah, but there's the other lad now, so even Gazza may have to allow the Slug a custody extension. Mind you, there must be records for Ellis clocking in with his handler when he was working undercover, giving him alibis, should they pin down a time of death for either stiff.'

'It's unlikely they'll be able to do that,' Billie answered. 'Slug shoved the crime-scene photos under my nose. Forgets that I'm not likely to produce the desired shocked affect when presented with close-ups of some poor sod in a nasty state. Don't know if he gets off on it. Trying to get some ridiculous confession about Ellis knocking people off and me playing his faithful sidekick. I would have laughed in his damn face but held back out of respect to the victim. It's a shame that Josta isn't still around to offer some saving grace for the deceased. Tricky business with old bones.'

'They're still searching around for someone capable of handling it. Most of the PMs are being carried out by the hospital pathologists. Can't get any big guns to head our way. Scarcer than hens' teeth these days, so they can pick and choose their patch. Word gets around and they don't like dealing with little pricks any more than I do,' Ash complained.

'Hospital pathologists are going to be scratching their heads with those two,' Billie pointed out. 'They specialise in the study of diseased tissue and there's not much left from what I saw. Needs a forensic anthropologist. Somebody who's at home with bones.'

111

'That big new forensic lab's just opened up.' Ash had taken another bite of his sandwich. Neither he nor Billie had ever been put off eating by talk of dead bodies, those having been such a regular part of their joint working lives until lately. 'If it was up to me, we'd be sending our new clients there. Word is they have the whole deal in one place. Specialists in every area of forensics.'

'It should be up to you,' Billie answered. 'You were the obvious choice to have stepped straight into my size sevens, not Slug.'

'Yeah, but no use crying over spilled milk.' Ash took a swig from his mug of tea. 'Done me a favour. I've got more time to spend with my girls and you've got other big investigative cases to deal with.'

Billie chuckled. 'If you only knew the half of it. Oh look what the cat dragged in.' Billie nodded as Perry Gooch swung the door open, looking dishevelled and hard done by.

'Full English with extra toast and jam and send over that whole vat of coffee,' she called over to the staff behind the serving desk. 'It's on *her* tab.' She nodded to Billie as she staggered over, hauled her bag onto the seat next to Ash and slumped down.

'I did tell you I've won major awards for investigative journalism, didn't I?' Perry huffed as she took her jacket off and settled into her seat. Billie nodded, well aware that she was about to get an earbashing.

'Been on a secret mission all night have you, cutting edge case?' Ash finished off his huge sandwich.

'The only edges I've been cutting are my bloody elbows and knees. I've lost count of the back garden fences I've climbed over. I also had a bucket of water chucked over me from an upstairs window, when Coco started with the love songs trying to woo some cool cutie at the far end of the neighbourhood. Then I lost my shoe in the dark, clambering through a hedge...'

'Sounds like you were chasing a cat burglar. Job for our lot.'

'Job for a nutter you mean. I was after a cat, not a burglar. The things I've had to do in order to keep my girls fed, clothed and educated...'

Ash pulled a puzzled face.

'One of the big investigative cases you just mentioned we have to deal with.' Billie filled him in, while Perry gladly accepted the hot cafetière of coffee put down on the table. She dug her hand in her bag and pulled out Coco's GPS collar.

'Little bugger went for me when I took it off.' Perry showed them a large scratch on her hand. 'Knows where its bread is buttered I'll tell you that. He spent half the night with a bunch of mates going through the bins of a posh house at the edge of the estate, one of those with a kitchen-cum-open-living area or whatever they call those wide-open spaces that have all the walls knocked out and a long glass door across the back of the whole house.'

'Like yours.' Ash nodded to Billie. Perry blew her lips out.

'Must have some dosh to go chucking all those leftovers out. The local cats are throwing parties in her back garden. M'laddo Coco was still feasting on a salmon fillet on the way back. Life of Riley he lives.'

'He's certainly got a devoted owner,' Billie agreed.

'Oh poor Coco is traumatised by that horrible collar.' Perry mimed a sotto voice which was quite a good copy of Edith Cutler's. 'The only thing that calms him down is that special cat milk, but woe is me, I don't have any left and my pension's not until–'

'Friday.' Billie ended the sentence as she wiped her fingers on a paper serviette and finished off her cuppa.

'Exactly,' Perry agreed as her huge English breakfast was

put down in front of her. 'So like an idiot off I went to the corner shop to get her some.' She took a large bite out of a fat sausage. 'You're getting the bill for that as well,' she added, her words muffled thanks to the chunk of food she had rammed in her mouth. Ash laughed.

'So are you off doing the same undercover operation tonight?' he teased. Perry looked fit to kill as Billie's mobile rang.

'Saved by the bell,' Billie joked, her demeanour changing to serious immediately as the voice started speaking. 'Hello. Mr Kingsnorth.' Billie turned away to face the window. 'I understand. So you have had notification from the coroner that Ozzie's body has been released. Of course. I'll get a second post-mortem request underway immediately and get back to you.' Billie pushed her chair back and stood up. Ash followed suit, draining his mug as he did so.

'Thanks, Perry. You've made an old lady very happy. As soon as anything else comes up–'

'Don't call me, I'll call you... if I'm really desperate,' Perry answered. Billie grinned. She hoped her friend was joking.

'What did you say the name of that new forensic centre was?' Billie asked Ash as she headed over to pay the bill. Ozzie was about to come into her care, and she would be absolutely dedicated to finding out the truth of his desperately early demise. Her hunch was that the truth wouldn't point to suicide.

As soon as Ash had read out the name after a quick search on his mobile, Billie had realised that she was about to come face to face with past events that she had struggled hard to deal with. Her stomach tied into a knot as she entered the smart reception area of King & Beech Forensics – a huge space created with glass and clean white walls dotted with exotic plants and beautiful artwork. An equally attractive receptionist, glossy and slick, smiled as Billie approached. Josta always did have an eye for a pretty face.

'Ms Wilde?' she asked, before Billie had even had a chance to speak. 'Dr King will be with you in a moment.'

Billie took a deep breath, turning to look at the decorations. She had to keep focused on Ozzie Kingsnorth, not the past, when her last investigation as a police detective had been so explosive for both herself and Josta that they had needed time away from one another, out of respect for the overwhelming losses both had suffered.

But there was no turning back time and Billie was determined to move forward with her own life and make a success of Wilde & Darque, proving to anyone who cared that her outstanding achievements truthfully weren't built on nepotism. Unlike Slug Harris, she had been devoted to her job, as had Josta, with a reputation as the best forensic pathologist in the business. It looked like she still was.

As Billie turned, she saw Josta standing at the top of a staircase leading from the side of the reception space to a wide bright mezzanine area. It looked like her old friend was ready to let the sunshine in again.

'Billie, my dear girl...' She trailed off, stopping for a moment, smiling hesitantly as Billie strode across the reception area and up the staircase, joining her at the top.

'Lovely to see you again, Josta,' Billie said and she meant it, suddenly unable to resist opening her arms wide to give Josta a hug. They held each other tight for a moment, their eyes brimming with tears, but no words were needed.

'Great place you've got here.' Billie waved her arm around in appreciation of the impressive premises.

'I put that down to my business partner. You well know that my great passion is for food rather than interior design.' Josta smiled. It was true. In the past Billie had often gone around to dinner at Josta's and been served a steak or other piece of meat with stab marks in it as Josta had finished work and then continued at home throughout the night using her store of knives to identify a sharp murder weapon. Josta looked smaller now, her intelligent eyes not shining quite so brightly, but she was still in one piece, Billie was relieved to see. They were both survivors.

'Oh, speak of the devil.' Josta smiled impishly as a tall, elegant, dark-haired woman wearing a white coat, approached. 'Billie, let me introduce you to Dr Lizbeth-Ann Beech. If there's a finer forensic anthropologist in the world, I have yet to meet them. She also insists on a healthy life/work balance, which is good for me. Lizbeth-Ann, this is Billie Wilde.' The woman smiled as she held out her hand to greet Billie.

'Josta's trying to tell you that I like to whisk her off on regular holidays. So pleased to meet you, Ms Wilde. I have heard so much about you already and your formidable reputation.' She glanced at Josta. Billie felt her body relax. It was clear that her old friend had chosen to move on with not only her professional but also her personal life, rather than wallow in the past.

'So very pleased to meet you, Dr Beech.' Billie knew that she was going to immediately like this woman. Not only because of her warm smile and obvious care for her old friend's welfare, but the fact that Josta had just announced that her specialism was bones and if there was one thing needed around the place right now it was a skeletal expert. She hoped Ellis had been released, though he hadn't called in yet, but if not, this woman could definitely be his get-out-of-jail card.

'Please, Lizbeth will do. Cecile, have the arrivals come in from the South Lane investigation yet?'

Bingo, Billie's inner voice called. South Lane was Ellis's address. It looked like even Slug had finally wised up to the fact that he couldn't get much mileage out of banging people in police cells without some proper scientific facts to back up his case.

'Just arrived and been admitted to examination suites two and three,' the elegant receptionist confirmed.

'Whilst Lizbeth picks over bones, I will be taking care of your boy. I've already looked over the notes from the first autopsy conducted at the hospital and I'm convinced that we can tell more of the poor lad's story. I believe they've had interns working like dogs over there due to staff shortages, so they can be forgiven for making one or two basic errors.' Billie's ears pricked up.

'Are you saying it might not have been suicide?' Billie remembered Richard Kingsnorth's utter heartbreak at the thought. She hoped that at least Josta could prove that Ozzie hadn't intended to take his life, that his death had in truth been some sort of accident.

'Indeed.' The pathologist led Billie down the staircase and then turned left, escorting her along a wide corridor with doors on either side. Josta stopped outside of a door marked *Examination Suite 1* with Josta's name printed on a tag below.

'Interpretation of findings from bodies recovered from a liquid environment prove to be a challenge even for those of us so long in the tooth that we're almost woolly mammoths. A few years ago, I had to correct the finding of drowning by a year one student, when in fact the body was already dead and in a coffin when it had entered water. This area is one of only three in the UK that allows burials at sea. I've occasionally had the pleasure of welcoming the odd drifter into my autopsy suite.'

'Really?' Billie was astonished.

'The official burial at sea sites are off the Needles Spoil Ground near the Isle of Wight, Hastings and near here in

Tynemouth. I'd recommend the scattering of ashes instead, alleviating the risk of the deceased washing up next to an unsuspecting sunbather tucking into an ice cream on the beach. Such events do rather put a damper on one's holidays.' It was the sort of fact that only Josta could throw into the most mundane of conversations. Billie had missed her dear friend more than she would ever know.

'I must warn you that he's not a pretty sight. Your new vocation may have allowed your memories of the criminally deceased to have faded somewhat.'

Billie wanted to say that all of the deceased that she had ever accompanied through their autopsies stayed in her memory forever. In truth they were never laid to rest, and some still continued to haunt her in the dead of night, but she didn't want to dwell on that fact right now.

'Criminally deceased? Are you saying that Ozzie's death wasn't accidental?' Billie followed Josta through the door where the unique smell of the autopsy suite hit her. She nodded to the technician, before taking a deep breath and looking in the direction of poor dead Ozzie Kingsnorth. It would be true to say that the body on the mortuary table bore no resemblance at all to the handsome and smiling young man that Billie had seen in the poster on display at Silver Darlings. Josta approached the body.

'Ozzie Kingsnorth, meet DSI Billie Wilde. If she can't get to the bottom of your early demise then no one can.' Billie smiled to herself, despite the sad sight. Josta had always had a way of talking to the dead with utter respect whilst she was working with them. It was as if they hadn't truly departed until their stories were finally told.

'Just plain Billie now,' Billie corrected, her heart full of sadness for the sorry state of the once vibrant young soul lying cold and utterly damaged before her now.

'You're still his best bet, my girl. DS Harris hasn't the stomach or aptitude for the job and someone has to bring the culprit to justice for this sad affair.' Billie realised that it was true that both she and Josta had always had a better understanding of the dead than the living.

'What can you tell me?' Billie scanned the bloated and bruised body. She could see horrific lacerations across his lower torso that she recognised as having been inflicted by a boat propellor.

'Luckily those lacerations that you are looking at were inflicted post mortem, by a small craft. Probably didn't spot the boy floating by.' Billie shuddered at the thought. 'But first things first. Ozzie was found about half a mile upriver, so it has been assumed according to the notes here on his first autopsy, that he drowned there. But my hypothesis is that he died out at sea and a fair way out at that, if our initial microbial findings are correct. The body then made the final part of its journey upriver via tidal surges at the mouth of the estuary where it meets the sea.

'He was certainly alive when he hit the water, although he had a nasty injury to the back of his head...' Josta trailed off momentarily as she showed Billie photographs taken before Ozzie's initial autopsy. 'This injury no doubt contributed to his demise. The initial examination wrongly deducted that it occurred when he was dead in the water, possibly by coming into contact with a rock in the river. Easy mistake for a student to make.' Billie loved the fact that Josta was forgiving with those who no doubt looked up to her as the ultimate figure in her field of forensic pathology. She also loved that Josta seemed absolutely sure of her own findings.

'Stomach contents show that he swallowed some seawater, in which we have found traces of heavy-duty epoxy coating, normally found in the water ballast tanks of large ships. He also had traces of partly corroded zinc deposits under his nails.

119

These are possibly from sacrificial anodes, which are secured to the side of the hull of such ships to offer protection. Again this points to the big ship scenario.'

'But wouldn't he have been sucked under the huge propellor on a big ship and been utterly cut into pieces?' Billie was having trouble focusing on the lacerations, which made Ozzie's torso present rather like a slab of pork with mincemeat spilling out of the long, wide-open cuts. Josta nodded.

'Precisely. The muscles on his left shoulder were torn and I found bruising on the left-hand side of his spine, localised, so suffered shortly before death, probably caused by a sudden jerk when his hand reached out and grabbed the square sacrificial anode structure. I'm guessing that the resulting pain and lack of grip area on these anodes forced him to let go, but he was still able to swim away at a right angle or similar from the ship and avoid death by propellor. However, the hefty thump to the head would soon have taken its toll.'

'Could he have hit his head on the side of the hull when he fell?' Billie wanted to be sure of the answer before jumping to conclusions. She didn't want to break the news of an even worse scenario than suicide to Ozzie's grieving dad. Josta shook her head.

'You don't get this sort of injury by falling from a ship. It appears to have been inflicted by a blunt instrument. My hypothesis is that he suffered exhaustion as a consequence of shock and loss of blood from the head injury and died because he was so far out he couldn't make it to the shore. There is a different process of osmosis between saltwater and freshwater drowning. It is clear that the boy suffered the former – basically one suffers death by drowning in one's own fluids. It's usually a slower death than that of freshwater.'

Billie shuddered as she absorbed the information.

'So, he was attacked, before being thrown or having fallen

off the side of a ship, tried desperately to hang on and then fought to survive by swimming away...' Billie closed her eyes tightly at the thought. It was as if the body lying alongside her was showing the last stages of his life via Josta's work. 'Died at sea, was cut up by a passing pleasure boat propellor and then was swept upriver to his final resting place.'

'That's about the sum of it, my dear. Go to the top of the class.'

'I can't bear the thought.' Billie's voice was hushed. She couldn't imagine the thought of telling Ozzie Kingsnorth's father either.

'Death by criminal means has always been hard for us to deal with.' Josta touched Billie's arm, knowing that their sorrow was shared and not only in connection with the sad ending to Ozzie Kingsnorth's life. 'But you and I have always been driven by the need to tell the truth, no matter what pain that might bring our way. I will inform the coroner of my findings and of course, the police. However, I think you will have to accept that your successor has little chance of getting to the bottom of this mystery. You might be the only hope of unearthing the full story of this poor young man's demise.'

Billie ran her fingers through her hair. Without the access she was used to as a police officer, the task was going to be fraught with difficulties and Ellis would probably quite reasonably argue that by passing on Josta's report to Ozzie's dad, Wilde & Darque's work was done, but she was determined to get to the truth of this sad scenario, even if it proved to be the death of her.

Chapter 17

Making Movies

'Is she alive?' Maya had woken only moments ago, shivering and shaken into consciousness by a rocking motion. She looked around her. There were lots of girls staring out of the darkness at her, all with the same wide-eyed shocked look on their pinched faces, scruffy blankets pulled around them. She only recognised one.

'Otilia, is she okay?' She reached out and grabbed the arm of the girl, who shook it away.

'Shush, you are already in enough trouble. If you don't keep quiet we'll all be killed by the border guards.' It was the girl with the blue-painted toenails talking.

'What's your name?' Maya whispered in anger.

'Bluey.' She wiggled her bare feet, the cheap blue nail polish already scuffed at the edges. 'My lover boy gave it to me when he took me away.'

'Kidnapped, you mean, and even took your name. Abused you, abused us all...' Maya was suddenly aware that her earlier wrap had been replaced by a cheap baggy dress, not in an act of kindness she guessed, feeling bruising and pain all over her body, inside and out. She couldn't see in the darkness what further damage had been inflicted upon her, only that her head was thumping, and her lower lip felt swollen and sore. She brushed her tongue over the wound and heard an involuntary whimper escape from her lips as she registered the metallic taste of congealed blood.

'You played your part. Thinking you were coming to save all the little children. It wasn't a real orphanage; you were told this before. Foreigners fall so easily for the tricky boys. It's all a game of make-believe so that the crazy people donate lots of money and send volunteers to do good work, even pay so that they can come and paint the building like Otilia said you did.' The girl laughed at the thought. 'She said they stayed in the dirty shed behind when no one came.' Another girl nodded her head in agreement.

'Yes, I was in an orphanage too. It was the same story. They sell us to men, even the babies, then when we are too old to play orphans anymore they sell us to work in other places where people want to buy sex.'

Bluey smiled. 'My lover boy says I'm different. He'll take good care of me.'

'What? If you spy on the other girls?' Maya hissed. 'Is that any way to live?' She was suddenly aware of the sound of an engine, wheel movement and rocking. Her guess was that they were travelling off-road in a lorry.

'It's the only way to stay alive,' Bluey whispered in answer, her face giving away the truth of her situation for a moment. She nodded towards the rough grey blanket crumpled beneath Maya's body. 'Cover up. The truck is refrigerated, and they want to keep you alive for your beauty. Otherwise you would have been killed like—' She suddenly clammed up. Maya felt her heart jump.

'What, *no*, where *is* Otilia?' Her voice rose as she tried to get up. Bluey pushed her back as someone banged on the side of the truck. Men's voices could be heard outside. Bluey looked scared.

'I told you to shut up!' she whispered. 'If they find us, who knows what they'll do?' The other girls looked terrified, but Maya wouldn't be silenced.

'Are you saying that we're heading towards a border? Then we'll be in another country. Police aren't always corrupt. We should cry for help, they'll free us. Hello?' She banged on the side of the lorry. The voices stopped outside.

A large girl next to Bluey sprang forward, pinning Maya down, her hand over her mouth. In other circumstances Maya would have put up a fight, but it was clear that she had been given some sort of drug after she and Otilia had been recaptured. Her head felt woozy, her stomach queasy. As she tried to struggle, the girl pinned her down with the entire weight of her body. Maya felt as though she might pass out, as the lorry moved forward once more. The girl finally rolled to one side, her hand still across Maya's mouth, eyes darting from side to side as she and the other girls listened.

'I need to find Otilia.' Maya pulled herself up defiantly to a sitting position, dragging the blanket around her as the iciness of the atmosphere began to bite into her bones.

'She's gone.' Bluey shrugged.

'With the others?' Maya suddenly realised that some of the group that she had been with before were now missing.

'The others went one way, we came another. You can have no friends here.'

'But Otilia needs me!' Maya couldn't believe what she was hearing. Sweet Otilia would be terrified, all alone at the mercy of the traffickers. The pain of that thought was even worse than that shooting through her body as the effects of the drug started to wear off more quickly now, making her injuries all the more painful.

'That girl doesn't need anyone now.' Bluey looked down, unable to meet Maya's eyes.

'What do you mean?' Maya gasped.

'She's dead,' the large girl said in a matter-of-fact way. 'I saw her being taken away, by the big man, after they had been making the movies.' She made a slicing movement across her throat.

'*No!*' Maya put her hand to her mouth, feeling sure that she was about to retch. 'No, you don't mean that, not Otilia.' She grabbed the edge of the large girl's blanket, willing her to engage further, to admit that she had made some crazy mistake.

'Yes, it was her. We all saw it happen. We all watched...' One or two of the other girls nodded, terror in their eyes. 'They wanted to give us a warning of what would happen to us all if we gave them any more trouble. You were lucky that your beauty saved you.' She rubbed her fingers together. 'You'll make big money. They film it all. Men on the dark web will be lining up to be your lover boy now. Bad for your friend, but good for you. Soon you'll be a movie star.'

Chapter 18

Stitched Up Like A Kipper

Ellis peered through the window. Flickering across the huge TV fixed onto the wall, he could see a preschool-age child's programme in bright colours, featuring piglets dressed as people. It was Connie's favourite. That meant that his ex-wife and daughter were at home, although his former wife hadn't answered either front or back doors and he'd been hammering for five minutes now. He knocked on the window. No sign of Connie in the room. He was desperate to see her.

Thanks to Slug Harris, who'd finally been forced to release him from custody, he'd missed his regular contact slot per the child arrangement order set by the courts. He'd instigated the court hearings when his ex had refused to let him see Connie at all, claiming that she didn't know him, his job made him a danger, he'd never had a child before and therefore wouldn't be able to handle a toddler, and a multitude of variations on those themes.

All of her claims had proven to be lies and then some. Connie now had a beautiful big sister and Ellis had changed jobs in order to be close to his child and have a little more control over working hours. Connie definitely loved her time with Dad and her new 'aunties and uncles' – Billie, Ash, Boo and Perry. Ellis reckoned that Ash's three kids were like sisters to her, and Connie adored playing on the beach at Alnmouth, where both Ash and Billie lived. Creating her very own room at his new house would have been the icing on the cake. He'd been looking forward to holding her fourth birthday party there, all the kiddie commotion, inviting all her little friends and getting to know the other parents. Now with the house having the real deal, as far as skeletons in the cupboard were concerned, it looked as though that idea had been knocked firmly on the head.

Ellis banged on the front door again, before peering through the letter box and shouting, 'Hello? Can you come and open the damn door?' Yeah, he had vowed to make these handovers more cordial, but his former wife wasn't making it easy for him, court order or not. The fact that he was late for his slot, thanks to the crazy custody situation, had clearly narked her. Ellis checked his watch. He'd finally been set free, not without a few choice words in Slug Harris's direction, but he was now a couple of hours overdue. 'Hello?' he yelled louder, hammering the door knocker with such force that it suddenly came off in his hand. He was still sheepishly looking at it when the door finally swung open. His ex's face looked like it had been slapped with a wet kipper. She stared furiously from Ellis to the door knocker, yanking it from his hand.

'This is criminal damage, you lunatic! I don't want you around here anymore,' she hissed, trying to slam the door shut again. She might have succeeded had Ellis not wedged his foot betwixt door and frame.

Storm Benbow had been his former wife's name when she had been a successful model gracing the front cover of glossy magazines and Ellis, still partly overshadowed by the glitzy businessman character that he had been playing as an undercover operative at the time, fell hook, line and sinker for the picture-perfect pout, sassy, short, bleached white hair and long legs that could perhaps even have given Billie's a run for their money. Now it was clear to see that Storm had been a well-chosen model name, her original childhood moniker long ago wiped out of history. Ellis had realised pretty soon after the whirlwind courtship and marriage that she was simply projecting a beautiful shell as hard as Kevlar, hiding a shallow and unforgiving soul, hell-bent on drama at any cost.

'So drop Connie off at my place in future. I'm sorry I'm late, I was–'

'Banged up!' Storm cut across Ellis's apology. 'I'm well aware of that! Should have locked you up and thrown away the key, making a fool of yourself in a bloody banana costume. The photos are all over the web!'

'I was working–' Ellis tried to explain again.

'I was working,' Storm repeated, using a whining voice as she twisted her mouth in a show of revulsion. 'No guesses for working out what everyone is saying online, I mean, what is your defence? The great undercover detective argues that he was just investigating the theft of a party bag – at a five-year-old's bash?'

'I can't share the details. The client wants confidentiality. I simply want to see my daughter as per the court order.' Ellis refused to be drawn into another argument.

'And take her where? Around to your new dosshouse? Don't think I haven't seen the cops crawling all over that too. Word is that they are finding dead bodies in every nook and cranny. What sort of a mother would I be to allow my daughter to be near someone who's a murderer and a paedo?'

'Now just hang on.' Ellis's resolve broke. No way was he standing for that sort of talk, even allowing for Storm's regular histrionics. 'If you spent less time looking at tittle-tattle on your phone and more time looking after your daughter, or hey, even looking for a job–' Ellis stopped mid-sentence, damning himself for rekindling this particular ongoing argument. It was true that Storm had long ago stopped the modelling work, through choice or lack of contracts because she eventually pissed off everyone she ever had a relationship with, he didn't know. But what he did know was that Connie spent long days at the highly expensive nursery that Storm had insisted upon, and he was happily coughing up for, yet his ex-wife seemed to spend almost every day being primped and pampered at various spas, ready to go partying at night. He paid up for the endless evening babysitters too, yet Storm would move heaven and earth to prevent him from having further access to his child.

'It's a full-time job being a mother. Not that you would know,' Storm spat back. 'You just have your fun and ditch the women to deal with the aftermath. Didn't the first one you got up the spout die all alone, riddled with cancer, leaving your precious kid dumped on the streets?' The accusation stung, even though Ellis hadn't been aware of Maya's existence at the time. He stepped forward.

'I just want to see Connie, even for a few minutes.' Ellis pushed the door wider at the same moment that an inner door opened. A man stepped out into the hallway. He was tall, well-built, probably mid-fifties, weather-beaten tanned face still just on the right side of handsome. His shirt was open. Come to think of it, Storm looked half-dressed too. But Ellis shoved any further scrutiny aside as he focused on the fact that this unknown guy was holding Connie, dressed in pink, piglet-print pyjamas. She was clutching a large pink toy rabbit with an even larger price tag still hanging from it, rather than her favourite stuffed piglet, the one that Ellis and she had found together at the toy swap at the local library.

'The kid's going to bed now. So fuck off.' The man glared in Ellis's direction. He was taken aback for a moment, both by the fact that his precious daughter was in another man's arms and the highly inappropriate language being used in her presence.

'Daddy's come to see you, sweetheart.' Ellis pushed past Storm as though she didn't exist. The man holding Connie flicked his thumb in the air.

'On your bike, mate, and don't come back. Storm and the kid are done with you. For good.'

'Says who? *You?*' Ellis poked his finger at the man, trying to keep the anger out of his voice, aware that his daughter was staring at him and only inches away. 'Come on, darling, give your dad a cuddle.' He reached out his arms to his child. He could smell baby shampoo and the strawberry soap that he recognised as her favourite.

'Leave it out.' The man moved sideways, hugging Connie against him. Ellis's heart nearly broke as she turned away from his offered embrace, instead snuggling into this stranger's side. 'The kid doesn't want to see you. They can sense a sweety man a mile off, kids. Nowadays they teach them early to steer clear of types like you.'

Ellis bristled. 'Do you want to put my daughter down and come outside and repeat that?' Ellis couldn't help himself.

'Bugger off, or I'll call the police,' Storm shouted. Connie started to whimper, peeping at Ellis from behind the huge stuffed rabbit.

'Where's Piglet, sweetheart?' Ellis tried to brush his hand against Connie's tiny foot. Clearly tired, she whimpered again and kicked her foot away.

'In the bin. Rubbish, just like you, mate.' The man poked his finger back in Ellis's direction. 'Now if I wasn't such a gentleman, I'd take you out there and smack your fucking mush in.' The man took a step back, turning towards the staircase. Connie peeped at Ellis over his shoulder warily. 'But right now, I'm taking this little lady up to bed for a story, isn't that right?'

His threatening face suddenly softened into a smile as he popped a kiss on Connie's forehead, glancing back to Ellis as he did so. 'Gonna tell you all about the big pink rabbit and the nasty pig. Nobody likes pigs, do they, Connie?' He smirked at Ellis as Connie shook her head in agreement.

'Pigs try to spoil everything and let's face it, once a pig always a pig,' he added, as he started to carry her away from Ellis up the stairs. Connie suddenly stuck her arm out, pointing her finger at Ellis. 'Bad pig, Papa!' she shouted, breaking Ellis's heart into tiny pieces. The man was almost halfway up the stairs now, as he made a loud pig snorting sound. Connie copied him with a piglet snort of her own before she giggled. The sound of the bedroom door shutting was like a nail being hammered into Ellis's coffin.

'Papa?' Ellis turned to Storm, simmering with pain and fury.

'That's right. Ed's her new daddy as far as Connie's concerned. We're moving and we've told her all about our big new house in the country. Going to build a whole fairground for her in the garden, buy her a real big white bunny and dye it pink just like the one Ed bought her today. She's so excited. We won't even be in England anymore. The further away from you the better.'

'You can't do that. I'll apply to the court for a prohibited steps order. You can't just take my kid anywhere without my say-so.' Ellis knew his rights, but after his recent run-in with the justice system, Slug Harris's section of it anyway, he wasn't sure that the whole thing was still fit for purpose. Storm gave a disparaging snigger.

'Yeah, well we'll see how far that gets you. Me and Ed are getting hitched, and I think the judge will take, like a second, to decide that a respected millionaire businessman and his wife, who's about to launch her own brand, are a much better bet as parents than a washed-up flat-foot whose home is a dumping spot for stiffs.'

'Brand? Does that mean you'll be tearing yourself away from the Botox house occasionally then?' Ellis hated himself for entering into this tit-for-tat spat, but somehow couldn't stop.

'Tearing my daughter away from a saddo embarrassment who's just been lifted playing with kiddies dressed as a fucking banana for God's sake. Now can you leave, before I ring up and get you arrested for trespass.' It wasn't a question. Storm flicked her head towards the door. Ellis glanced up the staircase, a scenario of him thundering up to Connie's bedroom and racing away with the child held tightly in his arms sped through his mind, before he realised that he was beaten, at least for that night.

'The only way you'll take her away from me is over my dead body.' Ellis had bent close and whispered into Storm's ear.

'Happy to arrange it, because nothing would give me greater pleasure,' Storm spat back, slamming the door shut the second Ellis had stepped over the threshold.

'There's a burial at sea area just along the coast from here, did you know that?' Billie asked Ash and Ellis. They were sitting on a low wall, facing the sea in the quaint fishing port of Amble, not far from her home, sipping coffee.

A pile of lobster pots stood to one side of them, fishing boats bobbing gently in the water only feet away. Coquet Island lay less than a mile offshore, where rare puffins, in season, and huge grey seals all year long, crowded together on the rocks around the lighthouse there. Above, the big skies of Northumberland were beginning to streak red, like lipstick smears across candyfloss. Yet Amble wasn't simply a tourist port. Right now, fishermen were still unloading their catch and washing down decks, ready for an early start again in the morning.

'An official burial at sea you mean?' Ash answered. 'My guess is that lots of our local ne'er-do-wells who go AWOL have ended up in Davy Jones's locker. Easy way to get rid of a body after all. Unless one washes up, before the fish have eaten all their fingers.' He grinned. Billie rolled her eyes.

'Looks like that's what happened to poor Ozzie Kingsnorth. Has Slug Harris reopened the investigation yet? Josta said she was sending the report straight over when I left.'

Ash shrugged. 'If he has he's not shared the details. He won't be a happy chappie, let's face it. He'd ticked the suicide/drowning box, so in his opinion no more work was needed. It'll be put on the bottom of the pile at best so don't go holding your breath if you're hoping for the full investigation before breaking the news to daddy dearest.'

Billie sighed. 'If you want a job doing, do it yourself.'

'Bugger.' Ellis had been listening to his mobile. He clicked it off, clearly still out of sorts. 'Looks like I missed a phone call from Maya when I was banged up yesterday.'

'What did she say?' Billie asked, all the while keeping her eyes on a target that she had been trailing for a client. Yet another husband playing away from home. She had been watching the man and his female companion from her position. They had walked the full length of the pier and were now heading her way, stopping to admire the view of mighty Warkworth Castle in the distance and the small flat-bottomed fishing cobles painted in bright colours unique to the area.

'Nothing much. The call was cut off. At least I know she's alive and thinking of her old dad.' He sighed and hung his head.

'Why don't you have an early night? Kip at my place. Can't get moved for stiffs in yours,' Ash joked.

'Don't I know it. A mate is going over to fix some CCTV

cameras outside the gaff. I wouldn't put it past Slug Harris to be planting maggot bait there. I can keep an eye out via my moby.'

Billie delved into her pocket for her house keys.

'Best off staying at mine. Don't want to give Slug any further cause to think Ash is hanging around with the enemy. Looks like I'm on the move...' Billie stood up and drained her coffee as the couple headed towards a beautiful restaurant, Lilly's Landing. Billie was already a regular at the modern, glass-encased chillout spot and her stomach was rumbling.

'I'm a bit peckish myself. Looks like they're cutting back on grub down in the cells as well as haemorrhaging staff with actual brain cells.' Ellis got up and joined Billie. 'It's not like we've got anything else on tonight. I checked the answerphone when I got back to the office, all our bookings bar this one have bailed out.'

'Count me in. The canteen scoff has gone right downhill recently with the endless cuts.' Ash jogged behind.

'Jeez, it's like taking the kids to work,' Billie joked, pretending to be irritated, but was actually grateful for the company. It would be easier to keep an eye on the target this way and she had a spare minicam in her shoulder bag which she would give to Ellis. Make him work for his dinner.

They entered the enchanting restaurant with views over the marina and took one of the bench seats on a long wooden table. The target and his female friend had already ordered a bottle of wine before perusing the menu, so it looked like they were in for the night. Billie relaxed a little. There were worse jobs in the world. She glanced out to sea.

In the far distance a ship sailed by, engulfing her in sadness for a second. She could only guess what drama had engulfed Ozzie Kingsnorth way out there, where the sea stopped being the backdrop to a jolly picture postcard scene and instead became a deadly location, a cold, deep watery grave, far beyond any desperate cries for help across the huge waves.

'Room for a little 'un?' Billie turned to see Perry slumping down alongside them on the bench. 'Don't worry, I'm not trying to muscle in on your all expenses paid meal, I'm just waiting at the takeaway next door for sausage and chips for my girls and spotted you lot sitting here living the good life.'

'Shame you didn't get a pic of Ellis entertaining the kids yesterday. Banana being arrested. You could be feasting on caviar tonight,' Ash quipped as Ellis tried to bury his face in his menu.

'Tell me about it.' Perry blew out her lips in dismay. 'Shame you didn't tip me the wink.' Perry flicked the back of Ellis's menu. 'Never said you did a sideline as a kid's entertainer. If you need an assistant any time, I can juggle. I'm managing four freelance jobs and childcare at the moment. Kids need new trainers. I wish to God they would stop growing.'

'Wish to God I could get to see mine.' Ellis finally put down his menu. Billie put her hand over Ash's mouth.

'No, don't you start,' she jokily admonished him. 'Everybody's having a fit of the morbs here and I'm working, so I can't get away from this parent pity party.'

'You'll see when your turn comes.' Perry checked her watch. 'Breaking my balls for my two and are they bothered? They've got to that age where they cross the street to avoid me embarrassing their friends.'

'Like how?' Ash asked.

Perry shrugged. 'Just breathing is enough. I have to keep reminding myself that I used to be an award-winning investigative journalist. I speak four languages, was once a clay pigeon shooting champion and see that waterborne knocking shop there?' She nodded towards a very smart boat coming in at speed to the marina, a suntanned hunk wearing sunglasses at the helm. 'I used to zip around in one of those, back in the day when I had a loaded husband and an expense account. Now I knock around getting Happy Hour meals, for ungrateful kids. How did that happen?'

'There's your chips.' Ellis nodded over Perry's shoulder where a woman at the takeaway van behind was waving in their direction.

'I've had my chips, love, and that's a fact.' Perry got up and headed for the door. Billie knew that part of Perry's downbeat demeanour was simply her particular brand of humour, but she guessed that there was some truth in her portrayal of a trapped and broke single mum. Billie vowed to put her first in line for extra work. That was if they should get any more clients after her front-page show and Ellis's equally high-profile debacle. At least they still had the Ozzie Kingsnorth case. His parents needed to know exactly how and why he died and if Slug Harris wasn't up to the job, Wilde & Darque would bring the story home. Billie just hadn't broken that news to Ellis yet.

'Fancy kippers for breakfast in the morning?' She kicked Ellis to get his attention. His mind was clearly miles away.

'Is that a chat-up line?' he replied, not breaking into a smile.

'Funny man. I'd rather eat my own spleen. What I'm saying is that we need to pay Teddy a call first thing in the morning and you might have to eat humble pie. Apologise to Smokey Boy Patel. That's the only way we're going to get more information on Ozzie.'

'We don't need more info on Ozzie. The brief was to prove it wasn't suicide and Josta's report appears to have confirmed that. Now it's over to Slug to sort out the reason why.'

'But–' Billie was about to argue that they couldn't possibly leave the case now, when her mobile rang.

'Saved by the bell,' Ash quipped as Ellis rolled his eyes and pulled a long-suffering face.

'Hello,' Billie answered, perusing the menu as she did so, before suddenly sitting up straight. 'Oh my God. No, no I didn't forget. I'm on my way. Of course I'll be on time.' She finished the call, jumping up and reaching for her jacket, surreptitiously unclipping her lapel camera and sliding it across the table.

'Forgot to tell you. This is your call tonight.' She nodded towards the romantic couple, still perusing the menu. The target picked up the woman's hand and slid her forefinger into his mouth, sucking it suggestively. She giggled.

'What's going on? It looks like you're on a promise.' Billie chose to ignore the slightly accusatory note in Ellis's question.

'Ash, can you give me a lift? Blues and twos? I need to rush home, get changed into something spangly and make the Grand Hotel in under an hour.' Ash jumped up.

'With you, boss.' He handed his menu to Ellis, who groaned.

'All right, just leave me sitting here on my tod,' he moaned. Billie winked.

'I've already offered you split kipper at nine in the morning. Don't be late, we've got a date,' she joked. Ellis gave a loud sigh.

'Been stitched up like a kipper more like,' Billie heard him whinge. Even before she and Ash had made it to the door she was sure she could hear Ellis humming the first few notes of 'All By Myself'. She couldn't help smiling to herself as she named the tune, despite Ellis's fit of the grumps as he glanced sideways at the ever more loving couple whilst ordering a sharing platter for one.

Chapter 19

Had His Chips

Billie jumped out of Ash's car and sprinted up the steps to the Grand Hotel, despite wearing glitzy heels and one of only two smart dresses that she owned. This was a clingy black velvet number, donated by Boo, which Billie was particularly grateful for tonight, as her other smart dress in green had been discovered, after her race home, to be living up to its description of crushed velvet, lying on the floor of her wardrobe. It would be true to say that neither garment got much of a run-out these days. Billie was more often to be found with her long legs encased in jeans, accompanied by a jumper and chunky boots.

'Thank God you're here.' Boo spun around in her powered wheelchair, and grabbed a trophy. She shoved it into Billie's hand.

'It's for Outstanding Achiever,' Boo quickly summarised, as the master of ceremonies of the event was glancing sideways, playing for time, centre stage, 'You met the winner yesterday – Abi.'

'Chill,' Billie answered, taking the trophy and sweeping onstage as though she had been in the building for hours. She was genuinely pleased to hand over the award to the pretty girl who seemed to have overcome so much and yet had picked herself up and was already helping others via her nurse's training. It was a lesson that Billie wanted to keep uppermost in her mind.

Although Abi managed a shy smile as she stepped up onstage, her striking large dark eyes were still full of the sadness Billie had seen the day before.

'Thank you, but I will only celebrate when my brother, Jemal, is here alongside me,' Abi whispered to Billie, before she turned and left the stage.

Billie fought the urge to immediately sit Abi down and interrogate her further about her missing brother. Despite what she had said to the girl before, she felt that it might be possible with a bit of persuasion, to tease out more information, put her thinking cap on and finally track the lad down, but Ellis was right that running a business required a different mindset to running a police department. She had to try and stay focused on the jobs that paid up and ensure that they fit the clients' remit, rather than running off on her own hunches and taking a whole team of detectives with her, as she had done in the past. Time was money and all that.

Abi was led aside to have her photograph taken with other award winners and Billie made her way to an empty seat that Boo had pointed out at the top table. She felt her heart sink slightly at the thought of sitting talking politely to a bunch of well-meaning strangers when she would much rather kick her shoes off right now and go for a quiet walk along her beach before the sun set completely.

'Dazzling,' she heard a man's voice say as she sat down, eyes still tracking Abi, who was attempting a smile for the photographer. Her heart went out to the girl.

'The light? I was thinking it was a bit dark, all these candles...' Billie answered distractedly, before turning to her dining companion, suddenly realising that the person who had spoken was James Checkley, looking particularly striking. Billie found her face flushing with totally unexpected embarrassment as he looked at her, eyebrows raised, a slow smile on his lips. Clearly the lighting arrangements hadn't been the target of his comment.

'I'm so pleased that you've finally arrived.' He grinned. Billie noted it was a nice smile but tried not to dwell on the fact. She wasn't in the market for a man right now, probably not ever again, not having the greatest record in the area of romance, even if she did sense a mischievous twinkle in those bright blue eyes. 'I thought I was going to be Billie no-friends all night,' James teased.

'I was just a bit tied up with work,' Billie answered. *If you can call snooping on a love-stricken couple work*, she found herself thinking but not admitting. She wished Abi's brother would walk through that door right now in order to bring the girl some peace, just like she wanted to crack on and investigate exactly what had caused Ozzie Kingsnorth's demise. She eased off her shoes under the table. The effects of the line-dancing session earlier that week still not having subsided.

'Quite the Miss Marple, I hear.' James poured some fizz into Billie's glass. 'Though I'm guessing that searching for someone's lost pup and suchlike doesn't give you quite the same buzz as being a top police detective.' Billie shot Boo an accusatory glance. She didn't notice, so busy was she organising attendees, but Billie assumed that she had given James Checkley that information.

'Oh, I don't know. I'm always up for new adventures,' Billie answered, though his question had hit a nerve. She thought of Edith Cutler and her cat.

'No dead bodies piling up though, I'm guessing?' Billie didn't answer, though she imagined a quick run through of the finer points of the crime-scene photos of the skeleton bride, Ozzie Kingsnorth and the new arrival at the bottom of Ellis's compost patch might put James Checkley off his dinner. 'I'm guessing those were meat and drink to you, growing up with a police chief as a dad as well as a godfather.'

'Do you always research your random dinner companions in so much detail?' Billie arched an eyebrow. James smiled.

'I might have moved a placemat or two. Some guests appear to be more interesting than others and you and I seem to have something in common. You inherited the family business just like me.'

'I wouldn't say mine was a family business,' Billie answered, slightly bristling at the comment. Even the slightest hint of nepotism in connection with her former job and the status of those closest to her made her hackles rise, but she had vowed to be less touchy on the subject. It was probably just an innocent throwaway comment, she reasoned. 'I worked my way up from the bottom without any sense of entitlement. But in any case, that life is well behind me now.'

'So I hear.' Billie arched her eyebrow once again, as though less than impressed at his prior knowledge on the subject of her life to date. He laughed.

'I always wanted to be a private investigator,' he teased. 'Oh, I asked them to save your starter.' James waved his hand to a waitress who swept in holding a delicate dish full of shrimp.

'Em, no thanks,' Billie said politely. Josta had once told her the story of examining every freshwater shrimp in a UK river near a major city and finding all of them full of cocaine. According to the forensic pathologist it wasn't an unusual occurrence these days, due to the widespread consumption of illegal drugs and the resulting contamination of waterways. It had put Billie off bottom feeders for the foreseeable future.

'Not your thing? Mine were lovely.'

'No, but shouldn't you have known that already, Sherlock?' Billie quipped back, taking a sip of her wine. 'I might have given you a chance, but you've just flunked the PI job interview. Shame. You'll never get to feel the gumshoe buzz.'

'Is that right?' James smiled once more, staring at Billie. 'Well, I'm definitely feeling a little buzz right now,' he answered.

'Old age does that. Best run off and get some treatment for it then.' Billie refused to be drawn into his attempts to flirt with her, though damn her light colouring, she could actually feel her skin flare pink under his stare. It was unexpected. She wasn't the slightest bit attracted to him, was she?

'Good idea, and I'm guessing that right now, you would rather be anywhere else but here too.' His comment wasn't actually true, not right at this moment, Billie suddenly realised. Not that she was going to admit the reason.

'I don't know about that. Boo is a close friend and she's doing amazing things with this charity. It's only right that I'm here to support her.' Billie took another sip of wine. If Boo was sitting next to her now, she would definitely say that she was pulling her Pinocchio face.

'Indeed, and the evening so far has been a great success. Boo doesn't need a babysitter. In fact, that dashing young man over there seems to be looking at her with sheep's eyes.' It was true. Boo's accident at work as an undercover police officer years back, resulting in her having to use a wheelchair, hadn't prevented her from having had a bunch of eager admirers since.

The waitress came back with a main course and was about to put the plates down before them, when James raised his hand.

'I don't know about you, but I'd say we've made our

donations, given out our prizes and the least we deserve is fresh air, a bag of chips and a walk along the river.'

'Now you're talking.' Billie pushed her chair back, waving at Boo who turned, clocked the situation and gave her a thumbs up. James caught the waitress before she moved away.

'Would you pop our food into a tinfoil tray and take it out with this bottle of wine, to the two homeless gentlemen I spotted under the railway arches across the street as I came in,' he asked, in such a manner that it was an order rather than a question. The waitress nodded and hurried away as Billie struggled back into her shoes, wondering what on earth she was doing. Hadn't she vowed to stay away from men for the foreseeable future? But James's thoughtfulness had struck a chord with her. Even more importantly, forget the gorgeous hunk, she was feeling ravenous now and event food fodder was unlikely to hit the spot.

'I knew that I could talk you round.' James's hand lightly touched Billie's back as they made their way to the exit door. A shiver ran up her spine.

'Sorry, but this has nothing to do with you,' Billie called over her shoulder as they weaved around the tables. 'I've never been able to say no to a bag of chips,' she explained.

'Harsh, very harsh,' James answered, trying to look sad as he caught up with Billie who was already gathering pace, despite her high heels, out of the main door, down the steps and along the pavement towards a chip van parked by the riverside.

As they sat on a park bench along the river from the brightly lit area where the chip van stood, Billie kicked off her shoes again. She so rarely went anywhere that required smart attire these days that her feet were seriously protesting about the discomfort level.

Billie felt the cool ground beneath her feet as she watched the lights further along the river from Newcastle's spectacular bridges, reflected on the dark water now that the sun had completely gone down. Here in the semi-shadows, away from the cheery and loud, rather inebriated customers hanging around the takeaway van, it was quiet and peaceful. Billie sighed.

'Good?' James asked as he finished off his last chip and returned from popping the empty takeaway tray into a bin.

'Yep,' Billie agreed. 'Hey.' She slapped James's hand as he leaned over and stole one of her remaining chips. 'Hands off. What's wrong, does this seem like some exotic food to you? Fed up with the caviar and white truffle that you usually nosh down on?'

James laughed. 'Don't come that game with me, Billie Wilde. I've done my investigations, remember. You come from a privileged background too.' Billie reflected that he hadn't dug too deeply in that case, but she wasn't about to open a closed part of her life and start unloading the truth for this stranger, no matter that they had become convivial takeaway companions.

'My family didn't run massive multinationals taking huge profits whilst exploiting workers and wrecking the environment. I'm guessing your big family biz has outposts in various Third World countries?' Billie asked.

James shrugged. 'A damning pronouncement indeed,' he answered. 'It's true that we have centres for our various endeavours in a number of countries, but we offer employment, a fair wage and try to give back with large donations to good causes, such as the one to this charity we've been celebrating tonight. Many of our business concerns are in Europe too.'

'Not tinned tomatoes, I hope.' Billie was referring to the widely reported abuse of agricultural labourers in areas of southern Italy, tomato pickers, living in squalid conditions for little or no pay.

'Nope. But are you telling me that you've never gone for the cheapest tin of tomatoes in the supermarket? Ever thought that might be due to someone along the line not getting paid very much? Customer demand for cheap food pushes businesses into sourcing cheap labour.'

'Good argument, but I'm guessing that the owners of the mega tinned tomato brands aren't taking less profits.'

'Tell you what, I'll start a chip company in good old Blighty if that would please you? Pay a king's ransom to potato pickers? Not that I know the first thing about the production workings from beginning to end. Most of our business is related to logistics and recruitment and I leave all the hands-on stuff to my brother. I deal more with finance and our charitable foundation.'

Billie made a mental note to stop making sweeping judgements on people. Her own donation had been huge due to her feeling the need not to keep what she saw as tainted money. She hoped that the unexpected inheritance would do good. She was reminded that the other big money donation via James had been even more substantial.

'I'm not saying that you're not right, Billie, maybe in the past when my father ran things, the little people *were* unfairly trampled down. But then we can't be forever responsible for the sins of our forefathers. I'm guessing that you, like me, have gained huge benefits from our ancestors' endeavours, whether those advantages have been due to malpractice or not. What are we to do? Go around in sackcloth and ashes forever more? We can only do our best going forward. At least I'm trying to do that...'

Billie was silent for a moment, letting his words sink in. She was still struggling with mixed feelings about her own family past – guilt, anger, sorrow. James was right, it was time to look forward not back. She gazed thoughtfully along the river into the darkness below a high stone arch, just making out the shapes of the two homeless men tucking into their unexpected feast.

'That was a really kind thing to do, sending our dinner over there,' she said, offering James her last chip. He didn't take it. 'Just out of interest, what was the pudding?'

'Sticky toffee,' he answered.

'Damn, my favourite.' Billie pretended to be less than pleased.

'I could always go and offer to buy it back,' James joked, taking her tray and heading towards the bin again.

Suddenly a movement further along the river caught Billie's eye, the glint of silver caught by a car headlight crossing the bridge in the distance and then the outline of a shape leaning over the low railings, where the water was as dark as treacle. A sixth sense, probably honed during her time in the police force, had Billie up off the bench and moving fast towards the figure. As she neared the shape, she could see that it was Abi, hunched over the railings, in danger of toppling forward. Was that what she was trying to achieve? Billie picked up pace, the girl's harrowing sobs filling the night air as she approached her.

'Abi?' Billie called, catching her around the waist as she slumped precariously close to tipping point. The trophy slid out of her hands into the river and out of sight. Billie pulled Abi away from the railings, holding her close, feeling her thin body heaving with wracking sobs. Seeing a taxi about to pass, Billie waved it down and pulled Abi alongside her. She had no intention of leaving the heartbroken girl to find her own way back to the charity hostel, not when so many of the staff were currently distracted by the celebrations inside of the Grand Hotel.

'You can stay at my place tonight.' Billie gently pushed the girl into the back of the taxi and joined her, giving the driver directions. It was only as she sat back in the seat, running her fingers through her hair, that she realised that the taxi had just swept past James Checkley having returned to the bench, now looking around bewildered.

'He looks like a man who's had his chips,' the taxi driver quipped, nodding to James as they passed.

'You're right,' Billie agreed, with a glance of regret. 'Looks like he has.'

Chapter 20

Slabs of Meat

Maya awoke, after a fitful sleep full of nightmare scenarios of Otilia's last moments as described in whispers by the other girls, during the journey. The large frozen slabs of animal carcasses all around them had been swinging from their hooks built into the roof of the lorry, often ricocheting into the bodies of the girls as the vehicle took a route that was obviously off-road. It was clear to Maya that the frozen animal corpses were simply different slabs of meat to the living souls on board, as far as their captors were concerned.

Maya was amazed that she had even been able to sleep in fits and starts, despite the ongoing feelings of nausea she kept experiencing, possibly due to revulsion and utter shock at the thought of what had happened to Otilia. She was thankful that the drugs she had been given seemed to have induced amnesia as to the horrors she herself had been subjected to, though the pain in various parts of her body made it clear that she had been exposed to violence and abuse of the most intimate and horrific kind.

The lorry suddenly came to a halt. Most of the girls were immediately on high alert, though a few seemed to remain in a catatonic stupor. Whether this had been due to the freezing temperature Maya didn't know. She remembered a lesson in school in which they had learned that refrigerator lorries reached temperatures as low as minus fifteen degrees. Strange how such random facts stayed somewhere lodged in one's brain, springing forth at the most ridiculous moments. But she also recalled that the refrigerated air meant that oxygen was present. The alternative, when the units were lifted from lorry to ship, was that only the air already inside was circulating. It would mean a slow and harrowing death to anyone trapped inside.

'Are we at a port?' she whispered, not able to avoid the note of terror impacting her words as men could be heard talking outside.

'We're in Germany. Quiet. They are about to unlock the door.' The big girl who had silenced Maya earlier, held her finger to her lips. The others pulled their ragged blankets around them, some reaching out to grip their neighbours' hands, despite most having been strangers only a day or two ago.

There was a jangling of keys, more voices and then the back of the lorry door swung open. At first Maya could see nothing, then the rails of frozen animal cadavers were pushed aside. Torchlight swept across them from the darkness outside, at first blinding Maya's eyes and the others, who held their arms over their faces or stared down hard at the floor. A gust of warm air blew inside the interior and the smell of sweat and garlic as Ubi entered. He was holding a gun. Behind him, other men stood. One was holding a baseball bat. Another grinned straight towards Maya, smiling and rubbing his crotch slowly as he looked her up and down.

'Eat.' Ubi flicked his head to someone behind him. A bucket was tipped onto the lorry floor. Stale-looking chunks of bread rolled out. A giant bottle of water was heaved in alongside it. The girls nearest pounced on the offering like starving hyenas.

149

'The clients want the merchandise smiling, not crying out for food.'

'I made sure that they stayed quiet.' Bluey wiggled her toes and smiled in a childishly provocative manner at Ubi. 'I kept an eye on this one as I promised.' She flicked her head in Maya's direction. Ubi already had his eye on her.

'You, come with me,' he said to Maya, ignoring Bluey completely. Maya shook her head, huddling back against the interior of the truck she had been so desperate to escape from until only seconds ago.

'Go with him. Do as you're told,' Bluey announced loudly, kicking Maya's leg, whilst looking back to Ubi for approval.

'Get her,' he announced to the baseball bat holder. He marched onto the lorry, followed by his grotesque companion who started kicking the carcasses of meat, as well as the girls, out of their path as Maya scuttled to the other side of the interior, in terror. But there was nowhere to go. She was hauled up, pedalling her legs, by the man holding the baseball bat. The other man made a grab for her ankles, running one hand along her legs and under her dress as he assisted in dragging Maya off. She heard the lorry door slam shut again behind her as she was carried into a building, trying to grab hold of the door frame, demanding to be set free.

A shot of pain suddenly ran through her as the leering man forced his hand higher between her legs, aggressively assaulting her as she was swept along a short corridor and then dumped hard on a bare floor. The door was banged shut behind her. Maya gasped for breath, looking up to see a small woman with an East Asian appearance waiting by a wooden chair. In front of her on a table, she had various make-up brushes and a mirror.

'You sit here.' The woman patted the chair. 'I make you look good.'

Maya shook her head as she pulled herself up onto shaky

150

legs. 'No way am I staying here,' she argued, despite looking all around and seeing no means of escape. The woman kicked the chair leg.

'You stay. You sit here. You going to be in film. You play game, or–' The woman made a slashing movement with her forefinger across her throat. Maya took a deep breath. Was she just about to meet the same fate as Otilia?

Chapter 21

Red Rag to a Bull

I n the end Abi had stayed for two nights with Billie who had been keen to ensure that the young woman's mental health had improved a little. Ash, Boo, Perry and Ellis who, until today, had still not been able to gain access to the interior of his own home, had joined forces to offer a protective circle around her. Their combined knowledge had ensured that Jemal Zerezghi's hazy photo and details were now listed on every missing persons register and website that they could find worldwide.

Perry had even taken the girl out the night before to meet her own teenage daughters, trying to forge new friendship bonds. Billie desperately hoped that it had worked, though Abi still appeared very subdued and had gone straight up to bed on her return. Billie guessed that it would take time. It was possible that Perry's tight-knit unit had even highlighted Abi's lack of family ties. Billie could get that. She had worked through issues of lacking any blood family herself. Perry had admitted that even using her best investigative reporter techniques, Abi had remained resolutely tight-lipped about her journey to the UK with her brother, Jemal.

That morning, reassured that Boo had put extra protection

measures in place at the hostel, Billie had dropped Abi off outside of her nursing college. It was on the way to Silver Darlings, where Billie had finally persuaded Ellis to have one last chat with Smokey Boy Patel.

'Poor girl, what a bummer.' Ellis sighed as Billie drove off. 'I feel bad enough about Maya having gone AWOL and she's left me two messages, well sort of. Abi's brother could be anywhere, maybe not aware or even caring about the heartbreak he's causing.'

'Have you managed to speak to Maya properly yet?' Billie asked.

'Nah, I keep leaving her messages, pointing out that as she's on a degree apprenticeship with the police, she can't just go swanning off whenever the urge takes her. She'll lose her job as well as her uni place and I've got enough aggro with the ex-wife and cleaning up the house without any more heading my way.'

'At least they didn't find any more dead bodies in there. Ash is certain that every nook and cranny has been explored.'

'Yep, only two stiffs. That's okay then,' Ellis grumbled. 'I hate to admit it, but Storm's right. It won't look good when I'm fighting to bring Connie over to stay.' He checked his watch. 'I've got to see my new solicitor in an hour, so we'd better make this gadabout snappy.'

'Well, we're a bit out of jobs at the moment,' Billie replied, trying not to pile more misery onto Ellis. At the moment, her friend, the happy-go-lucky crack undercover expert, seemed to have lost his mojo. 'So I think it's a chance to ensure that we've left no stone unturned for Ozzie's mum and dad.' She put her foot down, reflecting that when she had been head of the local police MIT she hadn't needed to negotiate with anyone before taking action.

'Fair point, but you've organised the second autopsy. Josta has confirmed that it wasn't suicide. Job done. That's what his dad wanted to know. That's what was written in the contract. We deliver that info, he pays.'

'But it's pointing to murder–'

'Yeah, from a big ship somewhere out at sea, probably in international waters. How does Wilde & Darque even begin to investigate that one? Job for PC Plod and possibly from more than one country. You would have argued the same yourself when you were head of MIT, if some PI had come along and told you they were taking on a suspicious death.' Billie overtook a car, giving the irate driver the finger when he beeped his horn in protest. Ellis was right, technically speaking, but Ash had made it clear Slug was either incapable or unwilling to follow it up anytime soon.

'Well, as we aren't doing anything else–'

'We should be looking for more clients. Look, I don't want to be awkward, Billie, but unlike you, I'm a bit strapped for cash. I can see this access business with Connie is going to cost a bomb and with everything else – I just haven't got a big money pot to dip into like you, allowing playtime off the job. Not unless I sell the gaff and who's going to want to buy the House of Horrors?' Ellis's comments had hit a still not totally healed scab within Billie's emotional protective shield.

'Playtime? Let me remind you that a young man has died here.' Billie heard herself using the sort of voice that she had reserved in the past for interrogating suspects. She damned herself, hesitating for a moment before speaking again. To her mortification, she could feel tears welling up in her eyes. 'As for my big money pot as you call it, I'd rather have my family back than the inheritance...' Billie trailed off, overtaking another car. Ellis rubbed his head.

'I know, I know. Christ, I'm so sorry, that didn't come out the way that I meant it.' He sounded genuinely pained.

'I offered to put more money in when we started the agency.'

Billie tipped her chin defiantly, shaking off the sudden self-pity moment. She'd long ago learned that such feelings were a waste of space. They weren't going to change anything.

'I don't want that. I want us to be *equal* partners, Billie. Things always go pear-shaped when one person has coughed up more dosh than the other and I've got enough partnership aggro with the ex.'

Billie bridled at the comment. 'Well, let's call this a probationary period, okay? If Wilde & Darque isn't working out the way we both want, we can always cut our losses. I'll stay wild, you can stay dark.' Billie slammed the brakes on outside of Silver Darlings. 'As you mentioned before, I'm maybe more interested in the dead than the living.'

'I didn't mean–' Ellis started to say, looking aghast, but Billie was already out of the car, heading towards Teddy Cook who she had spotted loading a van with kippers. Billie thought sadly for a brief moment that maybe instead of making a throwaway comment, she had hit the nail right on the head, that Ellis had been right. She was obsessed with murder.

'Hi!' Teddy rocked the same cheeky smiley demeanour that Ellis had when they had first met at work. Genes were a funny thing, she mused, hoping that Ellis would be back to normal soon. His usually mischievous twinkle was one of the things she loved, no, that she *liked* about him, she quickly corrected herself. Billie wondered if his recent fit of melancholy was her fault. She shook the thought away, aware of the many women she had met in the past who always blamed themselves for relationship issues.

Surely someone had to care for the people who no longer had a voice, she reasoned. In her mind Ozzie Kingsnorth wouldn't be properly laid to rest until his true story could be told and if she felt that, she could only imagine how his distraught family would feel if they were simply told, 'No, it wasn't suicide, nor did he die in a river. Go figure.'

'Here he comes, the bad boy of the family,' Teddy shouted cheerfully as Ellis, with a sheepish look on his face, hands deep in pockets, mooched towards them. He didn't look Billie in the eye.

'We won't keep you long.' Billie looked out across the harbour. Far out to sea on the horizon, a large ship was sailing past. Billie shivered, wondering if Ozzie had met his end falling or being pushed from a ship just like that. She shook the harrowing autopsy images from her mind.

'A couple of new facts have come up from the second autopsy on Ozzie,' Billie explained. Teddy frowned.

'Second one? Why can't they leave the poor lad alone?' Teddy looked pained at the thought. 'I don't know what his poor mum and dad must be going through. First, his suicide, and then chopping him around twice.' He shook his head. 'Sooner they get the funeral done and dusted the better. Had a big whip-round here for the wake.' He nudged Ellis. 'You'll have to come along. It promises to be a good night, but it's going to be a late one. Be a few wayward husbands on the pick-up. If you're here checking out any of our lot, playing away from home, tell the wives to get their rolling pins at the ready.' Teddy winked at Ellis as Billie bit her tongue. She knew it was all banter and she'd been on her high horse a bit in the car already.

'No, you're in the clear, mate,' Ellis answered with just a small smile. 'We're not investigating anyone here. We just want to ask a few more questions about Ozzie. Well, Billie does,' Ellis added.

'She's a right old Agatha Christie this one, isn't she?' Teddy joked as Billie rolled her eyes, arms folded, waiting for the banter fest to subside.

'That your boat over there?' Billie nodded to a boat in the harbour with the name of *Silver Darling* on the side.

'Yep, ten out of ten and go to the top of the class.' Teddy was a real Mr Chuckles today, Billie thought, glancing as she did so towards Ellis who was staring out to sea.

'Best fishing boat in the area.' Teddy proudly surveyed the brightly painted fishing boat.

'Not own any big ships then?' Billie asked, thinking of Josta's findings under Ozzie's fingernails. Teddy shrugged, his face darkening.

'Why would we need them? Those great big super freezer trawlers miles out to sea dredge up everything off the seabed. It's the reason the seas around the UK are getting emptier by the minute. Wipe them off the face of the earth if I had my way.'

'So Ozzie never went out on anything like that?' Ellis asked. Teddy shook his head, pulling a face that made it sound like a crazy question.

'Ozzie? He didn't even go out on this one. He just worked on the floor like the other young lads. Course, I can't vouch for any other jobs they might do on the side. You know what kids are like these days, always after designer kit, but those ships are out at sea for weeks on end. Ozzie worked here full time, weekends too when he wasn't playing football and wanted some extra cash.'

'He didn't go on a weekend jaunt with any of his mates over to Amsterdam and not come back then?' Billie suddenly thought of the big ferries that travelled daily between the Port of Tyne and Amsterdam. She'd been caught up in the middle of riotous hen and stag parties making wild weekend trips occasionally. Could that be how Ozzie had met his end? She'd have to remember to ask Ash whether Slug had looked into that possibility.

'Not that I'm aware of.' Teddy shrugged. 'Having said that,

I'm an employer, not a babysitter and I'm not skulking around checking what my employees are getting up to when they are not working here. Their time is their own business.' Teddy continued loading the crates of kippers onto the van. 'Got a minute, mate, can you give me a hand with these?' Teddy spoke to Ellis now, sticking a crate of kippers in his arms.

'Smokey Boy around?' Billie asked, wandering in the direction of the entrance. He would surely know if Ozzie had been away on any such trips. He'd probably been with him.

'No. Having a couple of days off and before you ask, I don't know what he's up to,' he called. 'Is she always in full Sherlock Holmes mode at work, mate?' he asked through a chuckle to Ellis as Billie looked through the door at the workers in the smokery busying themselves as they took their Silver Darlings through the various stages of cleaning, smoking and packing.

As she entered, the smell of smoking kippers hit her immediately and also the realisation that there was another room that she hadn't noticed, at the far end of the kipper smoking area. Through the plain glass interior window, Billie caught sight of the colourful thatch of hair, realising that Maya's best friend, Lily, was working at a desk inside. She marched across to the door, giving only the most cursory knock before entering. Lily looked up, almost jumping off her seat.

'Sorry. Didn't want to give you a fright. I didn't know you were working here. Thought you had set your sights on saving the world rather than dealing with small fish.'

'Um, I'm a bit busy actually.' Lily looked back at the PC screen as though she had already mentally dismissed Billie.

'Given up uni?' Billie queried.

Lily shrugged. 'Not back until next week,' she mumbled, her eyes still on the screen. 'I'm helping out with some clerical work to build up funds. Maya says you're loaded. You wouldn't understand,' she added, making Billie's hackles rise. There it was again, the accusation of being born with a silver spoon in her mouth. Even after having left the force, here it was still following her around like a bad smell.

'I did inherit on the deaths of my family members, yes, you are correct,' Billie answered. 'Thank you for reminding me. I'm also glad that you brought Maya up. Have you heard from her yet?' Billie asked. Lily kept on staring at the screen, but Billie noticed her blink.

'Nope. I'm her friend not her mum. She's free to do whatever she wants.'

'Except that her dad is getting worried. If she doesn't get back in the next couple of days then she might lose her degree apprenticeship and her wages. She's paid, not on a grant.'

'Well, maybe you could bung some of your money her way.' Lily clicked the PC screen off and reached for her bag. 'I've finished,' she mumbled. Billie blocked her exit. She was looking Lily eye to eye now.

'It's actually Ozzie Kingsnorth I've come to ask about.' A startled look flashed across Lily's face.

'Ozzie's dead,' she said. 'I mean, not that I knew him. I've just heard people talking.' Billie thumbed in the direction of the poster on the wall. 'Looks like you're standing right next to him on that poster over there, alongside Smokey Boy Patel and Maya. Did no one tell you that was him?'

Lily's face flushed. 'Yeah, well I mean I met him for a couple of hours that day, but I didn't really *know* him.' Billie recognised a Pinocchio face when she saw one. The question was, why was Lily lying.

'You know Smokey Boy Patel though?' Billie persisted.

Lily shrugged. 'A bit. Only through Maya.' She twisted her mouth. 'It was her who was really into him, not me.'

Billie frowned. Smokey Boy had told a different story.

'Maya's friends with Smokey Boy or Maya was friends with Ozzie Kingsnorth?'

Lily shrugged. 'Both, I guess. It was Maya who set the whole fashion shoot thing up. You know, she's registered with some local agency to do bits of modelling. She's not exactly flush with the apprenticeship wages and she's desperate to save up the deposit to get her own space. Who can blame her, if you lot are constantly firing questions all the time like this?' Lily pouted sulkily. Billie was simply relieved that the words had been directed at her rather than Ellis. It was the last thing he needed to hear right now.

'Before you head off,' Billie caught Lily's arm, 'let's just get this straight. Is Maya in a relationship with Smokey Boy Patel and if so, how come she's gone off with this other lad in Europe?' Alarm bells were starting to ring at the back of Billie's brain, though she wasn't quite sure why. Lily pulled her arm away, just as Ellis entered through the door.

'Who cares? As far as I know Maya's not exclusive. She can have fun with anyone she wants. It's her life. No wonder she can't wait to get away from you lot with the endless interrogations. I wouldn't be surprised if she decides to never come back!' Lily pushed past Ellis, who was looking gobsmacked. Billie decided it simply wasn't going to be her morning for making friends and influencing people.

'I'm sorry I've been like a bear with a sore head.' Ellis was following Billie in through the main door to their office premises, in an anonymous-looking building, that had seen better days.

'It's okay. It's not the first time that I've been told that I can be like a dog with a bone, so we're both animals.' Billie didn't want to fight with Ellis. She would never have agreed to team up with anyone who was less than brilliant at their job, and he'd arguably saved her life, more than once.

'We're all right then?' Ellis looked pensive.

'Well... if you're buying the chips next time we're on a joint snooping job...' Billie pretended to be undecided as to the answer.

'You drive a hard bargain, but okay, it's a deal.' Ellis finally grinned that cheeky smile that Billie had noticed could melt the hardest of hearts.

'You don't think she meant what she said, Maya's mate, about her not wanting to come back?' he asked. Billie couldn't help giving his arm a squeeze.

'Absolutely not. Teenagers know all the right buttons to press in order to make their parents feel guilty. Luckily I'm not a parent, so water off a duck's back to me.' Billie was pleased to see Ellis cheer up a little. What she wouldn't share was that she was suspicious that Lily still hadn't told the full story of Maya's decision not to come home at the same time as the rest of the students. Maya had impressed Billie when she had worked with her team. She was a loyal and intelligent girl who had shown no signs at all about feeling stifled by her newly found dad's utter devotion to her. Quite the opposite in fact.

Billie also still remembered the look on Lily's face as she had left the airport arrivals lounge with her own doting dad. Boo had clocked it too. Something wasn't right and she intended to find out what. Hopefully without loading more stress on Ellis. As they passed through the corridor heading towards their office, names of various companies were listed on doors to their left and right. Wilde & Darque was at the end.

'The door's open.' Ellis moved forward quickly, with Billie alert and following behind. He stopped so abruptly at the entrance that Billie nearly walked into his back.

161

'What the fu...' Ellis started to say, before Billie noticed Perry standing in the middle of the room.

'I was just about to ring you,' she said, looking around. The office was in total disarray, drawers pulled out, paperwork strewn across the floor and spray-painted graffiti across the walls. 'I came to drop off the spare key. I'm going to be on this temporary contract for a few weeks, in the press department again at your old gaff. I thought you might need it for someone else. The door was wide open...' She trailed off, nodding to words painted on the wall in black and red. 'Looks like someone's got the hump.'

Billie and Ellis surveyed the damage. The words scrawled in huge letters read KEEP AWAY FROM OZZIE KINGSNORTH.

'Someone's protesting too much,' Billie thought out loud as she read the words.

'Red rag to a bull this is.' Ellis's voice was firm. 'I take back everything I said earlier.'

'Sorry I can't stay to help scrub it off. I'm on duty in thirty minutes.' Perry reached for her handbag.

'I'll give it a lick of paint when I get back from my solicitor.' Ellis crossed the room to his desk. 'That's if I can lay my hands on the paperwork...' He started to hunt through the contents that had been spilled from a drawer onto the floor.

'Someone seems to have got wind that we've more info on Ozzie's death.' Billie got her mobile out and started to film, a habit she had found hard to drop, being second nature when attending the scene of a crime. 'They would be disappointed if they've been looking for evidence. I haven't got a copy of Josta's report yet. Slug Harris and the coroner are the only ones who've been informed of the full details.' Billie made a mental note to get a copy ASAP and go over it with a fine-tooth comb. This was absolute confirmation that Ozzie's death had not been an accident. Perry put her keys on Billie's desk.

'Window's the obvious entry point.' Perry nodded to the broken glass and gaping hole in a window behind Billie's desk.

'Must have been a small adult or teenager then.' Billie filmed the window area, at the same time thinking hard about who was aware of their investigation on Ozzie, other than their inner crowd and Josta's team. Teddy Cook certainly, but he couldn't have squeezed through the space left by the broken glass. Slug Harris would be aware by now that the second post-mortem request would have come via Wilde & Darque, but he would hardly use this means to stamp his authority over an investigation he appeared to be less than interested in. That left Smokey Boy Patel, who was not at work today and Lily, who had taken off like a scalded cat when Ellis had joined Billie in the office at the kipper smokery.

The two teenagers seemed to know each other better than they were making out. Billie was convinced they could spill more beans about Ozzie with a bit of firm encouragement and Lily could definitely tell more about Maya's extended holiday. The fact that Maya had allegedly spent time with Ozzie just before he was the victim of a suspicious death, sent shivers running down Billie's spine. It was definitely time for her to come home now, if only to supply vital information to Billie and Ellis. Billie was beginning to worry that the girl might be in some sort of trouble herself. Was that why she was delaying her return? Ellis finally pulled together half a dozen papers from the pile on the floor. He checked his watch.

'Sorry, I've really got to run. Leave all this and I'll help sort it out as soon as I get back.'

Billie shrugged. 'No problem. I'm not exactly rushed off my feet with jobs right now.' She was eager to brush the glass off her seat, make contact with Josta and get the second autopsy report sent over.

'I'm with you all the way on the Ozzie Kingsnorth

investigation now. Sorry I've taken all this convincing. I owe you.' Ellis was already heading for the door, flicking through paperwork.

'Yeah, a double portion of chips,' Billie teased as Perry headed after Ellis.

'Any chance of a lift? My car engine's just collapsed, and it might be a scrapyard job, even with my great engineering skills. Fixed the fan belt with my tights once. I'm on shanks's pony and the unreliable bus service until I can sort out new wheels.' Perry pulled the door shut behind her as Billie finished filming on her mobile and started the big clear-up. Five minutes later she still had dustpan and brush in her hand when she heard a knock on the door.

'Yep?' she called on hands and knees, picking up shards of glass which seemed to have ended up absolutely everywhere. She heard the door open and glanced up. James Checkley was standing in the doorway, a surprised look on his face that melted into a smile when they made eye contact.

'I think these must be yours?' He held Billie's silver shoes in his hand, the pair that she had been wearing when she had run off and left him standing on the riverside. 'I tried them on the two ugly sisters that I just passed coming in, but they didn't fit.'

Billie couldn't help smiling, though she was sure that Ellis and Perry would be less than impressed with James's description of them.

'They don't exactly fit me either. Hence me kicking them off. Sorry about the other night.' Billie straightened up and took the shoes from him. 'I'd offer you a drink but as you can see, there isn't anywhere to sit right now.' Billie still had the brush in her hand, waving it around.

'I'm happy to stay and give you a hand,' James offered.

Billie shook her head. 'No really. Thanks again for returning these, but I'm sure you have some glamorous ball to go to or something.' Billie glanced up at the wall with the warning sprayed across in bright red-and-black graffiti. She would crack on and get painting while she waited for the report from Josta. She had already texted her and now she was champing at the bit to get on with the investigation. The words scrawled on the wall had made her even more determined to discover what had caused Ozzie Kingsnorth's death. She was glad that Ellis now felt the same way.

'Quite an emphatic warning...' James looked at the wall and then back to Billie. 'Angry wife trying to scare you off?' Billie was aware of his sparkling blue eyes upon her. Was he fishing?

'I do deal with a lot of angry wives, that's true, but they are normally hiring me to follow their wayward husbands. This doesn't quite fit their normal modus operandi.'

'Well, I can assure you that I'm not married. Never have been, so how about another date now that I've returned your glass slippers?'

'Did we have a first date?' Billie answered.

'I bought you a bag of chips and that definitely counts as a date in my book. Got you extra ketchup too. Didn't you notice that?' James smiled mischievously.

'I did actually,' Billie answered through a smile. 'Clearly I'm not up to scratch with dating rules these days.'

'So let me take you to Moonshine, that lovely new restaurant overlooking the quayside, tomorrow night, where I can explain all?' Billie was about to answer 'no' automatically, but then suddenly thought, *why not?* Her history with men hadn't exactly been great, but she was a free agent and had to start seeing people again sometime. Either that or join a nunnery, so perhaps now was that time.

There was a sudden knock on the door, which stopped the conversation. It slowly opened. Billie was surprised to see Pandy Wood enter. She clocked Billie, James and the office mess.

'Oh, I'm sorry. Maybe this isn't a good time?' She took in the view, clearly, Billie noted, lingering a few extra seconds on James. Billie couldn't exactly blame her. He was looking like a rose in a garden of weeds right now. 'I just wanted to discuss a job...' She trailed off.

'No, stay, please, I'll just brush this glass off here–' Billie headed for one of the red sofas. Ellis was right. They needed all the work they could get. He'd come around to her views on the Ozzie case, she had to meet him halfway with his own concerns about generating income. James took in the scene, starting to head for the door.

'Look, I won't keep you. I can see that you're busy,' he said, starting to excuse himself. Billie felt her heart sink momentarily. The words were out of her mouth before she had time to think.

'Tomorrow night is good. Should we say 8pm?' Billie ran her fingers through her hair and looked up. James was staring straight at her. His face lit up in a smile.

'Until tomorrow.' He raised his hand and then was gone. Billie stared at the door closing and wondered what she had done, having vowed so recently to stay away from any relationships with a hint of romance. But this wasn't a romantic dinner, just new mates sharing a meal together, wasn't it?

'Wow. Some girls get all the luck.' Pandy sighed, tearing her gaze away from the door as it shut behind James.

'Just a client,' Billie answered, wondering why she was fibbing. 'How are you doing?' She could already tell by the look on Pandy's face that the answer wasn't hugely positive.

'I've used the money left by Aunt Sadie to start up a string of nail salons to compliment the hairdressing business. Thanks for making sure I didn't lose all my inheritance by the way.' Pandy sighed again.

'That sounds a good move.' Billie brushed the last shards of glass off the sofa and invited Pandy to sit, wondering why she was looking so down. 'Sorry about Rex, but better to know sooner than later.' Billie wondered if she was still recovering from the shock of finding out that her fiancé was already married.

'Yeah, should be, but that's why I've come to see you. No sooner did I set up my salons, then another chain popped up out of nowhere. They've been undercutting all my prices like crazy. If this goes on, I'll go bust before I've really got started and I was determined to pick myself up after Rexy...' She trailed off. Billie was aware that some such operations were used primarily to launder big money from criminal gangs, therefore could afford not to charge much for the services they offered as a convenient cover, but she didn't want to suggest the possibility without any evidence.

'The thing is, they don't pay proper wages to their technicians. One of them told me as much. Came running in the door one day, begging for a job, saying that they treat her like a slave at the place down the road. I'd just taken a new girl on, or I would have given her a chance, but that was the last I saw of her. I mean, I don't like dropping anyone in it with the authorities, but it can't be right that the owner will put me out of business when she's treating her staff so badly. Probably not paying any taxes or anything either, whereas I like to put in my fair share to support the rest of the community. If you could go in there and see what's what, tell me if I'm right or wrong. I mean, you're a great fibber. I had no idea that you were working undercover when you came to me for a haircut.' Billie didn't know whether that was a compliment.

'They'd have to be authentic nail technicians to do anything with these.' Billie waved her fingers. 'I haven't had a manicure since...' Billie tried to remember, with no luck. The memory didn't exist. 'I haven't ever had one actually,' she admitted. 'I just chew them into shape.' Pandy chuckled, but Billie wasn't joking.

'I admit they'll be a real test,' Pandy agreed. 'So will you take the job?' Billie saw no reason to refuse it, as she settled down to fill in the paperwork with her latest client. She had just waved Pandy off, having decided on a plan of action, when the phone rang.

'Dear heart, it's Josta.' Billie was just about to explain why she needed the full written second autopsy report when Josta continued, 'I've just had a meeting with Lizbeth re our various deceased clients and something rather strange has come up. Possibly a link between all three. Are you free to come over?'

Billie was out of her seat like a shot. This might just be the breakthrough she had been waiting for.

Chapter 22

A Look That Could Kill?

Ellis gave Slug Harris a look that could kill as the young detective's car swept past him and turned left into the police headquarters car park. Ellis quickened his step. He wanted a word, wanted to get the business with the bodies found in his house sorted out once and for all.

The solicitor advising him had pointed out that he had been released, after Slug's second ridiculous interview under caution, in a position of RUI. The solicitor didn't need to spell it out, not to an officer who had been at the top of his game. It meant that he had been released under investigation, and the investigation into him was still ongoing. Until his part in the crimes was confirmed to be negative there wasn't a hope in hell that he would get any further unsupervised access to Connie.

Even if he was successful in achieving supervised access via the family courts it meant meeting her in a special child contact centre, somewhere near her new home once Storm moved on, as she'd threatened with her new lover boy. Ellis didn't even know where that was. Not in England, his ex-wife had said. His heart lurched at the thought. He'd be under the gaze of a specialised health and social care worker to ensure Connie's safety, with all the rules, regulations and costs that would involve.

Ellis couldn't have even begun to imagine how leaving his high-flying job in law enforcement with the resulting drop in status would affect everything he did. It was especially irksome as he had given up the job specifically so that he could spend more time with his kids.

Slug Harris could have easily dismissed him as a suspect. The CPS would certainly chuck out any unsubstantiated charges in a moment, but now due to Slug's wish to be seen as the big man, eking out the pain, Ellis's mind was spinning. He could be hovering in limbo for years, police investigation processes having no time limit. Such a situation would sound the death knell for the business and definitely for Billie's involvement. She'd made clear that morning that she wouldn't be hanging around if Wilde & Darque wasn't working out.

The thought of that hurt almost as much as losing the chance of having a normal dad relationship with Connie. He suddenly thought of Maya. He hadn't even met her until she was eighteen and if her mate, Lily, had been telling the truth that morning when he had walked into the office, she hadn't bonded the same way he had. Is that what was about to happen with Connie too, due to this ridiculous situation? She'd soon get sick of meeting him in a room in some centre once she started going to school and it was clear that Storm was angling to have this new man take his place. Connie had even called him 'Papa'. Ellis closed his eyes tightly, trying to wipe that vision from his mind's eye.

Ellis quickened his pace. He'd have to eat humble pie, get Slug to see reason and get him to make it official that he wasn't part of the enquiry. Not that the kid seemed to have done much in the area of enquiries anyway, other than sit back and accuse Ellis, because the bodies had turned up in his gaff.

Ellis had done some bad things in his life, it was true. Working as an undercover officer it was an unavoidable part of the job. Had he taken action to the extremes on occasion to cover his back? You could bet on it. Not that he was about to come clean now, or ever, for that matter. It wasn't something he was proud of and technically some of those things could get him banged up these days. People didn't ask as many questions in the past and those who had never been in such dangerous situations judged through the eyes of sofa-surfing detectives.

In Ellis's opinion, it was the same with the war game. People for whom the most dangerous thing in their lives had been opening a packet of rough-edged pork scratchings criticised soldiers' actions when bang in the middle of the hellish theatre of war.

Ellis had crossed the car park and pushed the door into the reception area harder than he had meant to. It banged against the wall. A middle-aged female at the desk glanced up from doodling her shopping list on a notepad.

'I'd like a word with DS Harris, MIT,' Ellis announced, through pursed lips. He wasn't in the mood to live up to his usual cheery Jack the Lad persona today. The woman folded her arms.

'Like to come back in, close the door quietly behind you and ask again, this time politely?' She raised an eyebrow. Ellis could see that she was one of the types who imagined that she was actually part of the plod, rather than a civilian worker.

'Just pick up the blower and get him.' Ellis leaned on the desk, showing her he was going nowhere. She stepped back, seemed to consider challenging him and then thought better of it. Instead she reached for the phone handset and punched in an extension number.

'Hi. DS Harris? Yeah, there's an aggressive fellow down

here, saying he wants to speak to you, sir.' She listened before looking back at Ellis.

'What's your name?'

'Ellis Darque. He knows me–'

The woman cut over Ellis's words. 'Are you here to make a confession?' she asked. 'Apparently you're in the frame for the suspicious deaths.' She moved further away, and Ellis could see her eyeing the panic button on the countertop. He slapped his fist down hard on the surface.

'It's him who'll be the bleeding death of me. Tell him to get down here. I want a word about my status.'

'He's saying he wants to speak to you,' the woman whispered into the receiver, moving closer to the panic button. She listened, biting her lip before taking a deep breath and replacing the receiver. 'DS Harris has advised me to order you to leave the building, otherwise face a charge of police harassment. You are only to come back if you have a confession to make.' Her hand now hovered over the button as she tensed for Ellis's reaction.

'Muppets. Tell Slug Harris that he hasn't heard the last of this!' he shouted, turning on his heel and leaving the building, slamming the door so hard behind him that he was amazed that it hadn't come off its hinges. Furious, he glanced over to Slug's car sitting in the VIP area of the car park. Should he wait until he finally came out and then catch the little squirt unawares? One way or another, Slug Harris was going to pay for this.

Chapter 23

The Wasp Tattoo

Billie viewed the three large photos projected onto a screen in one of the many smart rooms within King & Beech Forensics. One of them featured the back of Ozzie Kingsnorth's head, on which a tattoo of a wasp was clear to see, situated at the base of his skull, behind his left ear. Above it was the gaping head wound that Josta had shown her via the same photo earlier, taken before his first autopsy. Billie hadn't viewed the tattoo as particularly remarkable at the time, but now, seen alongside the other two photos either side of it, a pattern was obvious.

'Clearly the information here is confidential, other than that fully available for your own client. However, both Lizbeth and I have discussed the situation and have decided to share these findings with you, as DS Harris has made clear that he has no wish to further investigate the two skeletonised bodies. He claims to already have linked the perpetrator to the location where the bodies were discovered.'

'Preposterous,' Billie said through a sigh. 'He'd need all the information that you can supply him with if he really wants to try and hang this on Ellis.'

'Quite,' Josta answered, 'hence our agreement to share this

with you. Our responsibility is to the police but even more so to the deceased.' Lizbeth Beech nodded. It was clear to see that she was a woman not easily persuaded to blab to all and sundry. She stood up now and walked towards the screen.

'The skull that you see on your left is the bride, discovered within the chimney. The body is largely skeletonised, and our findings are that it is firstly indeed a female. From our preliminary bone studies alone, estimated age was put at between seventeen and twenty-three years of age. In life, she was between five foot three and five foot five inches tall and Caucasian. There are some healed broken bones. One left rib and two sites on the right arm. All sustained antemortem, healing before the date of her death. On the left side there are distinct perimortem breakage patterns on the left wrist received shortly before death. A transverse fracture to the distal radius, known as a Colles fracture. This usually happens when trying to stop oneself with an outstretched arm during a fall, rather than a blow to the wrist.'

'So it looks like she fell or was pushed, down the chimney?' Billie's mind started working fast.

'Possibly the former. Though why a bride would willingly climb down a chimney in full regalia is anyone's guess. Certainly there isn't at this stage any obvious signs of a struggle which would have resulted in broken bones. No fractures to the skull and as we can see, some of the hair and skin are still attached in that region, having become mummified due to environmental conditions.

'Photos of the crime scene show salt contamination within the chimney,' Lizbeth explained, handing a pile of photos to Billie, who started to flick through them. To her untrained eye, it looked like a large damp patch above the fireplace. 'Salt contamination in chimneys is due to the long-term effects of burning fossil fuels such as coal and wood, in an open fire.

Contaminates are released into the chimney flue where they migrate into the brickwork. The salts are hygroscopic, meaning that they have the ability to absorb moisture. In this case around the area of the head of the deceased laid against the interior of the flue. The result, as you can see, is mummification as the skin becomes dehydrated and the normal putrefactive decomposition is inhibited.'

'On this photo,' Josta took up the explanation, 'we have magnified the visuals. We can see the skin at the back of the neck near the left ear. It is darkened by the mummification process to a mid-brown shade, but here–'

'It's the same wasp tattoo,' Billie finished. 'So how long do you estimate since her death?'

'Dating from radiocarbon testing alone is still a sketchy business. She was definitely born after 1950 as testing for nuclear weapons after that date dramatically increased the carbon 14 in the atmosphere and in all of our bodies. It's known as the bomb effect,' Lizbeth explained.

'That's shocking.' Billie gasped.

'Indeed. In 1955–1963 atmospheric radiocarbon levels almost doubled, then started to drop back. Using that information, I was involved with a USA research study in which we focused on tooth enamel and for teeth formed after 1965, enamel radiocarbon content predicted the year of birth to within 1.5 years. I have one of the students from that study with me at the moment, so it has been an interesting refresher for us both. We have also been lucky to have some tissue on this young lady still intact. We found during our research that radiocarbon levels in these tissues could predict the year of death, the radiocarbon level mirroring that in the atmosphere, as soft tissues constantly renew.'

'It's amazing stuff!' Josta interjected cheerily. She never failed to be impressed by new ways of communicating with the dead. 'So taking all of these things into consideration, we are finally putting her date of birth around 1977 and date of death in 1995 or thereabouts.'

'What? She's been up the chimney for twenty-seven years?' Billie was visibly astonished.

'That's correct, dear thing,' Josta confirmed. 'Making her about eighteen years old when she died.'

'But what about the wasp tattoo?' Billie ran her fingers through her hair. 'Ozzie's is identical, yet he wouldn't even have been born by the time she died...' Billie turned her gaze to the third photo. The body found in Ellis's compost heap. Lizbeth followed her gaze.

'Yes, this is what we wanted to put to you. We are just starting detailed examinations of this cadaver, which is not fully skeletonised and seems to have been moved at least once. But again, within the tissue available we can clearly see an identical tattoo.'

'In an identical spot.' Billie's senses were on high alert, trying to make sense of the links and suddenly wishing desperately that she was back in charge of the Murder Investigation Team. She, of course, couldn't go back but if Slug Harris wasn't going to do his job properly, she was determined somehow, to get justice for these victims.

Chapter 24

A Game of Make-Believe

As far as Maya was concerned the past day had been the most harrowing of her life. She knew by her muzzy head that she had been drugged once again and was now wearing different clothing, but despite the use of substances to perhaps subdue her or cause some measure of amnesia, horrific images still remained of the numerous men who had used and abused her body along with those of the other trapped girls.

She remembered a huge warehouse of a room with what looked like separate film sets created in different areas. She recalled being moved from one set-up to the next. Cameras on tripods always trained on her, directions spat out using words that she had either not understood, or now wanted to block out forever, along with the terrifying and shocking scenarios that she had been dragged into, involving different men, different girls. Each fragmented memory was like a deep, dark festering splinter that piece by piece was now emerging into her consciousness.

Maya suddenly felt nauseous, bile surging up into her throat. As she bowed forward on her wooden seat, female hands pulled her hair back off her face, whilst holding a bowl under her chin. It was the woman Maya remembered having painted her face with garish make-up, what seemed like a hundred years ago... or maybe she had done that more than once? Changed her hairstyle, before changing the scene? Maya retched again. Nothing came out into the bowl, but then she couldn't remember eating. Her body ached all over.

'I am going to make you beautiful again now. You sit still here.'

The woman put the bowl down and turned Maya towards her make-up mirror again. Maya registered that her face looked pale but had no marks on it, despite the sensation she was experiencing of being bruised all over. It was clear that her captors were professionals, largely ensuring that all the pain and horror experienced by their victims stayed hidden inside. She wondered if she had passed females in the street, to whom similar atrocities had happened and never guessed that they too had been violently sexually abused? The girls at the orphanage perhaps? Bluey had made clear that the place where she had been eagerly volunteering, believing she was bringing much needed help, had simply been another game of make-believe with victims hiding in plain view.

'This time, I'm going to make you look natural.' The woman smiled. Was she an abuser or abused too, a player or a victim? Maybe one now turned into the other? Maya shook her head, trying to clear her brain. She was down, but not totally beaten. There had to be some way out of this hell.

'Is she ready yet? My plane leaves in an hour.' Maya's heart leaped. It was an English voice. It was Mitch! Had he arrived to rescue her, come to take her to the airport?

Maya looked desperately into the mirror as Mitch appeared in the doorway. What had Bluey said about his name not really being Mitch at all? As he emerged into view looking as handsome as Maya had remembered with his soft features and gentle smile, she wondered if she was simply waking up and that Mitch was going to gently kiss her panic away. Perhaps he was here to tell her she was just having the worst dream ever?

'Mitch?' Maya's voice sounded hoarse. He stared at her momentarily with those striking eyes of his and then flicked his gaze away to the woman who was quickly sponging make-up across Maya's face.

'Get a move on. I've got to do this quickly.' He pulled a mobile phone out of his inside pocket and waved it in the air as he spoke to the other woman. Maya immediately recognised it as her own device.

'Yes, ring my dad. His phone number is in there, Mitch. Quickly!' Maya pushed the woman away and spun around in her seat to face him. He approached her and bent forward, a look of sadness on his face. He kissed her softly on the forehead, stroking his finger gently down the side of her face. The feeling made tears spring to the back of Maya's eyes, she wanted to hug him tightly, cling onto him as he swept her away from this terrible location.

'I'm sorry, Maya. This is not going to pan out the way you want.' Mitch moved back as he straightened up again, sidestepping Maya's outstretched hand. He swallowed hard as though he was genuinely sorry. 'You shouldn't have gone poking your nose into all this stuff, trying to phone your dad. You've made some people very angry. I don't want to do this–'

'So let's run away.' Maya could hear the desperation within her husky whisper.

'I can't. They know where my family live. They'll kill them if I don't do what they ask.' He held out her mobile again. 'You have one last piece of filming to do. Don't mess it up. They know where your dad lives too.'

'If you cause no more trouble, you might be sold on,' the woman added, rushing to finish Maya's make-up.

'Sold, to who, for what? A sex film? A *snuff* film?' Maya asked Mitch. A sudden memory sliced through her brain. Had a girl really been killed during one of the recent filming sessions that she had been forced into? Maya gasped, holding her hand to her mouth as the shocking truth hit her.

'You no do it right and then this will happen. Right here and now in this chair!' The woman pulled Maya's head around harshly to face the mirror, dragging an imaginary knife across Maya's neck. Maya tried to stop her body from shaking. What on earth could be waiting for her outside the door?

Chapter 25

Say Hello To Teddy Joe

'I dunno, there's something odd about it, even by Slug's low standards.' Ash shrugged as he, Billie and Ellis ate pasta at Billie's huge table, looking down onto Alnmouth's estuary. They were deep in discussion about Ozzie Kingsnorth, Skeleton Bride and Compost Man, as they had named the two as yet unidentified bodies. 'Clearly there's a link, but it's as though he's scared to do any further investigation.'

'Yeah, well he isn't scared about trying to frame me up.' Ellis sighed, taking a swig of his beer as he looked across to where Ash's children, Indie, Happi and Tani were playing hairdressers, with the box of wigs and hairpieces that Billie had hauled out of a cupboard in preparation for her undercover nail bar visit. She had made an appointment for the next morning. 'God knows how long it's going to be before my Connie is able to come here and play on the beach with your girls,' he added. Billie could see how much the thought pained Ellis. He'd hardly even registered the story that Billie had recounted about Pandy becoming a new client.

'Could it be that someone is pulling his strings?' Billie queried. It was no secret between them that weak police officers were sometimes targeted by criminals attempting to control them if they had some information to threaten blackmail with.

'What do you imagine Slug could have to hide? He's so clean he squeaks when he walks across the office,' Ash said with a chuckle.

'Well, someone's trying to scare us off looking into Ozzie's death. Maybe they stopped him from investigating at the beginning, hence the odd claim that it was suicide without a full investigation,' Billie suggested. Ellis's mobile suddenly rang its video messaging service tune.

'Thank God. It's Maya.' A look of relief immediately spread over Ellis's face.

'Hello, darlin'.' He smiled, a sight Billie was absolutely thrilled to see at last. Ellis's cheerful demeanour having been so sorely lacking in the past few days. Maya's face suddenly popped up onscreen. She smiled hesitantly, Billie noted, as she craned her neck to look over Ellis's shoulder, giving Maya a wave, wondering if the expression on her face was one of worry that Ellis was going to tell her off for her sudden change of plans.

'Hi, Dad.' Maya managed a wider smile. 'Sorry I've not been in touch, but I'm fine, don't worry.' Maya swallowed hard. 'I'll be back soon.'

'Not soon enough,' Ellis replied. 'Get yourself home now, we're all missing you here.' Ash called across to his girls, who Maya had nannied for a while.

'Come and say hello to Maya, girls.' Indie, Tani and Happi skipped across the room, giggling, wearing their various wigs.

'Hi, Maya!' Indie, the oldest, waved. Maya blinked suddenly, then answered.

'Hello, lovely. I'm coming home soon with Teddy Joe.' Indie didn't answer.

'Maya, we're playing hairdressers!' Happi shouted, waving. Maya waved back.

'Lovely! I'll bring Teddy Joe over for a haircut,' Maya answered. 'Teddy Joe sends his love.' Indie started to tug at Billie's top for attention.

'Billie...' she started to say as Happi started to tug at Ash's top in a similar manner.

'Got to go, Dad. Love you. Don't worry, I'm just taking a longer break. See you and Teddy Joe soon, girls—' Maya's words were cut off as the screen went blank.

'Well at least she's all right.' Ellis seemed to relax for a moment or two.

'Maya's in trouble.' Indie finally got Billie's attention.

'Yes, Maya's been captured by bad people,' Happi agreed, a serious look crossing her face. 'Teddy Joe is our special word, to use if we're in trouble.'

'What do you mean?' Billie frowned.

'Maya taught us to say that name if we were frightened or need help and wanted to come straight home. She taught us to ring her on our phones and say the words Teddy Joe and she would come straight and get us,' Indie explained, like a teacher speaking to three particularly dense students. 'Like this.' She lifted her little mobile phone out of her pocket, which had a couple of emergency numbers plumbed in. 'Hello, Teddy Joe,' said Indie, acting out the scenario. 'That's all we would have to say, then Maya said she would know.'

'Or if we were playing hide and seek and we wanted to be found.' Happi nodded sagely. 'Teddy Joe means come and get me now.' Billie, Ellis and Ash looked from one to another silently for a moment, as the girls went back to play.

'Is she serious?' Ellis asked Ash.

'Indie, is that the truth? Did Maya *definitely* tell you that?' Ash asked.

'Yes, Dad.' Indie nodded her head seriously. 'Ask Mum. Maya told her all about it. You'd better go and find her.'

'What was the name of the orphanage in Romania?' Billie asked Ellis, who had a look of utter shock on his face.

'Just a moment, let me check this out. I'll phone Jas.' Ash punched some numbers into his mobile, leaving the room as he connected with Jas, his former wife.

'I've got it somewhere...' Ellis got up, rubbing his head, as Billie rifled through her own mobile contacts.

'Found it. Well, the name of the place. Is this the number?' Ellis looked at Billie's phone, punching the numbers on show into his own mobile. He started walking back and forth across the floor, waiting for the number to connect. He stopped, pressed on the speaker so that both he and Billie could hear the disconnected tone. Ellis was immediately on the move.

'Sorry to leave you in the lurch, but I'm catching a flight over there right now. My passport's back at the house. I'll have to nip home to get it first...'

'Of course.' Billie started pacing the room in a similar fashion, as Ash reappeared.

'Looks like the girls are telling the truth,' he said, rubbing his face. Ellis was already rushing past him.

'There better not be some plod still standing in the way of me getting in my own gaff.' Ellis grabbed his bag and headed for the front door, followed by Billie, who hoped so too. It could only signal further trouble for Ellis if he punched a policeman to get to his travel documents.

'Let me know the moment you get there,' she said as he exited, jogging towards his car. 'Bring her back safely.' Billie watched him speed off, a feeling of foreboding enveloping her. She turned to see Ash emerging into the hallway, seemingly finishing another call.

'I hope this doesn't make Slug think he's gone on the run

abroad to avoid any more charges.' Billie sighed, then did a double take at the look of shock on Ash's face. He shook his head.

'No chance of that. Just got a call here on the blower. Slug Harris has been in a car crash. He's dead.'

Chapter 26

The Sale

'Please, don't go without me.' Maya reached out her hand to catch Mitch's arm as he clicked off her mobile phone and started to walk away.

'I've just told you. I've got no choice and you nearly dropped me in it with all that Teddy Joe shit. Do you think I'm stupid?'

'Just tell my dad what's happening, and he'll sort it out. He'll make sure that no one will touch you and he'll get us both home.' Maya could hear the note of desperation in her voice.

'Your dad will be dead if he comes here trying to push his way in and me, I am going home. Right now.' Mitch opened the mobile and took the SIM card out, throwing it into a dustbin in the corner, then dropped the mobile onto the ground and stamped on it hard, smashing the shell. The woman who had attended to Maya's make-up, in an attempt to make it look like everything was normal, pulled her away towards a door.

'You must come this way now. The sale has begun.' Maya tried to struggle as a large man stepped forward and grabbed her other arm, letting her legs give way as she was dragged across the floor, crying out for Mitch to return. He looked back only once, with what appeared to be regret and a hint of fear in his eyes, before leaving by a side door, closing it quickly behind him.

Maya was hauled through another door and then pulled upright. She found herself in a dark open area, with high walls all around it and a crowd of men gathered, spectators at what at first looked like some sort of cattle market. A roped-off square in the middle stood empty except for a lone girl, looking terrified. A huge man at the entrance, head shaved, nose looking like it had been broken more than once, casually held a gun, gazing around at the other males staring at the girl. Suddenly one man and then another, started bidding. Maya realised, as she was pushed into the queue of girls, that she was about to become part of a human auction.

'Do as you're told. They all have guns,' a girl in front of Maya and of a similar age and colouring whispered, as other girls were lined up behind her. 'They are from different places. When the auction is finished we will go on our next journey. Maybe to other countries. I want to go home to Italy. I may be able to escape from there. I have no hope in England.'

'So there's a buyer here from Britain?' Maya whispered back, her mind racing, wondering if anyone from her home country would help her.

'That man over there, in the corner. I've seen him bid already. I'm frightened he will want me, but my father is ill, dying. I need to get home to him, before it's too late.' Even in the darkness, Maya could see the girl's eyes fill with tears. As they finished speaking, bidding ended on the female before them. She was led away and the girl who had been talking was propelled forward into the middle of the roped-off area, where bidding began in earnest. Maya suddenly heard the English voice engage in the auction which continued for less than a minute before only the English man and another bidder were left competing. As the English man made the final bid, the girl let out a wail, scrambling over to the other bidder, begging in Italian for him to take her. An air of merriment filled the crowd.

'The whore must love Italian men!' the huge man holding the gun shouted, to more laughter as the losing bidder made a joke of pretending to unzip his filthy-looking jeans.

'She's not worth my money. I like the look of the one behind more.' He pointed towards Maya who was propelled into the middle of the roped-off square. Out of the corner of her eye, she could see the English man taking a call on his mobile, distracted. He didn't make a bid for her and in seconds it was over. She had been sold to the Italian. 'She has a little more meat on her. If I wasn't on overtime, I might try out the goods,' he joked as Maya was yanked away into the darkness so quickly that it had hardly registered in her shocked brain that she had crazily been disappointed that a particular man *hadn't* wanted to buy her body.

As her eyes became accustomed to the darkness, she saw now that the girls who had already been sold were congregated in a dark corner in separate huddled groups, associated with the different bidders. Maya slumped down, almost touching shoulders with the Italian girl she had just spoken to. The girl was sobbing, her tawny afro curls, so like Maya's own, covering her beautiful features. Maya patted her hand. Her mind racing as an idea suddenly formed. At the same moment, a loud wail could be heard, as Bluey realised that she and Ubi had just parted ways.

'No!' she cried. 'You promised to stay with me. You said you would take me to England. We would get married and have babies!' Loud laughter reverberated around the space at her screams. She was hanging on to Ubi's ankle. He tried to kick her off like a piece of dog dirt on his shoe.

'I have broken her in, but she needs more men to knock this lover boy crap out of her!' he shouted, playing to the crowd as he continued in his attempts to shake her off. But Bluey was clinging on for dear life, so that a commotion erupted, with the East Asian woman and the large man who had dragged Maya into the space, wading in to separate Bluey from a quickly angering Ubi, as the crowd of men laughed and cheered.

'Quick!' Maya grabbed the Italian girl's wrist to get her attention. 'Give me your dress.' Maya was already pulling her own shift dress off in the dark shadows. 'Swap places with me,' she whispered, shuffling quickly across to the group of girls heading for England as the Italian girl ripped off her own garment then pulled Maya's dress over her head. She moved quickly across into the space Maya had left in the knot of girls heading for Italy. A shot suddenly blasted out over their heads, silencing the crowd.

'Let's move. The show is over. We need to be out of here, pronto,' the large man shouted.

Almost immediately, different men split away from the crowd and appeared alongside the separate groups of girls, ordering them to follow, with threats of death if they made a sound. Maya reached out and squeezed the hand of the Italian girl, until their fingers finally slid free.

'*Viaggio sicuro,*' Maya whispered. The girl nodded, responding with the same words in English.

'Safe journey.' The girl kept her head down as she scrambled to her feet and followed the others in the Italian group.

Maya's cohort of around twenty girls was last and when they were pushed one by one into the back of another truck, Bluey was already on board, huddled up in the back, terrified and sobbing. It was plain for Maya to see that she was in shock, at last facing up to the reality that she was all alone and that the gruesome Ubi had never been her lover boy at all. Maya had some sympathy for the younger girl. She had just realised how much Mitch hadn't cared for her either. As she sat down next to Bluey, she put her arm around her, pulling her close and whispering into her ear.

'We don't need any lover boys, Bluey. We're going to get out of this and show them that they are messing with the wrong girls.' She hoped that she was telling the truth and that one of Ash's daughters had understood her call for help. All she needed to do now was to sit tight until they arrived in the UK. 'We'll be away from this hell, soon,' Maya added.

Bluey tucked her feet underneath her and sat hunched, chewing her thumbnail. She suddenly looked like a wary child, which after all, Maya sighed, was exactly the truth. Many of the other girls were as young as Bluey, looking equally childlike and terrified. Maya knew that what she needed to do now was to keep her head down, make sure that no one realised the swap and get to the UK. If she could simply manage to do that, then she would start rocking her heroine, Billie Wilde, who always fought back when the chips were down. Despite getting battered and bruised, *she* always ended up winning. Maya took strength from that thought, silently vowing that no matter what horrors might still lie ahead on this journey, *nobody* was going to stop her from heading home to her precious dad.

Chapter 27

Turning Tricks

'I leave these for you to choose colour.' The young woman spoke in heavily-accented English. 'My big boss will be looking after you today. She will come soon.' The woman glanced over her shoulder, having put down a long tray holding a vast assortment of coloured nail varnishes, before she scurried off. Billie was sure that she had heard a baby crying in the distance.

She looked around the smart nail bar. Nothing seemed untoward so far. The place was clean and bright. The smell of acrylic and acetone mixed with a floral perfume. The price list was much lower than Pandy's own, but that wasn't exactly a crime. Billie tugged down her straight, shoulder-length mouse-coloured wig. It was itching already. She tried to focus on the bright nail colours, unable to choose one. She pretty much hated them all. Suddenly her mobile rang. She glanced down as she answered. Ellis's name was flashing up.

'Are you there yet?' Billie asked.

'You sound just like my Connie two minutes into any journey,' Ellis answered. 'I've just touched down and grabbed a taxi straight over to the orphanage. I'm praying to God that Ash's girls were just spinning me a line, but better to be safe than sorry. Hopefully I can persuade Maya to come straight back with me. Sorry I'm leaving you with all the jobs today,' he added.

'No problem. Apart from Ozzie, we've only got this one and I'm just sitting in a nail bar about to have bits of plastic glued on my fingers, so chill out. Get Maya to take you sightseeing,' Billie replied, hoping like Ellis did that Indie and Happi had simply misunderstood what Maya had been saying in the video call.

'Plastic nails?' Ellis questioned.

'Yes. Eat your heart out. The job I told you about last night, you know, for Pandy Wood? Nail bar wars.' Billie tried to jog Ellis's memory but guessed that the information hadn't actually sunk in at the first telling the night before.

'Oh yeah, yeah,' Ellis answered. Billie could tell he was fibbing. She was just about to break the news about Slug Harris's demise, when she spotted a tall, slim woman crossing the room towards her. She had short stylishly-cut blonde hair and was wearing fashionable clothing.

'Look, I've got to go. See you later with that girl of yours in tow.' Billie ended the call.

'Hello. I have the pleasure of being your nail artist today.' She waved her arm politely in the direction of a seating area.

'Wow, this *is* an honour,' Billie trilled. 'The girl said that you're the boss and I thought you'd just launched a string of new nail bars?' The manicurist smiled in response, showing expensive snow-white teeth.

'That's correct, but I like to be hands-on, if you'll pardon the pun. This is a big new brand I'm launching and right now I want to ensure the staff are working to my strict specifications.'

Billie smiled, putting on her best 'great to hear it' face, as she followed and settled down in the black leather-and-chrome chair pulled out for her.

'Sorry, you've got a bit of a job on here.' She nodded to her nails. 'I was given this manicure appointment as a late birthday treat. It's not normally my thing.' She had already run through the explanation for being here in a nail salon when it would have been clear to see, even by a blind man on a galloping horse, that she had never been within a hundred miles of a manicure before, though she had raided a few nail salons in the past when still a police officer. *Best not strike up a conversation about that,* Billie silently joked with herself.

'That's no problem. We've got a special deal on today with both coffin and stiletto nails as far as the extensions are concerned.'

'Coffin? I don't like the sound of that.' Billie played the dizzy-head. Truth was she'd seen more than enough coffins in her time.

'Okay, well stiletto it is. I prefer the sharp pointed ends myself. All the easier for hitting those credit card codes in the cash machines at shops – my former husband used to moan.' The woman rolled her eyes and smiled. 'I'm glad to see the back of him, that's for sure. That'll be forty-five pounds please, to include the nail extensions and hand-harvested salt massage.' Billie noticed that the woman's own talon-like nails hadn't prevented her from whipping the cash machine out of thin air like a seasoned member of the Magic Circle.

'I prefer to pay in cash,' Billie answered. *Less chance of having a credit card tracked back to its true owner,* she omitted to say, as she paid over the money. She had already sussed that this woman was as sharp as knives, but so far there was still no obvious crime on show.

'So where are your other salons? I'm just on holiday here

and I could get hooked on this,' Billie fibbed, as the woman got to work.

'Oh, all over the place. It's so exciting. I'm moving to a big, big house in the country too, just over the Scottish border, so I'll have salons across the whole of the UK eventually. It's just a question of getting the staff. British employees are so lazy I find, whereas the foreign girls are happy to work like dogs...' She had started to file Billie's nails as she spoke. She suddenly looked up. 'Not that we would do that, of course, but they are so willing.'

Something suddenly caught the woman's eye through the large window facing onto the street. She looked over Billie's shoulder and flicked her head towards the door where a man was entering. The girl Billie had met in the reception area had taken the silent instruction and scurried across the room to let the man in, waving him quickly to a side door off the reception area, shutting it behind them. But not before Billie had seen the worried look from the young woman via a mirror on the wall and the stern stare from her manicurist, who suddenly fixed on a smile for Billie. She heard footsteps on a staircase and then briefly across the floor above them.

'Little bit of a language situation, of course, with some of them and here was me thinking that *everybody* has been taught to speak English these days.'

'I hadn't realised that manicures are so popular with men too,' Billie continued, with the innocent abroad act. 'Do you have another salon upstairs for them?'

The woman blinked for only a moment.

'Yes. It's true that the boys have tired of girls having all the fun. Let's face it, they all like a bit of mollycoddling from a pretty girl.'

Billie wondered if the man had indeed been led upstairs for a manicure. The woman turned away, a long nail extension in her hand as she reached for a bottle on a shelf immediately behind her. It was labelled MMA.

Billie almost dropped out of character. She was aware that this specific nail glue was banned in the USA, so strong that many people suffered injuries from nails ripping off and taking the nail bed with them as well as serious allergies. However, it was a cheap alternative to safer products. Billie wondered if that might be the explanation for the budget prices, but again MMA wasn't currently illegal in the UK, for some crazy reason.

The noise of a man groaning could fleetingly be heard from the room above. Billie guessed that the nail bar takings were being supplemented by sexual services income and that she was sitting in a combined nail bar and brothel. Storm flicked a switch on the wall. Background music filled the room.

'What did you say your name is, just in case I can manage to get another appointment with you?' The landline suddenly rang, distracting the woman's attention. Billie damned it.

'Em, Storm's the name, but we'll be getting in lots of new girls in a few days' time, so I'm not planning to be so hands-on. I'll be more of a ring mistress, cracking the whip... if you'll excuse me.' She pointed to the phone still ringing. 'Jack of all trades, that's me at the minute.'

'Can I use your bathroom?' Billie asked as Storm headed towards the reception desk.

'Yeah. It's just through the back there.' Storm waved her hand in the direction of a corridor at the back of the room. Billie moved quickly. She had no need to use the bathroom, but she slipped inside the small space and ran the tap on the sink to cover any other noise she might make. She peeped out and could see Storm in the distance, her back turned away towards the front window.

Billie snuck out and speedily moved along the corridor on tiptoe, almost bumping into the girl she had met earlier, coming down a dark interior staircase. The young woman jumped with fright. From the way she was trying to button up her top which was gaping open and tugging down her skirt, Billie could see that she had been doing something other than simply a manicure upstairs.

'Are you okay?' Billie asked, aware of the tearful look of stress etched across her face. The young woman nodded, trying to push past Billie and make her way into the bathroom. Billie blocked her way, catching her by the shoulders.

'Hey, are you being forced to do something that you don't want to do?' Billie whispered. The young woman shook her head, whilst trying to pull free.

'I need bathroom. I have another appointment for manicure,' she answered unconvincingly.

'Manicure or sex with men?' Billie asked. 'I can help you, take you away from this.' The girl pulled away, agitated.

'No! I need job and a home–' The sound of a baby whimpering cut through their conversation. Billie craned her head, looking to the left. The corridor opened out into a small room where a baby could be seen in a pushchair. 'I have baby. She's hungry.' The girl moved towards the baby.

'Look, I can take you to a place...' Billie wondered if Boo had any room free in her hostel.

'No. I need work to feed my baby. I am nanny.'

'And manicurist and prostitute? It sounds like you are being forced into this,' Billie whispered as the young woman lifted the baby from the pushchair. Suddenly there was a movement at the back of the building, where a door and small window looked out onto the road. Billie spotted a tall, broad, fair-haired man approaching.

'Look, you must go, or I will get big trouble!' The young woman pushed Billie away, replacing her child hastily into the pushchair. 'These people have helped me leave my country. I am working as nanny to pay back my fare. I cannot go back. Please leave me alone.'

'That's called bonded labour, slavery,' Billie started to say, but something else made her dart back towards the bathroom. The man approaching the side door was accompanied by a small child and if the child recognised Billie, then her game was up. She had just made it back inside, peeping through the crack in the door frame, when Billie saw Connie run into view.

'Mama,' Connie cried, 'Papa picked me up from nursery!' Billie slipped the door latch across, still looking through the crack. Her back against the wall. *What a moment to have met Ellis's ex-wife*, Billie reflected. He had never actually called her by name, but his descriptions of his 'ex' now made sense.

Storm had entered the corridor, glancing towards the bathroom door. Billie made a muffled cough, hoping it was enough to make Storm think that she was still in there, oblivious to the people outside the door, suffering from chronic constipation maybe, she didn't care what, but one thing was for certain, wig or no wig, Connie would recognise her immediately if she left the bathroom now.

'I'm with a client,' Storm answered, her words lacking any warmth. 'Take her home now. Eddie, you know better than to bring her in here when I'm working,' Storm snapped to the man.

'*You're* working? I've got some big business underway, and I just got back an hour ago. What's wrong with whatshername here picking her up. Isn't she meant to be your nanny?'

'Viku's doing nails and turning tricks. We've been run off our feet upstairs this morning. When the hell is that new consignment coming in?' Storm hissed.

'By the end of the week. All sorted.'

'Thank God for that. Give them a lift in the car home, Eddie. It smells of sex and baby milk round here.' Storm wafted her hand. 'It's enough to turn the client off.' She flicked her head

Billie's way. Billie pressed the toilet flush in response. She could see Storm Benbow thumbing Eddie, the young woman Billie now knew as Viku and Connie out of the back door, without as much as a goodbye kiss for her toddler daughter. Billie could only imagine Ellis's response if he'd been the one standing where she was at that very moment.

Chapter 28

Paris Of The East

The taxi driver had finally dropped Ellis off in an area of Bucharest far away from the busy streets full of spectacular architecture and pretty parks that, years ago, had earned the city the nickname 'Paris of the East'. On the stop-start journey through heavy traffic, Ellis recalled having travelled to this city once before, when the Linden trees were in full bloom. They had filled the air with the intoxicating smell of honey and lemon peel. It was the place in which he had proposed to Storm, in a mad, unthinking moment that he had long ago come to regret, except that the union had produced his beautiful younger daughter, Connie.

At this location the stunning buildings had disappeared, as though Ellis had been driven through a door into a different world. Crumbling and rusting Ceauşescu-era housing blocks and a ragtag collection of tin-roofed dwellings, slapped together with mud and scraps of wood were scattered along the potholed streets. Where buildings had decayed and collapsed, the spaces were filled with drifts of rubbish spilling from bags or simply piled high in the streets, along with the smell of blocked sewers.

Ellis was filled with admiration towards Maya for

volunteering to give up her holiday to work in the orphanage here. He had been blessed with both of his girls and was prepared to do whatever it took to protect them, vowing that from now on he would never be far away when they needed him. Billie had understood that too, which is one of the reasons that she made such a good business partner. He wished that she was here right now, that they could spend some downtime together, rather than focusing on wayward spouses, insurance claims and now also the emotional drain of dealings with the criminally deceased that they had both hoped to leave behind.

Ellis brushed the thought away as the taxi sped along with startling haste. There was absolutely no way that he could muck things up by making a move on Billie. However, memories of the one drunken night that they had spent together sometimes lit up his mind. The embarrassing situation had been a mistake caused by too many drinks in memory of a departed friend. The alcohol level had caused both of them to claim amnesia about the details and had resulted in an unspoken but clearly joint decision never to mention it again. In truth, Ellis reflected, he had retained some memories that he could never forget. Wilde by name, wild by nature, that was for sure.

He smiled at his hidden memories as he walked through the open gate where seemingly freshly painted iron railings surrounded what looked like a dilapidated Socialist realist two-storey block, with cracked bare grey brick walls. Ellis hoped that Maya and her fellow volunteers had made more headway inside, filling the interior with colour and fun for the orphaned children.

At first Ellis thought that he might have approached the building from the back rather than from the front, as he found a central door to be closed and locked with no doorbell nor rapper to alert anyone inside to his arrival. Skirting around the entire building, tripping over rusting rubbish and dumped bits of car, he came back to where he had started. The windows were either covered in dirty curtains or blocked with wood at the back, with absolutely no signs of life.

Ellis scratched his head, wondering if he had indeed been dropped off at the correct place. Suddenly he spotted a man sitting in the corner, on a pile of rubbish. He looked drunk, his head somehow appearing to be too big for his scrawny body. Ellis approached him.

'*Orfelinat?*' He pointed to the building, using the Romanian word for orphanage.

'*Da.*' The man nodded. '*Meu acasă*' Ellis scratched his head, he had picked up only the most rudimentary words during his first visit to the country.

'Your,' he pointed to the man, 'home?' He pointed back to the orphanage.

'*Da.*' The man nodded '*Terminant.*' He made the signal of a knife across his throat.

'Dead. Gone.' He attempted to clarify in English.

'Gone where?' Ellis asked. The man looked blankly at him. Ellis grabbed his mobile and scrolled through until he found a photo of Maya. He held it out to the man. 'This girl. Do you know her?' The man nodded, smiling. He held one hand to his heart.

'*Da.* Maya.'

'Where is she?' Ellis banged his finger against the picture.

'Gone,' the man answered before his face puckered up and tears began to fall from his eyes. '*Meu acasă*, Maya, *tot*. Left.' He began to cry more loudly now, to Ellis's shock. The man seemed alone and vulnerable, desperately in need of help, perhaps a grown-up orphan, Ellis questioned, left alone to fend for himself. But Maya would never have left the vulnerable man alone, not unless she was forced to do so, and he seemed to have known her by name... Ellis stepped back.

He had no time to offer a helping hand. He needed to find Maya.

'Where is she?' Ellis moved forward again, so close that the photo was almost in the man's face. The man held his arm up in defence as though he was someone used to violence and abuse. Ellis patted him on the shoulder, trying to calm himself down.

'Sorry. This is my daughter. *Meu fiică.*' He pointed to Maya and mimed rocking a baby, though in truth he had never even known she had existed when she was a baby. Ellis hated himself inside for that now. He prayed silently to God he hadn't let her down yet again. The man responded, nodding, holding his hand to his heart again.

'Maya. Good,' he replied. '*Maya luate.*' He looked regretful.

'What?' Ellis asked, he had totally reached his translation limit. The man gave a big sigh.

'Maya taken. By men.' He mimed a gun and walking fingers. 'Close door. Gone. Everybody gone.' He stared hard at Ellis, obviously having exhausted his own Romanian-to-English abilities. 'Goodbye,' he added as a final throwaway attempt to make any sense.

'Where?' Ellis tried, racking his memory for the correct word. *Unde?* he remembered as though his brain had sensed his near hysteria and thrown the word up from his subconscious. '*Unde?*' The man shrugged, shaking his head.

Ellis dug in his pocket and pulled out a batch of Romanian leu and shoved them into the man's hand. He hoped that at least it would allow him to access food and shelter for a short time. Turning on his heel he rushed out of the gate and onto the stinking street, rubbing his face as he scanned the potholed road in hope of finding a taxi. Meanwhile he had already started scrolling down his list of contacts on his mobile. He still had some mates in the National Crime Agency, who might have liaison officers currently in Bucharest. They would be his best bet for intel that could lead him to Maya.

Ellis had just punched in the number and heard it connect when he sensed movement behind him. It was the man he had just spoken with, somehow looking a lot livelier than he had a moment ago, rushing up to him now, only inches away. Before he could react, Ellis felt the broken bottle in the man's raised arm smash against his head with terrific force. He felt a metallic taste in his mouth before hearing but not feeling a loud thud as his body hit the ground.

'Take that, motherfucker. Maybe it'll stop you poking around asking questions in future.' The man spat on Ellis, scooping his mobile off the ground and speedily fleecing Ellis's pockets, before walking off with a jaunty step, reflecting, it appeared, on his unexpected good fortune.

Chapter 29

Late for A Date

'Thank God. Just the person I wanted to see.' Billie was paying the workman who had fixed the broken window, when Ash entered the office of Wilde & Darque.

'Ditto.' Ash blew out his lips. He looked stressed. 'Ellis back yet?'

'Nope. Haven't heard anything so far.' Billie was eyeing up the first coat of paint that she had covered the graffiti with, deciding that it definitely needed another one. 'But I've got to break some news to him, and I wouldn't mind a bit of advice before I do it,' she added.

Ash had been Billie's trusted wingman when she had been head of MIT and he was also close to Ellis. If her suspicions were correct and Ellis's ex-wife, Storm, was involved in trafficking, it would have serious consequences that would definitely have an impact on Connie's future, as well as Ellis's. A prison sentence would be the likely outcome once Billie alerted a police investigation team. Bearing in mind she had already met a vulnerable woman and child caught up in the situation, she felt that she really had no choice.

'It's all kicking off at work.' Ash sighed. 'I've taken over as SIO on the suspicious deaths.'

'That's good news for the deceased and congratulations, you should have had the job all along. But much as Slug wasn't top of my hit parade, I wouldn't have wanted for you to take over following such an awful accident.'

'That's the thing,' Ash answered. 'Mind if I make a cuppa?' He headed over to the kettle. 'I think you might need one too.'

'What's up?' Billie was immediately alert.

'The brake leads were cut on Slug's car. It was no accident.' Ash clicked the kettle on, rubbing his forehead.

'You are joking...' Billie trailed off, looking back at the warning graffiti, still visible through the first coat of paint on the wall.

'I wish I was. Problem is, Ellis is on record issuing threats Slug's way. More than once. He apparently put the wind up the staff member on the reception desk last night, kicking off, and he was seen on CCTV near Slug's wheels in the car park yesterday, not long before Slug got in it.'

'Surely no one thinks Ellis did him in? I'm guessing he's not the only one that Slug has rubbed up the wrong way recently. Me for one.' Billie joined him, chucking tea bags into cups as the kettle came to boiling point.

'But we have to bring him in for questioning. You know that, boss.'

'Correction. You're the boss now, but yep, you have to go through the motions. Trouble is, it's not exactly great for Wilde & Darque's business and *you* don't think for a minute–' Billie started before Ash interrupted.

'That it's him? No, of course I don't, but I've been trying to get him on his mobile to give him a heads-up on what's going to happen and his line's dead.'

'Dead?' Billie shook her head. 'It must just be a bad connection. After all he's—'

'Just left the country,' Ash said, finishing Billie's line. 'Tell me how I'm going to explain that to the big bosses without bringing suspicion crashing down big time?'

'I'm sure he'll be back by tomorrow.' Billie hoped that her prediction was true, and that Ellis would arrive back pronto with Maya in tow. She dunked tea bags in water, chucked in milk and ripped open the biscuit packet. She needed sugar.

'So what is it you wanted to see me about?' Ash took a biscuit and wolfed it down. He was clearly as much in need as she was. Billie swallowed hard. She couldn't risk inflicting more aggro on Ellis right now. She would look into the people-trafficking suspicions herself before saying any more. What on earth would become of little Connie, should her father and mother both end up in a police cell or worse, on remand in prison?

'Nothing. It'll keep. I can see your poor old brain cells are already overworked today.'

'That's right. Most of the MIT crew now are just kids, still training. Until last week most of them hadn't set eyes on a corpse, let alone four of them, including Slug.' Ash sipped his tea. 'He wasn't a pretty sight. Going about eighty when he hit the lorry.'

'Christ.' Billie sighed. 'They'll all be off on sick leave.'

'Exactly,' Ash agreed. 'That's why I had a word with the big bosses and asked for some outside help. Civilian detective, specialist in profiling serial killers. Clearly the forensics report links Ozzie Kingsnorth and the two partial skeletons. Three dead people from one source. No better expert than you on serial killers.' Billie said nothing as Ash continued, 'It would just be like taking any other job, except you invoice the police.'

'But I've just left the force. This is a mad idea.' Billie folded her arms around her.

'No one else thinks so. The powers that be want this cleared up quickly and I need someone on my side who knows what they're doing.'

'It's something I'd have to discuss with Ellis, when he gets back.' Billie sighed again, reflecting that a bit of consulting work with Ash would pay well and give her all of the inside info she had been longing to get her hands on in relation to the two skeletons. Lizbeth and Josta had been at pains to have given her only details which the two other victims shared with Ozzie Kingsnorth, for confidentiality reasons. Without being able to find anything else that they may have had in common, she still couldn't give a useful account to Ozzie's parents.

'Ellis has enough on his plate, Billie. The way I see it, it's a no-brainer. You continue to earn for Wilde & Darque, whilst working alongside the most charismatic SIO in the force.' Ash pulled a silly celebrity-style pose, giving Billie a wink. She couldn't help smiling.

'You're not exactly selling this gig,' Billie replied.

'I've got an appointment at King & Beech Forensics first thing in the morning. They've had a bit of a breakthrough with both of the partial skeletons. I can take you along, buy you breakfast first, if you say yes.'

Billie's ears pricked up. 'Okay. The full English, extra beans on the side and it's a deal.' She looked across to the faint warning graffiti still showing through the first coat of paint that she had put on. 'You don't think that Slug was getting messages like the one on our wall that he didn't heed?'

Ash shrugged. 'He didn't look like he was brimful of investigative information that he was about to spill to the rest of the world, but with you on board, we might find a link.'

Billie hadn't in reality taken much convincing. As Ash left, she grabbed her mobile and tried to contact Ellis. Ash was right. The phone immediately switched to the messaging service, saying that the person couldn't be contacted. She tried to stem her concerns. For all that she knew the orphanage could be located in a rural area, dicey for phone connectivity.

A knock on the door made Billie look up. Her heart sank. This was all she needed now. Edith Cutler hobbled in the doorway dressed once again in her Sunday best, glasses perched on her nose.

'Ah, Mrs Cutler. How nice to see you again. How's Coco doing?'

'He's been poisoned.' Edith Cutler took a seat opposite Billie, who was shocked at the unexpected answer. 'He's hanging in there, poor thing. He certainly won't be gadding about in the dead of night again, but it's not the first time I've had a pet nobbled.'

'Really?' Billie frowned. 'Did he not just nibble at some weedkiller-covered grass or something?' Billie recalled Perry telling her that he'd followed a fair old route across back gardens on his night-time outings.

'It's that cow, who leaves the salmon leftovers all over the shop. She's poisoned a bit. You mark my words.' Edith nodded sagely. 'If you'd actually listened to me last time and took proper action, my Coco wouldn't be crapping through the eye of a needle right now on my kitchen lino.'

'Em, I'm not sure I understand, Mrs Cutler—' Billie started to say, before Edith began talking over her.

'Your employee. The big lass, who Coco scratched when she went to take that tracker thing off. I knew she wasn't telling the truth. She would have reported back correctly what was going on had she *really* followed him up to that big house. You don't seriously think I came here giving a fig where my cat wandered every night? I was giving you a nudge in the right direction to investigate.'

'Investigate what was going on where?' Billie could feel her head spinning.

'Up at that big house with the glass back looking out onto the garden. Did it myself the other night. Bit of a bugger with my arthritis, but I got what I needed, and I took the pictures in to that young boy who was pretending to be in charge of the murder squad over at the cop shop. Harris his name was. Took one look and he could see straight away what was what. He knew I was telling the truth. Told me to keep quiet until he'd completed all enquiries...'

Billie was beginning to think the old woman was a touch mad. 'Em, Perry Gooch did report back that she had followed Coco as well as fitted and removed his tracker collar. We had breakfast the next morning. She had stayed out all night–'

'Yes, but not following my cat, Ms Wilde.' Edith reached into her handbag and pulled out a newspaper. 'See the local news the other day about the student fights in the town centre?' Edith asked.

'Yes, but what has this got to do with Coco?' Billie had heard the news of some drunken students causing a disruption during an all-night environmental protest. It had been on the radio in the café, on the morning that Perry had joined Billie and Ash after tracking Coco across gardens from dusk until dawn. Edith slammed the paper down on the desktop in front of Billie.

'See this picture taken at 2am? The credit and report went to one Perry Gooch.' Edith thumbed the paper open. There were more photos, with other photographers credited. In the middle of one stood Perry with her camera, recording the scene, surrounded by students.

'Got an identical twin sister, with the same name, has she?' Edith was suddenly looking at Billie with eagle eyes. Billie frowned. There was no doubt that the photo showed Perry, miles away from the back gardens surrounding Edith Cutler's home, where she had claimed to have been suffering all night. Billie slowly shook her head, remembering how Perry had given such a detailed and amusing account of her nocturnal outing with the neighbourhood cats.

'I used to be a magistrate in the local courts until I was chucked out aged seventy, Ms Wilde. I can spot someone telling porkies a mile off. If she'd really been following Coco, she would have seen this–' Edith hauled out some photos from her handbag. 'I developed these myself in my little darkroom...' Billie was beginning to think that she had seriously underestimated the woman, based on her age and earlier act of frailty.

'That bitch at the top of the road is bringing in girls. Trafficked I'm guessing. All shapes and sizes. Lot of them young. Saw it a lot back in the day. Different set-up, same old story. She's working them as manicurists through the day, turning tricks at night. You mark my words what's going on there.' As Billie scanned the photos she could see through the back window of the house that it did indeed look like a batch of scantily clad girls were collected together.

'Maybe it's just a party?' Billie didn't believe the words coming out of her own mouth.

'Somebody'll be having a party on the profits no doubt and she's got a young toddler in there too.' Edith slapped down a large photo of Storm Benbow leading Connie into the house. Billie swallowed hard.

'Sickening, isn't it? I told that young detective all about it. Said I'd be going to the papers unless he did something to get it stopped. He promised he'd get back to me but when I phoned this morning, they told me he wouldn't be taking any more of my calls.' Edith looked miffed. Billie couldn't find her voice, right at that moment, to explain that Slug Harris wouldn't be returning anyone's calls anymore.

'My guess is he did give her a call, told her it was me who'd put in the complaint, and she poisoned my Coco out of spite. Can't take it to *this one* at the papers, though, can I?' She poked her bony finger at Perry. 'This reporter can't be trusted. So I'm putting my faith in you, Ms Wilde. Somebody has to help me put a stop to this.

'Last time this sort of thing kicked off, my fellow magistrate tried to flag it up to the authorities and look where it got him – a suspect trip down his staircase, people claiming it was a stroke. If you ask me, he was given a push. He thought so too. Couldn't speak properly anymore, but I used to visit, and he told me to keep my mouth zipped, or the same might happen to me. But I'm too old to care anymore and I don't want to go to my grave knowing I turned a blind eye to what's still going on, especially when it's still kicking off today. It would be like I was spitting on poor Tommy Cook's grave.'

'Tommy Cook?' Billie recognised the name of Ellis's uncle.

'Yes. He used to run Silver Darlings Kipper Smokery, left it to young Teddy. Tommy used to dote on the lad. Happy-go-lucky type. You'll have met him of course?'

'Yes.' Billie nodded, wondering whether to call on Edith next time she needed an investigative subcontractor.

'No coincidence that he left his house to that nephew of his, your business partner, Mr Darque. In fact I countersigned his will and kept it safe for him. He was adamant the house had to go to him. He might have been dressed as a banana the other day, but I remember Tommy saying he was proud as punch of his half-sister Vera's lad. He'd heard that he'd gone to high places in the police force.'

'That's correct.' Billie nodded.

'Tommy said he regretted that he'd never got to meet him.

Planned to get him up here by leaving the house and I promised to make it my business to meet him and tell the story. I won't let Tommy down, Ms Wilde. This is the day we've waited for. I know that with Tommy's nephew in partnership with you, bearing in mind your own sterling record, the situation will finally be banged to rights.'

Billie hadn't realised that her mobile hadn't totally disconnected when she had been trying to get hold of Ellis earlier. Now she could hear the speaker on a loop reiterating the message that it could not connect to the owner. She hoped that Edith Cutler's confidence wasn't going to be sorely misplaced.

It was the flash of coloured hair that made Billie's head turn. Unfortunately that had been when Maya's friend, Lily, had jumped on a bus, which had immediately pulled away. Billie wasn't finished with the girl yet. If she didn't hear anything from Ellis or Maya by first thing in the morning, she was going to be down on her like a ton of bricks.

Just as Edith Cutler had left, Billie had taken two calls in quick succession. The first from Ozzie Kingsnorth's father, desperate to know whether Wilde & Darque had made any headway with his son's second post-mortem and when he might get Ozzie back in order to finally lay his precious offspring to rest. The second from Pandy Wood in her empty nail bar, also desperate to find out if Storm Benbow was using illegal means to undercut her, so that she could complain to the authorities and not lose the inheritance from her aunt that Billie had already stepped in to save once, from the bigamist.

It had been the two calls that had confirmed in Billie's mind that she had been right to agree to help Ash with investigating all of the recent victims. She'd had to fend off both callers, unable to hand over the vital information she had so far gleaned because of the risk of any knock-on effects. She needed more evidence, and that possibility could take a nosedive should interested parties spread the current info far and wide. Such an outcome could even put both Mr Kingsnorth and Pandy in danger, because it seemed that in both cases someone had a lot to lose if certain facts got out. Working with Ash was, Billie accepted, her best option for getting to the truth and the truth was everything to her, which was why she was entering the Cop-Out pub next to the police headquarters right now.

'Woo, guess what the cat dragged in. I'll have a vodka and diet cola if you're buying.' Perry raised her nearly empty glass in a cheers motion.

'I'm not staying,' Billie answered, sliding down in the seat next to Perry. She pulled out the newspaper left by Edith Cutler, with the photo putting Perry bang in the middle of the group of students rather than chasing Coco the cat. 'Just checking on that little overnight job you've invoiced me for.' Perry glanced at the paper and back to Billie before sighing.

'Okay, officer, it's a fair cop. I'll buy the next round.' Perry moved to leave her seat. Billie caught her arm.

'I don't want a drink. I just want to know why you didn't say you had another job on.'

'I *did* do an hour before I got a call about the students kicking off. Come on, Billie, lighten up. We're talking about stalking a *cat*. One that even had a bleeding tracking device on. It's not like I was investigating Jack the Ripper.' Perry rolled her eyes like Billie was making a big deal out of nothing. 'Forget the invoice payment. You can have my hour for free if that's what's bothering you and I won't bill you for the sticking plaster when the damn moggy scratched me when I took the tracker off. We're quits. Okay?'

Billie wasn't okay. She knew that she was being pedantic

about it, but she had always trusted Perry implicitly. It had been the journalist's crack work that had helped her solve a major case not too long ago and probably saved lives in the process. But if Perry hadn't told the truth about this night, then had she really been giving accurate reports on other investigations Billie had contracted her to work on for Wilde & Darque?

'It's not the cat. It's the fact you gave chapter and verse of the night you suffered following it.' Billie felt conflicted. Was she being pernickety? Maybe the fact that Ellis had gone abroad had knocked her equilibrium more than she was confessing – even to herself. If she could be duped by Perry over a cat, could the unthinkable be true, that Ellis might also be fooling her? Might he actually have been involved in Slug Harris's car crash? Billie shook the thought away. It was totally crazy to even give that idea a moment of her time.

'Oh grow up, Billie. Do you know what it's like to be so short of money that you haven't got two pence to rub together and yet have two teenage daughters to clothe and feed?' Perry's eyes flashed. 'We didn't all inherit money and status from the high-flying rellies.' Billie closed her eyes for a moment. Perry had hit her Achilles heel. Here was the nepotism accusation coming at her yet again. Perry seemed to realise that she'd gone too far.

'Sorry, that was below the belt. Let me buy you a drink.' Perry patted Billie's arm. 'I'm quids in again now I've got this work in the press office. It's just that things got pretty hairy there with the mortgage to pay and getting slim pickings with work. I feel terrible now about the cat. But think about it. He had the tracker on so nothing was lost.'

Billie ran her fingers through her hair. 'No, I know, you're right.' Billie suddenly realised how trivial her complaint must have sounded. 'It's not the cat. Edith thinks something illegal is going on at a house up the street and hoped you'd clocked it.'

Perry rolled her eyes. 'She's as mad as a hatter,' she

announced with feeling. 'Trust me. I've met loads of ancient biddies like her, obsessed with their pets and true crime channels on the telly. Nothing else to do than dream up tall stories in the short time left before they croak.'

'And Ellis has shot off to Romania thinking Maya might be in some trouble, so now neither of them are contactable.' Billie sunk back in her seat.

'Well, you might need a stiff one. Word is that Ellis is chief suspect for Slug being pulped into something resembling a tin of chopped tomatoes spread on the back of a lorry. We've already had calls in the office from my mates in the press who've got wind of it.'

'Please don't say anything,' Billie said through a sigh. She felt horrified about Slug's demise, whatever his shortcomings had been, as well as Ellis's position. Perry stood up, lifting her empty glass.

'My lips are sealed. Like I said, I owe you one. But nowadays police headquarters leaks like a sieve, I'm telling you. Someone is going to spill sooner rather than later. Want your usual?'

Billie nodded. She suddenly felt like she needed a drink. 'I'm going to be back in there with you in my old stomping ground for a bit. I've accepted a civilian investigator contract, assisting Ash with the recent suspect deaths.'

Perry stopped in her tracks, frowning. 'Result for Ash. At least I think it is. Whatever he says to you, word inside is *he* would have killed for that job. Everyone knows that you're still the star snoop around here. What's that saying about keeping your friends close and your enemies closer? Anyway, I thought you wanted to put all that dead body crap behind you. My old dad said never go back. But then he was an army bomb disposal expert.'

Perry winked and headed for the bar. Billie shivered. Was

Perry joking about Ash? Right now, she didn't want to pursue that line of conversation, nor could she tell her friend that Edith Cutler wasn't as mad as she thought, not without talking to Ellis first. She desperately wished that he would make contact. A barman headed over and nodded to a glass that was half full on the table.

'Your friend finished with that?' he asked.

'Sorry?' Billie came back from her thoughts.

'Girl with the coloured hair. Is she finished, only we're short of glasses?' He smiled genially. A picture of Lily popped into Billie's mind. She nodded, wondering why on earth Lily would have been sitting at a table for two with Perry. Her mobile suddenly rang as the barman carried the drink away.

'I'm starting to get a complex here.' Billie sat up straight on hearing James Checkley's smooth voice. 'Left in the lurch first time, now stood up again. Is this already the end of a beautiful friendship?'

'Oh damn, sorry. I'm on my way now.' Billie leaped up, wondering why her heart had started beating ten to the dozen.

'I've got a better idea,' James answered. Billie listened, waving 'no thanks' to Perry who had turned back from the bar with two drinks in her hand.

'Sorry. I'm late for a date,' Billie called, rushing out of the door, leaving Perry looking decidedly nonplussed.

Chapter 30

A Timpani Beat

Ellis opened his eyes slowly. They were swollen and tight. A timpani beat drummed in his head. His tongue felt thick, his mouth dry. He closed his eyes again, guessing that he'd been out of it for hours. The bright sun was no longer high in the sky, a cool breeze causing him to shiver. He was suddenly aware of small feet all around him, children giggling. He opened his eyes slowly once more, trying hard to focus, as one child probed him with the toe of his bare foot. Ellis suddenly remembered Maya having told him about the impoverished Roma minority children in the area she was heading to, where locals were regularly victimised, forced to live in mud huts with no basic amenities, no water, electricity or sanitation.

The child shouted something that Ellis didn't understand, as other children bent down and rolled him over. He guessed he was about to be fleeced again but was still not capable of defending himself. He seemed to lose consciousness once more for a moment, then opened his eyes to further shouting all around and a blurred figure walking towards him. The small feet seemed to run backwards and then a woman bent down over him. She had dark hair and eyes.

'I've been mugged,' Ellis said, not expecting for a moment for the woman to understand him.

'British?' she asked. Ellis managed the tiniest of nods. 'It's okay. I'm the community nurse. I can help you. Your little friends here came to get me,' she added, as the children helped her haul Ellis up to a sitting position.

'My name is Adelina,' she said. 'Where are you going?' She opened a bag and took out a bottle and a pristine clean gauze pad, deftly pouring the liquid onto the material. She started to bathe Ellis's head. It stung like hell.

'To find my daughter.' Ellis felt panic rise up in his chest once more. He had lost time, lying here in the dirt. Hours seemed to have passed. His mind was fighting to regain clarity.

'Where will you find her?' She delved back into her bag, lifting out a pair of tweezers before starting to pick shards of glass from Ellis's wound. He winced – at the question, more than the pain.

'I don't know. She was working here at the orphanage. Volunteering.' His voice was hoarse. A small, serious faced boy reached into Adelina's bag and lifted out a bottle of water. He unscrewed it and handed it to her. She thanked him, holding it to Ellis's lips to drink. He took a mouthful gratefully.

'They were trafficking children there. It is common. We have lost many local kids that way. They pretend to be running orphanages, getting money from volunteers who pay to work, thinking they can help. Then they run, taking the children, open up elsewhere and repeat.'

'But where do they take them?' Ellis wondered why he was asking. He had worked for long enough in organised crime. The bigger question was why they had taken Maya with them. Billie and Boo had said that all of her friends had arrived back on the plane as planned.

Adelina shrugged. 'They could end up anywhere in the

218

world,' Adelina answered. 'Anyone who tries to stop them will end up dead for sure. We can only hope that our children look up to the stars in the sky and know that we are also looking at the same stars and making a wish that we will meet them once again.'

Chapter 31

The Big Bear

'It's absolutely amazing,' Billie whispered. She was lying back on a huge beanbag inside a glass-domed folly, looking up at the ink-black sky which appeared to be scattered with a thousand sparkling diamonds, relaxing at last, after the myriad tensions of the day.

'Northumberland has some of the darkest skies in the entire world.' James Checkley lay alongside Billie, hands behind his head, dressed in casual white shirt and jeans. 'It's amazing what you can see without any light pollution blinding us to the beauty of it all. When I'm not travelling and I'm back here in the area, I spend more nights in this folly than up in the main house.'

The 'main house' James was referring to was a beautiful Georgian mansion in acres of countryside deep in Northumberland. It was the alternative place that James had suggested Billie meet him at after she had missed their restaurant slot, claiming that he would grab a takeaway and meet her there. But this was unlike any takeaway Billie had experienced before, with a mezze-type banquet to die for, laid out on a low table.

'There's the big bear!' Billie pointed to the constellation

Ursa Major. 'My dad used to say that was him.' Billie sighed at the childhood memory when everyone and everything in her world had seemed so perfect. She'd spent hours looking at stars then, astronomy being her dad's at-home hobby. She didn't want to think about his other murky pastimes. 'When I was six, I saved up my pocket money and had a star named after him for his birthday. I actually thought it would be an authentic thing, listed on proper astronomical charts forever.' Billie laughed at her childhood naivety.

'You seem to have spent some special moments with your dad.' James looked across at Billie. It was true that she was able now to remember some good times. It was amazing what time and space could do to painful memories.

'My dad spent much of his time in betting shops or wheeling and dealing.' James spoke quietly as though deep in thought. 'If I'm honest I steered clear of him as much as I could. He had something of a volatile temper. My big brother was his favourite, daring and brave, very like him, whereas I was a bit wet.' James laughed softly. 'I don't do conflict that well, I'm afraid, so I still keep my distance a bit.'

Billie looked across at the man, his handsome profile caught in the starlight. 'Yet you're in the family business?' Billie thought she'd better check that her limited knowledge on him was correct.

'Well, my dad is long gone and to give him his due, he built up the different areas of the business from scratch, though I don't think his financing was altogether legal at the start of it all...' James trailed off, turning to Billie with a smile that she just caught in the darkness. 'Should I be telling a former senior police detective such things?' he teased.

'Yeah, well my own dad wasn't always totally whiter than white.' *Even though he was the Chief of Police*, Billie thought to herself. But she'd come to terms with that at last. James turned to look up at the sky again.

'I used to mull over it for years when I was young, that our family was benefitting from the proceeds of other people's loss. At least that's the way I saw it, making a profit. I even set out to build a new career as a surgeon, fixing people back together. A shrink would make something of those couple of years of medical school madness, no doubt. But it wasn't really for me. My dad persuaded me to come back into the fold before he died, and we finally made our peace. In the end I decided that the only thing I could do was move forward and give as much back from the family business as we take, with good working conditions and the charities and so forth. All legal now, I hasten to add.'

'Are you on better terms with your big brother these days then?' Billie imagined that running a vast multinational business came with more conflict than ever.

'I'm capable of forcefully arguing my corner now, let's put it that way. My brother and I are never going to be bosom buddies, but we stick to our own areas of expertise and respect each other, I think, for our different talents. It all seems to jog along nicely these days.'

'Yay, look, a shooting star!' Billie pointed up to the sky.

'Think that's your dad then, giving you a thumbs up?' James asked. Billie didn't answer. James sat up and reached for an open bottle of champagne on the table. 'Another glass?' he offered Billie. She pulled herself up to a sitting position.

'No really, I'd better not. I have to drive home.' Her voice was filled with regret.

'You could always stay here. Don't worry, there are lots of spare rooms in the house if you so choose.' Billie paused for a moment, though she didn't want to mull over her less than perfect past anymore either. Time to wipe so many memories away and make a new start at last. She was ready to live in the moment.

'I'm fine just to stay here all night... if you are...' She picked up her glass and leaned forward, fully aware of what James was really offering and what she was accepting. He took the glass from her hand and put the bottle back on the table as he leaned forward and brushed her hair from her face as their lips met.

Chapter 32

A Communal Grave

'I still miss my Ubi. He would protect me,' Bluey sobbed as the lorry slowed down. It had been stopping and starting over the past few minutes, rather than travelling at a steady pace for hours. 'He will forgive me for upsetting him and come and find me soon. I know it. We will be together in Britain, like he promised. We will have a house and a big family...'

Maya sighed. She was tired, from the journey, the fear and the madness, and from also endlessly trying to convince Bluey that her 'lover boy' was nothing of the sort, that he was an evil monster, who didn't care about Bluey or any of the other girls, nor without any doubt, the others who had travelled this route before them and would after.

'What is his full name?' Maya asked. She was going to make a mental note of it and ensure that when she broke free and came forward with her testimony he would pay dearly for this.

'Ubi means *love*,' another girl advised Maya. 'There is no Ubi. There is no love.' Maya knew that for many of the girls squeezed into the truck alongside her that would have been the case since the day they had been born.

'But I will have my baby soon.' Bluey's face was swollen and wet with endless tears. The penny had finally dropped for Maya. The young girl wasn't simply plump, she was pregnant and much as she wanted to fantasise about the conception, she couldn't possibly know who the father might be.

The lorry stopped for a moment. Voices could be heard outside. All of the girls fell into silence. Maya had no idea which country they were now in, or how much time had passed since they had been loaded onto the vehicle in Germany, only that at one point they had stopped for a long time in a lay-by, presumably for the driver to get some rest. A bucket had been thrown in then, for them to defecate in, along with bread and water, before the door had been hastily slammed shut and bolted several times from the outside. Maya had heard cars passing by only inches away, their occupants totally unaware of the slaves being held inside this metal prison, as though existing in a horrific parallel universe.

There had been whispered conversations when snoring had finally been heard from the cab. Maya and some of the older girls had made weak attempts to break free, but it had been impossible, such was the design of the interior of the unit.

'In any case, if we are taken back to Romania, we will be captured again. It happened to my sister,' one girl recounted. She hadn't been an orphan, simply a schoolgirl taken from the street on her way home. The trafficker was well known in the village where they had lived, apparently a location where child trafficking had long been considered the norm within the local mafia. He had simply smirked at the family when they had gone to him begging for her return. Eventually her parents had sold their business to raise the money to buy her back.

'And now it has happened to me also... all of us. There is no one to help. In Britain the police will be the same.'

'That's not the case. When we get to Britain, I will break free and get help, I promise,' Maya vowed. 'But tell no one that I am English, or we may have no chance.' Another girl at the back of the lorry shrugged.

'You can try. But most of us, we will just be sent back to Romania where we will be taken away again. It is an old story. This is our life, our destiny.'

'No way!' Maya had watched Billie Wilde at work, absorbed some of her feistiness. 'This is not how we're going to end up, certainly not me and not any of you either!'

Suddenly there was the sensation of the lorry backing up before it jerked to a halt. The driver got out of the cab. Maya heard and felt the ISO twist locks being clanked open as the girls looked from one to another wide-eyed. The driver cleared his throat before spitting on the ground outside. The girls all appeared to hold their breath.

Next, heavy footsteps could be heard as the driver headed back to the cab and jumped inside. The engine started and just as Maya breathed out again, there was the sensation of the unit slowly lifting at the driver's end, where she was crouched. She flung her arms out to try and steady herself from sliding down the length of the lorry as Bluey was now doing, with a cry of terror, kicking into the bucket that the girls had been forced to use as a toilet. It toppled over, covering Bluey and the other girls at the back with excrement as they scrabbled and cried out, tumbling hard against one another. With a loud bang the unit slammed down on level ground now. The lorry could be heard lurching forward and then driving away, as the girls, fell silent, gripped by fear.

'I think we've been dropped off in a port. Waiting for a ship to England.' Maya hoped her voice sounded calm rather than full of the utter shock and horror that she was truly feeling.

'But what if we are loaded on with other units all around and on top us?' another girl answered, her voice unable to hide the terror she was clearly feeling. 'We'll all suffocate in here. This prison will become our communal grave.'

Maya closed her eyes tightly, unable to take any more for the moment. She knew the girl was right. She, like most of Britain, had watched the TV news reporting the dreadful story of thirty-nine Vietnamese people smuggled from Belgium to England in a similar container, by people traffickers. They had died excruciating deaths from heat and suffocation. Despite her show of bravado Maya wondered if, in truth, an identical fate might be about to face them all right now.

Chapter 33

Captured By Slave Traders

'Just in the nick of time. I thought you'd been captured by slave traders,' Ash quipped, checking his watch as Billie flew through the door to King & Beech Forensics, startling the receptionist. 'I gave you a knock this morning. Thought you might like a lift here, but hmmm... those look like the clothes you were wearing yesterday. My first thoughts would be that you've had a night in the car getting intel on yet another spouse playing away from home, if it wasn't for the fact that you're rocking that flushed, newly-shagged look yourself,' he teased. The receptionist looked down quickly, fiddling with some papers on the desk.

'Get you, Sherlock Holmes,' Billie managed to answer between breaths. In truth she had woken early, her body entwined with that of James Checkley. The dawn of the new day had filled the folly where they had spent the night, with the glow of a spectacular sunrise. Somehow, Billie had been persuaded to stay a while longer than she had planned. 'I never had you down as the curtain-twitching type of neighbour,' she added, trying to suppress a smile, as she referred to the fact that Ash lived in the flat below her house by the sea. One of the things that in truth, she loved most about living there. 'Do I go snooping when you spend the night out on the tiles with a hot new man?'

'Chance would be a fine thing,' Ash scoffed. 'Still, it saves me treating you to that early morning breakfast I offered. Looks like you've already eaten.' He nudged Billie, who rolled her eyes in response, just as a buzzer rang behind the desk. The receptionist coughed to get their attention.

'Drs King and Beech will see you now. I'll take you along.' The receptionist, who Billie now recalled was named Cecile, appeared from behind the desk, all long legs and perfect make-up and manicure. Ash and Billie followed.

'Ah, my dear friends, good morning, please help yourself to coffee and tea.' Josta waved to a tray placed on the table in the middle of a small but smart meeting room. It was certainly a step up from the waiting room at the mortuary in which Josta King had conducted autopsies in the past. Lizbeth Beech was at the end of the room. She turned now to face them, dabbing her nose as she did so. Billie immediately noticed that she appeared to be upset.

'You will forgive Lizbeth, my loves, she's a bit out of sorts today. This terrible business with DS Harris. I did tell you that it wasn't wise to observe my autopsy on him, didn't I, dear?' Josta said, gently chastising Lizbeth. Billie exchanged glances with Ash, their frowns mirroring each other's as Lizbeth nodded. Billie imagined that just like her, Ash was wondering why an autopsy would upset a forensics specialist.

'He was my godson, you see,' Lizbeth explained to Billie and Ash. 'I think you met his mother, Judge Pennington?' She looked down momentarily in what seemed like an attempt to compose herself, Billie doing the same. No wonder Slug Harris had it in for Billie and Ellis. They had publicly embarrassed his mother and potentially him, by revealing that his father was a bigamist.

'I had no idea...' Billie trailed off.

'No, well, he liked to keep that side of things low-key, his mother being a judge. She's absolutely heartbroken of course. She adopted him long before children of her own came along. Doted on him. But he was adamant that he didn't want to be accused of achieving his high-flying position at such a young age due to nepotism. He was aware of your own situation. I think that's why he was such a stickler for proper procedure. Even as a teenager he could recite obscure laws in detail, trying to prove he wasn't profiting from family connections.'

Billie closed her eyes for a minute, realising that a lot of the oddities about Slug Harris had just been explained. She had experienced similar feelings herself, being the daughter of a police chief. A fact that Lizbeth Beech had just alluded to. Who knew that they could have had so much in common?

'He was affected by ASD, of course. Not brilliant at social interaction but nonetheless, very high functioning, hence his career success. He was remarkably focused and persistent but once he got an idea into his head he couldn't be persuaded to change it, hence our disagreement over further investigation, following our findings over the recently deceased. I feel very sorry that I was so dismissive of him at the time. I should have made allowances bearing in mind the news about his father, though I don't think the connection ever leaked to the press...'

'I'm so sorry.' Billie glanced at Ash. By the look on his face, he clearly felt the same. She realised now why it had been so important to Judge Pennington to keep the investigation into her husband's infidelity hushed up.

'His mother had concerns about his chosen career, despite being proud of his achievements. She was well aware that his condition would lead him to make enemies. But cutting his brake leads? Really, no one could have imagined that anyone could dislike him *that* much.' Billie flung aside the picture of Ellis that flashed into her mind.

'Put it out of your head for now, my dear,' Josta said, handing Lizbeth a black coffee. 'Our meeting this morning concerns our dear young skeleton bride and due to Lizbeth's sterling work, we are pretty sure that we can give you a positive identity.'

Josta clicked on her laptop and a photograph suddenly filled the screen that almost covered the far wall of the room. A pretty, dark-haired and dark-eyed teenage girl was smiling at the camera.

'You have already met Irina Subašić, of course. But here she is full of life. In this photo she is at her home, surrounded by her family in Srebrenica. The town was in a largely Bosniak area in the former Republic of Yugoslavia, a beautiful spa location known for rich deposits of silver in the surrounding mountains.'

'And the Srebrenica Massacre in July 1995 during the Bosnian conflict,' Ash added.

'Indeed.' Lizbeth nodded in agreement. 'It was the location where Bosnian Serb forces perpetrated the massacre of more than 8,000 Bosniak men and boys and buried them in communal graves as they tried to flee from the town.'

'But you said that our bride, Irina, probably died in the same year, here in England?' Billie questioned.

'Correct.' Lizbeth nodded. 'Unfortunately for her family, but a stroke of good fortune for us years later, her grandfather, the man you see standing behind Irina in this photo, was killed whilst trying to escape the village. He was a silver miner and here in the picture as well as recovered from Irina's skeletonised finger, you can see the silver ring that he made especially for her.'

'Oh my goodness. That poor family.' Ash rubbed his face, no

doubt, Billie considered, thinking about his own precious daughters.

'Yes. Irina's grandfather was buried in a mass grave.' Josta moved to a harrowing scene of a huge exhumation taking place at a beautiful clearing surrounded by a forest.

Billie shivered at the thought. A dark cloud had swept across a day which had started so full of sunshine, as Lizbeth picked up the explanation, working in tandem with Josta who now clicked the screen back to Irina's happy family photo.

'Luckily, DNA advances have resulted in the International Commission on Missing Persons successfully revealing the identity of thousands of people who had remained unaccounted for, after the fall of Srebrenica. I was involved at one point with the project. We worked on bones exhumed from mass graves, matching them to blood samples from living relatives. Since then ICMP has provided assistance to investigators all around the globe.

'Irina's grandfather's remains were linked by DNA in his bones to a living relative in 2009. Both DNA details were still available, and yesterday we received news that both samples flagged up a family match to Irina. I was successful in speaking to Irina's aunt yesterday. She sent us some details on her background as well as this charming photo.'

'I expect the poor woman is devastated.' Billie ran her fingers through her hair. Lizbeth nodded in agreement.

'Indeed, but the family had long ago guessed that something had gone badly wrong. They all agreed that it would be unthinkable for Irina not to have made contact by now, had she been able to do so.'

'Did her aunt say why Irina came to the UK in the first place?' Ash asked. It was Josta who answered.

'In 1993, trouble was already looming and a charity in England offered to take some young women to safety abroad to continue their education. Irina had always achieved top marks at school and could speak English, so her family grabbed the chance. Their home was already overcrowded, as family members from far and wide had headed to Srebrenica thinking it was a safe place. Everyone was so happy for Irina, despite being sorry to lose her, but they thought the family would only be split up for a short while. Sadly as history now shows, they were wrong on all counts.'

'Did the aunt know the name of the charity?' Ash asked. 'It could offer a useful lead to finding out what happened to Irina when she arrived here.'

Lizbeth shook her head. 'No one in the family can remember. They have, of course, endured extreme distress throughout the years since. Several male members of the family, including Irina's fourteen-year-old brother went missing at the same time as her grandfather. The women were moved to refugee camps and didn't have time to take much more than photographs with them. Memories are more precious than personal belongings after all.'

Billie and Ash digested the new information, quietly munching biscuits and drinking coffee whilst Josta and Liz left the room; one to put the new information into a file for them to take away, the other to chase up developments on the cadaver found in Ellis's compost patch.

'It's a real bummer.' Ash took the last biscuit off the plate, broke off half and offered it to Billie. She took it, comfort eating had often been their joint response to deathly scenarios. 'That young girl had so much life left ahead of her.'

Billie nodded. 'It's so odd, the whole thing. A bride down a chimney... how come no one noticed she'd gone, then reported it?'

'Because they had something to hide. Usual story,' Ash answered. 'Question is, what?'

'Didn't Teddy Cook say that he grew up in the house next door to his uncle?' Billie suddenly recalled. 'Let's show him the photo. See if it jogs his memory.'

'Heard anything from Ellis yet?' Ash asked, already knowing the answer before Billie shook her head.

'You don't think I would shield him, if he was involved in any of this?' Billie asked Ash. She hoped that she was sure of the answer herself. 'I mean, would *you*?' She nodded to the photo of the pretty teenager and her grandfather smiling down on them.

'Course not.' Crumbs sprayed out of Ash's mouth as he answered. 'A mate's a mate but this would put the strongest of friendships to the test. Not that he *is* involved.'

'No way.' Billie sighed. 'I just wish he, or Maya would make contact. Something's wrong, Ash. I hope they're not both in trouble.'

Ash rubbed his head. 'Ellis is anyway. The chief got on to me at dawn. He's reviewed the CCTV both at the reception desk and outside, near Slug's car. Ellis had a face on, looking like he was fit to kill. We both know how he can appear when he's got the hump, but to an outsider... I can't hold off sending out a Red Notice, if he doesn't ring in or turn up soon...'

'An Interpol alert? Christ no.' Billie knew the drill off by heart but an international wanted persons notice was still a nightmare scenario for both personal and business reasons. 'That would finish him off as far as access to Connie is concerned.' *And kibosh the credibility of Wilde & Darque too*, she didn't add. Josta suddenly bundled through the door, putting an end to the subject.

'I have to say, the state-of-the-art 3D CT scans have been a game changer. Regarding our friend found in the compost heap, we have made a copy of the individual's skull precisely, using CT scans. They have been manipulated with a wonderful new programme in our stereolithography department, to give an opportunity for a variety of tissue reconstructions. I have a few to get us going here. We can also print any of them out with our 3D printer, giving us a solid head. Wonderful fun!' Josta announced cheerfully.

Josta handed Billie the first printout, showing a handsome young man with dark tanned skin and huge black eyes. She swallowed hard. He was the double of his sister.

'Jemal Zerezghi,' she said, showing the printout to Ash.

'Eritrean by any chance?' Josta's specs slipped down her nose as she looked at Billie with interest.

Billie nodded. 'How do you know that?' she answered. Josta handed over another photograph. It showed a tiny square cellophane pouch containing dark brown powder.

'We found this sewn into the inside pocket of his singlet. It's sand from his home village, we assume. It is a common practice among Eritreans to take a physical reminder of their homeland before leaving, knowing that they may never return.' Both Billie and Ash were struck into silence by the thought for a moment.

'I have witnessed it on several occasions, during the time I took off last year, when I assisted identification of unsuccessful refugees fleeing Libya by boat to Sicily.'

Billie had wondered what had become of Josta during their joint annus horribilis. Now this explained it. She had run away to play with the dead. It was her comfort zone.

'There was no register, you see, of victims of such events, yet families were crying for assistance to find loved ones who hadn't arrived as expected. With Eritreans we regularly found pieces of homeland such as these, so it aided us in precisely identifying the area of origin. It can be harder with other refugees unfortunately. Many of them are adolescents and die with the same football team emblems, spare change and designer branded trainers one might expect to find on any of our own teenagers on their way to school.'

'How long has he been dead, do you think?' Ash questioned. 'I saw the body in situ. He was far from fully skeletonised.'

'Well, he had been moved, let me make that clear first of all. That may well be important to your investigation. When a body has lain in one place for some time, one might see nitrogen in the soil spike up to fifty times higher than with a typical soil sample. We have not seen anything like that sort of change in the samples we took from around the body. We have also identified pollen and spore samples intermingled with dried blood that cannot be matched to any such samples taken from the garden, compost heap or surrounding vegetation. As far as the question we forensics types hate more than any – "How long has he been dead, doc?" I can tell you that my best guess is around a month, maybe a little longer. It has been rather cold recently and dry, which affects the speed of decomposition. But there are so many variables that further work will be necessary in order to be any more precise.'

'So Ellis is hardly going to kill someone and then drive them home and dump them in the back garden at the same time he's moving in. Slug's idea that Ellis could have been involved is preposterous. Looks like someone wants to set him up. Maybe the same person who knocked off Slug,' Billie reasoned.

'But the big bosses insist that's *Ellis*...' Ash answered. 'We're going round in circles here.'

'Ellis's ex, Storm Benbow, wanted to get rid of him, he's made no secret of that and Edith Cutler claims that she told the police that Storm was involved in sex trafficking. Edith fears that Storm got questioned by Slug Harris and tried to kill her pet as a consequence.'

'Well, Slug kept it under his belt if he knew anything about it. So have you, actually. Ellis's ex is a people trafficker?' Ash looked aghast at the thought. 'When were you thinking of sharing this?'

'Once I'd broken the news to Ellis himself. We've got a lot of catching up to do. Looking at the background of Irina and Jemal I think we're looking for killers who traffic vulnerable foreigners for sex, slave labour...' Josta gave a little cough, no doubt to remind them that she was still present in the room.

'And organ harvesting,' she added. 'Mr Zerezghi was missing both kidneys and indications are that it was due to them being removed rather than decomposition.'

'You what?' Ash gasped in horror.

'He may have donated one, of course, to finance travel from his home country. Organ sales are big business the world over and not an uncommon discovery during examination of boat people who had drowned. Illegal transplantation is estimated to account for five to ten per cent of all global transplants, generating nearly two billion pounds a year, with an illicitly traded kidney transplanted at the rate of one an hour. A sobering thought to ponder on.'

'But how on earth can it happen without someone somewhere in a hospital reporting it?' Billie frowned.

'Using a series of middlemen to muddy the waters. Specialist medical personnel, blood and tissue testing labs, pop-up surgical theatres...' Lizbeth suddenly entered the room holding a file. She handed it to Billie.

'How much would you get for a kidney then?' Ash asked. Josta looked to Lizbeth, who frowned as though she was simply trying to recall an item from her shopping list.

'The sums involved are significant. We're talking around £50,000 for a kidney, as much as £150,000 for a lung, £30,000 per cornea...'

'Jeez,' Billie gasped. 'I'm imagining the donor doesn't get to see much of that?'

'Nope,' Lizbeth agreed. 'Should they survive, they pretty

soon end up in debt once again, usually due to medical costs related to a botched operation and little aftercare.'

'The various stakeholders are often in different countries. Hence the trafficking,' Josta explained. 'Victim from country A, recipient from country B, hospital country C and so it goes on, adding to the complexity of law enforcement.'

'Also the recipients are often in desperate need and will die without the transplant, so the price goes up. It's win-win for the organ traffickers, especially if they can source matches via donations from poor people,' Lizbeth added. 'If they are trafficked, then they can use them first to make money by selling sex or in forced labour. The profits that can be made are vast.'

'It could be the case that Jemal was considered more valuable because his kidney was a good match for a donor who was willing to pay top dollar, than for his other contributions to the traffickers' coffers,' Josta pointed out.

'This has got to stop.' Billie rubbed her forehead in utter disbelief. If Edith had more info about Storm Benbow, then that was currently their best chance of getting to the main players as well as clearing Ellis's name. 'Come on.' Billie jumped up and headed for the door.

'Where are you going?' Ash got up and waved adios to Josta and Lizbeth as he followed Billie out of the door and into the corridor where she was picking up speed, heading for the exit.

'To see an old woman about a cat,' Billie shouted over her shoulder, already out of the building and jogging towards her car.

'Edith, are you there?' Billie hammered on the back door of Edith's house.

'Newspaper's still stuffed in the front door,' Ash called as

Billie ran around to the front and joined him. She had filled Ash in with all the details that she had about Storm and Edith along the way.

'Oh shit.' Billie peered through the letter box. 'Oh bugger, she's at the bottom of the stairs. Let's get the ambulance in.' Billie was already kicking at the front door. She managed to smash a hole in the flimsy panel and thrust her arm through, loosening the lock. The door swung open. Billie, closely followed by Ash, burst into the hall.

Edith lay with her head on the floor, legs and sensibly slippered feet, splayed out on the stairs behind. Her neck was at an odd angle. Billie shook her head as she took Edith's pulse knowing before she even touched the ice-cold skin that the woman had already long ago departed. Coco, despite the commotion, had remained steadfastly by her side, giving a soulful miaow on realising that Billie had failed to rouse his mistress.

'Maybe she fell over the moggy.' Ash frowned, looking around. 'Can't see any signs of a break-in.'

Billie immediately recalled the conversation with Edith only yesterday when the old woman had told her about the suspicions she had that Ellis's Uncle Tommy had been silenced via an allegedly dangerous staircase. 'Or maybe she was pushed.' Billie ran her fingers through her hair.

'You've been here before. Has anything been taken?' Ash asked. He handed her scene-of-crime gloves and foot coverings, the sort of thing that she herself had always carried around when she had been head of MIT. She slipped them on and carefully looked around the small house, finding it completely tidy, just as she had recalled from her first visit.

'Nothing?' Ash asked, finishing his call for the CSI team to attend. Billie suddenly stopped at the entrance to the kitchen and looked right.

'She mentioned a darkroom,' Billie said as she noticed a door handle to Edith's understairs cupboard. Billie opened the door, peering inside. She could tell by the paraphernalia laid out on a long tabletop fitted to the wall that this was indeed the room that she had been looking for, but it appeared to be strangely devoid of photographs. 'Here it is, but there are no pictures.' She flicked on the light. A string with clips hung above the countertop, where she would have expected photos to be in situ, but there were none. The filing trays were empty too. 'Maybe they've been taken,' Billie wondered aloud, 'or handed over to Slug Harris in evidence.'

'She sounded like a wily old gal though.' Ash nodded to the broken figure lying on the floor. He picked up Coco and gave the cat a stroke. 'Wouldn't she have hidden copies somewhere?'

Billie suddenly had a light bulb moment. She swept past Ash, carefully stretching her legs over Edith's prostrate corpse, before taking the stairs two at a time.

'Under the mattress!' Billie called down to Ash, heading towards Edith's bedroom where a large iron-posted bed held a patchwork quilt and cushions with intricate needlework. Billie guessed Edith had embroidered them herself. She seemed to be a woman that left no detail untouched. Billie heaved the mattress up.

'Bingo,' she whispered to herself as a large file was revealed, rather than the old money that Edith had hinted she kept there. Billie lifted the file and pulled out the first photo. It was Storm Benbow in the back room of her house surrounded by girls. The second photo had zoomed in on the scene. Billie could clearly see the girl named Viku that she had met at Storm's nail salon, holding her baby and looking scared. A third print showed Storm Benbow entering the house alongside a tall, muscular fair-haired man who was carrying Connie. Billie thought immediately of Ellis's pain had he been alongside her now witnessing that particular photo. She carefully came back down the stairs as a paramedic now in the hallway confirmed life deceased.

'This is Storm, Ellis's ex.' Billie showed the photo to Ash. 'Any idea who the guy is?' Ash took the photo from Billie.

'Yep. You been living under a rock for the past year? He's a bit of a Bobby Big Baps round here these days. Fingers in lots of business pies. Had his nightclub raided a few weeks back. Didn't find anything untoward but he knows who to pay the backhanders to. He's a non-dom. Comes and goes, no doubt to avoid paying taxes. Name's Eddie Checkley. His brother James gave that big wodge of money to Boo to start her charity off.

'I told her to make sure that it hadn't been laundered. This Eddie is a straightforward bully by all accounts, but James, the other one, isn't as sparkling white as he makes out in my opinion. I told Boo that I wouldn't touch him or his dosh with a bargepole. But hey, you know what you women are like. You fall for any man with bulging pockets and a pretty face.'

Billie knew that Ash was just teasing and expected her to retort with an equally abusive and cheeky reply, but she couldn't quite bring herself to see the joke.

Chapter 34

A Sobering Thought

'What's happening now?' Bluey pinned herself onto Maya's side, clinging on for dear life as voices could be heard outside of the unit along with the sound of clanking and squeaking chains and a bone-shaking thud on the top and sides of the metal box, as though the whole unit had just been gripped by a giant crab. The refrigerator unit suddenly lurched upwards fast and then started to move sideways. Maya grabbed the slippery sides with her free hand, trying to gain some purchase, holding Bluey around the waist tightly with her other arm.

'I think they're loading us on a ship,' she said, swallowing hard as she tried to hide the terror in her voice. Her face was no doubt a reflection of that of her fellow travellers. All of the girls looked wide-eyed, like frightened rabbits, as they tried to grip the side walls or each other. She heard one girl whispering a prayer. It sent a chill through Maya. Not that she was in the mood to believe in any god after this.

'Oh my God, we will die!' another girl screamed out as the unit now started to move downwards, the sound of the hydraulic action partly drowning out her voice. The girls heard movement around them as though the unit was being secured in place and then silence for what seemed an age, as they stayed on high alert, whispering concerns interspersed with attempts to calm one another as they waited for other units to be loaded on top or to either side of them, wondering if the air they were presently gulping in would soon run out.

'I think these units have their own system for keeping the contents at the correct temperature,' Maya said, attempting to dredge up something about the subject that she vaguely remembered learning at school.

'Maybe, if one is transporting tomatoes, but these people are not professional exporters,' another girl argued.

'I wouldn't be so sure about that,' Maya answered. She doubted that this was the first time that girls had been trafficked on this route. 'They need to keep us alive. We have no value to them unless they can sell us off again.'

'Yes, that's right.' Bluey's tear-stained face brightened momentarily. 'Hopefully they will treat us just like they do when transporting animals abroad. For slaughter...'

It was a sobering thought. Maya closed her eyes and leaned her head back against the metal wall as another unit was suddenly slammed down beside them.

Chapter 35

Needle in a Haystack

'Upside is you've always wanted a cat.' Ash glanced at Coco, ensconced in the cat carrier on Billie's knee as he changed gear.

'When did I say that?' Billie questioned as she hugged the cat carrier. Taking on the care of Coco was the least she could do in the circumstances. Of course, proper enquiries would have to take place to try and verify if Edith's death was due to accident or ill intent, but Billie was pretty sure what she believed. First Coco had been poisoned, as a warning, and when that hadn't worked... Billie tried not to dwell on the picture of Edith's lifeless and broken body, still shuffling through her mind's eye. Turned out that she'd been a brave woman. If someone had indeed given her the push, Billie was determined to make that person pay.

'The girls have been on about wanting a pet for ages.' Ash smiled. 'They'll be thrilled by the new arrival.'

'Okay, we can share.' Billie hadn't been able to find any obvious next of kin for Edith via her initial enquiries, so it looked like a done deal.

'Did you say Storm Benbow's house is the next turning?' Ash knocked on his indicator.

'Yeah, according to Edith. She had scribbled the address on the back of the photo of Connie and her mum,' *and Eddie Checkley*, Billie didn't add – her heart was still sinking at the thought that they were about to drag her new lover's brother in for questioning, but then romantic relationships never had exactly run smoothly for her. Billie's mobile suddenly rang. She reached for it, relieved, putting off the moment that she would have to come clean with Ash as to her amour of the night before.

'Hello.' Billie listened to the caller's response. 'Thank God. It's Ellis.' Billie clicked on the loudspeaker.

'Where are you?' Ellis asked as they pulled up outside of Storm Benbow's house. Ash's team had already got a warrant from a magistrate to search the house. The front door was open, and Billie could see people milling around the entrance.

'Where are you?' she answered swiftly, reversing the question as she exchanged glances with Ash.

'British Embassy in Bucharest. Nightmare. I was mugged, passport, the lot gone. But I might not be heading back yet–'

'Mate, you've got to come straight back,' Ash said, cutting over Ellis's words.

'What? Has Slug Harris got nothing better to do than drag me in for questioning again? Tell him to bog off!' Billie and Ash looked at one another again. Billie relaxed a little. At least that proved Ellis had no idea what had happened to Slug. She quickly broke the news. Ellis was silent for a moment.

'Shame but these things happen. Shows the power of collective thinking,' he added. Billie wasn't sure if he was joking.

'That's a bit harsh,' Ash responded, through a pained looking expression.

'What's harsh is that Maya's gone!' Ellis bellowed in response. 'I've got to find her.'

'Gone where, travelling with her boyfriend?' Billie tried to make sense of Ellis's obvious distress.

'The whole bloody orphanage is gone. Apparently people traffickers work in the area. Set up rogue orphanages, get dosh from gullible travellers paying to do the bloody dumps up and then move the kids on. They've taken Maya. I knew there was something up. God knows why I didn't suss it and act earlier. She could be anywhere now, it's like looking for a sodding needle in a haystack.' Ellis's voice actually started to crack as though he was tearful. It shocked Billie to the core. She'd never heard her friend in such emotional distress.

'Come straight back, and we'll put our heads together. We're working on a people trafficking job right now,' Ash said as one of his team headed towards the car. Ash popped his head out of the window.

'Place has been entirely cleared out, guv. It's totally empty. No sign of where they've headed. Neighbours said they never even spoke to anyone, but there was lots of coming and going.'

'Just get on the first plane back, Ellis.' Billie had heard the exchange between Ash and his officer, only briefly registering that a year ago, all of the officers outside would have been answerable to her.

'What for? Maya's not likely to just turn up there,' Ellis started to argue. 'I've got a few contacts here that might—'

'Ellis, we need your help here. We need to find Connie.' Ash blew out his lips and Billie bit her own as they registered the moment of shocked muteness on the other end of the line. It was clear that Billie's words had hit home.

'What?' Ellis sounded winded.

Billie squeezed her eyes shut for a second. When she opened them Ash gave her a nod. Looked like she had just been given the job of breaking the devastating news. Ellis's darkest day was just about to spiral into an emotional black hole.

Chapter 36

Press Gangs

'We're definitely moving.' Maya sat up straight. For the past few hours there had been noise and commotion all around the unit, but now it was quiet, save for the rocking motion similar to that which Maya had been familiar with on school trips abroad, when a ferry had left the dock.

'I feel sick,' Bluey mumbled, scrambling across on hands and knees to the bucket that was already full to the brim once again. Maya wondered how that was possible. It had been ages since they had eaten or been given a drink.

'They'll have to feed us soon,' she said through a sigh. Not that she felt hungry at all, but she remembered her mum reminding her that she had to eat when she felt unwell and in truth she had never felt worse. She knew that the other girls would be feeling the same. Low blood sugar, together with shock and physical, as well as extreme emotional injury, had made them either jittery or catatonic.

Suddenly Maya heard movement outside. Bolts were being hauled back, before the doors slammed open wide, caught by the huge gust of sea-salty wind that blew into the unit, causing the girls' hair to swirl around their faces. Two burly men stood at the doorway. One flicked his head back.

'Walk, ladies, walk.'

The girls gingerly pulled themselves up, holding their thin dresses and wraps around them as the fabric was tugged by the strong wind. Outside, a choppy expanse of grey sea topped with white froth was all that could be seen beyond the deck, except for the hint of land that they presumably had left, just visible on the horizon. Maya immediately registered that there was absolutely nowhere to run to.

As the girls filed out and turned left, through a heavy metal door into the interior of the ship, Maya suddenly spotted a young man, about to shut the door. She blinked, thinking she was imagining things, but she wasn't. She recognised him.

'Hey!' she called. She was looking at Jake, the student who had posed for the environmental charity photo with Ozzie and the gang. She couldn't understand what on earth he could be doing here. Had she been so wrong about him as well?

'Got a feisty one here. I'll take care of her.' Jake suddenly slammed his hand over Maya's mouth and propelled her quickly backwards into a corner, almost making her fall over. The other men were following the last of the girls into the body of the ship. They both chuckled.

'Give her one from me, mate,' one of them said. He gave a wink before stepping over the lip of the door and closing it behind him. Maya rebalanced herself, now pinned against the wall of the ship. She started struggling.

'Shush or you'll get us both killed,' Jake whispered urgently as he moved Maya even further into the shadows.

'What the fuck is going on?' Maya pulled her shift around her as it whipped up in the blustery sea breeze. 'Did you know what I was walking into all along, you and Ozzie and–'

'Shut it!' Jake hissed. 'I'm not part of this, I'm investigating it! Well, not people trafficking...' He trailed off for a moment, looking almost as shocked as Maya felt. He swallowed hard then stared wide-eyed at Maya. 'You've got to keep calm, Maya. They killed Ozzie.' Tears rose to his eyes. He swept them away with his hand.

'We came on board undercover as part of Green Planet, you know, the environmental group we did that poster for? This fucking monster is one of those super freezer trawlers. They stay at sea for months on end, bottom-trawling, taking everything in their path, including porpoises, dolphins, everything in their mile-long nets, just sucked up like the ship's got a giant vacuum cleaner on board.

'This one has been fishing in the UK's Marine Protected areas, taking hundreds of tons of sea life every day, and me and Ozzie, well we'd studied as sea cadets at school, so they took us on when we applied for holiday work. We told them that we were starting maritime college. They had no idea we knew one another, or that we were gathering info under cover of being navigation officer interns. My mother is from Vietnam, so I can understand what some of the crew here are saying.

'But... they *killed* him?' Maya felt her whole body shaking and not only because of the cold.

Jake nodded. His eyes filled with horror. 'We had cameras hidden on us and when we found out that it wasn't just the mass fishing, that they had also tricked most of the factory crew on board, holding them with no way off...'

Maya shook her head, not understanding. Jake looked over his shoulder to check no one else was in the vicinity, dropping his voice. 'It's just like a modern-day version of press gangs. Ships like these are lawless, out at sea for months on end, far from authorities in any country.

'The foreign crew have often been tricked on board, working night and day. It's non-stop – processing, freezing and sometimes canning the catch. It's like a giant factory at sea. The crew working that side of things are bought and sold to different companies, swapped at sea, often made to work for little or nothing to repay some random debt to the owners. They beat them badly if they don't work fast enough. We were recording as much as possible, but someone caught Ozzie at it.'

Maya slapped her hand over her mouth. 'Slave labour. Just what they are planning for us. Thrown overboard if we don't comply,' she said through a gasp.

Jake looked around again. 'Crew who have tried to stand up to them have disappeared and there's nowhere safe to run to. They told me that someone watched Ozzie jump off when he was drunk but I know that's bollocks. Look, I've got to be quick. I've overheard what they are planning for some of your group, but they have no idea that I know. I'm due to be lifted off this afternoon. I said I'm due to start my navigation officer course and my uncle is one of the lecturers. I claimed that I really wanted to stay onboard, but he would kick off if I didn't return on time. They've been happy with my work and seem to think I'm unaware or just plain stupid, so I'm good.

'A bigwig is coming on board when we pass down the coast, near Amsterdam. His boat will drop him off and pick me up with a couple of the other navigation crew who are due leave. Got a flight booked straight back to Newcastle. As soon as I hit home soil I'll tell the authorities what's happening here. You must have police contacts?' Maya nodded. 'Okay. Just sit tight for a few days and keep schtum. Don't tell *anyone*. You may be in for a bumpy ride but if your police friends aren't all bent, too, then I'm hoping to help get at least some people off this hellhole.'

'You are telling the truth, aren't you?' Maya didn't know what to believe anymore.

'I only wish I wasn't. Ozzie was a good mate. The best.'

'Yeah, I thought that about Mitch too,' Maya replied, allowing Jake to grab her now by the wrist and pull her towards the dark innards of the ship.

Chapter 37

Just Like Old Times

Ash came into the office holding reams of papers, as Billie cleared through Slug's office, partly to give Ash somewhere to move, bearing in mind the number of additional staff being brought in to assist the MIT who were rapidly filling up desk space in the main office, and partly to keep out of the way, so that any old-timers didn't come to ask her for advice first, before speaking to Ash.

Despite her friend's protests that he didn't really want this top job he truly deserved it and she wanted the best outcome for him – for them all. She wasn't going to rain on his parade and technically she was simply a civilian detective, here to offer advice specifically on serial killers. Was Slug Harris the victim of one of those, or did he have other enemies? Right now no one knew.

'Did your latest forensic phone wizard agree to track Maya's mobile?' Billie asked.

'Yeah. Great idea of yours. He owes me a favour and as she was using the PC over in the corner when she was last in, he reckons it's just a matter of logging into her Google tracking history. He'll nip in and do it a bit later on when it's quiet. I told him we're worried about her.'

'We're worried about everybody right now. It's just like old times,' Billie reflected.

'Any word back from Silver Darlings yet?' Ash asked, as Billie, who had been trying various keys, finally whispered 'bingo.' The top drawer of Slug's office desk had finally slid open.

'Teddy's due back later tonight. Seems that he's away at some sort of kipper-smoking convention,' Billie answered, as she looked through the top drawer. It was as neat and tidy as she would have expected from Slug. 'Who knew such things even existed? I tell you it's a never-ending education this job...'

'Nothing on Storm Benbow, nor Eddie Checkley yet,' Ash updated Billie. 'Her real first name is Mavis, by the way. Nail bar is closed. Connie isn't at her nursery as usual either. Hopefully she's with that nanny. We've got someone posted at the house in case they've just been off to the ice-cream parlour.'

'Oh hello...' Billie crouched down. Her outstretched hand had made contact with a pile of crumpled papers at the back of the otherwise organised drawer, holding a notebook and identical pens that looked box fresh. Billie dragged out the papers and dumped them on the desktop, exchanging glances with Ash who was staring at them. She reached for the neatly folded protective gloves, ripped the clear bag open and slipped them on, lifting each piece out of the pile and smoothing them one by one out on the desktop.

'Same writing as in our office,' Billie pointed out, grabbing her mobile from the desktop and clicking on the photos she had taken of Wilde & Darque's graffitied wall. STAY AWAY FROM OZZIE KINGSNORTH. 'The warning is similar too.' Billie perused the rest of the ripped slices of paper. LEAVE OZZIE KINGSNORTH ALONE, OR YOU WILL BE NEXT read another.

FORGET THE SKELETONS said a third. Billie looked to Ash. 'Surely this clears Ellis totally from all investigations. He's not likely to come along to our office, break in and warn himself off.'

'You might do something like that if you were a killer though, mightn't you? Put people off the track. I probably would. But to alleviate our eternally suspicious minds, one of the team has been out speaking with Judge Pennington. She said that Slug gave her a lift to the opera the other night at about 7.30pm. They picked up a friend on the way and the brakes were perfectly all right then. She remembered that clearly, as someone swerved in front of them, and Slug had to slam the brakes on hard. If they had been tampered with then, she claims they would have all ended up in the morgue like her son.'

'So that clearly proves that Ellis wasn't the one who cut the brake lines. He was with us from about six o'clock until he ran out to catch the plane and you got the call to say that Slug had snuffed it practically the moment he had left my house.' Billie hoped she was keeping a clear head here and not protesting too much.

'Judge Pennington said that Slug was meant to accompany them to the opera. He had a seat booked and was looking forward to it, but something came up at the last minute, somebody he had to meet urgently. She said he seemed distracted, on reflection, so of course she's blaming herself for not asking if something was worrying him.'

Billie was suddenly filled with sympathy for the woman. 'Jeez, first the husband is found to be a bigamist and next her favourite son smashes into the back of a lorry. Life can be a bitch.' Billie ran her fingers through her hair. 'Any chance he gave her a heads-up who he was meeting? Someone equipped to slice through brake lines for example?'

'If the brake lines had been cut right through, the pedal would have hit the floor as soon as he tried to put the car into gear though. Surely a heads-up that the brakes were shot?' Ash seemed perplexed. 'Even Slug would have guessed that, and the scene-of-crime lot are certain it's a DODI.' Ash was using the police slang for Dead One Did It. 'The lorry driver wasn't at fault. He was only touching thirty miles per hour. Couldn't have been suicide, could it? God knows this job can get to us all.' Ash sighed. 'Can't say I don't feel a bit guilty about all of this. None of us exactly offered him much of a helping hand.'

Billie looked up from the warning notices sent to Slug. 'I'm not buying it. Slug didn't strike me as the type. Maybe he was in a hurry to get away, so he wasn't about to put his head under the bonnet and do a spot of maintenance, even if he did think his brakes were suspect. Car driver said that he overtook her at speed before he turned the bend and said a big hello to the lorry. Have you ever known Slug to break a speed limit? Doesn't sound like him, though I never had the pleasure of being his back seat driver.'

Ash shook his head. 'That is a point. Slug usually drove like a snail–' His mobile suddenly rang. 'DS Sanghera,' he answered, listening for a moment. 'Okay. I'm on my way.' He looked across to Billie. 'Got a possible suspicious death across town. Uniform just called in wanting me to give it the once-over. Chances are it's nothing to do with this. Will you go and see if Teddy Cook can throw any light on Irina's contacts?'

'Yes. I'll go and break the news to Abi Zerezghi on the way.' Billie accepted the coffee in a plastic cup that Ash was holding out to her and took a sip. Her face creased into a grimace as she put it quickly back on the countertop again.

'Thanks but no thanks. I see the canteen has gone downhill since I checked out.'

Ash grinned. 'Your tastebuds have just recovered, that's all. For some of us, beggars can't be choosers.' Ash raised his cup in a cheers motion. 'I'll catch up with you over at the kipper smokery.'

As Ash headed out Billie picked up the phone and rang Boo. She had already given her a heads-up about Jemal and Boo had agreed to be present when Abi returned from the local hospital after a long day training to be a nurse, to hear the news that her beloved brother had no hope of joining her in her new life.

Billie checked her watch. On hearing that Storm Benbow appeared to have gone AWOL with Connie, Ellis had made arrangements to get the first flight back to the UK. He was due to arrive early evening. Billie braced herself. Stress beckoned in every direction. Certainly they had no jolly reunion celebration planned for later that night.

Chapter 38

Everything Passes, Love remains

S treaks of blood red slashed the dark-grey sky, over the little enclosed courtyard garden strung with fairy lights, in which Billie and Boo had gently broken the news to Abi about her beloved brother, Jemal. Billie had watched her move through all of the different emotions one experienced having found that a loved one had died in horrific circumstances. She'd been through them all herself, after all.

On seeing the 3D printout Abi had at first been disbelieving, though even to Billie, who had only seen a hazy photo of the young man, there could be no doubt as to identity. Tomorrow, a blood sample would be taken from Abi to verify for her, beyond any doubt, that Jemal had been the body found in Ellis's back garden.

Anger was now simmering in Billie's blood, along with sympathy and heartache for the beautiful girl, trying to follow a career putting broken bodies back together, when her own heart would clearly be forever broken. Abi was calming now as Boo held her hand gently. Tears had run dry. She simply hung her head and gave the odd juddering sigh as she stroked Jemal's picture. Billie and Boo exchanged glances. Billie had to start asking questions. She knew that Abi was holding vital information which could lead in the direction of Jemal's killer. She simply *had* to get any new facts that she possibly could from her.

'*Kullu yihalif, fiqri yiterif,*' Abi finally whispered through a sigh.

'Sorry?' Boo questioned.

'An Eritrean saying. *Everything passes, love remains.*' She looked up, suddenly angry.

'You must make them pay. The people who did this to Jemal!' Billie saw a flash of fire in her eyes. It had undoubtedly been needed for Abi to have dealt with the seemingly insurmountable challenges that she and her brother had faced on leaving Eritrea. Billie breathed a sigh of relief. The girl was going to be okay.

'We want to do that, Abi. Currently there is a child missing and she may be with the traffickers. She probably won't be harmed but others–' Billie thought of Ellis for a split second and those sad souls on the move around the world, just like any other form of merchandise that people had an insatiable taste for.

'I will tell you everything I know. Now I have nothing to lose. I don't care if they come for me–' Abi was talking fast now. '*Tsibuq zereba 'atsmi aganinti yisebbir.* Another saying from my home country that has come true. It means *nice talk can break the bones of a ghost.* By talking nicely and saying nothing I have broken my own brother's bones–'

'No, Abi.' Billie smoothed her hand over the young woman's hair. 'That isn't true.'

'I will go to my grave knowing that. But now I will talk.'

Billie reached in her pocket for her notepad as Abi took a sip of the fruit juice before her. 'From Libya, we came by boat to Europe. Italy. Jemal and I would have been happy to stay there – anywhere safe where we could have started a new life.

We thought we would be free then. But the people who brought us said we owed them more money. We had already paid them everything we had. We now had nothing left but they said the debt had risen and we couldn't go until we had paid it all.'

'Typical bonded labour. People tricked into working for little or no money and the debt keeps going up, so that it can never be repaid.' Boo shook her head in anger and dismay.

'Yes, we were stupid, but they had guns and had found out details about our loved ones left behind. Our grandmother, our older brother in the army. They said they would make them pay if we didn't. We could not just walk away.' Abi wrung her hands together.

'This is not your fault,' Billie was at pains to reassure Abi. 'It happens to thousands of people all over the world, but you are fighting back now, by telling us this. You are not walking away.'

'We crossed many different countries in a lorry. I do not know them all. Sometimes we stopped and some people were sold to other traffickers. We were paraded like cattle. Look at this.' Abi lifted her hair back and showed Billie the tattoo of a wasp on her neck. Billie felt sick. It was the first time that she had seen it on someone still alive. 'Buying and selling us like animals, some to go one way, some to go another.'

'The people who brought you here to England, where did they meet you?' Billie asked, desperate to have pick-up and drop-off points in her head. It would be at least something to go on.

Abi took a deep breath, her mind clearly full of horrors. 'It was Germany, I think. Yes, Germany. Then we were taken by lorry again to a port in the Netherlands and loaded on a ship, still in the container. We were very scared. Jemal protected me when I cried that we would all die. He said that he would always keep me safe...' Abi trailed off. A tear sprang from her

259

eye, tracing a tiny river down her face. She wiped it away with a big sigh.

'We stayed at sea for a while, maybe a day and night. We were kept underground in a hold. Many people were very sick with the rocking of the ship, but they were lucky. Some of us were taken by the crew for sex. Jemal was strong but he could not stop it. He was given some work, cleaning the decks. It was dangerous. High waves would sometimes knock people overboard if they were not strapped down. Jemal told me that another person he met on the deck was from Malaysia. He had taken a job advertised on the ship, but now he could never leave. He owed too much money and they knew where his family lived just like us. He has to stay on the ship and work forever.'

'This is an absolute nightmare.' Boo sighed. Different scenarios, but identical modus operandi.

'Abi, do you know the name of the place where the ship docked when you left it?' Billie asked.

'It did not dock. It stayed at sea. It was a huge ship. I saw it when we were loaded off onto the little boat and taken to the place where we were picked up,' Abi explained.

'Where was that? A beach perhaps?' Billie referenced in her mind news stories she had watched on TV, smugglers bringing people on small boats to southern English seaside locations.

'No, we were still in the middle of the sea. The little boat took us to a wind farm. We saw some in the desert on our journey when we left Eritrea. Here, there are five maybe, very big, in the middle of the sea. We had to get off the boat at one of them, climb up a ladder and were locked in a room where we waited. We were alone. The boat left. Then eventually another boat came with other people, and they took us away. A man and a woman.'

'Can you describe them?' Billie was writing the details down fast.

Abi paused. 'The man was big and tall. Had fair hair. They were all wrapped up against the wind and the cold.' Billie nevertheless registered that the description would fit Eddie Checkley.

'And the woman?' Boo gently encouraged, but Abi was getting emotional again.

'I cannot say. It was so cold. They were wearing big rain jackets with hoods, and she had a scarf over her face... It was so frightening. Huge waves, and I slipped off the ladder and nearly fell in the water when we moved back onto their boat. Jemal grabbed my arm. He saved me...' Abi started to cry again now, like a tap that had been turned on and would never completely be turned off. Billie looked at Boo. She knew that she could push the young woman no further right now.

'Let's get you up to your room,' Boo said. Billie knew Boo wouldn't allow more questioning anyway. Billie thanked Abi, reiterating how helpful she had been. She mimed a phone call and Boo nodded. Billie hoped that her friend and former office manager in the MIT would be able to get more details out of Abi once the initial shock had worn off. She had just opened the door to leave when her mobile rang.

'Hi, it's Ash. I'm still at the location of the female suspicious death. She's just been dragged out of the lake.'

'Want me to come out and give you a hand?' Billie asked.

'No, to be honest, I'm feeling a bit crappy. Think it's that horrible coffee I drank. I really need to get off home and get some zeds once Josta's arrived and given it the once-over. I don't want to throw up and contaminate the scene.'

Billie also didn't want to appear to be muscling in on the normal day-to-day activities of the MIT. She reminded herself she was contracted specifically to help out with what appeared to be serial killings, but she also registered that Ash must be feeling really unwell. It wasn't like him to be thinking of clocking off at such a crucial moment.

'I can come and pick you up if you'd rather not drive.' Billie was anxious for her friend.

'No, I'll be okay. I'll get one of the team to ferry me back if I'm at death's door. Listen, I'm just about to forward details of Maya's phone history. Maybe shed some light on her whereabouts. I'll also send a photo of the deceased here. Hopefully confirm that it's not Storm Benbow, or the nanny. Bear in mind she's been submerged, poor lass, so identification might be difficult.'

Billie headed for her car, her mind racing. She hoped to God that the poor dead female was neither Storm nor Viku. Because if it were to be, the next chilling question was, what had happened to Connie or Viku's own baby?

Chapter 39

The Wolf Moon

Billie tried to concentrate on the road as she drove towards Silver Darlings. In truth, though she had texted Ash to confirm that the body in the lake definitely wasn't Storm Benbow because of the dark head of hair, she wasn't sure if the woman pulled out of the lake was the nanny or not.

It was too early for death and water to have totally distorted the female's features and Billie was guessing that the body hadn't been in the water that long, but Viku had been animated yesterday when Billie had met her at the nail salon. The body, like all cadavers Billie had ever viewed had the look of an empty house. Wherever the dead person had gone, regardless of whether it was Viku or not, there was simply an empty shell left behind. Billie's thoughts were also clouded by thoughts of Viku's baby. She desperately didn't want the corpse to be the young mother.

Her car phone rang. Billie answered, expecting Ash but instead Ellis's voice, taut with tension, filled the car. Billie, however, felt a little of her own anxiety lift on hearing his voice.

'I'm back. Where are you?' he asked.

'On my way to Silver Darlings. See if Teddy can shed any

further light on the skeleton bride,' Billie explained, updating him on Irina's identity. She knew that Ellis would be as focused as she was on getting to the truth of the situation. Billie was determined to find out if Teddy could link Eddie Checkley somehow not only to Ozzie Kingsnorth and Jemal Zerezghi's deaths, but also to Irina Subašić, the skeleton bride. The three young people caught living at the wrong time and being at the wrong place, with devastating consequences.

'On my way. I'll meet you there.'

Billie could see that Silver Darlings was still in darkness as she arrived, save for the glow through the long paned windows that edged the smokehouse, where the little night fires had been lit in groups of five below each batch of herrings, slowly smoking throughout the night. Teddy's house next door was also in darkness.

She pulled the car up in front of the harbour, deciding to wait for the arrival of both Teddy and Ellis there. The rising Wolf Moon was almost full tonight, casting a silver reflection on the rippling dark water. Rolling down her window, Billie looked out, surveying the star-spangled sky, hearing the waves crashing softly out in the wide open sea beyond.

Billie's thoughts turned to James Checkley. The night before had been full of enchanting moments, in which both had been transfixed with the moon and the stars and each other. She shivered now. This morning she had felt that she had been ready to make a fresh start, even possibly learn to love again, but now she felt conflicted. Could sweet, gentle James really be so different from his brother, Eddie? Billie, more than most, knew well that looks could deceive.

She still hadn't fessed up to Ash that she had any connection with the Checkleys. She felt guilty about the fact but had made some gentle enquiries herself after finding a bouquet of red roses left outside of her office door when she had nipped back to check some messages. Those had included one left from Pandy Wood announcing that Storm Benbow's nail bars seemed to have shut down, so she wouldn't need Billie to do further investigations. Little did she realise the truth of it.

Billie had sent a text to James thanking him for the flowers. He had sent a message back to tell her that he was heading abroad later today for a few days but hoped to see her as soon as he returned. Billie couldn't deny that her heart lifted at the thought. But was this the start of something really special at last, or a relationship that was doomed before it had even begun?

As though some collective unconscious vibe had been sent out, Billie's mobile suddenly rang. It was James's name that flashed up. Billie grabbed it like a guilty schoolgirl caught hanging around with the wrong crowd, certain of how Ash would view the connection despite his teasing that morning. She didn't even dare think of Ellis's reaction. She brushed her misgivings away. It was vital to discover the whereabouts of Eddie Checkley after all, not only in connection with trafficking, but to pin down the whereabouts of Storm Benbow and Connie and there was a good chance his brother would know better than most.

'Hi,' Billie answered, 'I do hope that you're not checking up on me already?' she joked.

'Just asking for confirmation that you are snugly tucked up and sad that I'm not wrapped around you. The Wolf Moon is looking pretty much full, from where I am tonight.' Billie could hear that James's answer was through a smile.

'So not that far from me. I'm looking at it too, right now.' Billie wondered if James's trip abroad had been cancelled. She felt her hopes lift for a second and then sink, wondering how she would square that up with Ash and Ellis. 'I'm now an expert on moons,' she added. Until last night, Billie hadn't even registered that all full moons had names.

'You are an expert on many things, Ms Wilde,' James answered flirtatiously. 'Just watch out for any marauding wolves howling out there.' James had explained the night before that the January moon was originally named after wolves howling for more food in this icy month when the prey that they hunted was able to hide in the darkness. It was a good moment for Billie to bring up what was on her mind.

'Is your brother with you?' Billie asked. James was silent for a moment, then his voice quizzical in reply.

'My brother... Ed you mean?'

'Do you have other brothers?' Billie replied, trying to keep her voice light.

'No. One is enough, I assure you. But why on earth do you ask?'

'It's just that my partner, I mean my business partner,' Billie made clear, wondering why on earth she felt she had to clarify that and why she also felt guilty for emphasising it, 'used to be married to your brother's girlfriend, Storm Benbow. He's trying to get hold of her to pin down child access. They have a young daughter together.' That was the truth anyway.

'Oh, I see. I've never met the woman. Sorry, I wouldn't have a clue where she or indeed he, is. We're really brothers in name rather than nature as I explained last night, and we have various bases around the world. We meet fairly regularly at the boardroom table to discuss our different businesses under the company umbrella. But that's more a sharing of essential facts and figures rather than family bonhomie, I'm afraid.'

'You sound like the William and Harry of the international business world.' Billie tried to make her comment sound like a joke. To James's credit, he did give a soft chuckle.

'We're a bit less on the amigo scale than that, in truth. I hardly know my brother at all. He had left education and had started working with my father around the time I was sent off to boarding school. I was more fixated on the tuck shop and football stickers than what Ed was up to.'

'So you wouldn't know where to start looking for him?' Billie gently persisted.

'I'm sure I can get a message to him via our respective PAs if your partner is desperate. Get mine to speak to his. Tell her to pass the message on to my brother that his girlfriend's former husband is on the warpath. At least that's what it sounds like.' James laughed.

Billie decided to leave it for the time being, Ash and Ellis would have agreed that any further pressing would have flagged up trouble looming, were James to have been involved in the trafficking business too, *or maybe I can't bear to believe that could be true*, Billie chided herself. A sudden banging on the car window made Billie almost leap out of her skin. Ellis was bending down staring at her.

'Everything all right?' James asked, suddenly alert, undoubtedly having heard the noise.

'Yep. Just a mad wolf baying for my blood. Got to go.' Billie waved at Ellis who was pacing back and forth outside, full of pent-up tension, Billie imagined.

'Well, tell him to keep his filthy paws off. I'm planning to take you back to my own lair again as soon as I get back.' James's voice sounded husky.

'With lines like that you could be waiting a long time,' Billie answered, unable to completely wipe out the flirtatious tone to her own voice. Ellis suddenly banged on the window again. 'See you soon.' Billie quickly ended the call. She hoped her words would come true and that this wasn't yet another relationship that was about to go totally pear-shaped.

'Doesn't look like Teddy's here yet,' Billie called to Ellis, whilst opening the passenger door. She suddenly remembered the info on Maya's phone tracking that Ash had forwarded on to her. She hadn't looked through it, but now seemed like a good time. 'I've been instigating a bit of Maya investigation myself, come in and let's see where her mobile's been.' Ellis was inside the car within seconds.

'What a bleeding nightmare this is.' He rubbed his face as Billie brought up the file. 'Billie, you are an angel. I could kiss you for this.' He looked at her and for a moment Billie thought that he really meant it. Instead, she patted him on the head.

'Ow.' He pulled away. 'That's the spot where I was bottled.'

'Well you shouldn't threaten me. If this gives us Maya's location though, you owe me a bag of chips on the way home.' Billie opened the file and Ellis bent in next to her to view it.

'The first call that she made, last Sunday, the day that she was due back, was made from the orphanage, as you can see, if that's the correct address.' Billie showed Ellis the Google Maps timeline of Maya's mobile.

'Yep, that's it.' He sighed, rubbing his head in an absent-minded fashion, the address no doubt having brought back memories of the location where he had been mugged.

'Then the video message on Friday, that was sent from Germany.' Billie had her head bent close to the screen.

'Christ. She could be anywhere now. I'll get on to Ash, give him the address. Get him to contact the German cops pronto—' Ellis started to say before Billie put her hand up to stop him.

'There's mostly red Missing Travel messages, offering no location details. Maybe the SIM card has been taken in and out but look at this. The day she sent me a message from her phone. Monday, at the office. You were dressed as a banana, remember?' said Billie.

'To my dying day,' Ellis replied. 'Where did she send that from?' Billie looked up at the sound of a car passing theirs and parking in front of Silver Darlings.

'Right here. It even records the exact location. Silver

Darlings Fish Smokery,' Billie replied, as Teddy Cook alighted from his car and headed for the main door.

The little fires revealed glowing embers everywhere as the smoke rose up and around the hundreds of herrings on tenterhooks turning from silver to bronze in the process. Teddy Cook had only half crossed the floor, on the way to his office, from which a dim light spilled out casting shadows, when Ellis flew at him.

'Where's my daughter?' Ellis shouted, knocking a totally shocked Teddy to the floor. Billie had raced after Ellis and caught up with him now, dragging him back as he lunged over Teddy, heaving him up by his jacket lapels to face him.

'Ellis, get a grip.' Billie pushed between him and Teddy, who managed to pull free. A smoking ember had attached itself to his jacket. Billie hastily brushed it off as he scuttled sideways, away from the fire.

'What's going on?' Teddy looked wide-eyed from Billie to Ellis.

'That's what I want you to tell me! How come my daughter sent a message from right here on Monday when she was in Romania the day before and Germany a couple of nights back?'

'Who, Maya? I thought she was extending her holiday.' Teddy looked genuinely bewildered.

'She's been kidnapped!' Ellis pushed Billie away and hauled Teddy back towards him.

'You're having a laugh, aren't you?' Teddy tried to pull free, clearly not amused. 'Why would she be here? I've been working my socks off as usual, all hours every day this week until today. No way has Maya been here. Have you had a drink or something?'

Billie turned her mobile phone screen to show Teddy.

'Look, Google Maps tracks where people have been using their phone data, times and places. It's definitely showing that Maya was at this location. Maya or her phone...' Billie suddenly added as her brain started firing on all cylinders. 'Has anyone here been to Romania, come back and then gone to Germany–'

At that moment the door to Teddy's office opened slightly and two figures tried to slip out unseen, yet the glow of the little oak fires everywhere made that impossible.

'Hey, you two, stop. We want a word.' Billie had just identified Maya's friend, Lily, with Smokey Boy Patel. They both took off at speed along a back corridor, Billie giving chase with Ellis hot on her heels. They arrived at a storage room packed high with boxes and crates. Billie was across the room in two strides leaping to catch Lily's ankle as she scrabbled up the packing boxes, making for an open window through which Smokey Boy Patel had just flung himself.

'I'll cut him off by the front,' Ellis called, turning and racing back the way they had come, whilst Billie dragged Lily down in an avalanche of packing containers. She pulled the girl upright and marched her back towards the office entrance, flicking the switch to allow full light to spill into the room.

'Get off me!' Lily squealed as Teddy joined Billie.

'Not until you tell me exactly what the story is with Maya and don't play the innocent again. My patience is wearing thin, madam.'

'I don't know, I keep telling you...' Lily tried to protest, but her earlier show of bravado was slipping, Billie could see. Ellis suddenly appeared, breathless and disgruntled.

'No idea which way he went, could have gone into the sand dunes. It's pitch black there...'

'He just lives down the road,' Teddy started to say when Lily cut over him.

'Don't tell them anything,' Lily hissed, trying to pull free from the vice-like grip Billie had her arms in, behind her back. 'You know what'll happen if we say even a word.'

'What do you mean?' Teddy frowned. Billie figured that his show of ignorance was genuine. Either that or he should swap careers to actor and try for an Oscar. Lily hung her head down.

'What do you *mean*?' Ellis bent down and tipped Lily's chin up to face him. Lily suddenly started sobbing.

'I mean look what's happened to Maya! She sussed what was really going on in that orphanage, wanted to play Daddy's Girl or copy her heroine Billie Big Baps here and save all the little children. But look where that got *her*?'

'Where exactly has it got her, Lily? Maya was your *best friend*.' Billie tried to sound calm, but she was struggling. 'Don't you care about her well-being?'

'Ask him.' Lily nodded her head towards Teddy. 'He's probably in on it. Eddie Checkley's his cousin, Smokey Boy says.'

Billie and Ellis looked to Teddy who opened his arms out, shaking his head.

'He is but I've never had anything to do with him.'

'He's lying,' Lily argued. 'I've seen one of Eddie's men coming here every Friday to collect money. I've seen the accounts. Money goes out to them every week.'

Teddy nodded slowly. 'That's right. I've had to pay that out to his lot since the day I took the place over and I'm not the only business in the area who has to do likewise. I've had to just accept it as part of the game or sell up. Told me at the beginning that they'd take the business down otherwise. I tried to refuse the first time, but they smashed the place up and me with it. We're talking Eddie Checkley here. He was a thug when he was a kid, demanding dinner money with menaces at school and word is he rules most of the county now. But straight up, handing over weekly protection dosh – that's as far as my involvement with him goes.'

Ellis and Billie exchanged glances. It wasn't the first time in a long chalk that they had come across small businesses forced into paying protection money to gang leaders.

'It's the same with Smokey Boy, they make him do things and he's got no choice,' Lily added. 'They know where his dad lives, and his little sister is disabled. They told him they would make sure that the whole family would die in a car crash. When I was going to come and tell you all about Maya, cos I've been worried sick, whatever you might think...' Lily started sobbing again, 'they said that if I didn't stick to the boyfriend story, her going off travelling, they would cut the brake cables in my dad's car. They know where we live and everything.'

'Who's *they*? I'm guessing Eddie Checkley doesn't spend all day hanging around threatening kids?'

Lily wiped a hand across her nose. 'I've been told that they've got people watching us everywhere, making sure that everyone keeps in line. Even in the police...'

Billie gave a little groan. She'd had dealings with corrupt officers in the past, so knew that it was a possibility. 'So Maya was going to spill the beans about the orphanage scam?' Billie wanted to clarify.

'Yeah, she thought she could save all the kids and make her dad proud, with him having been a crack serious crime investigator and all that...'

Ellis looked like he'd been slapped in the face. He wiped his hand across his eyes. Was that a tear that Billie had spotted about to spill out?

'Yeah, well I'm not doing such a good job of that right now, am I? Can't even save my own girls.' He sighed.

Billie loosened her grip on Lily a little. She could feel the fear pulsating through her shaking body, her earlier smart girl posturing forgotten now.

'Will my dad be all right?' Lily's face crumpled up. 'I couldn't bear it if anything happened–'

'So *please*, tell us absolutely everything you know,' Billie pleaded. 'Do you have any photos of this Mitch, for example? You might not know him, but he may actually live locally if the gang have that much info on you. Maybe someone can pinpoint a young man who has travelled abroad twice in the last week.'

Lily paused, before finally answering through a sigh, 'I've got a photo of him on my mobile.' Billie released her arms and let Lily delve in her pocket for her phone. She held it up. It was a photo of Lily on one side and Maya on the other, with a young man in the middle. All were posing with wide smiles outside of the Romanian orphanage.

'But that's Smokey Boy Patel,' Ellis gasped, looking around in the mad hope that the young man was actually skulking in a dark shadow.

'They made him do it,' Lily whispered.

'Mitch Patel, that's his real name,' Teddy confirmed. 'Smokey Boy is his nickname.'

'Where is his gaff?' Ellis cut in, just as a loud smash rang out along with a hail of glass from one of the large windows in the smoking room. Billie caught a quick glimpse of Smokey Boy's face, looking desperate. A bottle seemingly stuffed with a rag, landed smack in the middle of one of the little oak-smoking fires before bursting into a ball of flames, tracking with breathtaking speed across the room as one little fire merged into the next and surged upwards. A wall of flame had blocked off the open exit route within a matter of seconds.

'Run!' Billie pulled Lily behind her as she raced into the office, hoping for an escape route through the window.

'It's got bars on it!' Teddy shouted as the fireball roared

across the ground almost to the open door, in a plume of dark smoke and the overwhelming smell of now burning kippers. Billie turned, spotting a fire extinguisher on the office wall. She yanked it off and aimed it at the flames licking the door frame as Ellis grabbed Lily and pulled her out of the office. The fire had already reached the ceiling and was tracking across the smoking room towards them at an incredible pace.

'There's a window in the back room,' Teddy shouted as Billie gave up with the fire extinguisher and followed them as fast as she could, the heat already almost unbearable. Thick smoke was already coming into the packaging room, but Ellis had hold of Lily's wrist, attempting to pull her behind him as he clambered up the crates and cardboard boxes. She suddenly dropped, seemingly losing consciousness. Teddy was almost through the window, coughing and spluttering but he turned and hung back, reaching out his arm in an attempt to help. It was too late. Billie caught Lily in her arms as Ellis lost his grip and the teenager tumbled back through the boxes, taking Billie down with her.

There was a loud bang as the fire devoured some combustible materials possibly in the cupboard Billie had noticed in the corridor. The effect was that the fire burst into the storeroom, shooting along to the boxes which caught alight immediately.

'Billie!' Ellis yelled. Billie, coughing, had no time to respond as she dragged Lily across the room.

'Go! I'll get them.' Billie suddenly heard Smokey Boy shout, as he scrambled back through the window and jumped to the floor. He raced across to Billie, picking up Lily by the ankles, whilst Billie lifted her under her arms.

'There's an old coal access door over in the corner, behind those crates,' he shouted over the roar of the fire and between hacking coughs. Billie kicked the crates away and spotted what

Smokey Boy was directing her to – a tiny door in the wall. Billie was gasping for breath. She hoped that they could get Lily through it. Suddenly the door was kicked open from outside. The fire behind roared up in response, as Teddy's face appeared in the opening.

'We're over here, give her to us,' he shouted, as Billie and Smokey Boy struggled with the lack of oxygen and weight of Lily's body. Ellis now came into view, having flung himself down on the ground outside next to Teddy. Within seconds they were in grabbing distance. The two of them seized hold of Lily, yanking her out through the desperately small space, like men involved in a tug of war. As her legs finally disappeared, Billie waved Smokey Boy forward.

'Go,' she cried, almost choking with the fumes and smell of burning fish. Smokey Boy sat back on his knees, sweat dripping from his brow. He shook his head, struggling for air.

'No. Get out. I'm staying. I don't know what I was doing. I didn't mean for that to happen, I wasn't thinking. I just wanted to protect my family.' He held his head in horror. Billie lunged for his arm.

'It's not your fault, you've been coerced, we can explain it all, you can give us more facts!' She jumped back as the cardboard boxes erupted into a huge bonfire. Billie felt as though her lungs would burst. 'Let's go.' Billie took a step forward, but Smokey Boy, sobbing now, scuttled back out of reach.

'No. I couldn't live with the shame. I can't put my family through that. I love my family...' He turned and stood upright, staggering towards the flames, when a beam along which the fire had been licking suddenly caught fully alight. It fell down with a deafening crash and flared up, a curtain of noise and heat cutting off any further hope of a safe exit for Smokey Boy Patel.

'Billie, for God's sake hurry!' Ellis had slid halfway through the tiny door, his large frame not allowing him to enter any further, but it was enough for him to grab a handful of Billie's shirt and yank her back towards him. Devastated, as well as aware that her flesh felt as though it was melting, she finally turned and flung herself out through the coal door and onto the grass. Ellis pulled her away swiftly to where Teddy crouched alongside Lily as locals gathered, trying to help him revive the girl. Billie could hear and then see fire engines and an ambulance arriving, the smell of smoking and burning herring filling the atmosphere.

'There's a teenager in there!' she screamed, as the first fireman jumped from the still moving truck. 'He's just an innocent young lad,' she cried, as Ellis pulled her close in a hug. She felt tears of shock and horror spill down her cheeks as Ellis stroked her hair. 'He was just a boy,' she sobbed.

Chapter 40

A Good Heart

In the end, Smokey Boy Patel had a good heart in more ways than one, Billie mused sadly, as she sat in the hospital corridor. The young man had finally died outside of the A & E entrance to the hospital, following more than one resuscitation attempt during the journey. The long wail from a small room just inside the building, followed by his father running out and leaning against the wall, utterly heartbroken, had announced the final ending.

Neither Billie nor Teddy, sitting with his head in his hands, nor Ellis marching up and down the corridor, restless and looking as though desperate to take some sort of action, was in any doubt as to the outcome of Smokey Boy's final journey.

Despite the fact that the young man had started the fire and had clearly been involved in Maya's disappearance, Billie felt tears spring into the back of her eyes. In the end, he had saved her life and explained the reasons for his actions, though she could tell by Ellis's appearance that he was absolutely distraught that the secrets that Smokey Boy had held had died along with him.

Teddy, though heartbroken by the fact that his home and business had been reduced to burning embers, had nonetheless insisted on accompanying Billie and Ellis to the hospital, genuinely desperate, Billie was certain, to offer support to Lily and Smokey Boy. He got up from his seat now, crossed to Smokey Boy's dad and wrapped his arms around the shoulders of the sobbing man. Another family member emerged from the room and led him, still weeping, from the building.

'I feel so responsible,' Teddy said through a sigh, as he took his seat next to Billie again. 'If I'd flagged up the protection racket years ago, things may never have got this far.'

'Or your business might have been burned down earlier,' Billie replied. She knew that there was no easy solution to violence instigated by local gangs, let alone international ones. 'Here, take a look at this. Do you recognise her?' Billie clicked on her mobile and brought up the photo of the skeleton bride as a young girl in Srebrenica.

'That's *Irina*! She looks younger than I remember her, of course, but what's she got to do with anything? She must be in her forties now.'

'Unlikely to have made it out of her teens, I'm afraid. She's the skeleton in the chimney.' Billie registered the look of total shock and horror on Teddy's face.

'But, I thought she'd ran away...' Teddy rubbed his hand over his mouth. Billie thought he might be about to throw up.

'Ran away from what, Teddy? Look, Irina, the body found in Ellis's back garden, and Ozzie Kingsnorth all appear to have been branded with a wasp tattoo. We think they are linked to people traffickers and that Eddie Checkley is at least high up in the pecking order. Was Irina trafficked?' Teddy scratched his head, deep in thought.

'Eddie's dad and mine jointly bought up all the old terraces

278

on one side of our little street, bar Uncle Tommy's place. He was more a distant relative, especially with being a magistrate during his spare time, at the local court. My dad and Eddie's were always wheeling and dealing so they kept him at arm's length. He was my favourite, though, and I was always bunking off to his to get a bit of peace.

'At our gaff, Eddie's dad and mine were always kicking off, squaring up to each other. We were the original dysfunctional family. I'm pretty sure they used the terraces as a brothel when I think about it now, but then, as a kid, I had no idea why all the new girls kept arriving, many of them foreign. They kept piles of dicey stuff up in the attics too. I once saw a gun in a bag there and sacks that I'm guessing were full of drugs. That all seemed to kick off big time after my dad died in a car accident. Spun off the road and hit a tree. Hadn't had his brakes checked apparently. Eddie got all the houses then.'

Billie exchanged glances with Ellis who had stopped dead in his tracks.

'Where was Eddie's brother, James, during all this?' She had to know.

Teddy shrugged. 'Off at some posh boarding school. He was just a little kid then, younger than me. And he had a different mother to Eddie. Bit like he lived on another planet really. Never saw him around our street growing up.'

Billie breathed out a quiet sigh of relief.

'So what do you know about this Irina?' Ellis asked Teddy. 'Did you know she was stuffed up the chimney all this time?' Billie could see that with his girls both currently AWOL, Ellis wasn't in the mood to gently coax out information. Her own judgement so far was that Teddy was simply another victim of Eddie Checkley's various illegal and cruel endeavours.

'No!' Teddy protested, so that the receptionist looked up

279

over her specs and held her finger to her lips. 'No,' he answered again, quietly but firmly. 'But I think some of those foreign girls were married off. Fake weddings to get a passport maybe, or for Eddie's mates to claim extra benefits perhaps...'

'How old were you when your dad copped it then?' Ellis looked like he still needed some convincing.

'Twelve,' Teddy answered. 'Mum had long ago done a runner, so Uncle Tommy took me in. But I knew how to access all of the houses, through the top attic rooms. They were joined, you see, and when I was a kid, I used to take out certain bricks so that I could squeeze through from one to the other. I showed Irina how to do it one day, after I'd seen Eddie hitting her, through a hole in the floorboards above one of the houses.'

'So you spoke with Irina?' Billie's ears pricked up. Teddy nodded sadly.

'Yeah, Irina was kind to me, and she wasn't that much older. She told me that she wanted to go back home. She'd been sent to England to finish her education, because of that fighting kicking off in Bosnia, remember? But she said she was trapped. She missed her grandad...' Teddy wiped his eyes. 'So I showed her how to get across to Uncle Tommy's attic. I told her that I would leave the front door open when I went to school, so that she could get across and run away. I thought she had. Never saw or heard from her anymore...'

'Did you never light a fire in the room then?' Ellis looked confused.

'No. We never even went in from one month to the next. Back then, the front room was always kept tidy. Just like everyone else, we only used that when visitors came and me and Uncle Tommy, well, we never had any. More or less lived in the back of the house, overlooking the garden.' Teddy closed his eyes tightly. Billie guessed that he was imagining the awful scenario that had taken place as Irina had slowly died a harrowing death, only a room away. 'Maybe someone sussed what she was up to, chased her and she couldn't make it out of the attic, so tried to hide in the...'

'How's the girl?' Ellis stopped a doctor who had raced to take Lily inside on arrival from the ambulance.

'Too early to tell,' she answered. 'She's being treated now and is stable, but not conscious yet.' Ellis spun around, blowing out his lips in exasperation as Billie's mobile rang. It was Josta.

'Hello, dear heart, I'm just ringing to see how Ash is getting on?'

'Ash?' Billie frowned. 'I haven't heard from him since he was at the crime scene with you. He said that he was heading home to bed, he had a bit of an upset tum—'

'Oh, my apologies, haven't you heard? He collapsed and was whisked off to the hospital.'

'I'm at the hospital now, but I didn't know that Ash was here.' Billie ran her fingers through her hair as Ellis stopped pacing and Teddy looked up, worried. Ellis marched over to the receptionist sitting at a desk.

'Has a DS Ash Sanghera been admitted tonight?' he asked.

'Ward five,' the receptionist replied. Billie, who had overheard the conversation, had ended her call and was already marching at speed along the corridor, following signs with ward directions listed on them. Ellis and Teddy followed close behind. As Billie stopped outside of the ward and pulled the door open, a tiny but fierce-looking nurse descended on her like a Rottweiler.

'You can't come in here, it's well after visiting time,' she announced, at the very moment that Ash appeared in a hospital gown, dragging a drip behind him.

'Ash,' Billie called, moving the nurse firmly to one side as she rushed over to her friend.

'Make it quick,' the nurse snapped, clearly realising that she wouldn't win the fight, but standing against the door to ensure that Ellis and Teddy didn't follow.

'Are you okay?' Billie held Ash's shoulders, looking aghast at the paleness of his face.

'Yeah, yeah, just a spot of food poisoning they reckon. They're keeping me in on fluids overnight and running a few tests. I'm feeling like a right wuss, taking up a bed when someone else needs it.' Ash sighed.

'Don't be crazy. You deffo look like *you* need it,' Billie reassured Ash.

'Hey thanks. You know how to make a guy feel better,' he joked weakly.

'So what have you eaten?' Billie took Ash's arm and helped him towards the bed area.

'I only had that coffee. We've been way too busy to knock back any sarnies today after all. But you had a coffee too,' he added before turning quickly. 'Oh, I need the bathroom again,' he moaned, trying to pick up pace towards a door off the nurses' station.

'I didn't drink it,' Billie explained. 'It tasted bitter... hang on, did the canteen staff make it for you or–'

'No,' Ash started to say before he picked up more speed, dragging his drip clumsily into the bathroom behind him and slamming the door shut. The final word of his answer was muffled, as he concentrated on making it to the toilet just in time.

'Who gave it to you then?' Billie held her ear against the door, having failed to catch his answer.

'I need the netty.' An old man had appeared in the corridor, walking towards the nurse like a pyjama-wearing zombie.

'There's another one just along the corridor, Wilf, pet. Look, you really need to go,' the nurse snapped at Billie.

'Ash, who gave you the coffee?' Billie called more loudly.

'Nurse!' Another voice bellowed from one of the side wards. 'I can't sleep for all the racket out there!'

'Too late,' the old man announced, emptying his bladder on the floor. Tears of embarrassment started to trickle down his cheeks. The nurse closed her eyes for a moment, looking completely at the end of her tether. Billie could hear nothing but moans and bowel-emptying sounds from the direction of Ash.

'Don't get yourself upset, Wilf. Come on, I'll get you cleaned up. It's no bother.' The nurse managed to paste on a sympathetic smile. Billie sighed. Maybe she was letting her imagination run amok. She stepped away from the bathroom door and enveloped the diminutive nurse in her arms.

'What you need, my love, is one big hug.' Billie almost lifted her off the floor with her bear hug before releasing her. The nurse blinked, looking astonished.

'I'm on till seven in the morning. I'll keep a close eye on him,' she whispered as Billie, reminded herself that the small nurse with the big heart could probably beat her hands down in a shit day at work competition. The moment was broken as Ellis suddenly slung the door open. It crashed loudly against the wall.

'Got to run.' He waved his mobile phone towards Billie. 'Just got an alert from my new CCTV system. Someone's skulking around my gaff.' The sleepless patient started complaining loudly again. Billie nodded a thanks to the nurse as she gave up trying to interrogate Ash and instead headed after Ellis who had already turned and started moving fast along the corridor. She jogged alongside him.

'Any idea who it is?' Billie asked as she steered him out of the way of a hospital trolley he was in danger of smashing into, so intent was he at monitoring his mobile phone screen. Ellis shrugged.

'Dunno, but one thing's for sure. With my luck, it's hardly likely to be the tooth fairy.'

Chapter 41

Live in the Moment

'Stop here,' Ellis instructed Billie as she turned her car into his street. He was still looking at his mobile. 'They're still mooching around, probably dumping another stiff. Here's hoping they drop down dead with fright when I tap them on the shoulder.'

'You don't think they really are?' Teddy whispered nervously to Billie, as she cut the engine. Ellis had already opened his door and jumped onto the pavement, staying close to the garden walls, his dark shadow merging with the those of the trees and shrubs as he moved stealthily along the quiet street.

'We'll soon find out. Stay back here in the car, if you like,' Billie added. She opened her own door to follow. Sometimes she had to remind herself that not everyone was comfortable with killers and corpses.

'No way, we're family, and family stick together.' Teddy slipped out of his own seat and alighted onto the pavement behind Billie. Sometimes she thought Teddy was under the impression that Ellis and she were a married couple rather than business partners, but now wasn't the time to remind him of that, or the fact that Eddie Checkley was part of his family too and hadn't exactly done him any favours.

'Just stay quiet and stick behind me,' Billie answered. She followed Ellis's route via the shadows to where scraps of scene-of-crime tape, the sad streamers of death, still fluttered in the late-night breeze. Billie could hardly believe how recently it had been that they had all been having a jolly time painting the house, getting ready to pick up Maya from the airport, with Ellis full of plans to host Connie's birthday in the garden. The words 'live in the moment' held a special resonance for Billie. Although it was Ellis whose life had currently been flung into such turmoil, she knew from her own experiences that no one in the world ever knew what life was about to throw up at any moment.

'Gotcha!' Billie heard a small squeal of shock even as she approached the gate. Ellis was clearly not in the mood to waste time. She whipped out her torch, flipped it on and was alongside him in seconds, years of police training instantaneously kicking in. A young man with dark curled hair screwed up his eyes in discomfort at the strong beam of light, as Ellis propelled him back towards the porch.

'Who are you and what's your game here? Spill.' Ellis's voice had a threatening air.

'I'm Maya's friend.' The young man spoke quietly.

'She's not here,' Ellis answered. 'When did you last see her?' Billie noted Ellis immediately springing into interview mode. Never one to miss an opportunity.

'Lunchtime today,' the young man replied, shocking them all into momentary silence.

'Where is she?' Billie suddenly found her voice.

Jake looked around. 'Can I come in? I need to tell you everything, but you'll have to act quickly, or it'll be too late.'

'I have to admit, this sounds crazy, mate. You're not stringing me a line?' Ellis scratched his head as Jake took a breath from recounting his story and paused for a swig of strong tea. Jake shook his head.

'Maya gave me your address, so I came straight here. The word is that there are people placed in the police working undercover for the gang, so I didn't want to go there to report it. I mean it's not that far-fetched an idea. We come across a lot of that stuff with our environmental group Green Planet. Undercover cops. You would think that they would put their energy into catching people traffickers rather than those of us trying to save the planet.'

Billie tried not to catch Ellis's eye. She knew for a fact that he'd been there and done that in his past.

'Maya's mum was a big environmental activist,' Ellis said quietly.

'Yes, when we did that charity modelling gig, she told me all about it.' Jake smiled for a moment. 'It's probably the sense of wanting fair play from her mother's genes and bringing people to justice via yours that's got her in this fix.'

'I swear to God, I'll kill the bastards that have done this!' Ellis banged his mug down on the table, slopping the contents over the side.

'So, you've explained how Maya has come to be on the ship. Where is it going to dock, so that we can get her off?' Billie was keen to pin down hard facts.

'It's not going to dock anytime soon. It was in port in the Netherlands yesterday briefly to stock up on supplies, which included Maya and the other girls. Super trawlers stay out at sea for months, that's how they can hide the crew. No one can see what they are up to, and they move from one sea or ocean to another, skirting constantly around national jurisdictions, by re-registering, re-flagging and renaming the ships. This one is currently sailing under a British flag and is named *The Wasp*.'

'But you have some idea of where it's heading?' Ellis demanded.

Jake nodded. 'Yes, supplies are brought to and taken from the factory ship by smaller vessels. Time is against us now, but I took photos of the navigation charts and I'm pretty sure that some of the girls, hopefully to include Maya, are going to be transferred from *The Wasp* out at sea, around dawn and then dropped off at a pick-up point about four miles off the coast here. It's where they take the people who have been matched for organ transplants.'

'What?' Billie gasped, the hazy photo of Jemal sweeping through her brain.

'I'm afraid so. I couldn't believe it myself at first. Does anyone have access to a boat?'

Ellis and Billie immediately turned their gaze to Teddy, who looked like a man with nowhere to hide.

Chapter 42

Birds In A Cage

'What time is it do you think?' Bluey asked. She had just woken from a fretful slumber. The girls were lying on sacking in the dark hold which had been rolling for hours on the waves. 'Dunno, maybe the middle of the night,' Maya answered. It was largely quiet above decks now, save for the crashing of waves against the side of the ship and the loud noise of the fish factory seemingly never-ending, somewhere even further below. The girls had been given overalls to wear and fish and rice to eat, along with water, all of which had been devoured as though they had been starving animals, but they had been otherwise left alone and untouched, for which Maya was hugely grateful.

She had heard noise and clanging hours ago now and desperately hoped that it was the sound of the boat arriving to take Jake home. Maya felt a sudden surge of emotion. She so wished that she had been leaving with him. Amsterdam was only just over an hour away from Newcastle, her home airport, where Jake had been heading. Hopefully he had made contact with her dad and Billie by now and they would be waiting with an army of police at the next port they stopped off at. Then this complete nightmare would be over.

'What's that?' Bluey jumped at the sound of boots on metal, running down steps towards them at the same time as a thud knocked against the side of the ship. The bolts of the door were suddenly drawn back followed by it being flung open.

'Okay, let's go.' A man shone a torch around the girls, who gingerly got to their feet and started walking. He put his hand up.

'Only the ones with red boiler suits,' he said to a girl who Maya could now see in the torchlight had been given blue overalls. He shone his torch up and down Maya.

'It seems you have good body parts, baby.' He winked at her. 'You too, come.' He waved at Bluey and a couple of the other girls.

'What does he mean?' Bluey asked, clinging to Maya's side.

'We are being processed, just like the fish,' one of the other girls whispered. 'The tests they did on us in Germany.'

Maya frowned. 'What tests?' They were being hustled by more than one man up the metal staircase from one deck to another.

'You swapped with that Italian girl, right?' the fourth girl said. 'Don't worry, your secret is safe. The rest of us here had tests before the auction, blood tests...' Maya thought she might be sick. 'My cousin had her kidney taken when she was kidnapped. She became very ill. No good for the men anymore so she was dumped back in my home village.'

Her words caught on the wind that hit the girls with full force as they alighted onto the main deck, clinging onto anything they could, as the waves crashed against the side of the ship sending spray high up into the air. Maya caught her breath as the icy spatters hit her face, the wind tearing at her hair. Above, a Wolf Moon and a thousand stars twinkled brightly. Before them stood the tall fair Englishman who had bid in the auction. He didn't seem to realise that he had been duped and right now Maya didn't feel like telling him. If she had swapped with a valuable organ donor then the grim-faced buyer might throw her overboard, like Ozzie Kingsnorth.

'Okay, let's go.' He snapped his fingers like a man not used to waiting. Suddenly Maya heard a loud whirring sound and stepped back, her attention caught upwards to an onboard crane. It had started to lower a bell-shaped enclosure down towards them. It was open save for the arched rods of steel sitting on what looked to Maya like a tyre.

'Get inside.' The man who had spoken to Maya earlier, now poked her in the back.

'What...?' Maya started to ask, before the Englishman flicked his head and the discussion was over. Maya was picked up and thrown into the cage with Bluey right behind her. The other two girls, kicking and crying, were similarly hauled inside, like birds trapped in a cage, before the door was slammed shut and fastened.

As the contraption started to move upwards, swinging perilously in the gusting wind, like a crazed fairground ride, the girls held on to the steel rails for dear life. A smaller boat to one side of the ship was visible now. Maya hoped it was that, rather than the sea, that was to be their destination. She stared at the Englishman, refusing to show her terror. If she ever got out of this, she would never forget his face, even though the haunting screams of Bluey and the other girls clouded her brain for a moment, before being torn away by the wind, somewhere far off across the dark rolling sea.

As the crane swung out, huge waves roared up around them, the taste of salt stinging Maya's lips. She closed her eyes, feeling her stomach lurch as the crane steadied its movement and started to winch them down. She hoped this was all part of the plan that Jake had found out about, desperately praying that the four of them weren't about to be spirited away in another direction, far out of reach of her dad and Billie Wilde.

Chapter 43

A Room With a View

Nautical twilight made an enchanting entrance as Teddy Cook, assisted by Jake, edged his small fishing boat, the *Silver Darling*, nearer to the huge wind turbine. It soared over 100 metres high, taller than Big Ben, and was one of a handful of offshore structures standing about four miles off the coast.

Billie could see nothing but waves in all directions, save for the lightening sky, streaked with crimson on the horizon, topped with a pale band of yellow then blue, the inky dark sky above still scattered with a million stars. The sensation was breathtaking, making Billie feel very small in the world. She hoped it wouldn't be the last view such as this that she would ever witness. She was in no doubt, especially now that they had arrived at the location, how easily this quickly cobbled together plan could spin totally out of control.

The sun would be up within half an hour, Teddy explained, hence the need to drop Ellis and Billie off quickly. During the night, Jake had passed on all of the information that he had managed to glean. Hopefully Maya and a handful of others would be dropped off at the wind turbine, owned by the same international company as *The Wasp*. Eddie Checkley would be with them, though Jake couldn't confirm if he would be alone or accompanied by other crew members. He had heard that a haul of other items of a dubious nature had already been deposited at that location. Possibly drugs or weapons.

Soon after the arrival of the girls, another small boat would arrive from the UK coastline and take the combined stash of merchandise to land. The girls would then be taken onwards by road to their specific destination.

'I'm willing to stay, if you'd like,' Jake offered. Both Ellis and Billie shook their heads, mutually preferring to rely on one another and their high-level police training. Though grateful for the offer from the brave young man, they had both made the unspoken judgement that he would only get in the way, should any trouble kick off and Billie was certain that it would be impossible to completely avoid it.

'Don't let me down, mate. I *can* trust you, yeah?' Ellis slapped Teddy on the back as he brought the *Silver Darling* tight alongside the structure.

'You've just seen the state of my place. If I can build it up again, I want to get free of the Checkleys once and for all. Anyway, where am I going to doss down if my old cuz doesn't return the favour by letting me stay at his place for a bit?' he said, trying to make a small joke. 'But seriously, mate, take care of yourself. I'll be back with the cavalry as soon as we've waited long enough for the drop-off and have the all-clear from you.'

Billie hoped that he was telling the truth. She had her mobile on her, but the chances of calling for help from four miles out in the North Sea would be hit and miss. She had left a message on Ash's answer service, giving him an overview and requesting assistance. She prayed that he was waking up about now and would be well enough today to act upon it.

After much thought both she and Ellis had decided not to try and rouse any of the police MIT themselves. Ellis still wasn't completely cleared in relation to Slug's death and if the threats made to keep people quiet were true rather than a ruse, then they might have alerted the very people who were allegedly on Eddie Checkley's payroll. It was certain that should that happen, then both she, Ellis and more importantly to both of them, Maya, would end up following Ozzie Kingsnorth's watery journey.

On the other hand, if the police weren't crooked, then they would surely have banned both Billie and Ellis from attending, on the basis that they weren't arresting officers. That thought wiped any idea of officially spilling the beans to anyone but Ash permanently from their minds.

Billie balanced on the edge of the boat as it swayed crazily up and down, bounced by the high waves crashing against the side of the turbine's normal landing spot from which a bright-yellow-painted transition ladder led fifteen metres up to the first landing stage. Ellis had already made it across and was clambering up to a base platform, but it was by no means an easy transfer. Billie knew that one slip-up as she crossed would suck her down into the depths of the sea. Teddy had explained that normally carabiners would be used to transfer safely. No sane technician would even think of following in Ellis's treacherous footsteps.

Billie gritted her teeth, silently telling herself that beggars couldn't be choosers. She balanced, waited for the right moment and then half stepped, half jumped across to the lowest rung, gripping the slippery metal for dear life, before quickly scuttling up to breathlessly join Ellis, the waves surging up even as she reached relative safety. Teddy backed the *Silver Darling* away as Ellis opened the metal door leading to the interior of the white tower.

'Jake said that the haul already dropped off will be in the nacelle.' Billie looked around the metallic interior which largely consisted of a tube with metal ladders leading upwards. 'Where's that?'

'Up at the top. Better get cracking. I want to have eyes on them before they get a chance to have eyes on us.' Ellis patted the binoculars strung across his chest. 'Just one hundred metres or so to the next bit.' Despite the fact that his face until now had been etched with worry, he actually managed a wink and a smile. 'You go up first. If I fall at least I'll get a good view on my death bed,' he joked.

'Perv.' Billie elbowed him. 'Woke police would have you cancelled for life for a remark like that.'

'I feel like I have been cancelled for life, so nothing to lose there then. Get a move on.' Ellis waved to the ladder. Billie looked up. She was pretty fit, but the climb looked never-ending with no safety net in view should she slip on a rung and despite Ellis's jesting, the chances were that she would take him down with her. She took a deep breath and set off, trying not to think of the distance between her body and the floor as she climbed ever higher.

The nacelle, Billie discovered as she lay panting for breath on the floor of it, was the heart of the wind turbine, a large pod holding the rotor blades at one end attached to a hub and all of the engineering paraphernalia needed to make a turbine work inside. The room was slightly swaying from side to side.

'Talk about a room with a view.' Ellis had already descended the final small staircase, opened the hatch and popped his head out, using his binoculars to scan the surrounds.

'Any sign of them yet?' Billie asked, finally managing to come to a sitting position.

'Not yet. But I'm guessing that stuff loaded up over there is worth a pretty penny, so we're unlikely to be stood up.' Ellis's attention was taken by a pile of black bags partly tucked underneath the large controller unit. He crossed over and unzipped them. The bags seemed to be full of what appeared to be packets of heroin and cocaine. 'There could be firearms amongst this stuff too. Let's not underestimate who we're dealing with,' he said, a steely tone to his voice.

'So we have to keep our heads.' Billie pulled herself up, worried that Ellis wouldn't be able to resist springing into action the moment he set eyes on Maya.

'If I have my way, someone will be losing theirs,' Ellis answered gruffly. 'I'm guessing they will be hanging out here waiting for the pick-up, or in the yaw chamber we climbed through, right below. There's nowhere else, so let's remove this little lot out of harm's way.' He picked up two of the bags holding the stash. Billie reached for another two bags. 'Follow me, ma'am, whilst I take you to the best room in the house.'

Ellis led the way up the short metal staircase. Billie followed, emerging onto the very top of the turbine, stunned by the view for miles around, with only a waist-high, bright-red fence between them and the sky and sea. She could imagine what it felt like to be a bird. She also realised that up here, there were few places to hide from view.

They moved up and down the staircase, piling the bags in a row rather like sandbags in a war bunker, around the edges of the red fence.

'At least this gives us some cover while we're waiting.' Billie lay flat on the platform zipping her jacket up high as she did so, against the whipping icy cold wind. Ellis lay down in a similar position, scanning the view with his binoculars. Billie looked down at the crashing waves. It was a spectacular sight but there was no way anyone could survive a fall into the water. If they weren't dead on impact then the temperature of the sea would freeze them to death, sucked into a watery grave within minutes. Clearly Ellis had been thinking the same thing. He had started humming an ancient song that Billie's dad had been fond of, 'The Ocean Burial'. She wished he would stop. He lowered his binoculars having scanned the horizon.

'Sorry I got you into this, Billie. I know it's madness, us stuck up here like sitting ducks should a boat full of Eddie Checkley's cronies arrive with him.'

'All for one and one for all, my fellow musketeer,' Billie said, trying to make a joke of it, though right now, she was trying hard not to have second thoughts herself. Ellis gave a rueful smile.

'You are one in a million, Billie. Honest. There's no one else I'd rather be perched on the top of a giant windmill with. I'm just hoping the other brother isn't with him. Chances are he's as bad.'

'No, he's okay.' The words tumbled out of Billie's mouth before she could stop them.

'You know him?' Ellis must have recognised the look that Billie tried to hide too quickly, because he appeared momentarily shocked then hurt. He turned away and shrugged.

'Hey, none of my business. No skin off my nose if one brother is shagging the ex and the other one my business partner. Probably both have had a go at my oldest daughter and God knows about the youngest—'

'That's not fair!' Billie said, shocked by Ellis's reaction.

'You said it,' Ellis snapped back, holding his binoculars up again. Billie noticed his demeanour stiffen. 'Something coming our way. You haven't made a date for today with lover boy, have you?'

'What? Are you accusing me of being in on this thing?' Billie was stunned.

'I don't know who I can trust anymore and that's a fact. For all I know Ash is the inside copper and he's the only one we've told.'

'Yeah, well he voiced similar doubts about you the other day, when you were seen on CCTV hanging around Slug Harris's car not long before the brake leads snapped, just after you'd made threats.'

'I felt like killing him.' Ellis lifted his binoculars and scanned the scene again. 'But I didn't. Look, I'm sorry about what I just said there.'

'Forget it,' Billie answered tersely. 'This is all part of the investigation into Ozzie Kingsnorth's death, so let's just cut the happy chat and concentrate on the job.'

'Yeah. I said I'm sorry... it's just... look, I do appreciate this, what you're doing. It's none of my business who you hang out with. I'll pay you back for this, I promise.' Ellis rubbed his face sheepishly.

'Knock yourself out. If either of us is still alive,' Billie answered, not in the mood to kiss and make up right now. It was one thing for her to lie here wondering if she'd made yet another major cock-up with a lover, quite another for Ellis to flag it up.

They both fell into an awkward silence as they watched the little boat becoming more than just a speck on the horizon. It was definitely moving in their direction.

Chapter 44

A Final Journey

Maya shivered as she was prodded up the short staircase of the small boat onto the slippery wet deck. The sky was steely grey streaked with pale orange, but it was the view looming in front of her that grabbed Maya's attention. She, and the other girls huddled alongside her, were staring at a vast wind turbine rising so high up from the sea that it seemed to penetrate the clouds above.

The boat was so close now, tossing from side to side like a cork, that she could hardly see to the very top of the tower, save for the three gigantic blades, white and smooth and still against the stormy sky. As they approached the yellow-painted base, waves gurgled and crashed with force. The journey from the huge boat to this vessel had been terrifying enough, but Maya had a feeling that this transfer was going to be even worse.

As a crew member tied the boat with some difficulty to the metal steps, the surly-faced English man moved from boat to metal stairs and upwards like someone who hadn't been making the perilous crossing for the first time. He opened the door to the interior of the tower and shouted, 'Move.'

'No, I can't do it, I can't!' Bluey cried in a terrifying wail that reflected the way that Maya was feeling, though she tried hard not to show it. She glanced up to the sky, praying that there was someone up there looking out for her, but all she could see was the red cage at the top of the tower, edged with black, rather than any guardian angel smiling down from the clouds. She stiffened, determined to brazen it out.

'I'll go first, then you follow.' She hugged Bluey close, before the screaming girl was dragged back to allow Maya to step on the edge of the boat. One of the crewmen took her arm, nodding encouragement. For one warped moment, Maya thought that he looked like a sweet encouraging father, before focusing her mind on the situation that she was truly in.

A huge wave suddenly crashed against the side of the boat, taking her breath away with the icy coldness of the water, which almost dragged her overboard and deep down as it sank. The man steadied her.

'Go quickly,' he said. Maya took a leap and grabbed the slippery wet rails, feeling her legs being dragged away from her with the force of another huge wave. She gripped tightly, refusing to give up, paddling her legs furiously until her feet made contact with the rungs, then pulled herself up, almost collapsing at the feet of the English man.

She turned to wave on Bluey who was trying to wrestle away from two other crew members, screaming madly, before the other girls took their own leaps of faith and followed her up the ladder. Both scuttled on hands and knees behind Maya into the safety of the interior of the tower, gasping for breath and trying to control tears of shock and terror. Maya pulled herself up and made for the open door again. The English man moved his leg to prevent her leaving.

'Get a fucking move on!' he shouted as the two crew members hauled Bluey onto the side of the boat, Maya's helper moving back to try and control the vessel, which was rolling even more now, as the wind and sea whipped even higher.

'You can do it, Bluey.' Maya defied the English man, leaning her body out to encourage the desperate girl, who looked at her for a moment, seeming to calm herself. She stretched her plump leg out nervously, bare feet still showing chipped blue toenails, before taking a small leap just at the moment a huge wave crashed against the steps. When the blinding whirlpool of spray cleared, Bluey had totally disappeared from view.

Maya could hear a piercing scream fill the air, but it wasn't Bluey or any of the shocked-looking crew members making the noise and certainly not the furious English man. She suddenly realised that the ghastly sound was actually coming from her.

'Oh my God, that's my baby!' Ellis tried to scramble to his feet from behind the bags disguising their whereabouts, on hearing the scream below. Billie pinned him down, with her arm firmly around his shoulders.

'Don't move. Maya's okay. I can see her. She's okay,' Billie whispered.

'But...' Ellis started to argue.

'Someone else didn't make the crossing,' Billie said quietly, taking a moment to still herself. From her vantage point she had seen Bluey fall into the water. No matter how hideous the scene was, nothing that she nor Ellis could do would save the girl. It was already too late.

'Oh Christ,' Ellis half sobbed into his sleeve. Billie kept her arm around Ellis, trying to steady her breathing, their spat and joint silence of the last half hour now history. She was well aware that every fibre of his body would be urging him to spring into action with his darling daughter so near and yet still in such terrible danger. But the wrong move could sign all of their death warrants.

'We've got to stay still, stay focused. Wait for the boat to leave,' Billie whispered.

'Fuck off now, you idiot, that'll be another one hundred grand on top of what you already owe me! That one was a triple match. We'll have to stand down a whole medical crew this afternoon, you utter tosser,' Eddie Checkley shouted across to the white-faced man who had helped Maya to make the crossing, as the boat rapidly backed up away from the wind turbine and turned to face the direction from which it had come.

'I swear to God,' Ellis muttered, clenching his fists. Billie didn't know if she could keep him pinned down much longer. She was having trouble staying still herself.

'Look, it's going. There were four men on board. Three have left. Seems only Eddie Checkley's staying with us.'

'I'll kill the bastard...' Ellis swore. Billie had no doubt he meant every word yet didn't feel it was the perfect time to remind him that they needed to keep Eddie Checkley intact – if only to find out where Connie was.

As the boat that had deposited Eddie Checkley and the girls disappeared into the distance, quiet seemed to envelop the turbine for a matter of minutes. Billie and Ellis pulled themselves up to a sitting position, straining their ears in order to hear any movement over the roar of the waves.

'There's no way he'll risk bringing the girls up the ladders,' Ellis whispered. 'But he's going to have to come looking for his drugs stash and when he can't find it down below here, he's going to be coming through that hatch. I'll be waiting.' He held up the heavy bit of steel equipment, much like a spanner, that he had found whilst rummaging in an open box of tools in the nacelle. Billie had something similar clutched in her hand. She hoped it would be enough. In this day and age, international traffickers of people and drugs were hardly likely to stick to the UK's gun licensing laws. In their desperate haste, they had come woefully unprepared.

Billie glanced down at her mobile. She had set it to silent and until now, there had been a *no signal* sign, but as the sun had come fully up and the sea had calmed a little, she tried once again to text Ash, warning him to bring an armed cavalry ASAP. She hoped that this time the message would hit home.

'Here comes the collection boat.' Ellis ducked down again, pulling Billie with him, as a speedboat could be seen heading towards them fast from the direction of land.

'It might be Ash.' Billie prayed that she was right.

'It might be a pile of Checkley's cronies armed up to the hilt too. Oh, here comes lover boy now.' Ellis stopped speaking to listen. The sound of footsteps climbing the tower clanged up towards them. 'Maybe I should go down there and stamp on his fingers. That would finish the bastard off good and proper.'

'We need him to tell us where Connie is.' Billie finally said the words she'd been hedging around. Ellis looked crestfallen at the reminder but nodded his head in agreement.

'I'll just have to cosh him with this when he sticks his head through the hatch here. You got your cuffs on you?'

'Yes,' Billie whispered. They could hear Eddie Checkley right below them now. His heavy breathing, huffs of annoyance and then his voice on his phone. At least that meant that there was a possibility that her own messages had got through.

'Where the fuck is the stuff? This has been a total cock-up. Just lost two kidneys and a good heart and now the stash isn't in position...' He seemed to be listening. 'Yes, I've looked everywhere except up the top and who would be fucking crazy enough to stash it out in the open air?'

The speedboat could be seen arriving up against the landing ladders below. Billie could observe only one person driving. She had no idea if they were male or female, so wrapped up were they against the weather, with hooded oilskin and scarf around their face. If there were other crew Billie expected them to be below deck. The sound of Eddie Checkley now starting to climb the short staircase up to the hatch meant that there was no more time to dwell upon the matter.

Ellis quickly moved behind the hatch opening, in order to catch Eddie Checkley unawares. Billie slid behind a pile of bags to the side, exchanging glances with Ellis and holding her breath as the hatch door was suddenly flung open. Before Ellis had an opportunity to lean forward and swing a carefully aimed spanner at their target, an arm shot out holding a gun and fired four shots, the first one aimed backwards, the three others in a circle, one missing Billie's head by millimetres. She ducked, then looked up again as she heard Ellis groan and fall back on the flooring with a resounding thud.

'Thought there must be something up, motherfucker.' Eddie Checkley had quickly rushed up onto the deck and was now leaning over Ellis. Billie scuttled behind him silently on hands and knees, her heart in her mouth. From the noise that Ellis was making it sounded like he had been seriously hurt. 'Oh dear, if it isn't my girl's old shag boy. Well, this will be the end of the child access malarkey.'

Billie knew that she probably only had one chance at this as she swiftly moved towards him, both hands holding the steel tool. She raised her arms high and brought them down forcefully, whacking Eddie Checkley as hard as she could with it. The implement made contact with a sickening crack, followed by a gasp as he dropped forward onto the deck.

Billie kicked the gun to one side, pulled his hands back and cuffed him, before shoving his body away to attend to Ellis who was covered in blood and gasping. Billie tore off her jacket, using her scarf to stem the blood pouring from Ellis's head somewhere near his left temple, hyper-aware that at least one other gang member must be on the turbine now. She wondered if this would be the end of the game, for her as well as Ellis.

'What the fuck's going on?' The new arrival was a woman, who had expertly secured the speedboat and arrived at the base of the tower, to the screams of the girls. They had heard the commotion up above and were hoping that somehow, technicians already in situ perhaps, had apprehended their captor and might be able to call for some sort of help.

'Shut it, bitches!' the woman shouted, skirting around the bodies who were cowering on the floor, surrounded by nothing but curved steel walls, the seemingly endless ladder going up, and the door out into the sea. Maya kept her head down. She knew that if her true identity was sussed she would be following poor sad Bluey. Tears trickled down her cheeks at the memory of the vulnerable girl's horrific end, as well as the thought that her own short life was possibly also about to be curtailed.

'Eddie, are you up there?' the female called. She sighed heavily when no sound was heard in reply and with an annoyed look on her face, started climbing the metal stairs upwards. Maya held her breath, following the woman's journey until her body and then feet disappeared from view.

'Eddie?' Maya heard her breathlessly call again from way up above. She had been hatching a plan. It was a crazy one, but the way Maya saw it, she wanted to live her life, as she was sure the others did, and this looked like a chance that was too good to miss. She kicked her foot out, touching the legs of the other girls.

'Let's go,' she whispered.

'Where?' one of the other girls whispered back.

'To freedom.' Maya waved them after her.

The door was still open out onto the landing base. Maya took a deep breath. The sea was calmer now than when they had arrived, but their escape still meant descending the precarious, wet, yellow-painted ladder on the outside of the tower, before leaping across the choppy waves crashing against the tower base, onto the speedboat. She turned around to the other two girls perched beside her on the landing deck. They looked terrified.

'I can't do it,' one said.

'What choice do we have?' Maya answered, before starting to descend the stairs. The others gingerly followed, terror rather than bravery urging them forward. In the end it took only one brave leap for each before they were in the boat and Maya was quickly untying it. As soon as the rope slid free, the boat drifted quickly backwards from the tower, pulled by some unseen current.

'What do we do now?' one of the girls cried, as a wave lifted them high.

'Learn how to drive this thing quickly,' Maya answered. Her dad had bought her car-driving lessons for her birthday, but she guessed that wasn't going to be much use right now. However, she had been on a boating weekend with a mate's family and had even had a little try at manoeuvring the vessel herself, so at least she had enough knowledge to get them the hell away from here. She pushed down the throttle and moved as quickly as she dared.

'Keep your heads down,' she called to the other two girls, sure she had heard gunshots from above earlier. She really couldn't face any other horrific surprises today.

'Ellis?' Billie moved Ellis into the recovery position. The trouble was, he didn't look much like he was recovering. Blood was already seeping through the scarf that she had tied around his head. Eddie Checkley suddenly groaned. Billie reached for the tool and whacked him over the head again. She wasn't in the mood to play Florence Nightingale with him. Her main concern right now was Ellis.

'Ellis, come on, wake up. Don't go checking out on me now.' She sat back on her knees, glancing up as she heard the speedboat quickly moving away, wondering whether she should shout for help, but telling herself instead, to get real. She couldn't imagine that there was anyone in the speedboat who would want either Ellis or her to stay alive.

Billie grabbed her mobile and tried to ring Ash again, leaving an urgent voice message as she ran her fingers through her hair in distress, well aware that it would surely only be a matter of time before some of Eddie Checkley's people would come looking for him. Sooner than she thought, as it turned out. She hadn't heard the woman emerging through the hatch behind her.

'Oh dear, Billie. Why did it have to end like this? Honest to God, I'm going to miss you.' Billie spun around to see a woman pulling down her hood and unwinding her scarf with one hand whilst holding a gun pointed towards her with the other. Billie was stunned to see such a familiar figure. She swallowed hard.

'Don't do this, Perry.' She glanced from Ellis to her erstwhile friend. 'He looks badly hurt. We need to get help.'

'We all need help, Billie.' Perry sighed. 'The trouble is some of us haven't got daddy's trust fund to help us out when times get tough. Some of us have had to make tough choices, in order to feed and clothe our kids. My two daughters don't come cheap.'

'But the lives of other young girls do?' Billie reasoned. 'And what about Ellis? He's got two girls—'

'Believe me, little Connie will be okay. Her new dad here is a Checkley after all and poor old Maya, well, she'll be earning her own keep by now spreading her legs somewhere.'

'You're bigger than this, Perry,' Billie persisted. 'A top journalist, great investigator, you've even won awards you said—'

'Yep. All that and more, Billie, and where has it got me, eh? Chasing my mortgage payments month to month, living hand to mouth, always trying to tell the truth of a story. Well now the truth is that I'm looking after myself for a change. Me and my own kids. I've tried to make an honest crust, but honesty doesn't pay these days. This job may be less than regular but when the call comes to play, it pays big money and I want my girls to have the best. Give them the sort of start that people like *you* had in life—'

Perry's words were cut off as she looked up and suddenly realised that the speedboat had already sped away across the water. Billie didn't quite know what was happening, but the outcome didn't look good, for any of them. She could see by the shock on Perry's face that the boat leaving without her definitely hadn't been part of the plan.

'Looks like you've been left in the lurch again,' Billie answered. 'All right, you might have saved him,' she flicked her head Eddie Checkley's way, 'but he won't thank you for it. Not even if you let Ellis die and then kill me too. Loose lips sink ships, so to be on the safe side you'll just go missing. People will think the two of you have been in cahoots. Gone on the run or something. He's already in the frame for killing Ozzie Kingsnorth.' Perry touched Ellis with the tip of her boot. 'Or maybe that was you?' Billie realised that it suddenly all made sense.

'The threatening notes, so easy to send to Slug Harris when

you're working in the police headquarters. Your access to the same car park. You fessed up in Lilly's Landing that you know your way around the guts of a car. I'm guessing that it was you who bought the coffee Ash drank?' In her mind's eye, a memory flashed into view, of Perry standing by the graffiti on the interior wall of Wilde & Darque. 'I nearly caught you at it with your spray can at our place, after all.'

'Yeah, you always were the clever one. But that's not much use to you here and now,' Perry retorted.

'You're the clever one, Perry. You must be able to see that you know too much. Like I said, it'll be you or both of your girls washed up on the beach next. That's the way this business operates, and you know it.' Billie spoke slowly, trying to sound calm, though her heart was hammering against her chest. But even as she spoke she had heard a new noise in the distance now. She touched Ellis's hand hoping that time was with them.

'And anyway, the game's up. Ash knows all about this. Sounds like him and the MIT coming now...' Billie glanced behind her. Up in the air a helicopter was heading towards them at the same time that a Border Force cutter and a marine police vessel could be seen speeding their way.

'They don't know anything about me,' Perry answered, but Billie could see her mind working fast.

'How are you going to play this then? Say that you just dropped in to say hello when you swam out a bit too far?' Billie needled. 'You've got time to knock off me and Ellis, but as Steady Eddie here isn't exactly looking like Action Man right now, that's two murders you'll be taken in for. Bet your daughters would thank you for that and if you get time inside as you most surely will, your boss here will have you hanging in your cell way before you can give evidence against him. More shame for your precious kids.'

Perry suddenly gazed around her, the sound of the helicopter now almost overhead. She gave a shuddering sigh.

'You're right. It's always the little people who suffer in the end, the ones so desperate to make ends meet that they'll sell their souls to the Devil. But tell my girls this, Billie, that I loved them with all of my heart, and I tried to do *everything* in my power to give them a good life.' She turned, pointed the gun at Eddie Checkley and shot him in the head.

Billie was so startled and stunned that she was unable to stop Perry as she took an odd little run before launching herself over the safety fence, somersaulting downwards in a sickening spiral to the sea so very far below. She disappeared from view like a missile rocketing into the turbulent waves. Shaking, Billie jumped up, scouring the surface with her eyes. She even called out Perry's name once, madly thinking that perhaps her old friend could be saved, but her body was nowhere to be seen.

She had no more time to search. Ellis moaned loudly as he regained consciousness. She rushed over to help him, aware by the sound all around that help was finally at hand. Had Billie turned back a split second later to look one more time over the side, she might have noticed another body floating silently by. It was that of a young girl, real name unknown, her only crime in life that of having been born in the wrong place at the wrong time. As she was caught on a swell, small feet with chipped blue nail varnish on chubby toes were the last things on view, as Bluey changed direction and was swept away with her unborn baby on her final journey.

Chapter 45

Good Samaritan

Billie checked the clock on her dashboard, blowing out a sigh as she clambered into her car. It was nearly midnight, and she was bone tired, with so many emotions running through her mind. First of all, relief that both Maya and Ellis were okay. He had been airlifted straight to hospital thanks to Ash's foresight in bringing a well-equipped support team with him. The blood that had covered his head had been caused by the bullet taking off the top of his ear, Billie thanked God, rather than half of his brain.

He had been out of surgery and propped up on pillows in a ward for an hour now, thrilled to have Maya at his bedside. She had been showing him various silly face mock-ups featuring him wearing crazy wigs, on a phone app she had downloaded, suggesting he use one to disguise the new disfigurement. Billie reflected that it was always a good sign when someone was well enough to have the mickey taken out of them.

She smiled at the memory of some of the photos Maya had generated, full of admiration for the guts and strength the girl had shown in the face of such harrowing adversity. Maya had been kept in overnight, whilst the other two trafficked girls had been taken away after being interviewed, to some reception centre from which Billie desperately hoped a better future for them would be planned.

Billie only allowed herself now, all alone, to dwell on the vision of Perry's death. The memory would no doubt haunt her for years to come, another addition to the collection of PTSD images she had amassed by having lived a far from ordinary life. She hoped that Perry's girls would be okay, at the same time experiencing a disturbing thought, that perhaps the night that Perry had taken Abi under her wing, after the girl had been suicidal, had in fact been filled with threats and warnings rather than the budding friendships that Billie had hoped would ensue from that outing. A quick visit to Lily, thankfully recovering now, had confirmed that Perry had indeed been the 'police insider' she had hinted about. Billie shivered. It was time to go home.

As she turned on the car ignition, Billie's mobile rang. She answered it, hoping that Ellis hadn't had some sort of relapse. The feelings of utter panic and desperation that she had felt when Ellis had been shot hadn't escaped her, even hours later. It was impossible to imagine life without him. He was a much-loved mate and that was the truth. Was it *all* of the truth? Billie shrugged the thought away, deeming it unworthy of her time.

'Hello. Billie Wilde,' she answered, already opening the car door and dropping one leg out in case she had to rush back up to Ellis's ward.

'Hi, Billie, it's Pandy.' Billie blinked for a second, checked the clock on the dashboard again. 'Pandy Wood,' the hairdresser added, clearly taking Billie's lack of response to be due to a memory lapse rather than a reaction to the late time of the call. 'I'm at the shop. Can you come over please?' she asked.

'What *now?*' Billie inwardly groaned, seeing her huge

bedroom, bed piled high with soft pillows and windows overlooking the stunning Alnmouth Estuary, in her mind's eye.

'I've been trying to get in touch all day, but I couldn't get any answer,' Pandy explained. Billie could have run through all of her out-of-contact locations that day, including offshore wind turbine, high seas and various hospital waiting rooms, but Pandy already sounded stressed enough. 'Truly, it's urgent and I can't speak to anyone else.' Billie relented, reminding herself that it was always nice to be wanted, though that need had got her into trouble more than once.

'Okay, on my way. I'll see you in ten.' She ended the call, pulling out of the hospital car park as rain started to pelt the windscreen. She switched on the radio, turning it up loud to help her stay awake. The haunting song 'Stay Another Day' filled the car, before the radio DJ announced that Billie was listening to a competition, in which night owls had to ring in and guess the date of which New Year's Day the song had been top of the charts. Thelma from Gateshead announced that she'd got the CD along with a brand-new Discman, in her Christmas stocking in 1994.

'So I'm pretty sure it was still top of the charts on New Year's Day 1995.' Thelma sounded like she was catching her breath in excitement. Immediately a loud cheering jingle blasted out. The DJ announced that Thelma was a winner.

Billie thought of Irina the Skeleton Bride, who had died that same year. Had this song played out the background music to her last days on earth? She certainly hadn't been a winner. It was at that moment that Billie finally gave vent to her emotions, her nerves frayed to shreds by the various stresses and griefs of the day.

It wasn't the Billie Wilde that she liked anyone else to see, though for a short moment in time, she had thought that James Checkley might have been the soul with whom she could have finally shared her true emotions. She wondered if perhaps she was grieving the lost possibility with that relationship too after the day's events, or maybe experiencing conflict about her real feelings for Ellis? The release of emotions had been like a pressure cooker blowing. At the end of Pandy Wood's street, she stopped the car, blew her nose, wiped her face and steadied herself before moving forward again. Pandy was already out on the street awaiting her arrival.

'Oh, thank goodness you're here.' Pandy ran towards Billie the minute she had cut the engine and opened the car door.

'What's up?' Billie asked, playing it cool, though Pandy was clearly so tied up with her own emotional turmoil that she hadn't even noticed Billie's puffed eyes and blotched skin. Pandy grabbed Billie's wrist and propelled her forward into the shop. She slammed the door behind her, making sure that it was triple locked and the blind firmly down.

'You can't be too careful. If this gets out and people get the wrong end of the stick, it'll be curtains for me. Go through to the back,' Pandy added, gently pushing Billie forward through the hairdressing salon. Only the crack of light from outside, shining through the edge of the window blind, prevented Billie from tripping over one of the chairs.

'Well, if you can tell me—' Billie started, before she was given a little push in the back into a storage room. Pandy shut the door firmly behind her and finally switched on the light.

'Auntie Billie!' Connie shouted, jumping off a sofa where she had been snuggled alongside Viku, the young mother with the baby who Billie had met in Storm Benbow's salon. Billie swept Connie into her arms and gave her a tight hug, fearing that she might come over all emotional once again.

'I saw it on the news last night,' said Pandy. "Police are worried for the whereabouts of Connie Darque and her mother". I wanted to say, "Connie's here with the nanny and her

315

baby. I was just trying to be a Good Samaritan". But if I'd come clean, then Viku would have been carted off–'

'I do not have the visa, you see.' Viku looked nervous. 'I come from Ukraine where we have troubles... my husband was killed.' She paused, looking down to compose herself, gripping the baby close. 'I had to leave my town, Mariupol. My mother was killed too, in the war. I was told I can have visa, just to wait. My papers are still with visa office in Lviv. Then Connie's mother, she got in touch with me on social media and said that she could give me a home and a job. They had someone meet me at the border. Me and many other women, some with children. I don't know where they all went but I was brought here.'

'To work as a slave.' Billie looked from Viku to Pandy, grim-faced.

'Viku's the girl that I told you about before, who came asking for work at the salon,' Pandy explained as Viku looked worried about Billie's response and desperate now to explain her situation.

'But Storm found out about me trying to leave and said that she would tell the authorities. I haven't got any papers to prove that I was waiting for proper visa and she took my passport. She said that I would be arrested by the police. She said they would take my baby away.'

'So when she turned up in a right state just when I was closing the salon the other day, dragging the two kids, I hid her here–' Pandy was interrupted by Viku.

'I overheard them talking about selling body parts. I have the list here. I saw her write it down...' Viku dipped into her handbag and lifted out a folded sheet of paper. She handed it to Billie. 'I was scared. I heard her say that they needed a heart for a baby. When she finished her phone call, she said that I had to give her my child, that it needed a medical check later, to get

British documents. I did not believe her. I am not an idiot even though you might see me just as a worthless sex worker. I ran my own business back in Ukraine. I know that my baby is well. I also know they wanted my little one's body parts, so when Storm left to visit her gym I ran and ran, but I could not leave Connie in the house all alone.'

'I understand.' Billie had also noted that at no point had Storm Benbow registered Connie missing. She was either more interested in saving her own skin once she'd got wind that the police were on their case, or not around anymore to tell the tale.

'I mean, Viku's a good worker. She owned her own health spa in Ukraine. It would be great if we could join forces and run my new chain of nail salons together, with crèche facilities for kids. Women helping women. What do you think?'

Billie realised that her very first conversation with Pandy Wood had been about being careful with her inheritance money. The alarm bells had rung out loud and clear then, but this time the idea sounded right, for both women, and she silently vowed that she would do absolutely everything in her power to help them achieve their aims.

317

Chapter 46

Freedom Angels

A cheer went up from the crowd in the memorial garden, which had been speedily created next to the land earmarked for a centre named Freedom Angels, committed to helping those who had suffered from people trafficking. Boo would be heading up the new charity, assisted by Maya, with plans for Abi to become the healthcare advisor once her nurse's training was complete.

Pandy and Viku, her visa now confirmed, had pledged their support and willingness to train up youngsters to be able to find employment in the hair and beauty business, so at least they would learn skills to earn money of their own and so avoid falling victim to people traffickers again in the future.

But the amazing new project hadn't been all plain sailing. It had been James Checkley who had immediately donated the vast amount required to create the state-of-the-art building, having been found not to have had any involvement in the illegal activities carried out by his brother, under cover of running a respected international logistics company. Ellis had been highly vocal, however, about his opposition to financial aid being accepted from *any* Checkley, heartbroken and furious about the experiences that Maya and others had been through. He had even fallen out with Boo, claiming that she was taking blood money.

'It's a cover up job. Somebody at the top has been paid to brush it all under the carpet. I've never known an investigation wound up so quickly,' he'd ranted. But nobody had wanted to listen. No donation would have meant no Freedom Angels, so even Billie had refused to be drawn into the row.

It had been Maya who had quietly intervened and finally accepted the donation, having argued that she was in a unique position to make that choice. She couldn't change history, she announced, but she could help change lives going forward. Turn a negative situation into a positive outcome and just like James, both she and Ellis had some, albeit distant, blood connection to the Checkley family. They couldn't change that, nor be forever blamed for it.

Ellis had backed off but had nevertheless sullenly refused to come to the ceremony today, claiming that he had better things to do, such as investigate yet another insurance scammer. Billie guessed he would come around in time. She was certain that Boo and Maya would create an amazing success story, overcoming any challenges that may step in their way.

As Billie sat on a low wall, face turned up towards the unexpected cool winter sunshine, she felt a movement next to her. She opened her eyes to find herself looking straight into James Checkley's own. She hadn't seen him since the night that they had spent together, but despite her vow to stay clear, she couldn't help but feel her heart lift at the sight of him.

'You haven't answered any of my calls,' he said, gently.

'I felt it would be for the best,' Billie answered, turning to look at him and immediately regretting her decision. His beautiful blue eyes looked sad, his soft smile showing no sign of anger about the many unreturned calls.

'Shame. I thought we had an understanding about not being blamed for the sins of our families.' He spoke quietly. Billie looked down. He was right, she had found out things about her own clan that were terrible too and wouldn't like to feel that she would be forever judged for something that she had no part of.

'I don't blame you, James. Though the set-up of huge multinational companies such as yours doesn't exactly lend itself to fair treatment of people. Easy for crimes such as your brother's to have taken place in plain sight under cover of a perfectly well-run corporation.'

'Well, thanks to you, that's all in the past and my brother is gone for good.'

'Don't ask me to say I'm sorry he's dead,' Billie answered defiantly.

'I'm not sorry either, in truth. I lost any sense of family loyalty when I discovered what he'd been up to. As I've said before, I hardly knew the man.'

The two of them sat in silence for a few moments, watching balloons lift into the sky, every one of them had a name of a known trafficking victim written upon them, along with one balloon dedicated to Ozzie Kingsnorth. His parents had attended, having found some small comfort in having discovered the part that their precious son had played in helping to fight for those without a voice. Maya had set free one balloon in blue. It was larger than all of the others and had a tiny replica attached with ribbon. It took flight quickly, dancing up towards the sun. Billie had heard Bluey's story. She was certain that the girl would never be forgotten as long as Maya was alive.

'Might it be too much to ask for us to try again, Billie?' James said, biting his lip as Billie glanced at him. She suddenly felt a little stupid. Maybe she was growing too much like Ellis, getting grumpy and stubborn these days. She quietly asked herself how she would feel if someone chose to blank her forever, based on her father's illegal and life-changing deeds? She was tired of fighting her genuine feelings. Ellis had his own very strong views, but she had always vowed to follow her own truth.

'Maybe we could give it a go,' she finally said. James smiled. Sliding his fingers along the wall to brush hers.

'Thank you. I'm leaving in a couple of hours on business. You could always come with me for a few days? Got some great stars where I'm going.' He smiled.

'Maybe next time.' Billie finally returned his smile. 'I have my own commitment later today. Though I am a sucker for a few well-placed stars and under a full moon, well, anything could happen.' She knew as she said the words that she wanted this. She wanted to be with James and also that, in truth, had she not been helping Ellis with Connie's party that afternoon, the one that meant so very much to him, she may have just thrown caution to the wind and ran off for a wonderful romantic break, not worrying for a short time, about everyone else. She'd done a lot of that after all, recently.

'My loss.' James got to his feet. 'Until next time then?' He bent down and kissed Billie slowly on the lips, before walking away towards a chauffeur-driven car purring at the kerbside. Billie smiled to herself. She hoped that it wouldn't be too long.

Chapter 47

The Winner Takes It All

E llis walked away from the airfield, hands in pockets, whistling a tune, 'The Winner Takes It All'. He didn't know why it had popped into his head just now, but it was true that he didn't like losing. If Eddie Checkley had lived, Ellis would have torn him limb from limb for what he had done to his precious girl. There was still no sign of Storm but that suited him fine. Win-win situation, in fact. Maya had once been nanny to Ash's kids and she had volunteered to look after Connie in between setting up the charity, now that his smallest child had been officially placed into his care.

Way he saw it, life should be perfect, except one thing kept gnawing away at him. What if Billie hadn't stopped Eddie Checkley from blowing his head off? He would have left his girls high and dry. Much as he didn't like to labour the point after Maya had been through so much, he had no doubt that in any case, their intervention had simply been a small glitch in the people-trafficking operation. Also, no way did he buy the idea that Eddie Checkley was the kingpin of the organisation. From all accounts he wasn't that bright, and it took a mastermind to run something on that scale. Billie surely knew it too. She just didn't want to face up to the fact.

Luckily, Ellis's background at the Serious Crime Investigation Agency meant that he had made some useful contacts. He'd put out feelers far and wide and discovered that the secretive but smart brother, James Checkley, was likely to be the organ grinder behind the whole operation. Always played the part of an angel whereas in truth he was the Devil incarnate. He'd even trained as a surgeon, hence the private hospitals around the world, set up to carry out illegal organ farming, some of them pop-up affairs in normal urban houses. It was said that he personally checked off every one of them. Bit kinky in that respect.

One or two old schoolmates Ellis had tracked down even said that Checkley had a pad at the bottom of his mum's garden, in Northumberland. Used to hang out there when he was a kid during school holidays. Some sort of glass domed folly, where he would spend days and nights on end dissecting live trapped animals. The more beautiful, the better. Too quick and clever to get anything to ever stick on him though.

Still, Ellis had been able to pull the wool over people's eyes himself a good few times, many of those whilst he was undercover, posing as somebody completely different. The glitzy but bent businessman for example, whose fake identity had still been overshadowing him when he had met Storm. That character was a man who often did bad things. Ellis had sometimes wondered where that act had stopped, and his real personality had begun.

Funny how he had dropped so easily into the persona again after four years, to meet the useful contact today. He was perfectly positioned, and still owed him a big favour or so the guy thought, though the person that he thought he was in debt to didn't really exist. Always useful to have friends in high places Ellis once remembered his mum saying, and this one didn't give him access much higher.

Ellis gave a grim smile. He had remembered once telling Billie that she was more interested in the dead than the living. He recalled how the comment had hurt her and how sorry he had been. Truth was she'd done everything to keep him alive, whereas he was the one who *definitely* wanted someone dead.

Chapter 48

Gone With a Bang

'Well, you said that you wanted it to go with a bang.' Billie laughed, as Connie's party was in full swing and one of the kids running around at their feet burst a balloon right behind Ellis.

'I nearly had a heart attack,' Ellis gasped, clutching his chest playfully.

'Who wants to help me bring in Connie's cake?' Billie whispered to Ash's oldest girls, Indie and Happi, who both jumped up and down, hands in the air, as though responding to a teacher in class. The event was clearly a big success, with the paintwork completed and party decorations hanging everywhere, spilling into the room that had housed the skeleton bride. All vestiges of that sad scenario had been wiped away now, in the brightly painted TV room, Maya now having nabbed the whole top floor of the house for herself.

Billie looked around at the lively chatter and fun-filled house, thinking that it was odd that the last time the core group had been together, Perry had been in the middle of everything. It was a thought that Billie determinedly pushed out of her mind. It was impossible to turn back the clock, no matter how much she might have liked to. Maya was in fine form, hosting the various games and Connie was making a great fuss of Uncle Teddy who was staying temporarily with Ellis until his own place was resurrected from the flames. Billie smiled to herself. Ellis now had nearly as many lodgers as she had once housed. It was lovely to see him happy in the centre of his family, where he belonged.

As the girls skipped after Billie to the kitchen to help light candles, the front room fell empty for a moment. Ellis quickly reached for the TV remote and pressed buttons. The TV news flashed up on the screen. Ellis glanced around him whilst turning the sound to mute. Footage of a horrific helicopter crash filled the screen, with a crawler text-band underneath the pictures of rescue workers picking their way through the burnt-out shell. *Millionaire Businessman James Checkley Killed in Shocking Helicopter Crash*, the words read. Ellis swiftly turned the TV off. His contact had just repaid his debt. Billie re-entered the room surrounded by children as they sang 'Happy Birthday' to Connie. There was suddenly a squeal from a small child as Billie placed the cake on a table heaving with food.

'What's up, mate?' Ellis asked the small boy.

'It's a wasp!' the child cried, dodging the insect which had escaped from the direction of the fireplace and was now flying at speed around the room. 'Kill it!'

'In January?' Maya questioned, as the wasp skittered around the sugary treats on the table. Billie headed over to the window and opened it wide.

'Yeah. It's a queen. They sometimes hibernate inside chimneys. Spot of warmer weather like we're enjoying today can bring them out.' The wasp left the table and flew across the room, hovering at the opening to the window, it seemed.

'It's woken up at the wrong time in the wrong place,' Billie explained as the wasp finally took flight out into the cold fresh air. Suddenly a burst of unexpected sunlight shone out from behind a cloud, washing the room in brightness. 'But if we treat it kindly and set it free, then we might just give this January wasp a chance to survive.'

THE END

Acknowledgements

When discussing each of my books, the first question interviewers always ask is, 'What was your inspiration?' In the case of this book, the answer is easy.

The inspiration behind *Buried Dreams*, came from my husband Bob Whittaker, who mentioned that when he was an angst-ridden young man, he had once penned a poem called *The January Wasp*. That's all he could remember about it. The title. He became an award-winning journalist, so I have no doubt it was a fantastic poem, but in truth, to me it needed no other words. The title said it all, telling the tale of a creature born in the wrong time at the wrong place.

I was trying to jog his memory about the rest of the poem, whilst we were walking along the harbour at Amble, a tiny fishing port, a few miles from where we live in Northumberland. A car-boot sale was underway and as we weaved through the sea-salt kissed stalls overlooking the fishing quay, I spotted a wedding dress for sale. The family who were selling it had just arrived fresh from the conflict in Ukraine. The idea that became *Buried Dreams* had started to take shape in my mind and so the title of the poem, the wedding dress, people travelling the world in search of a safe haven and the harbour at Amble all play a part in the resulting story.

Of course, that first idea would not have become a fully-fledged novel without the dream team at Bloodhound Books, led by Betsy and Fred Reavley helping to bring my final story to life. I can't say thank you enough to Tara Lyons, editorial and production manager extraordinaire, Editor Ian Skewis, who is an absolute star and who I am so lucky to have had working with me on all of my books. Hawk-eyed proofreader Shirley Khan and ace Marketing and PR Manager, Hannah Deuce. A big shout-out also to friend Sam Brown who gave me advice on offshore structures.

A book, of course, only comes to life when readers become involved in the story. One of the joys of being an author is getting to know lots of fellow bookworms and inviting them to be part of my writing journey. In *Buried Dreams*, a number of readers actually helped inspire the names of several characters.

When Bloodhound Books ran a fundraiser to help refugees from Ukraine, Liz Turnock very kindly made a donation in return for having her own named character, Lizbeth Ann Beech, featured in my book. Members of reading group Book Swap Central: Donna Cook, Sarah Cutler, Julie Cornelius, Shelley Benbow and budding author Megan Benbow, Sarah Kingsnorth, Ramila Patel and Lynda Checkley all assisted in the most fun way with character names. Their precious pets helped even more. Thank you all!

As you can tell, the readers of my books are very special to me, and I love to hear from them. You are very welcome to come and chat via –

My website, at https://marrissewhittaker.com.
My Facebook page – https://www.facebook.com/MarrisseWhittakerAuthor
Twitter – https://twitter.com/MarrisseWhitt
Instagram – https://www.instagram.com/marrissewhittakerauthor/
TikTok – https://www.tiktok.com/@marrissewhittaker

Thank you for reading!

A note from the publisher

Thank you for reading this book. If you enjoyed it please do consider leaving a review on Amazon to help others find it too.

We hate typos. All of our books have been rigorously edited and proofread, but sometimes mistakes do slip through. If you have spotted a typo, please do let us know and we can get it amended within hours.

info@bloodhoundbooks.com